FORTUNA'S
DEADLY
SHADOW

FORTUNA'S DEADLY SHADOW

LESLIE SCASE

Gomer

First published in 2018 by Gomer Press,
Llandysul, Ceredigion SA44 4JL

ISBN 978 1 78562 288 5

A CIP record for this title is available from the British Library.

This book is published with the financial support of the
Welsh Books Council.

Printed and bound in Wales at
Gomer Press, Llandysul, Ceredigion
www.gomer.co.uk

All characters and events in this publication, other than those clearly in
the public domain, are fictitious and any resemblance to real persons,
living or dead, is purely coincidental.

The maps of Pontypridd and Treforest from the 1890s are adaptations
of OS maps kindly provided by Pontypridd Library.

To Janet
for her love and support

ACKNOWLEDGEMENTS

My sincere thanks go to Meirion Davies, Susan Roberts, Ashley Owen and all the team at Gomer Press for their help and encouragement. Thanks also to my wife Janet for her assistance with my research.

Map 1.
Pontypridd town centre 1895

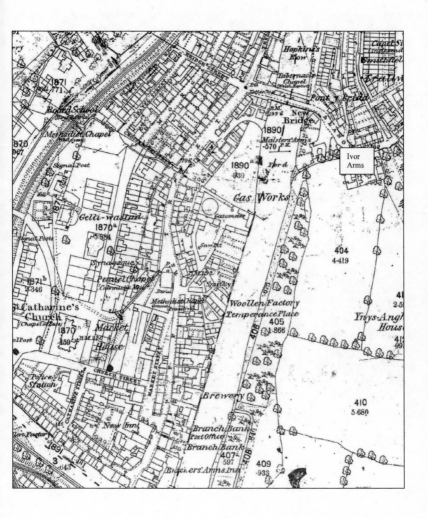

Map 2.
Pontypridd Station, Graig and Tumble Area

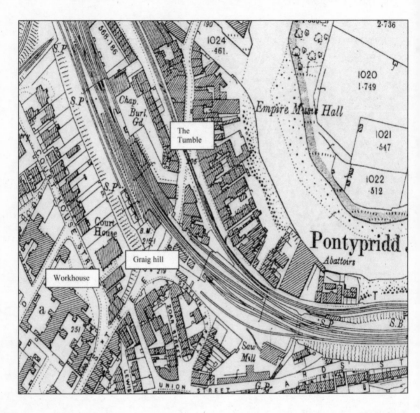

Map 3.
Central Treforest

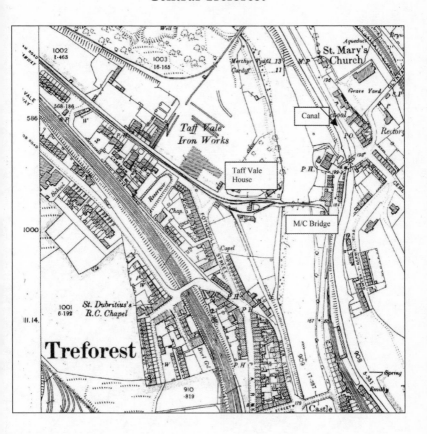

Map 4.
Treforest South

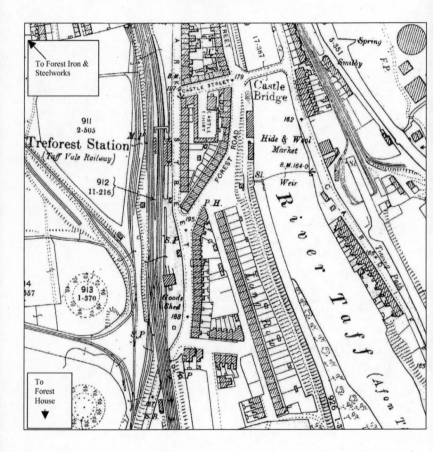

PROLOGUE

He opened his eyes.

Water crossed his face and obscured his vision. He felt the wetness against his cheeks.

Occasionally stars were just visible but then would disappear only to come again, shining faintly as a raincloud would pass. Strangely the stars seemed to be turning, rotating in the sky. Perhaps he himself was rotating, slowly or maybe quickly, he wasn't sure. He had a body, he knew he did, but he couldn't feel it. Everything vanished and then reappeared again, then he could hear.

He could hear rushing water, roaring at times, then it would go silent and he was in a place of tranquillity. Once more the stars re-appeared and the sound returned. Then the shock kicked in as he realised where he was and what would now inevitably happen. There should have been panic, there really should, he told himself. Instead he felt nothing, there was just acceptance. He knew he was in the river and reasoned that he must actually be floating then submerging, moving around in the current then coming to the surface. That he was slowly drowning seemed logical and he thought with a sense of detachment that even now the water must be entering his lungs. They must be burning, struggling to function and feeling as if they are about to explode. The pain should be horrific, yet he felt nothing, just peace.

The stars re-appeared and glimmered in the sky and maybe that was where he was going, to heaven. He didn't deserve it but the alternative was a thought that was too hard to bear. He began to pray silently and closed his eyes.

The river, in full spate from a week of heavy rain carried its burden downstream, beneath one bridge then onwards to another. The by now lifeless body hit the pillar of a second bridge, stayed trapped for some moments before being freed by the current.

On it swept down to a weir where it crashed over the edge to be submerged for some moments then tossed like a rag doll before being hurled ever onwards. Here it was pitch black and no one observed the corpse as it drifted for another quarter mile until it was sucked deep by an eddy and lodged deep within weeds along the eastern bank of the river.

A thick submerged tree root caught upon the sturdy leather belt of the dead man's clothing and stuck there, keeping the body hidden below. There it stayed.

CHAPTER ONE

SPRING 1893

The railway carriage was full. A cross section of humanity filled the confined space with a cacophony of sound. A group of men, alcohol heavy on their breath, argued over the relative merits of their favoured rugby football teams. A woman, respectably dressed, tried without success to control the continual wailing of the three children she held in tow. An elderly gentleman harrumphed and muttered in discontent as he tried to read his daily journal whilst being pressed by the corpulent passenger seated alongside. Incessant chatter seemed to flow like a wave from end to end.

One passenger however, remained silent. A swarthy, unpleasant-looking individual who sat, head resting against the side window of the carriage looking outside to his right, with his cap pulled low on his brow. He gazed at the verdant pastures of the Taff Valley as the train hurtled along. At times it ran parallel to the River Taff and the spring sunshine would glint on its waters before the river disappeared from view only to reappear beyond woods or small groups of cottages.

The silent man felt a tap on his arm and he turned to a florid-faced cheery gentleman who remarked, 'Well, sir, we are fair clipping along, are we not?'

There was no response.

'I said, sir, we are fair clipping along,' repeated the man who assumed he hadn't spoken loud enough the first time.

This time the response was an icy stare. The cheery man started to repeat himself once again, but slowed the words and gulped as he took in the cold, hard features that faced him.

The silent man turned back to the window. Despite his

natural demeanour he raised an eyebrow in surprise as he looked across the valley to see, perched on the hillside, a castle that seemed to have come straight out of a fairy tale. This was indeed a surprising part of the world.

The train was now much higher than the valley floor, clinging to a hillside as it swept along, the carriage swaying rhythmically and the click-clack of the tracks created a soothing effect that helped make the noise generated inside the carriage a little more bearable.

'We won't be long at this rate,' exclaimed one of the men who had been arguing over the rugby teams earlier.

'We'll have time for an early snifter in the Clarence I reckon,' slurred one of his compatriots.

'It usually slows down near to Devil's Bridge and if we stop at Treforest station it might be a bit longer – but we'll have time for a few jars anyway,' chipped in another.

The silent man returned to his thoughts. It had been a long journey getting this far but as soon as he had got on the Taff Vale Railway train at Cardiff he had felt the comfort of knowing that soon his travels would be at an end.

He absent-mindedly tapped his jacket pocket where he kept his wallet. Plenty of money there, he reminded himself, and importantly nothing to identify himself. His personal documents and most of his belongings were stored safely in the left luggage store at Cardiff station.

The vista outside the train was gradually becoming less bright as the sun fell behind clouds and ahead in the distance, as the train rounded a long gentle curve, plumes of smoke could be seen emanating from the Treforest Tinplate Works.

The train continued to power onwards, not slowing at any point as it continued further down the line. No one could foresee what was about to happen. The continuous wet weather had slowly taken its toll on the hillside and one part, under which flowed an underground stream, had become sodden. Just a few yards of the hillside slipped away, but it was all that was needed.

The silent man, despite himself, had started to relax and let his mind wander, when suddenly he was jolted by a loud bang, an ear-piercing screech of metal grinding against metal and then suddenly time seemed to stand still. For what felt like an eternity he experienced absolute silence and the world appeared to be tilted at a forty-five-degree angle. In fact this occurred in a fraction of a second and his senses soon reeled to a wave of shouts and screams as the carriage, together with the one attached behind, derailed.

The cheery gentleman that had tried to start a conversation was now wedged against him and several people had fallen out of their seats. The woman with the three children was shrieking hysterically and her three offspring were crying loudly.

The carriage stayed derailed but at a stable sharp angle, though being at the bottom of the slant he knew that if it toppled further he would have the full crush of passengers fall on him. Ignoring the screams, shouts and curses he quickly hauled himself up to his left hand side and started to claw his way upwards. A child screamed louder as his boot trod on its small arm and a man tried to hurl him back as he grabbed a handful of hair as he moved upwards. Then, suddenly, the carriage started to move again. Real panic set in and his breathing froze as he realised the carriage was going to go over.

For a second he felt almost weightless as he fell backwards onto the passengers he had just climbed over. There was a loud bang and a shattering of glass which mingled with further screams and shouts of panic as the carriage landed on its side and slowly start to slide down the hillside.

Realising that he wasn't hurt, the panic started to recede, as although the carriage was sliding he was not at the bottom of the press of bodies. Despite the screams that still almost deafened him he realised that there was a chance that he could come out of this unscathed.

Then, suddenly, there was a stomach-turning realisation that everything was topsy-turvy, the carriage had started to flip over, and once more a feeling of weightlessness came to him as he was hurled around like a leaf in a hurricane. He felt the impact as his leg hit the side of the carriage whilst the bulk of his body slammed through a window, shattering it. Launched through the glass, he felt the pain of the resulting lacerations and of the now-broken leg. Hitting the ground hard he rolled down the slope, daylight obliterated by the blood that seeped into his eyes from his badly cut face. He came to a stop suddenly, aware of other things, whether people or bits of broken carriage he knew not, rushing past him. The air was full of noise and movement. Suddenly he felt a terrible crushing pain on his head and he gasped. Unable to breathe he panicked but could do nothing. It was an experience of pure terror that seemed to last forever.

Then there was a feeling of stillness. He was without vision and wasn't even sure if he was breathing. He supposed that was the case, because he could hear sound. He could hear groans and cries and screams but there was no pain. At least I'm still alive, was his last thought before darkness came to him.

*   *   *

The crash could not and did not go unnoticed, such was the dreadful commotion.

Some of the workers at the tinplate works down in the valley had seen the horrifying accident happen and ran to tell their supervisors.

Meanwhile, a handful of travellers on the turnpike road

which ran on the hillside above the railway line had rushed to the road edge to look down at the scene below them. The more agile of them clambered down towards the railway line whilst others just stood and watched the drama unfold. One occupant in a jet-black carriage with silver trim deigned not to get out but sent his footman down to the site to report back.

At the Treforest Tinplate Works the foreman had notified the works manager who had reacted calmly and efficiently. Despite its name, the works was actually some three miles from the village of Treforest which had actually become a suburb of the large town of Pontypridd a further mile distant. Arrangements were made to send a telegram to the police station at Pontypridd, whilst working parties were put together under control of their foremen and chargehands to attend the site of the disaster.

The sight that greeted them when they arrived was not a pleasant one. Some of the passengers had been thrown clear of the wreck, but those were mainly lying like rag dolls – some missing limbs, others groaning pitifully, some weeping and others perfectly still. Inside the carriages were possibly worse sights. The mother who had been trying to control her children lay dead alongside two of her dead offspring, whilst the third lay alive but crying pathetically. The cheery gentleman lay distorted, his neck clearly broken. There were some groans, some very lucky survivors, but many were silent.

'What are we going to do with them, Dai?' asked a young tinplate worker of his older workmate.

'Simple, Tom, just see if we can find any we can help. We need to sort out who is dead, who is alive and of those, how badly they are injured. Any walking wounded can be cared for back at the works for the time being, but the seriously injured will have to go to the infirmary. The foreman has got a team making makeshift stretchers and I am sure that someone will have arranged for transport. At least the weather is fine today, the rain we've had these last few days, especially the storm last night, would have made this far worse'.

Making their way through the carnage, Tom stopped briefly to vomit as he came across the body of a man whose leg was broken at an unnatural angle and whose face had been squashed to a bloody pulp by a broken chunk of metal that was still embedded in his flesh.

'*Iesu Mawr!*' he blasphemed in Welsh. 'Look at this poor bugger!'

'No point in helping him; he's beyond help. Let's move along to the next one,' responded Dai.

'No! Wait! I think I saw his fingers twitch.'

Bending over, Dai checked the body. 'You're right. He's still alive, but only just.

He'll take some handling though, he is a big lump. We need to get him to the infirmary as soon as we can get a stretcher over here.'

* * *

May Roper had been looking forward to finishing work early at the infirmary when the telegram came in. The infirmary was part of the large workhouse complex on the Graig hill only a few hundred yards above the railway station at Pontypridd, which was very close to the County Court building. Pontypridd had no hospital, the nearest being up the valley in Porth, so the infirmary provided a useful service to the town in case of emergency as well as looking after the workhouse inmates, many of whom were aged or infirm.

As soon as she read the contents of the telegram May rushed into the office of Dr Henderson, the workhouse medical officer.

'Miss Roper, kindly have some propriety, barging in here like that,' he snapped.

'I am ever so sorry, Dr Henderson,' apologised the attractive auburn-haired secretary, 'but this is ever so urgent.' She handed him the card and watched his grey eyebrows rise in alarm. He lifted his corpulent frame out of his chair and stroked his drooping grey moustache.

' "Train crash STOP. Prepare many casualties coming your way STOP",' he quoted. 'We had better jump to it, Miss Roper.'

'Yes, Dr Henderson.'

The doctor had seen action in the military as a younger man before circumstances eventually led him to this current position which, although not well paid, was secure and not too demanding. His experience came to the fore as he rattled out a string of instructions.

'I'm sure that they will have telegrammed Porth hospital as well but, just in case, send one from us, asking for at least one doctor and half a dozen nurses, plus any suitable equipment they might think appropriate. We have our small theatre room here if needs be, but it is difficult to plan properly on the information we've been given. We can take action here on broken limbs and give morphine to the poor devils that need it. Our main role will be sorting the injuries to determine the best way to proceed.'

'In what way, Doctor?'

'Well, for instance, even the hospital has limits on what it can cope with in terms of numbers, and so far we have nothing much to go on. For those with broken limbs we can set them here. If they have amputated limbs, internal injuries or head injuries then we can assess if they are mortally injured or if they can survive any more travelling. If necessary I might even have to operate here.'

'Shall I fetch Nurse Bayliss and Nurse Harris for you to brief them, Doctor?'

'Yes, at once, and make sure that there is enough space in our cold room for any unfortunates that don't make it. Take one of the inmates with you to help. Oh, and by the way, I will expect you to work on tonight and man the infirmary entrance to guide in the arrivals'

'Of course, Dr Henderson. I'll send a message to my parents later.' May rushed off to find the two resident nurses, then with one of the trustworthy inmates who acted as porters, went towards the makeshift mortuary, used on a temporary basis when inmates passed away.

Dr Henderson waited for the nurses, and then briefed them, giving them further instructions.

'We probably will not have enough beds, so get some of the workhouse lads to move the existing beds to one side of the infirmary. Then make up temporary beds on the floor on the other side of the room using blankets and anything else you can lay your hands on.

'I will assess the patients we've already got in and either move them back into their dormitories, or if necessary, they can go on the made up beds on the floor.'

'All we can do now is wait,' he murmured to himself as the nurses hurried off.

CHAPTER TWO

It was an hour later when the telegram arrived at St Dubricius Catholic Church in Treforest.

Father McManus had been on the point of leaving the vestry when he met Jenny Norton, one of his parishioners.

'Hello Father, I have been meaning to have a word with you.'

'Very well Jenny, I have five minutes now if you would like to go back inside the vestry with me'.

'Thank you Father. That would be most kind of you'.

Just then their conversation was interrupted by a red-faced telegram delivery boy who clearly had been running as fast as he could.

'Telegram, Father McManus. It is really urgent and I can't stop. I need to deliver one to Father Clarke at St Mary's straight away.'

'Dear me, if there is something so important that both Catholic and Anglican churches have to be notified immediately then I had better open it.'

He turned to Jenny. 'Please excuse me, Jenny, whilst I open this first'.

As he began to read the contents his facial expression changed from one of calm benevolence to one of pure horror.

'Oh dear me, no!' he exclaimed. 'There has been a train crash with dozens killed or mortally injured. They are being taken to the infirmary. I must go there at once in case there are any of our faith. I will get what I need from the presbytery.'

'I will go to Park Street and get a hansom cab for you. There is usually one near Treforest station,' offered Jenny.

Nodding his agreement, the priest hurried to the presbytery whilst the young woman set off on the relatively short walk towards a small bridge over the railway line that led to Park Street, moving as briskly as her skirts would allow.

Fortunately, there was indeed a hansom cab waiting for fares outside the entrance to the small station, and after she had a quick word with the driver, he set the two-wheeled cabriolet off in motion in the direction of the Catholic church.

As Jenny turned, deep in thought, someone caught her eye and she called across the street to a young man of medium height in workman's clothes with dark hair, a neat black moustache and a roguish smile.

'Jack, oh I am pleased to see you.'

'I'll come over,' he responded as he eagerly crossed the road; his voice tinged with an accent that identified him as being one of the many foreign newcomers to the area.

Jack's eyes scanned the statuesque beauty that was Jenny Norton who lived just two doors away from his own home, on the very street where they stood.

He had moved to the area only a year ago, and had found work at the local Taff Vale Ironworks. Jenny had herself only arrived two years prior but was well settled in, with a clerical job in the payroll office of the same ironworks.

Jack took in her tall figure, lustrous black hair, perfectly proportioned face and dark mysterious eyes. He knew that if she were to smile he would probably become too enamoured to talk coherently. However, she was clearly not about to smile.

'There has been a terrible train crash, with dozens badly hurt. They are being taken to the infirmary and I've decided I would like to offer my help. The infirmary won't have enough people to cope with an emergency of this size.'

'Why don't they take them to the hospital in Porth?'

'It's probably too far away for those who are very badly injured. Our infirmary does at least have some facilities and an able doctor. Anyway I have decided that I would like to go but it is early evening now and I don't want to have to return unattended. Will you come with me?'

'Yes, of course,' Jack quickly agreed.

'There isn't a train due, so it'll be quicker to walk down to the Tram Road and catch a brake,' suggested Jenny.

They both set off down the north end of Park Street, along Fothergill Street until they reached the broad Tram Road which was the main route to Pontypridd.

They were very lucky, in fact, to catch one of the wagonette brakes that regularly provided transport into the town, because many had been commandeered by the authorities to help transport victims of the tragedy. One rattled past as Jack helped Jenny up the tailboard steps of the vehicle. They made themselves comfortable sat facing each other on the longitudinal seats, the driver cracked his whip, and the horse-drawn brake set off.

*   *   *

May stood at the door of the workhouse infirmary. It had taken some time for the casualties to be recovered and transported to Pontypridd. It was very slow progress for some, with a fine balance having to be made between getting them back quickly to alleviate their pain and, on the other hand, taking care not to make their injuries worse by jolting them as the various carriages travelled down the Tram Road. This complication meant that there was a mixture of injuries arriving depending on the ease of transporting them. The workhouse governor had arranged for staff to be on the main gates directing the carriages to the infirmary. Six corpses had already been sent to the cold room, two of whom had died on the journey. Another fourteen had come with fractured limbs or ribs. Two others in comas. In the chaos, May had also had to deal with organising a number of ad hoc visitors offering to help. These included two local chapel ministers, the Catholic priest from Treforest, the vicars of St Mary's and St Catherine's, a local private doctor and of course, the press.

'No, Mr Morgan, you cannot go in. This is an infirmary and no one is in a position of being able to talk to you'.

'Well, my lovely, I only want to help, see.'

'First of all, I am not "your lovely" and secondly, you only want a story. I suggest you go and speak to the governor because if you don't go away I will have you removed.'

This was said with such determination that the reporter muttered something of likely obscenity under his breath and moved away, hoping to catch a word with one of the drivers who were waiting in the yard. Just then, a jet-black carriage with silver trim drawn by two large perfectly groomed horses entered the yard. Out stepped an immaculately attired young man in a grey velvet collared frock coat, carrying a black cane in one hand and a top hat in the other. He strolled almost casually over to May and made a slight bow of his head.

'Excuse me, miss. I have a fellow in my carriage who is not in the best of health. Frankly, he might be dead. I wonder if you could tell me what to do with the chap.'

For a moment May didn't respond. There was something about the man's bearing and appearance that was quite striking, particularly his face. He was quite simply the prettiest man she had ever seen. Not handsome, that would imply some form of masculine attraction. He was undeniably pretty. A face that was delicate, with a flawless complexion, clean shaven, with eyebrows that had been trimmed and shaped to perfection.

'Miss …?'

May was jolted back to present matters.

'Oh, certainly …' she faltered. She called over her shoulder to a pair of inmate porters, 'Evans, Walters, there's a patient in the black carriage over there. Move him inside, get him stripped and in one of the beds. Apparently he is in a bad way.'

The two porters moved somewhat lethargically down towards the carriage, carrying a stretcher.

'May I ask how you came to help the injured gentleman?'

'I was on my way to my temporary residence when I heard a commotion. I sent my footman to enquire and, looking over the roadside wall, he could see that there had been an accident on the railway line below. In order to get down below the railway and help, I had to continue into Treforest itself, under the railway bridge there and then back around via the road to the tinplate works. This particular fellow was in such a bad way that they needed a vehicle with a well-sprung frame to give him a chance of surviving the journey'.

They watched as the porters carried the injured man from the carriage into the infirmary. May blanched as she saw the pulped face go past.

'Would you mind terribly if I was to stay awhile, just to see what transpires with the fellow? I promise not to get in the way,' added the stranger with an expectantly raised eyebrow. 'After all, having gone to the inconvenience of bringing him here I think it is understandable that I am rather curious to discover his fate.'

'Well I don't know ...'

'I am terribly sorry, I have failed to introduce myself. My name is Mr James Dorsett, and I am a guest of Mr Crawshay at Forest House.'

The Crawshay family name carried a great deal of weight and May decided to acquiesce.

'Very well, you may wait in our office for the time being. My name is Miss Roper. May I take your hat and cane?'

'There's really no need, I'll keep them with me,' Dorsett

replied, fingering the weighty top of his cane which was in the form of a beautifully designed silver leopard's head.

Whilst the conversation took place, May could hear Nurse Harris's shrill voice in the background.

'Evans! Hurry up with that patient and get the screens around him.'

Dr Henderson was busily tending to the injured so May was able to escort Dorsett to an empty office, before returning to her post.

A fresh casualty was in the process of being carried in. A woman with a face contorted with pain was being carried on a stretcher by two workmen from the tinplate works.

'We think it's her insides, miss,' they explained.

May directed them to Nurse Bayliss who attracted the attention of Dr Henderson.

Having second thoughts about allowing Mr Dorsett to loiter in the office, May quickly went back inside. She noticed that the screens were now around the patient that he had brought in, so she approached the visitor.

'Mr Dorsett, the man you fetched in is now in bed. You can take a quick look to see that he is comfortable but then I must ask you to leave.'

They made their way out of the office to the relevant screen and May turned to speak to Dorsett. However, before she could say a word she noticed him suddenly stiffen and his lips moved as he muttered something to himself.

Instinctively May turned around, to see a young man and woman walking through the door.

'Excuse me, but who are you?'

Both new arrivals had already halted hesitantly and there seemed to be a flicker of recognition in both their eyes.

'My name is Jenny Norton and I was with Father McManus when the telegram came informing him of the crash. There he is, talking with the vicar of St Mary's,' said Jenny, pointing to the far end of the room where Father McManus was indeed in close conversation with another clergyman. 'I came to offer some help and this is my friend, Jack Ross.'

'Haven't I seen you somewhere before?' asked May.

'I don't think so,' replied Jenny quickly.

'Perhaps we had better go if we aren't needed,' suggested Jack.

'I think I was about to be asked to leave,' said Dorsett softly, 'but I was just going to take a look at the injured man I brought in first'.

Just then there was a commotion at the door as another arrival was being brought in, screaming in pain.

'Take a quick look and then please go. We've got more medical staff arriving shortly and we need room to work.'

'Yes, Miss Roper, of course,' replied Dorsett.

May dashed off leaving the other three by the screen.

'Would you care to join me,' suggested Dorsett with a smile. He gestured Jack and Jenny to come behind the screen, and there lay a pitiful large figure with unrecognisable facial features. His clothes were piled clumsily on a chair at the side of the bed. The sheet was turned back showing cuts and bruises on his torso and underneath the sheet it could be seen that one of his legs was at an unnatural angle. He was very still, the only movement being the odd twitch of his fingers.

Jack turned white and initially stepped back but then went forward to lay a hand on the shoulder of Jenny who had sat on the edge of the chair and instinctively grabbed the hand of the patient. They lingered a little while at the bedside until Dorsett gave a polite cough and spoke.

'I don't think we should stay. I do believe he is not long for this world.'

Dorsett ushered them out, went over to the bed one last time, patted the sheet and then left.

More casualties were arriving as they made their way towards the door as were a number of hospital nurses.

'Can anyone not directly involved in the medical treatment of patients please leave immediately!' exclaimed Dr Henderson.

They went outside.

'Can I offer anyone a lift in my carriage? My man will have cleaned the furnishings of anything unpleasant whilst I was inside.'

'If that would not be too inconvenient,' answered Jenny with a smile. 'I wouldn't normally enter a strange carriage but as Jack is with me.'

Dorsett looked at her companion and raised an eyebrow quizzically.

'I have to go,' said Jack, politely nodding before turning and walking to the main gates.

That is odd, thought Jenny. Jack seemed to want to follow her around whenever he could find an excuse. Wiping the thought from her mind she nonetheless smiled at Dorsett and let his footman help her into the carriage.

* * *

Next morning Dr Henderson went straight to his office.

'You are in early, Miss Roper.'

'There is so much to do, Dr Henderson. I need to type the records of those treated here to send off to the hospital. Also some of the patients will be staying with us because they aren't well enough to move. A few have yet to be identified so we are unable to contact relatives.'

'What was the final total? Frankly I lost count.'

'I am sorry to say, sixty injured and fifteen dead.'

'Hmm, I see. Well I think I'll quickly do my rounds. I'm interested in the fellow with the disfigured face. When he first arrived he could merely twitch his fingers but just before I left last night he could move one arm.'

May hesitated.

'I am sorry, Doctor, but I am afraid he passed away in the night. Nurse Harris found him dead this morning.'

'Oh what a shame,' commented Henderson, genuinely saddened. 'Do we know who he was or where he came from?'

'I searched his clothes myself to try and find out some details for my records.'

'And ...?'

'There was nothing in his pockets other than an empty wallet and a pocket watch. His name was engraved on the inside of the watch. Apparently the unfortunate gentleman's name was Michael Blake.'

CHAPTER THREE

SPRING 1895

Thomas Chard absent-mindedly scratched one of his sideburns as he stared out of the train window. There was nothing to see, the damp spring weather had made for a murky, depressing outlook during the day and now night was starting to close in.

'I should have set off sooner', he told himself as he glanced at his Bradshaw's Handbook and tried vainly to catch a glimpse of the fairy tale folly that was Castell Coch across the valley.

Was he really doing the right thing, uprooting himself from his native Shropshire to come here, somewhere so relatively strange compared to his rural community? Shrewsbury, where he had worked, was a busy county town admittedly. However life in the small town of Wem, where he had lived, was decidedly quiet.

It wasn't that he was unfamiliar with Wales. Shropshire was a border county on the Welsh Marches, but the rural communities of Mid Wales were a far cry from where he was heading.

His reverie was interrupted by a sharp call.

'Tickets, please', demanded the conductor, a rotund, fussy-looking man with pince-nez spectacles.

Chard reached into the ticket pocket of his waistcoat and handed it for inspection.

'Thank you, sir. Newbridge Junction.'

'That is close to Pontypridd I understand?' enquired Chard as the conductor began to turn away.

'Yes indeed, sir. In fact it is Pontypridd itself.'

'So why is it called Newbridge Junction?'

'Because Pontypridd was called Newbridge until they

"Welshified" it,' he retorted. 'The new maps may have us as Pontypridd Junction but we aren't going to change the name of our stations willy-nilly, so it stays as it is. I take it you have not been down this way before, sir. Are you visiting Pontypridd?'

'I am going to live there, hopefully for some time to come.'

'So it is your first time and you are arriving on a Saturday night,' he replied smiling mischievously. 'Good luck'.

'Why do you say that?'

'You'll find out in good time, sir.'

With that he walked off, moving in cadence with the train as it rattled along the track at significant speed, leaving Chard to return to his thoughts of his beloved Shropshire.

'Perhaps when the scandal blows over.'

The train swept on, the dark sky illuminated by the red glow of the tinplate works as it travelled to Pontypridd, and soon after it pulled in at the small Treforest station, where two or three passengers alighted, before proceeding to Pontypridd/ Newbridge Junction where it arrived a few minutes later.

Chard turned the solid handle of the train door and stepped down onto the platform.

On taking advice he had already sent his luggage ahead the previous week and it should in theory have arrived safely at the New Inn in the centre of Pontypridd.

The station was larger than he expected and as with all stations the air was heavy with the smell of burning coal. The air was chilly so Chard did the buttons up on his overcoat, adjusted his derby hat (which he felt was more stylish than many British bowlers) and set off towards the footbridge to the other side of the tracks.

He wished he had arrived earlier because the refreshment bar facilities were now closed and he had a ravenous thirst, so he would have to take his chance in the town.

His feet echoed down the broad exit staircase which

seemed to go forever downwards, for the railway was perched high above the town. As he progressed he became aware of a gradual increase in noise that started as a background murmur but expanded to a discordant roar. As he emerged into the station yard and out onto the street he was taken aback by what confronted him.

Nothing could have prepared him for the pandemonium that met his eyes and indeed his ears. Every other building seemed to be licensed premises. Indeed there was one in the station yard behind him, there were a couple down the road to his left, on a corner across the way was a short squat building, its sign 'The Clarence' painted on its wall was lit by an adjoining gas lamp. Light and music came from premises named The White Hart directly facing him and another licensed establishment premises with a painted dog as its emblem. Closer to his right was the well-signed Half Moon in a curious rounded shape which in turn was next to the Red Lion.

The streets were rowdy and Chard's eyes were drawn to a series of individual dioramas, the sum of which made him feel inclined to retrace his steps back to the station platform and take the next train out of town.

A heavily bewhiskered man sat upon a rearing horse, yelling loudly with one hand on the reins whilst the other grasped a beer bottle; two women fought, grabbing each other's hair whilst a small crowd gathered around cheering them on; in the shadows there were glimpses of women, bodices cut low, trying to entice passers-by; one man in a flat cap was vomiting against the foot of a lamp post, another was urinating openly in the street.

Chard took in the wider view. He was standing on a junction of several roads. The main thoroughfare seemed to be a broad roadway running from his right front, bearing around to disappear northwards to his left. To his front left there seemed, by the light of several premises and the limited gas lighting, to be a narrow road leading down to what he presumed to be the town centre. Finally, behind and to his right there was a road leading underneath the railway station bridge and up a steep hill on the other side. It was from this direction that a two-horse carriage suddenly appeared at terrific speed causing him to jump back in alarm. Horses foaming at the mouth and the driver cracking his whip, it swung to the left in front of him heading north at such speed Chard felt sure that the carriage would fail to take the change in direction without overturning. In fact his premonition almost came true for the vehicle went up on two wheels before crashing down again on making the turn and disappearing into the night.

*　*　*

Not too far away in the town hall a polka was in full swing at a charity dance attended by the higher echelons of society. The sons and daughters of local industrialists and owners of nearby estates danced energetically beneath gaslight chandeliers whilst their elders mixed convivially at the outer edges of the dance floor.

'Nice to see you back again, James,' commented a white-haired worthy to his much younger companion. 'You seem to be coming to visit ever more frequently. When you first came about three years ago I thought, "Hello, this chap is just down here to splash a few sovereigns, make a killing on his investments then clear off back to England for good" but you can't seem to get enough of the smell of coal.'

'Well, you know I have to keep on top of my interests, Mr Kelce,' replied an elegantly attired James Dorsett.

'That's one interest I wouldn't mind keeping on top of,'

replied Kelce with a nudge, as a petite blonde would-be debutante passed closely by in the arms of her beau.

Dorsett gave an amused smile.

'You really are quite incorrigible you know,' he scolded light-heartedly.

'We must find you some pretty little thing. There you are decked out in your finest yet no young lady is hanging on your arm.'

'There really is no need …'

'But I insist, my boy. Ah, I have it! I know just the person. Now, I am going to a little soiree towards the end of the evening and I think if you come along you won't be disappointed. Distant relation of Lady Llanover, a lovely girl.'

'I am afraid that I have other interests that must attract me away a little later, but I thank you for the kind offer.' With a polite smile Dorsett nodded and turned away towards the refreshment area where punch was being served from an ornate silver serving bowl.

'He's a strange fish,' muttered Kelce to himself.

Sometime later James Dorsett quietly left via a back door, checked he wasn't being followed, then slipped into the darkness.

* * *

The small boy looked up at the well-dressed, slightly stocky man of medium height who was looking into the street with such a grim expression on his face. That visage didn't seem to hold much promise, but he thought it worth a try. He put on the most pathetic expression he could muster.

'Can you spare a penny, mister?' he asked hopefully.

Chard looked down at the waif who had somehow appeared at his side unnoticed.

He took in the boy's skinny frame, grimy ragged clothes and wide-eyed pathetic expression and guessed he was about ten years old.

'What's your name, boy?'

'Dilwyn, mister.'

'And how old are you?'

'Twelve and a half, sir.'

Clearly undernourished, thought Chard. He gestured towards the ongoing chaos. 'Is this normal for the town?'

'Well, it's Saturday night up the Tumble,' he replied

'The what, boy?'

'The Tumble. It's what they call this bit of town. I don't know why. Mam used to say that it was because so many carriages used to crash here but I think she made it up.'

'And where is your mother?'

'Dead, sir. She passed away with the typhoid a couple of years ago.' He worked harder on the pathetic look and felt more hopeful.

'What about your father?'

'He's got a job, but it's night work, so I'm on my own.'

'Well then, young Dilwyn, I am new in town so perhaps you can give me a recommendation. I have accommodation but I always like to find somewhere that I can go for a quiet drink when I want a bit of peace and where I am not going to get my throat cut. Do you know of such a place?'

The boy held his hand out expectantly.

'Name first, payment after,' insisted Chard.

'The Ivor Arms, mister. Gwen will look after you. It's right up the far end of town and over the bridge, but as you are a stranger I would leave it until the daytime to go looking for it.'

'Gwen?'

'Trust me, mister,' he replied holding out his hand once more.

Chard put his hand in his pocket and with a smile hovering on his lips, he took out a threepenny piece and put it in the boy's hand.

'*Diolch yn fawr*, mister,' thanked the lad, clearly delighted.

Chard watched the boy turn and scamper up the road and then turned his mind as to what he should do next. He could go straight to his accommodation at the New Inn which purportedly was in the centre of the town, or he could forget about the boy's advice and go looking for this Ivor Arms rather than wait until daylight. He decided on a third option. He needed to get used to this town, which would be his home for the foreseeable future, so why not face up to the worst it had to offer, and quench his thirst at the same time? Scratching his sideburn by his right ear, he looked around at his options. He should have asked young Dilwyn which of the pubs on the Tumble should definitely be avoided, but he hadn't, so it was down to pot luck.

He started towards the Half Moon, but seeing a couple of ladies of negotiable affection heading towards him, he veered to the right and headed for the Red Lion. A man hurrying past towards the railway bridge nearly knocked him over. Chard turned to remonstrate but the man was already under the bridge, looking nervously over his shoulder as he walked quickly on. Chard decided to ignore the incident and carried on towards the Red Lion.

*   *   *

The nervous man stopped just under the bridge and watched Chard enter the pub. He kept staring back towards the Tumble. He was sure he was being followed. Was that a movement in the shadows across the road? He shivered as a train rumbled overhead and his footsteps echoed off the white-tiled walls of the underpass as he walked quickly up towards the Graig hill. He looked once more over his shoulder to see if he was being followed and that was his undoing. A large fist came out of the shadows and dragged him into a narrow alley. Though it was almost pitch black he could make out the silhouette of the man in front of him. He wept as he soiled himself for he knew who the man was and what he wanted. The crying man never saw the hammer being swung low, but he heard the cracking, splintering sound as the metal hit his kneecap, and felt the white-hot pain, the indescribable agony as his body collapsed, writhing to the ground.

✳   ✳   ✳

Chard gripped the brass door handle and turned it firmly.

The door was stiff in its frame, needing a shove with the shoulder to force it open. There was a step down into a smoky room made welcoming by a roaring fire in an ornate wrought-iron fireplace. Three aged men sat close to the flames conversing in whispers, oblivious to the newcomer's entrance.

Wall mounted gas lamps lit the way through into the adjoining bar area. A group of four men stood at the right hand side of the bar, cursing and arguing amongst themselves, clearly the worse for having had too much to drink. Chard made his way to the left hand side of the bar where a customer leaned, holding two terriers by a lead. He bent down to pat them.

'Careful, or they'll take your hand off,' warned their master, but they just wagged their tails delightedly and licked Chard's hand.

Straightening up, he placed a foot on the metal footrest and gestured to the barman.

'I'll take a pint of pale ale, please.'

The barman, a scruffy young man with a goatee beard,

nodded an acknowledgement and pulled a pint of golden liquid that looked enticing.

'That'll be tuppence,' grunted the barman.

Chard put two pennies on the bar and took a sip of the beer, savouring the delicate hoppy flavour. He gave an appreciative nod and moved to the far corner of the bar, taking a seat where he could observe the room. An old man and woman sat at a table close by. This clearly wasn't the most popular pub in town and perhaps the reason for that was manifesting itself at the opposite end of the bar, where a group of four men was creating a commotion.

'They're a bad lot,' commented the old woman who could see that Chard was staring in that direction.

'Local men, I take it?'

'They work at the new slaughterhouse across by the Tram Road. It only opened last year,' informed the woman who then went into a series of hacking coughs.

'That big one there with the black beard, he's Slitter,' chipped in her companion through teeth heavily stained with tobacco. 'You know, Slitter Watkins? He plays in the front row for Cilfynydd rugby. You must know him,' he insisted.

'Sorry, I don't. I'm not from around here. Charming name, by the way.'

'Well, it's his job, isn't it?' rejoined the old woman. 'Kills the animals in the slaughter house. I wouldn't do it. It would drive me *twp*,' she said firmly, tapping the side of her head.

'He's not got all his marbles, that's for definite. Just look at him now,' added the man drawing their attention to Slitter who had one of his companions by the throat.

The other man was much smaller and he stared with goggle eyes as he tried to breathe. His fingers grabbed desperately at the fist that held him. Meanwhile the other two were holding on to Slitter's arms trying to make him let go.

'He didn't mean it. It was only a joke,' said one of them who wore a blue workman's jacket.

'Yes, cool head now. You don't want to kill him,' cajoled the fourth man who, with grey hair and a creased face, looked much older than the others.

The pressure was not being eased and from his seat Chard could see that the small man was having the life choked out of him.

Chard was not a particularly big man, but he had been blessed with a fine pair of lungs and a commanding voice when he chose to use it. He stood to his feet.

'Put that man down! NOW!' he boomed.

Everything went quiet. Slitter and his companions stood stock still. Slowly he let go of the man who slipped to the floor with a thud. After a pause that seemed to take forever, he turned around.

'Who the fuck are you?' he shouted, spittle spraying from his mouth.

Chard considered his options. Ideally he would try and calm the man and talk his way out of the situation, but looking in his eyes, that wasn't going to be likely. The man was too drunk and too angry. This was not going to end well because the only real option was going to be to fight him, and he hated violence. However, that wasn't to say that he didn't know how to use it. Slitter was taller and heavier but he was drunk which hopefully would even the odds.

'I said …'

'I know what you said.

'The name is Chard, Thomas Chard. Maybe we should calm down, have a drink … and sort things out quietly.' Perhaps there was a chance of avoiding violence.

There wasn't.

'Calm down, my arse,' grunted Slitter as he stepped forward and threw a haymaker of a punch.

Chard dodged the blow and instinctively aimed his straightened fingers at his assailant's throat. The attempt was ill-timed and had been made without taking proper aim and as a result it missed, his hand landing harmlessly in mid-air. Slitter gave a roar and, picking up a bottle from the bar, aimed a swing at Chard's head. The heavy blow also missed and took him off balance, the momentum carrying him past his target. Chard saw his opportunity and, grasping both hands together, brought them down in a hammer blow on the top of Slitter's back. The impact clearly had an effect as he dropped his weapon, which rolled across the floor and under a table. He straightened up, turned to face Chard and cracked his knuckles.

'I'm going to make you wish you'd never been born. I'll have your balls for breakfast.'

His face full of fury, Slitter made a grab for Chard's right arm but he easily twisted out of the grip, grabbed an ashtray from a nearby table and slammed it down on his opponent's left collar bone. Slitter let out a bellow of pain and made a lunge for Chard who calmly stepped to the side, evading the attempt easily. He then aimed a punch to the side of Slitter's head which should have felled him, but it was like hitting a tree. Chard drew back, nursing the bruised knuckles on his right hand.

His opponent tried to seize the advantage this time with a clever kick which looked like it was going for his stomach but, as Chard drew back out of the way, it missed its original target and caught him on the inside of his right thigh instead.

'That's got yer!' Slitter cried, before following up with another kick, this time to the left shin. Chard gave a yelp and reached out a hand against the wall to prevent himself from falling over. With a triumphant shout Slitter threw a punch at his ribs but Chard was able to block it with his free arm, deflecting it outside the point of intended impact. Then quickly putting his thumb on the inside of his attacker's wrist, with his other fingers on the opposite side, he twisted, putting his opponent into a wristlock.

Using this as leverage he slammed Slitter into the edge of the bar with all the force he could muster. There was a tremendous bang like a trap door slamming shut and Slitter slid to the floor, out cold.

Chard breathed a sigh of relief and, rubbing his bruised shin, he turned around. He had a smile on his face which soon vanished as he saw the bottle coming towards him and suddenly everything went black.

'He put up a good fight, but we'd better throw him out before Slitter comes round or we'll be witnesses to a killing,' said the man in the blue workman's jacket.

'Aye, *chwarae teg*, he gave Slitter a good lamping there. We're doing him a favour. I hope I didn't hit him too hard with the bottle,' worried his grey-haired friend.

They took him by the arms and legs and the small man who had been in danger of being choked opened the door for them. With three swings they let go and Chard landed in the gutter.

He was woken only five minutes later by the prod of a boot in the ribs.

'Hello, what piece of gutter shit do we have here?'

Chard shook his aching head and cleared his vision. He looked up at the decidedly unpleasant face of a man in a police uniform.

'The piece of gutter shit that will make your life hell if you don't help me up. I am your new inspector.'

CHAPTER FOUR

Chard woke with a start. His head hurt damnably and his eyes squinted as sunlight shone through a gap in the curtains of his room. He reached across to the bedside table and checked his pocket watch. It was late morning. He recalled that the previous night he had been assisted to the New Inn by a reluctant Constable Jackson and had given orders to the night clerk that he was not to be disturbed. Rubbing his eyes he got out of bed and went to the china washbasin, poured some cold water from the decorative jug placed alongside and splashed his face. The shock of the cold liquid hitting his skin made him shiver.

Pulling the curtain aside he could see that there were blue skies with bright sunshine for the first time in days.

After his ablutions Chard dressed and made his way out of the room and down the elaborate, impressive, staircase which he had not been in a condition to appreciate the previous evening. His shin still hurt and he grimaced every time he took a step downward. He was greeted at the bottom of the stairs by a prim, elegantly attired middle-aged lady who carried a stern expression on her face.

'Good morning Mr Chard. I am Mrs Miles, the owner of this establishment.'

Chard anticipated that he was in for an admonishment.

'Mr. Chard, I would like to have a word with you regarding your arrival last night,' continued Mrs Miles. 'I am informed by my staff that you were escorted here by a police constable and it appears that you had been involved in an affray,' she continued. 'I would have you know that this is a very respectable establishment and our reputation is paramount. Do you have anything to say on the matter?' she demanded.

Chard decided that a charm offensive was the best way

forward, so he lightened his normally grim expression with a polite smile.

'I do most humbly apologise if I caused your staff and your good self any concern, dear lady. Actually, I am the new inspector of police but unfortunately I tripped on some steps and had a nasty fall,' he lied.

The lady proprietor was mortified.

'Oh, you poor man. Here I am confronting you as if you had done something wrong when you have come to take up such an important and respectable position in our community. I am most dreadfully sorry.'

'Not to worry, Mrs Miles. No harm done. I intend to take a stroll around the town as it's such a nice day. I shall dine in tonight but thought I might get a midday meal somewhere on my walk.'

'There are several establishments that provide midday meals, but no alcohol of course, as it's the Lord's day. If you are unsuccessful we have our coffee room open but the bar will of course be closed.'

Chard expressed his thanks and made his way outside onto the main street. Although sunny, there was a slight chill in the air when the breeze blew and he was glad of his warm tweed jacket.

He recalled that on the previous night the constable had led him past several public houses, then a theatre, over a bridge with iron railings underneath which the River Rhondda flowed to meet the River Taff a short distance beyond, past a left hand junction and then a few yards on to his current location. Chard had no particular desire to go back in that direction so decided to turn left and take a stroll down the town's main shopping street. He remembered the urchin outside the station and his recommendation of the Ivor Arms, so, with nothing else to do in particular, he decided to seek it out.

The street was decidedly quiet. There was a gig parked outside the Butchers Arms, a large establishment almost opposite the New Inn and the occasional snort of its horse was the only sound to break the silence. It was as if he had been transported magically to a completely different town from the one he had experienced the previous night. He passed the small junction leading to Market Street which then ran parallel to and above Taff Street on which he stood; the streets separated by a row of shops and a high wall. On the corner of the road was Thompson & Shackell's New Music Salon, but no sound came from within. Chard passed a wide variety of premises; a pawnbroker's to his left, a jeweller's to his right, both heavily shuttered; here a chemist shop, there a sweet shop. He stopped briefly to tip his hat at a pair of attractive young ladies in extravagant hats who gave him a nod of acknowledgement as they passed by.

He continued past a baker's shop, and paused at a lamp post where Market Street re-joined Taff Street, in order to allow an overweight man with unruly grey hair to pass on the pavement. The man was being taken for a walk (for it could not be said otherwise) by a panting boxer dog that pulled him onwards far faster than he really wanted to go.

A graveyard wall was now on the left side of the road, belonging to a large grey stone chapel. There was singing coming from within, interrupted by the clatter of horseshoes on cobblestones as a cart appeared from behind a large ironmonger's shop across the road. Just a few yards further on he came to a square with shops either side, which was dominated by the front edifice of the chapel and also an extraordinary piece of unfinished construction work. It was a large ornamental drinking fountain which by his estimation was at least fifteen feet high. It had a finely sculpted base, roughly square in shape with moulded drinking basins on each side. Four ornate pillars supported a richly decorated canopy which was surmounted by a lamp base, either side of which were two wrought iron dragons. These supported the rounded gas lamp itself which was topped by a delicate small cupola. Clearly this was a new installation as the area around it was rubble and there was much more to be done.

As he was admiring the craftsmanship Chard became aware of a hubbub behind him. It was a pleasing sound, like the buzzing of bees on a summer's day. He turned around to see that morning service had finished and the congregation was now emerging, all in their Sunday best, smiling and talking happily.

Their happiness was contagious and Chard felt his own spirits lifted so that the previous day's bad start was fading into the background. He noticed that he had stopped limping without realising it and even his sore head was much eased.

On he walked, past yet more shops as he realised that the town was bigger than he had originally thought. He recalled the urchin's directions as being 'the other end of town and over the bridge' so he pressed on, ignoring the small side streets. The variety of shops was endless. Fancy goods, sweet shops, jewellers, pawnbrokers, tailors and the inevitable licensed premises led to a road junction. Looking to his right Chard smiled. There was the bridge, or to be correct, there were the bridges in question.

* * *

Jenny smiled to Father McManus as she stood by the church door.

'Wonderful service, Father, you must have made the sun come out'.

'Thank you, my child, but I am sure I had nothing to do with it. Shall we see you at the parish meeting on Wednesday?'

'Of course, Father. I will look forward to it,' she replied before smiling and walking out into the fresh breeze.

Such a lovely girl, thought the priest to himself. It would be nice for her to be married here someday. Thinking of which …

'Good morning, Jack,' he said aloud.

'Good morning, Father,' he responded clearly not really wanting to stop to chat.

'You are looking a little flushed. Are you alright?'

'I am fine, Father, really I am. I am sorry, I must go,' he added hastily, and before Father McManus could say another word he was off as quick as he could in the same direction as Jenny.

The priest watched him go, shook his head and then turned back to talk to the rest of his emerging parishioners.

* * *

One of the few things that he knew about Pontypridd was the pride the people had in their Old Bridge. Now used solely as a footbridge, it had been one of the longest single span stone bridges in the world at the time it was built in 1756. However, when it was completed they found it was far too steep and in some cases too narrow for farm carts and other commercial vehicles. Consequently a century later, another three-arch bridge had to be built alongside. The New Bridge had been very controversial at the time because the aesthetics of the Old Bridge, with the River Taff flowing through the valley, had drawn many artists to the view, which was now largely spoiled.

The morning was still very quiet with only the few occasional pedestrians on their way home from church or chapel and Chard continued his walk across the New Bridge in relative silence.

To his right, just over the bridge, was the Maltsters Arms and further ahead he could see a large lime-washed establishment clearly signed The Ivor Arms. He just hoped that the long walk had been worthwhile.

As soon as he opened the door he realised that maybe he was in luck as the smell of roast gammon hit his senses.

The interior of the inn was a little dim and the room not as big as he had expected, though a side door hinted that there were additional rooms beyond. The floor was constructed of bare flagstones and the walls were whitewashed, no doubt to help lift the room's brightness. There were bench seats around the edges of the room with several tables and accompanying chairs scattered around. The bar took up much of the left hand side of the room and it was from this general direction that he heard himself addressed.

'I'm sorry, we are closed,' said a firm female voice.

A woman had appeared from another door behind the bar in the far left hand corner which, from the delicious smells emanating, had to be the kitchen.

'My apologies,' he replied, and he meant it for his stomach was starting to rumble. 'I could smell food.' He took in the quite remarkable lady in front of him. She was as broad as she was tall with an enormous bosom primly covered by a high-collared dress which struggled to contain its contents. Her hair was piled high with twin curls allowed to drop either side framing a round pleasant face with a slightly turned up nose and a wide mouth.

'That's only because we have some paying guests staying overnight. We don't open on a Sunday as we obviously are not allowed to serve alcohol on the Lord's day.' She turned to go back to the kitchen.

'You were highly recommended to me.'

She turned and raised an eyebrow. 'By who?'

'A small boy. He said that if I came here, someone called Gwen would look after me.'

She laughed. 'Well, I am Mrs Williams and this is my establishment. Everyone knows me as Gwen but it's come to something when I have small boys recommending me. What was his name?'

'He said his name was Dilwyn.'

'Oh Dilwyn. Poor little bugger.' Remembering it was a Sunday she crossed herself and whispered an apology.

'Seemed like a nice lad. He said that his mother died of typhoid.'

'Yes, and his father is no bloody good.' She crossed herself again. 'Oh well, as Dilwyn recommended you, perhaps I can make an exception just this once. Our guests want to eat in their rooms so I'll just take their food up and then I'll sort you out. Do me a favour though and put the latch on the front door. I don't want anyone else turning up.'

Chard turned and did as he was told, his stomach rumbling once more in anticipation. He took off his hat and jacket, placed them on a spare chair and sat down.

A few minutes later the landlady reappeared carrying a tray with two steaming bowls of food which smelled delicious. She put it down on a table, opened a door across the room and could then be heard thudding her way up a staircase.

When she returned she nodded towards Chard, 'Will *cawl* do for you?' she asked.

He looked blank.

'*Cawl*,' she repeated.

Still a blank look.

'Sorry, you're English and obviously not been here long so you don't understand. I'll get you some anyway.'

Moments later she came in with a steaming bowl of thick broth with chunks of gammon, leeks, potatoes and carrots for him.

'I'll get you some cutlery and bread, and then after you've finished you can tell me all about yourself.'

Chard tucked in with relish. It was difficult to get the balance right between wolfing it all down and slowly savouring the flavour in each mouthful.

After he finished, he slouched back in his seat and patted his stomach.

Mrs Williams appeared, took his empty bowl away and placed it temporarily on the bar.

'It's a pity there's nothing to wash it down with,' said Chard regretfully.

'Well I don't break the law, but I can give you a free cup of coffee.'

The landlady went into the kitchen and when she eventually came back it was with two steaming hot mugs of black coffee.

She sat down opposite him. 'You have me at a disadvantage, so start by telling me your name.'

'Well my friends, of whom, after that meal, you are definitely one, call me Thomas.'

'Well then, you can call me Gwen like everyone else around here. So, Thomas, what brings you to Ponty?' she asked sipping her coffee.

'I have the honour of being the new police inspector,' he replied raising his mug to his lips.

Gwen looked concerned. Chard took a sip of his drink.

'My, this is special coffee,' he coughed as the unmistakeable hit of brandy reached his throat. He glanced up and noticed the landlady's expression. 'It's OK, your licence is safe. You gave me a cup of coffee, you didn't sell it. I don't want you to think that I turn a blind eye to things though. If I had seen anything serious then I would have to do my duty.' Chard gave a reassuring smile. 'If you are wondering why I came here, I will explain. I know from experience that because of my position I will be expected to join a social circle, perhaps a gentleman's club and so on. I will then be pestered for favours or for my opinion on this and that. Everything I say or do will be scrutinised and I won't be able to relax. I just wanted to find somewhere to get away from things when I need to think and I do my best thinking with a pint of beer in my hand.'

Gwen seemed to relax. 'You will be welcome here but I will have to put the word around to the regulars about who you are. We don't have any villains coming in, I see to that, but I don't want any embarrassment caused if any of the lads say things that put you in an awkward situation. I think that they'll be pleased because if you start coming here then I suspect the constables will stay clear, including that awful Constable Jackson.'

'I met him last night,' grimaced Chard.

'Nasty little shit,' spat out the landlady who then realised her bad language, crossed herself again and whispered another little prayer of forgiveness. 'My husband used to think the same.'

'Is Mr Williams still …?'

'I lost him three years ago,' interrupted Gwen.

'I am sorry, it must be difficult being a widow and running a pub on your own,' responded the inspector sympathetically.

'Don't be sorry. He's living in sin somewhere in Newport with an Irish tart,' explained Gwen with a shrug. 'He was a right arsehole and I'm glad to be rid of him,' she continued, with one more apology to the heavens.

Chard didn't quite know what to say next, so was relieved when Gwen changed the topic of conversation.

'What do you think of Ponty so far?' she asked.

The inspector pondered. 'To be honest I don't know what to think. I arrived last night and it was like a scene from hell. I became involved in a fight and ended up having to be escorted home with bumps and bruises. Then I come out this morning and everything is as genteel as you could wish for. It's very confusing.'

'Well, Thomas, I'll tell you something for nothing. The people here are good and warm-hearted and there are better conditions here than some of the places up the valleys, but we still have our share of poverty. We have also had outbreaks of cholera and typhoid over the years. Most of the working men around here have got hard backbreaking jobs. Ponty is surrounded by coal mines such as the Maritime and the Great Western, then there's also the chain works, the canal, the Forest Iron & Steel works, Victoria brickworks, Taff Vale Ironworks...'

'I get the picture,' interrupted Chard.

'The point is it is a hard life and it can be a short one. If you are too ill to work you end up homeless. Nobody wants to end up dying in the workhouse. So what happens is, come payday, everybody forgets their troubles and lets loose on a Saturday night. Not that there aren't any villains, but if they come in here they go out through the window.' She flexed her mighty forearm as she said this. Chard laughed as did she.

Suddenly, there was a rap on the door.

'Ignore it,' said Gwen.

The rap came again, and a few moments later it was repeated. Gwen sighed realising that it wasn't going to go away. She got up and opened the door. In slid the shiftiest-looking human specimen that Chard had ever seen. Led by an enormous bulbous nose which covered a drooping black moustache, a man entered wearing a long brown coat that came down to his shins. There seemed to be something inside the coat that was weighing it down as he moved. He wore a flat cap on his head and his eyes moved swiftly from side to side finally resting on Chard. He whispered to Gwen who whispered back, then with his eyes still fixed on the inspector he sidled sideways towards the kitchen and disappeared inside.

'Who is that?' asked Chard.

Gwen laughed. 'Old Dic Jenkins. He is a purveyor of the finest salmon, trout, pike and perch.'

'From …?'

'Ask no questions and I'll tell you no lies.'

Dic reappeared shortly afterwards, his coat clearly much lighter. He tipped his cap in Gwen's direction then, with a final anxious look at Chard, quickly opened the door and left.

Chard finished his coffee. 'Well, Gwen, I think I am going to fit in here, but don't think of me as an inspector. I am just Thomas.'

'I'll make sure that you are made welcome but my barman is an odd so-and-so. He is good at his job but can be a bit grumpy, so don't take offence.'

'I'll bear that in mind. Anyway, it has been a pleasure.' With that he put on his jacket and hat, bade farewell and went out into the street feeling less pessimistic about the future and looking forward to his first day at the police station.

CHAPTER FIVE

The following morning Chard presented himself at the forbidding grey-stone building that housed the police station. It stood in the shadow of St Catherine's Church just outside the town centre. In the reception area there was a desk manned by a burly police sergeant with thinning hair and missing front teeth.

'Inspector Chard. I believe I am expected.'

'Yes sir. I'll let you through,' he replied with what passed as a smile. The sergeant disappeared for a moment, then with a loud rattle of a bolt, a door to Chard's right was opened to allow him to pass through.

'I am Sergeant Humphreys. I'll take you through to Superintendent Jones, Inspector'.

Chard was led through the common room where a handful of officers were gathered. Two men sat at desks writing whilst the others were being briefed by a very large bearded sergeant. Humphreys knocked on a polished wooden door in the corner of the room.

'Enter!'

Humphreys held the door open and Chard went in. A distinguished man with sideburns and a bushy moustache stood behind a large oak desk. He wore his superintendent's uniform of navy blue with black braid, and the silver insignia on his collar had been finely polished. His face was stern and he was clearly not a man who would suffer fools gladly. He looked Chard up and down like a lion regarding its prey.

'Inspector Chard, I presume.' His voice was strong, commanding and intimidating.

'Yes sir. Pleased to make your acquaintance, Superintendent.'

There was a pause as Superintendent Jones fixed him

with a stare. Chard felt uncomfortable. The superintendent eventually broke eye contact, glanced at his desk, before looking back up.

'It is a great disappointment to me that I hear you were found lying in the gutter after a drunken brawl on Saturday night,' he stated sternly.

Chard was taken aback with surprise that the superintendent had come to hear of the incident, and the injustice of the implied accusation.

'Well sir, I had been attempting to break up a fight and I certainly was not drunk,' he argued.

'Do you deny that you were lying in the gutter after a brawl?'

Chard cursed Constable Jackson inwardly.

'No sir,' replied Chard sheepishly, for there was no way he could refute the allegation.

'It is only because I happen to know your former superintendent personally, having served with him in South Africa, that I am allowing you to stay. If it were otherwise you would be going back to England on the next train. Do I make myself clear?'

'Yes sir,' answered Chard quickly. The sooner this is over the better, he thought to himself.

Another uncomfortable pause. The superintendent coughed.

'Very well then. I hope there are no further incidents. Take a seat.'

They both sat down, the superintendent leaning forward, both hands clasped on the desk in front of him.

'What do you know about this town?'

'I have read a little about Pontypridd in my Bradshaw's Guide sir. I know it is heavily industrialised and the town seems to be very proud of its Old Bridge. My experience of the people since I have arrived has been very mixed. It can be as rough as Bristol Docks on one day and as genteel as Bath on the next.'

Superintendent Jones nodded, furrowed his brow and began to speak.

'Your home town of Shrewsbury has been in existence as a fully developed town for nigh on a thousand years. Two hundred years ago Pontypridd, as such, didn't exist. It was just a crossing point, a ford on the river. Fifty years ago the population was around two thousand souls. Now, if we include the adjoining urban districts of Treforest, Cilfynydd and so on, the population is somewhere in the region of thirty-five thousand.'

The superintendent paused again to let the words sink in. He was pleased to see that Chard's face was very serious and, satisfied that his statements were having an effect, he gave a wry smile and continued.

'We are the gateway to the Rhondda valleys and the Merthyr Vale. The anthracite coal mined here and in the valleys is the best in the world. It fuels homes, factories, railways and very importantly the Royal Navy. It is a major part of our export trade and the economy relies on it. The iron and steel industry is not as strong as it was, in fact it's going through a bad patch, but it is still important. Also, in Pontypridd we have the Newbridge Chainworks. Have you seen that photograph of Brunel standing in front of the enormous chains of the Great Eastern?'

'Yes, it's quite famous.'

'Well those chains were made in this town. Then there's the tinplate works down the river …'

The superintendent halted his speech, got up and started to pace backwards and forwards behind the desk as he continued.

'We have four main commercial routes that run through the town roughly north to south. There is one principal road to Cardiff, the Glamorganshire Canal from Merthyr carries much commercial traffic, and then there are the two railway lines.'

'Two?' asked Chard with a raised eyebrow.

'Yes. You will have come up from Cardiff on the Taff Vale Railway into what they still call Newbridge Junction, but if you were to go a few hundred yards up the Graig hill you would find another station belonging to the Barry Railway Company. It travels through a tunnel almost a mile long to its own Treforest Station, then onwards to Barry Docks. It only takes commercial traffic though, no passengers. The employees of the two companies hate each other and cause no end of trouble, which comes to my final point. The people.'

Superintendent Jones sat back down and leaned forward again as if to emphasise the importance of what he had to say next.

'I mentioned earlier how long Shrewsbury has been established. You come from a town where families have lived for decades if not centuries. The social structures are all in place, there is a common culture and people of importance are respected. Here, the social order is not so firmly established, the common culture of the valleys is only in its infancy. Only a small percentage of people can trace their roots in this town over more than a century. Apart from those who have moved here from other parts of Wales there are also Englishmen from the West Country who came here when their rural economy collapsed thirty years ago, miners from the North of England and from the Midlands, plus get-rich-quick investors from the cities.

In addition we have Irish, Polish and even some immigrants from the Ukraine. In fact we've probably got half the world's destitute that can't afford to get to America coming to the South Wales valleys. With the cheap labour the working conditions are in the most part terrible, especially in the coal mines. There was the strike two years ago when troops including the 14th Hussars were deployed to keep order, and no doubt you will have heard about the disaster at Cilfynydd last year.'

'Indeed I have, sir, though not in great detail.'

'Well many of us here dealt with the aftermath and frankly we would rather not talk about it. I would advise that for the time being you refrain from mentioning that terrible event.'

'I have been told that there is a lot of poverty in the area, especially further up in the valleys,' commented Chard.

'Correct, which helps to fuel industrial unrest. The railway employees are currently kicking up a fuss and the last thing we want is a strike. Politically this is a powder keg waiting to blow and the government is afraid of communist influences. On top of this of course we have got the day-to-day problems of law and order; drunkenness, pickpockets, assaults and so on. So you can see my problem when I tell you that my command here, including yourself, is twenty officers.'

'That certainly seems a challenge, sir. Are the powers that be not able to provide more men?'

'Unfortunately, not. The Glamorgan Constabulary is stretched to the limit and the most recent recruits have been sent to Merthyr Tydfil which is the area with the biggest problems. However, we might have our own challenges highlighted now that we have a new local authority. Pontypridd Urban District Council came into being at the start of the month. Colonel Grover, the clerk of the council, is a fine fellow and I am sure the new authority will be supportive.'

The superintendent seemed to relax a little and leant back in his chair.

'Now, as to your duties. As inspector I expect your role to be largely one of administration.'

Chard's face dropped.

'I have one desk sergeant who is near retirement, two other sergeants, one of whom is on the sick list and likely to remain so for at least a month, and sixteen constables who work shift patterns. In addition we allocate responsibility for some of the outlying areas to individual constables, usually based on where they live. So for example, minor crimes in Treforest are dealt with by Constable Preece because he lives locally and the residents know how to get hold of him. These men and these arrangements need to be managed and that is your role.'

'Will I not be working on any crimes, sir?'

'Only if they are major crimes, by which I mean murders or physical attacks on respectable women, and thankfully there are few of those.'

'Major crimes or respectable women, sir?' asked Chard innocently.

'Do not be flippant!'

Chard looked into the superintendent's eyes and wished that he had kept his mouth shut.

'I will shortly call in Sergeant Morris who will show you around and then you can start your duties. However, there are another couple of things to discuss before I do. We will start with your uniform.'

'My uniform, sir?'

'Yes. I understand that Shropshire had been experimenting with a detective branch like they have in London, Nottingham and a few other cities where inspectors swan around wearing what they like. However, that does not happen here. Your first task at your desk will be to requisition your uniform from our stores in Cardiff. I will not have men under my command that are improperly dressed. Do I make myself clear?'

'Yes sir. I understand,' replied Chard, a little disappointed.

'The other thing that I wanted to mention is that I

appreciate you are new here and may take some time to get accustomed to things. Particularly the paperwork. So I am going to allocate one of the constables to assist you. Not full time you understand, he will have his other duties which I am sure you will allocate to him but the officer I have in mind may be quite suitable for your needs.'

'Would that be the Constable Preece that you mentioned, sir?'

'Yes, exactly. He is a little different to the average constable. Not as robust physically as the others and a bit of an intellectual. Both his parents were teachers and I dare say that if his father hadn't been killed during a robbery he might have gone to private schooling in Cardiff and ended up in a university.'

'His father died in a robbery you say?'

'Yes. The culprits were never caught. I think it's the reason he joined the force.'

The superintendent got up from behind his desk, walked to the door and gestured to someone outside. It was the large bearded sergeant that Chard had noticed on the way in. As he came closer to the door Chard could see that he was a veritable man mountain with a barrel chest and huge arms.

'Sergeant Morris, this is your new inspector. Mr Chard.'

'Pleased to meet you, sir.' His voice was unexpectedly soft for such a leviathan.

'Show the inspector around the station, Sergeant. Mr Chard will be at his desk thereafter as there is much for him to do on his first day, but I think that tomorrow morning it might be useful for you to take him for a walk through town. Show him some of the less obvious places of interest.'

The superintendent then gave a curt nod before returning to his inner sanctum, leaving the inspector and sergeant to themselves.

Sergeant Morris led the inspector into the centre of the room.

'Listen up lads,' he commanded in a clear yet still surprisingly quiet voice.

'This is our new inspector, Mr Chard.'

The constables stopped what they were doing and stood to attention.

'This here is Constable Jenkins. Very fine boxer for the force.'

Chard nodded towards a tall young man with peculiarly set ears, as if they had been stuck on the side of his head as an afterthought. He looked quite formidable, as did the next in line, again a tall young man with a rosy complexion and an untidy beard.

'Constable Matthews. A good officer when he isn't larking about.'

'Who me, Sergeant?' he replied with smiling eyes.

'Yes you,' but the sergeant was smiling himself.

The next constable was just over regulation height but stocky and thick set with mutton chop whiskers.

'Constable Morgan. Plays rugby for the force and our best player.'

They continued to walk down the line as the sergeant introduced the final two constables in the room.

'Constable Scudamore and Constable Davies make up our happy band today. The others are out on patrol.'

Scudamore was a tall, slightly older man with ginger hair and a bearing that would easily point him out as a policeman anywhere in a crowd. Davies on the other hand would easily fit in behind a butcher's counter. Large and carrying an undue amount of weight, Chard could not imagine him running after criminals.

'Thank you, Sergeant. Pleased to meet all of you. I am sure

that we will become properly acquainted once I have my feet properly under the table. You may return to your duties.'

The room returned to normality and the sergeant proceeded to give Chard a tour of the rest of the building. The first floor was in a state of general disrepair and used only for storage of building materials ready for future renovation. On the ground floor there were six cells, two being occupied by a couple of sorry looking individuals, two store rooms, a locker room, a mess room with a stove, and eventually they came back to where they started. In the far corner of this room, at the opposite end to the superintendent's office, his own office awaited him.

Chard entered, hung his jacket and hat on the stand next to the desk, looked at the paperwork that was already stacked thereon awaiting his attention, and wondered if he had done the right thing.

* * *

It was dark in the lane behind the row of terraced houses. No rays of light escaped from the windows. Fortunately there was enough moonlight to guide the man's footsteps, not because he didn't know the way, but the path was strewn with loose stones and pitted with holes that could turn an ankle. It was cold and he felt the chill stinging his facial scars. There, up ahead, was a small red glow from a lit cigarette. He absent-mindedly let his left hand stray to the pocket of his large coat and stroked the handle of the heavy lump hammer that lay within. Not that he would need it any more this night. In fact he didn't ever really need to carry it. Only one man had ever bested him, and he wasn't around anymore. It did inspire fear, though, and that could be useful. Not that there would be any fear shown by the person he was about to meet. Quite the reverse in fact. He was not overly big in stature but there was something about his eyes, something dark and predatory.

A voice came from behind the cigarette smoke.

'About time.'

No other words were spoken.

The man with the scarred face took a canvas bag off his shoulder, took out a smaller cloth bag and handed it to the cigarette smoker. He in turn opened his jacket, reached into an inside pocket and handed over the contents.

The scarred man nodded, turned on his heel and disappeared into the darkness whilst the bag was taken indoors and carefully locked away.

CHAPTER SIX

The following morning found Chard standing on the Tumble outside the Clarence Hotel accompanied by Sergeant Morris. The inspector was pleased that his uniform would take a while to arrive and wore a smart herring bone pattern grey suit with a navy blue waistcoat.

'Right then, Mr Chard. We will take a little stroll down through the town and I'll give you some local knowledge that may be useful.'

'I can't wait to be educated, Sergeant,' Chard responded with a smile. Morris was clearly a very affable gentle giant and he felt relaxed in his company.

'Well sir, let us start with the public house by there.' He pointed across the street to premises with a bay window and a door to the side. 'That is the Bunch of Grapes and it hasn't got a particularly good reputation.'

Chard nodded. 'That seems straightforward.'

'Yes sir, but it isn't the only Bunch of Grapes. We have another one near the chainworks and that one is excellent. So you wouldn't want to send men to the wrong one would you, sir?'

The sergeant didn't wait for the obvious answer but continued speaking as they walked further down the road.

'Now then, this here on the right is the Vic, I mean the Victoria, sir. My advice is not to go in there at night unless you've got one of the lads with you. If you go down the alley next to it you'll come to the Empire Music Hall. A bit coarse for my tastes sir, my good lady would rather go to the Clarence Theatre.'

They crossed a bridge over the River Rhondda which flowed from left to right, joining the larger River Taff a few yards downstream. Not far ahead Chard noticed the New Inn as it came into view.

'You'll have seen the Butchers Arms, sir?' asked Sergeant Morris pointing obliquely to the right.

'As it's directly across the road from where I'm staying I could hardly miss it,' Chard replied with pleasant sarcasm.

'Quite so sir, but I was just going to point out that in the yard behind it there are often sales and auctions. A good place to keep your eye on if you know what I mean, sir.'

'Ah, I see ...'

The sergeant pointed to a street that branched off to their left.

'Down that direction there's flour mills and ...'

Before he could finish there was a shout of '*Shwmae* Sergeant Morris.'

Chard turned to see a smiling bearded man sat upon a two-wheeled cart pulled by a small brown pony. He wore a bowler hat, a rather shabby jacket and through the bottom of one of his trouser legs poked a wooden peg leg.

'*Shwmae* Tom,' called the sergeant in response to the greeting. I see your peg is outside the cart today so the weather's staying fine is it?'

'Certain to be, Sergeant. Can't be sure whether it will be more than a day or two. Good for the cockles though.'

With that he gave the pony a nudge and they continued up the street towards the Tumble.

'That's Tom Cockles, as we call him. He says he feels the weather through his wooden leg. Must be nonsense yet he is usually pretty accurate. He is a well-known character in these parts. Sells shellfish in the market and has a small shop.'

They watched him disappear up the street, then Chard turned to the sergeant.

'By the way, Sergeant, if you don't mind me asking, there are a couple of things I would like to ask you.'

They resumed walking as they continued their conversation.

'Yes sir, what is it that you want to know?'

'Well as you may be aware, Shrewsbury is not far from the border with Mid Wales so I am not unfamiliar with Welsh people. I have heard Welsh spoken but I cannot understand it, spell it or say it properly.'

'I had noticed, begging your pardon, sir.'

Chard gave a frown.

The sergeant indicated that they should continue directly ahead on Taff Street, rather than take the fork into Market Street.

'The market is best experienced on one of the main market days, namely Wednesday, Friday or Saturday. Literally thousands of people turn up. They come from miles around,' he said proudly.

Chard put the conversation back on track.

'Do you speak Welsh as your first language, Sergeant?'

'No sir. I have never spoken Welsh as such.'

'Come now, Sergeant, I just heard you.'

'Well, you just pick it up. On one hand we have some people here who are born and bred in Wales who still use Welsh as a first language. However we also have, for example, Polish people who have been living here for some time who will watch a boxing match and if one wins over another they will say '*chwarae teg*' meaning 'well done, fair play' without even realising they are speaking Welsh.'

'You never know I might pick up a bit myself.'

'I am sure you will, sir.'

The pavements were getting busier as they proceeded further down Taff Street but the sight of the formidable sergeant ensured that the crowds of shoppers parted to let them through. Chard stopped to admire a magnificent white stallion ridden by a distinguished gentleman in a long riding coat. He liked horses and could just about ride one but had no illusions about his abilities; he was no horseman.

The sergeant interrupted his thoughts.

'I may as well mention that in these parts we do also have our own little turns of phrase that you might notice.'

'Such as, Sergeant?'

'Oh, just this and that. For example, if we ask someone for a description of a suspect he might point at you and say, 'He's about your dap'. Meaning about your size. Then again we refer to sports shoes, what you English call pumps or plimsolls, as daps. Someone's friend is known as his butty so a greeting might be "Alright butt?" ' The one that really annoys the superintendent, and I caught myself doing it when I was talking to you earlier, is that instead of saying 'here' and 'there', we tend to say 'by here' or 'by there'. Constable Matthews often does it deliberately when the superintendent is around just to get a reaction.'

Chard suppressed a smile and wondered what Superintendent Jones would think if he picked up that habit.

'Nearly forgot to mention it, sir, but that alley we just passed leads down to a brewery next to the river.' He gesticulated back up the street. 'There, next to the parked gig.'

'I hadn't noticed it before even though I have walked down this street more than once since I have been here,' replied the inspector.

'Which is why Superintendent Jones suggested it might be useful for me to show you around, sir. Now here we come to Penuel Square. On your right there is a lane which leads down to the gasworks and also to the Cambrian textile mill. If you listen carefully you can hear the sound of the great waterwheel that powers the mill.'

Chard strained his ears and could indeed hear the mill, but only faintly over the sound of the street. It was busier than he would have expected for a weekday. There were well-dressed ladies discussing the displays in the shop windows, errand boys scurrying to and fro, tradesmen moving stock into their premises, the occasional itinerant fleeing for cover at the sight of the sergeant, all parts of the social fabric of the town. The atmosphere was vibrant and Chard felt enlightened. It was a good day to be alive and surely nothing was going to spoil it.

*　　*　　*

William Williams strolled down his weed-strewn garden path whistling happily, a newspaper held beneath the crook of his left arm whilst holding a small broken chair in his right hand. He had enjoyed himself the previous evening through strong drink and good company and he had time to rest this morning before starting an afternoon shift at the foundry. Getting to the bottom of his garden he swung his arm, hurling the chair over the hedge down into the river below. The back gardens of his terraced cottage and those of his neighbours stood over twenty feet above the east bank of the River Taff and the few residents that were untidy, lazy or inconsiderate (or indeed in Billy Williams' case all three) were inclined to throw their rubbish over their hedges resulting in a less than appealing view from the opposite bank. The dense foliage below several of the properties was festooned with household detritus that hung down to the weed-strewn lower bank at the water's edge.

Nevertheless, no concern passed the mind of Billy as he entered the small hut, his *tŷ-bach*, next to his unkempt garden hedge. He put his paper to one side, dropped his trousers and sat on the cold wooden seat. There was enough light filtering through the top and sides of the badly constructed wooden door that enabled him to read so he took up his copy of the *Glamorgan Times*, oblivious to everything bar the roar of the weir a few hundred yards upstream.

'BILLY WILLIAMS!' The screech was followed by a hard banging on the toilet door. Billy's heart jumped in his mouth.

'Billy Williams, you come out of there this instant!'

'I'm busy, woman. Go away.'

'I don't care if you are halfway through a shit. If you don't come out right now I'm going to break that damn door down and drag you out by your ear!'

Billy hastily stood, pulled up his trousers and emerged looking sheepish. There was no point in arguing with his Mair when she had her blood up, and though she was small, she was ferocious.

'What's the matter *cariad*?'

'Don't you *cariad* me you old bastard.' She stood red faced with fury, holding up his jacket from the previous night in one tiny fist.

'Blond hairs! Blond hairs!' she repeated. 'It's 'er isn't it? 'Er down the road. That trollop, Blodwen.'

'I don't know what you're talking about,' he cringed.

'You weren't working an extra shift last night were you? Oh no, you were out gallivanting with that woman.'

'I wasn't.'

'Don't you deny it, don't you bloody dare deny it. I'm not having this jacket in the house ever again after what it's been touching.'

With that, Billy's wife took a run and threw the jacket over the hedge.

Billy held his head in his hands.

'There's money in there, you stupid woman,' he cried out without thought, because normally he wouldn't have dared to insult her when she was in such a temper. It didn't matter however, because she was in too much of a rage to take in what he had said.

'And the next time it'll be you that goes in the river,' she yelled before stomping back up the garden path, into the kitchen, and slamming the door behind.

Billy stretched his neck and attempted to look over the hedge. He had to get the jacket back, but it was a long way down. Fortunately, despite the recent damp weather the river level was quite low for the time of year. The jacket had landed on a small tree that was growing out of the bank near the water's edge, close to some bones of what looked like a dead sheep that had been tangled up in some matting. They had been there for ages but were only visible whenever there was low water. He couldn't risk climbing down, there were rats down there and one thing Billy hated was rats. No, someone else would have to go. He went to the fence separating his small garden from that of his neighbour and gave a yell.

'Dai? Are you in, *bach*?' There was no response but he yelled once more and to his relief a small boy came out of the adjoining property's back door.

'Yes, Mr Williams?' The boy looked fearfully through the hedge in case Mrs Williams was about.

'How would you like to earn thruppence?'

'What do I have to do?' he answered cautiously.

'I've accidentally dropped my jacket over the hedge,' lied Billy, 'and I can't climb down because I've got a bad back. If I tie a piece of rope onto this fence post will you climb down and get my jacket back?'

'Where is it?'

'You can't see it from where you are, but it's by the side of the river on a small tree next to some old sheep's bones.'

'OK, Mr Williams, but give me the thruppence first please.'

Billy took out three pennies from the odd coins he kept in

his trouser pocket and gave it to the boy and they set about preparing for the climb.

Dai was very nimble and not afraid of a few scratches from the brambles and ragged branches on the bank as he made his way down to the river's edge, gripping the rope tightly as he went hand over hand. Unfortunately, the rope wasn't quite long enough so he had to stretch out a leg to try and hook the jacket with his foot as he got to the bottom. This he did and he then let go of the rope with one hand in order to take hold of the jacket. Suddenly to his dismay he felt his other hand slip and he began to fall. He landed with a crunching sound on top of some old bits of cloth or matting partly submerged in the water. Cursing with words that should have been unknown to a small boy, Dai got to his feet and kicked away the bones that had caught his left foot as he stood. Dead animals were a regular feature in the river. Everyone was used to seeing their remains, usually unwanted dogs and cats but sometimes there would be sheep or cattle that had been washed away by occasional floods. Then again, Dai thought, as he glanced through the low water beneath the cover of the foliage, they didn't have human skulls. He stood rigid with shock, then forgetting about the jacket, he gave an almighty yell, jumped up to grab the end of the rope and climbed hand over hand for all he was worth until he reached the top of the bank.

CHAPTER SEVEN

Sergeant Morris and Inspector Chard stopped in Penuel Square to look at the progress of the roadworks around the new fountain.

'Looks like it's nearly finished,' said the sergeant. 'When it's completed there will be a civic opening of the fountain by its donor, Sir Alfred Thomas, our member of parliament. Then there will be a grand fair to complete the celebrations.'

Just then they were alerted by a shout.

'Stop thief!' shouted a portly, red-faced man as he waved furiously after a young boy wearing a flat cap and torn clothes who was scampering away from him, head down, as fast as he could go. Unfortunately for the boy, by concentrating on speed rather than alertness, he didn't see Sergeant Morris until the flat of the policeman's mighty hand struck him full in the ear, sending him crashing into the stone wall between two shops. The lad fell to his knees. Sergeant Morris grabbed him by the collar and hauled him up. Seeing the boy was dazed and had a bloody nose the sergeant loosened his grip. He held out his hand and the miscreant placed a shilling coin into it.

'Good, you've got the little beggar!' exclaimed the portly man as he caught up.

'Here is your money, sir,' said the sergeant with a smile, handing over the shilling.

'Do you want me to come to the station to make a statement for the magistrates?' asked the man.

'No sir, we have all we need. We saw it all. Didn't we, Inspector Chard?'

Chard had been standing back slightly astonished at what he thought had been the rough handling of a boy that could only have been about eleven years old.

'W-well we didn't quite ...' then he saw a knowing look from the sergeant, and nodded his confirmation, '... I mean yes, we saw it all.'

'Oh, you are an inspector,' said the man. 'Tell me, why aren't you wearing a uniform?'

'It's being cleaned,' replied Chard, coming up with the first thing that came into his head.

'We will deal with everything from now on, sir,' interrupted the sergeant. 'We needn't bother you any further.'

'Thank you, Sergeant, I will be on my way then,' and with that he turned and headed up the street.

As soon as he was out of sight, Sergeant Morris grabbed the boy tighter and hit him firmly across the other ear. He then pointed in the opposite direction to which the portly man had gone and let the lad go. The boy ran off, wiping his bloodied nose with his sleeve as he went.

'I dare say you'll have some questions about that, sir,' said the sergeant in his usual soft tone of voice.

'Indeed I do, Sergeant. Indeed I do. The blows you gave that child would have floored a grown man.'

'Well sir, you must remember there are only twenty of us and minor crime is rife. That lad would have taken up one of our cells for maybe a week until he was taken before the magistrate. If he was lucky he might get a dozen strokes of the birch but the sentences are even harsher in this neck of the woods so he might even have been sent to prison. He won't forget those clips across the ear he got from me and as a result will think twice about doing it again. If I catch him thieving once more, then it's the cells.'

'In the circumstances I can follow your reasoning, Sergeant, but I am not entirely comfortable with it,' replied Chard. 'I realise I am new to this station so I will let it pass on this occasion until I have a better understanding of how things work on a day-to-day basis.'

'Fair enough, sir.'

They continued their walk and a few dozen yards further on the sergeant pointed to a lane down to the right.

'At the end of that lane is Fairfield. That is where the festivities will be after they have the civic opening of the fountain, sir. It's right next to the river.'

'Perhaps we could walk down and take a look, Sergeant?'

'Certainly sir … Hello, what's this?'

Hurrying towards them was Constable Davies who was beetroot red in the face from trying to move his bulk at a fast pace.

'Constable Davies, whatever is the matter?' asked Sergeant Morris as Davies reached them.

The constable took a deep breath. 'Message for the inspector. A body has been found in the river at Treforest. It's below the garden of a house belonging to a Mr and Mrs Williams on Cardiff Road, not far beyond the weir. Constable Preece is there and Constables Scudamore and Morgan have gone to assist.'

'I'll make my way there now,' replied Chard, relieved to find an excuse to put off the paperwork on his desk.

'I know where it is, sir. I had better come with you to show you the way,' volunteered Sergeant Morris. 'The constables will have taken the gig from our stables but there is a spare one for our use at the rear of the White Hart. Constable Davies, you take your time on the way back to the station and have a sit down when you get there.'

*　　*　　*

When Chard and the sergeant arrived at the house in Cardiff Road they found Mr and Mrs Williams arguing heatedly outside their front door whilst a dozen or so neighbours looked on with interest.

'How on earth can it be my fault?' argued Billy Williams.

The tiny woman facing him shook her little fist in his face.

'If you hadn't sent young Dai down to the river I wouldn't have policemen coming through our house with their big boots, creating a nuisance ...'

'But it was you that threw my jacket down there ...' interrupted Billy, but with no success as his wife continued to shout over him.

'... and just what is going to happen next? I say what is going to happen next ...'

'I don't know,' answered Billy.

'... I'll tell you what is going to happen next. They are going to fetch a body ...' She paused for effect, 'a DEAD body, through our home and I repeat, it's all your fault.'

'If you hadn't thrown my jacket, though ...' was as far as Billy's sentence was allowed to go.

'So it's my fault is it?'

Billy held his head in his hands then waved his arms animatedly in frustration.

'Well yes!'

Chard and the sergeant watched bemused as Mrs Williams slapped her husband's arm.

'Did I say I was working an extra shift last night?' asked the enraged wife. She hit him again and he began to back away.

'Did I lie to the person that I married?' Another blow and he backed off again. Some of the neighbours in the watching crowd started to laugh which only made Mrs Williams angrier.

'Did I let some slattern drape her hair and goodness knows what else over my body?' She hit him once more, this time much harder.

'Mair, *cariad*, it's not like that. Not in front of the

neighbours,' he tried to whisper, glancing in the direction of the crowd of onlookers who were being royally entertained.

'That's enough I think, Sergeant,' Inspector Chard said firmly.

Sergeant Morris walked over and held Mrs Williams' arm just as she was about to let loose with a slap to the face that would have stung Billy Williams considerably.

Mrs Williams looked up at the sergeant and with a grimace, turned on her heel and went inside. The two policemen followed her inside along with Billy who made sure that the police officers were between him and his wife.

They made their way through the parlour and the dining room, into a small kitchen that had been extended on the property and out into the garden. There they found Constable Scudamore in his shirtsleeves, steadying a thick rope, and looking over the hedge at the bottom of the garden. Another constable stood watching his colleague and he turned on hearing the sergeant's heavy footsteps. He was of average height, slim in build and with a face that carried a studious expression.

'Inspector Chard, this is Constable Daniel Preece. He's the local officer for Treforest as he lives just over the river in Long Row,' explained Sergeant Morris.

'Pleased to meet you, Constable Preece. How are you progressing?'

'We had some difficulty getting a suitable rope, sir. The body was discovered by a small boy who had climbed down to try and retrieve a jacket belonging to Mr Williams. The rope the boy used wasn't strong enough for an adult but we finally got a stronger one from one of the neighbours. We've managed to secure it properly and Constable Scudamore is steadying it whilst Constable Morgan makes his way down.'

'I'm there, Tom,' came a shout.

Constable Scudamore let the rope go slack and leaned further over the hedge.

'Can you tie your end of the rope around it to drag it up?' he replied.

'Hold on.'

With a great deal of trepidation Constable Morgan put his hands around the rotted, stinking material that housed the remains and gave a tug.

'It's not shifting and I am afraid to pull too hard or bits will fall apart.'

'Is it caught on anything?' queried Constable Preece.

His colleague down below put his hand under the water and felt around.

'It stinks,' he complained. 'It's absolutely disgusting down here.'

'Stop moaning and get on with it,' shouted down Sergeant Morris.

'There's a branch or root or something caught in the clothing. I'll need something to cut it away. Got anything sharp up there?' replied Constable Morgan.

'What about my jacket?' interrupted Billy Williams who had been hanging back.

'Sod your jacket,' snapped Constable Scudamore. 'Have you got something sharp for cutting back hedges?'

'No. I don't bother.'

Sergeant Morris took charge. 'Constable Preece. Get over to the ironmongers in Park Street. Get a billhook and some tarpaulin to fetch the body up in, plus some extra rope. Take Scudamore with you. Constable Morgan can stay where he is until you get back.'

Both officers set off to get the equipment, taking one of the gigs and twenty minutes later they were back.

'Here we go,' said Constable Scudamore as he started to tie

the billhook to the new piece of rope. 'I can't just drop it down, I might miss and take Idris's head off,' he joked.

He lowered the tool down to Constable Morgan who was getting impatient.

'About bloody time, Tom. It's horrible down here. My trousers are soaking and it's bitterly cold. I hate rats and if one more comes sniffing I'm climbing back up, rope or no rope.'

'Stop complaining. We'll have you up in no time.'

With the billhook in his hand, Constable Morgan started to hack away. After a few attempts the underwater growth was cut away and with a gentle pull he could tell that he would be able to move the remains.

'Right, drop the tarpaulin down and I'll move this mess onto it.'

Over the hedge came the tarpaulin, falling close to Constable Morgan so that he could pull it next to the bank. He tugged at the body.

'It was caught up due to this belt,' said Morgan as he grabbed it and pulled out the broken wood that he had needed to cut away with the billhook. 'Shit,' he suddenly shouted.

'What's the matter, Constable?' called down Chard who had remained silent as he watched the men of his new command in their endeavours.

'Cut myself, sir.'

'You should be more careful with that billhook,' called Sergeant Morris.

'It's not the billhook, it's the bloody belt, begging your pardon, Sergeant. The buckle has sharp edges on one side.'

Chard decided to step in and take charge.

'Sergeant we need two men down there not one. Send Preece down to help Morgan and they can put the remains into the tarpaulin and tie it off with the two ropes. I will then help you and Constable Scudamore to raise the tarpaulin and take it to the gig.

Then we will drop the ropes down again to fetch up our men. One gig with Scudamore and Morgan can take the remains to the mortuary where they can be looked at in the morning. Afterwards Morgan can be taken to the infirmary where he can get his cut looked after. Even if the cut isn't serious I don't like the idea of any river water having got into it. Sergeant, you and I can take the other gig. Preece can get home, change his wet trousers and then get back on duty.'

'What about my jacket?' came a cry.

'Oh, and have Preece fetch up this man's jacket,' sighed Chard.

The policemen were impressed with Chard's decisiveness and the manner in which he took control and before long the tarpaulin containing the remains of the body was being carried through the house watched by a grim-faced Mrs Williams.

When all the police officers were settled in their respective gigs, Inspector Chard called across to Constable Preece.

'You can accompany me to the mortuary tomorrow morning and afterwards help me with the paperwork.'

Tipping his hat to Mrs Williams, who stood apart from her husband as he happily counted the money recovered from his jacket, Chard tapped Sergeant Morris's arm to indicate they should leave. The sergeant gave a quick shake of the reins and they set off back to the police station.

* * *

Jack Ross entered the Commercial public house in Treforest and ordered a pint of bitter. He noticed that there was an animated discussion taking place at the end of the bar but decided to ignore it. Moving towards a seat by a window Jack sat down and reflected on his problems. His wage paid the rent but his money, his real money, was dwindling. It was his own fault. He should have moved on months ago, but there was Jenny. She was out of his social class, he knew that, and being a foreigner didn't help. His cause was doomed to failure, yet somehow hope refused to release him from its grasp. If only Jenny would show some interest in him beyond the friendly smile that she gave everyone. He had nearly said how he felt after work yesterday evening. Despite waiting for her as she left the ironworks, he had been disappointed when she came out smiling and laughing with her work friend Lizzie Hawkins. They were always together and unless he came up with some excuse to knock on her door unannounced he wasn't going to find the right situation to tell her how he felt. Then again there was the guilt that had stopped him doing that over all these months. How could he hide from her the terrible thing that he had done, yet the truth could not come out. Not here, not now, maybe not ever.

CHAPTER EIGHT

The following afternoon found Inspector Chard and Constable Preece entering the bleak stone building that housed the mortuary. They had hoped to visit earlier that morning but the attending general practitioner was not available until after midday. Chard was not in the best of moods. He had by necessity had to deal with dead bodies in the past but it was the most unpleasant part of his duties.

They walked into a white-tiled room that gave that peculiar smell only found in hospitals, infirmaries and other medical premises. A white sheet had been draped across a table in the middle of the room and from the doorway Chard could see that the recovered remains had been laid out carefully. A man in a frock coat stood with his back to them fussing with a bag of medical implements. Chard gave a polite cough. 'Good morning, I am Inspector Chard and this is Constable Preece.'

Preece stood a pace behind Chard and removed his helmet.

The man in the frock coat turned slowly and gave a smile.

'Good morning, Inspector. Dr Ezekiel Matthews, at your service.'

As they shook hands Chard took in the appearance of the doctor. He was of average height and build, with combed back wavy brown hair, a thin waxed moustache and a pointed face. As he spoke the doctor's nose wrinkled involuntarily causing his moustache to twitch in a manner that reminded Chard of an inquisitive rodent. The smile, however, did appear warm and genuine.

'Pleased to meet you, Doctor. I see you've been busy.'

'I've had a bit of a look and a bit of a poke about,' he jested.

His voice was heavily accented. Most definitely Welsh but not from the local area.

'Do you know when he drowned?'

'Well, to begin, perhaps you want to ask how long he has been in the river. That is your first question.'

'I assume it is the same thing, but very well, how long has he or indeed she, been in the river?'

'Definitely a he, but as to how long, I have no way of saying other than a very long time. Certainly not a recent death, even allowing for the predations of fish and rats, though they have indeed had a bit of a go. Look at these various marks on the bones here and here for example.'

Chard declined the offer.

'I am afraid I am unable to be any more precise. This could have been someone who died several years ago,' continued the doctor.

'So we can't say if he drowned say six months ago or five years ago for example,' enquired Chard.

'Ah, and there's the other issue and the missing question. The one you have so far failed to ask.' The doctor's nose continued to twitch which, for some reason, Chard found irritating. There was a pause as the inspector failed to react to the medical man's prompt. The doctor shrugged his shoulders.

'The question is, he was found in the river but did he drown? Was that the cause of his demise?'

'Very well, did he drown?'

The doctor smiled. 'Maybe yes, maybe no.'

Chard turned to Constable Preece and raised his eyebrows in frustration before turning back to Dr Matthews.

'Please enlighten us.'

'The skeleton is more or less in one piece held within the clothing which, although rotted in places, seems to have stood the test of time. Some splintering here and there which may have happened post mortem, and there are the scratches from the wildlife, but there are two points of note.'

The doctor waved Chard closer to the table and he reluctantly stepped forward.

'Firstly the little finger on the left hand is missing. This doesn't really trouble me too much. It could have been due to an accident years ago, or indeed as the hand wasn't encased in clothing, fish may have nibbled away at any remaining sinews as the body decomposed. I mention it purely for completeness.'

Chard nodded whilst trying to get the image out of his head.

'Now this is what does interest me. Look at this damage here, to the neck vertebrae.'

'If someone fell in the river during a storm then surely they would be knocked about,' suggested the inspector.

'Yes, of course, but these vertebrae took a lot of impact. So in an accident that caused this impact we would be looking at say, a fall from a bridge perhaps, or hitting a large rock going over the weir?'

'That would seem reasonable, Doctor,' agreed Chard.

Dr Matthews smiled. 'However, if that were the case we would expect to see damage to the bones around it. What we have here is not a huge crashing blow across the body. This is a very heavy blow hitting a relatively small area.'

'So what caused it?'

'Well, and this is only supposition on my part, a blow delivered with force from a heavy instrument before the victim went into the river. As the flesh is gone I cannot determine what sort of instrument, it could be anything from a small rock to a lump of metal. I cannot be absolutely certain that it is the cause of death though.'

'That does seem to be what you are suggesting.'

Dr Matthews frowned. 'There must of course be an inquest. I cannot sign a death certificate given the circumstances. I will give my opinion to the coroner that the blow contributed to the death of this man but I cannot be certain that the blow actually killed him. It may have paralysed him or possibly just rendered him unconscious. The cause of death may still have been drowning.'

'You mean that someone may have rendered him helpless and then just pushed him in the river?'

'Yes, I am afraid so. We had a couple of incidents in my home town of Swansea some years back. A whack on the back of the head or neck and into the dock rather than a river. Pockets were weighted down there though, just to make sure. Turned out to be gang killings of police informers.'

Chard scratched his sideburns as he pondered the remains on the table.

'Of course we still don't know this fellow's identity. Have you got the clothing?'

'In the ante room.'

The doctor led the way followed by the two police officers and once in the ante room he pulled a bag from a cupboard and laid it on a table.

'Constable Preece. Open it up and let's take a look,' commanded Chard.

The constable opened the bag, screwing his face up at the smell of decay that came from its contents. The clothing material had largely rotted into rags, there were two leather boots, a leather belt and a wallet. The wallet contained a few coins but the paper contents just fell apart.

'Nothing to identify him, sir,' commented the constable.

'Pass me the belt, Constable.'

Chard took the belt from Preece, straightened it out and examined the buckle.

'This might help us. I think this buckle is silver, or more likely silver alloy. Badly tarnished obviously after its time in the water. There is some sort of design on it.'

'I see what you mean, sir,' responded Constable Preece, looking closer. 'Perhaps if I take it to one of the jewellers in town, they might be able to clean it up.'

'Good idea, Constable. They probably have solvents for cleaning metals. Do that and then we can try and ascertain if anybody in the local area can identify it. Careful how you handle it, though. Two corners of the buckle are rounded but the other two corners look as though they've been ground down to give sharp edges. That's why Constable Morgan cut his hand.'

Constable Preece took the belt and carefully rolled it up. Turning to Dr Matthews, Chard offered his thanks and made to leave.

'I take it I will see you at the inquest, Inspector?' asked the doctor.

'Certainly. I just hope by then we will have made some progress with our enquiries. I had thought this would be a straightforward accidental death but this is a puzzle and no mistake.'

* * *

The following morning, Constable Danny Preece collected the belt buckle from Otto Faller's jeweller's shop in Taff Street where he had left it to be cleaned.

'How has it come up, Mr Faller?' asked the policeman when the jeweller retrieved the object from behind the counter.

'It has come up remarkably well, Constable.'

Mr Faller spoke with a strong German accent which several years of living in Pontypridd had failed to alter.

'Here you can clearly see a design of three entwined snakes. It looks similar to one I may have seen before. Possibly it is Indian in origin, perhaps brought to these parts by a returning serviceman.'

The policeman thanked the jeweller and set off back to the station.

Inspector Chard had given the constable clear instructions before settling down to his mountain of paperwork so when Danny got back to his desk he drafted out a public notice. Then it was a walk to the printers to order two dozen small posters to be collected the following day.

* * *

It was late. The man, wrapped in dark clothes so as to remain unseen, made his way carefully along the narrow path. There was the faint glimmer of gaslight in the distance but the way through the trees was guided by the moonlight that breached the canopy of foliage above. His heart beat faster with every step. There was a sharp snap as a twig broke beneath his foot and he silently cursed himself for his clumsiness. The river was not far away now and he could hear the sound of flowing water as a background murmur. Something scurried in the undergrowth to his right causing his heart to miss a beat and he stood for a while until he regained his composure before continuing onward as stealthily as possible. Suddenly he was at the edge of a small clearing and it was just possible to make out a figure standing close to a horse chestnut tree with a split trunk. This was it, this was what he had spent all day waiting for and as he crept closer the figure became more distinguishable. Carefully now, he told himself, only ten paces away, his heart pounding in his chest. He started to move more quickly, disregarding the risk of breaking another twig.

When he was just a yard away, the figure turned. 'You will have to do a lot better than that if you want to creep up on me unawares,' came the admonishment.

Then they fell into each other's arms.

CHAPTER NINE

Danny Preece sat in a wooden armchair, picked up his book and started to read by the light of an oil lamp resting on the window sill. His mother sat across the room knitting contentedly. Occasionally she would glance up and look at her son. Since her husband died he had become the centre of her life and she was very proud that he had become a policeman.

Danny had been kept waiting for what seemed like an age by the printers that morning. When he finally had the posters he gave some to his colleagues then set off on his beat, distributing the posters and stopping to talk to the local gossips in order to spread the word. It had felt good to get home to Long Row and get out of uniform.

Long Row was a peculiar-looking street and one of the oldest in Treforest. It appeared as if the houses had been built back to front. The two-storey front facades faced the garden. Beyond the garden was a small tram road with an accompanying water feeder channel, fed by a sluice from the weir that led over a mile to the tinplate works. Ten feet lower than the water feeder was the west bank of the River Taff. The roof of the house sloped down on the reverse, street-facing side to cover the single-storey rear of the property which housed the kitchen and pantry, the back door of which led directly onto the street of Long Row. It was on this door that someone started to knock urgently.

'I'll see to it,' said Danny to his mother. She smiled and nodded in reply.

He opened the door to see Stephen Jones, an old friend, standing with an excited expression on his face.

'C'mon Danny, down to the pub.'

'Why, what's so important?'

'It's that poster you've put out. Someone mentioned it at the bar. He knows the belt but wasn't going to come forward because he thought he would be wasting your time. I've told him to stay where he is. No time to get into uniform, mind.'

'Alright, wait a minute for me to get my jacket.'

The two young men were soon hurrying up to the end of Long Row and into the Commercial. There were a handful of people in the smoke-filled room either stood at the bar or sat at the few tables that were scattered about. Danny paid them no notice other than the little old man in the flat cap that Stephen was pointing at.

'That's him Danny. Have a word.'

Danny approached the small, wizened character and tapped him on the shoulder. The man turned to face him.

'Good evening. I am Constable Preece.'

'Constable? Where's your uniform then?'

'I didn't have time to put it on. Any of the regulars here will vouch for me.'

'Well, I can't see me being able to help you anyway.'

'I understand that you recognise the description of the belt buckle on the posters I put up.'

'I've certainly seen one like it. I used to rent out a room to the owner, but it can't be his,' responded the man, shaking his head. 'He died a couple of years ago.'

'Yes, well we just found his body in the river,' replied Danny.

'Bloody clever if you found him in the river when they piled six feet of earth on top of him two years ago. He'd been killed in a train crash.'

'Who was he?' asked Danny.

'Mickey Blake. A nasty bastard. If I had known what he was like I would never have rented to him. He came from London way and got a job at the Taff Vale Ironworks. He used to do a bit of debt collection on the side. That's why I remember the belt buckle. He showed me himself how he used to fight with it. He would wrap the belt around his wrist and his hand with the buckle on top of his fist. He had sharpened two edges of the buckle so that they would cut whoever he was hitting. I have seen more than one man with a scarred face in this town because of him,' he said, nodding sagely.

'That's certainly the same belt, no doubt about it. He must have sold it on,' suggested Danny. 'Anything else you can tell me about him?'

'Nothing, I am afraid, other than he was a large fellow, otherwise unremarkable ...'

Danny thanked the man turned to leave.

'... apart from the missing little finger on his left hand.'

* * *

It had been a busy week and Inspector Chard felt that he deserved to unwind in the evening. This day in particular had kept him at his desk, too busy even to take a midday stroll to experience the Friday market in the town centre. As the first major street market day since he had arrived, Chard had been looking forward to see if it met his expectations, but other than the increased noise drifting across the town the experience had been denied to him. So far he had been happy to eat in the dining room of his hotel, take drinks in its small cocktail bar and pass the time in its well-equipped billiards room. Tonight however he thought it was time to make a second visit to the Ivor Arms so he got changed and stepped out onto the street.

The town centre was reasonably busy and the other public houses that he passed were doing a good trade. Most working men would have work next day but a Friday night was considered by some to be a trial run for the Saturday night. He was feeling in good humour and looking forward to sipping a pint of beer hopefully in good company.

On reaching the Ivor Arms after a pleasant stroll he gave the stiff front door a push and stepped inside to see that it was clearly well patronised on a Friday night. All of the seating was already taken. There were a couple of groups standing in the centre of the room and three men stood at the bar talking to the barman. As Chard walked in there was a definite lull in conversation as everybody turned to look at him. As he stepped further into the room he noticed that one of the men at the bar was Dic Jenkins. The barman was a tall, cadaverous looking fellow with shoulder length grey hair and a thin slit-like mouth. Jenkins leaned across and whispered something in the barman's ear which caused the latter to stare in Chard's direction. Chard approached the bar and as he did so Dic Jenkins and his two companions sidled around to the far side but continued to watch in silence as the barman spoke.

'You must be the policeman,' he grunted.

Chard tried to put on a friendly smile.

'Not at the moment. My name is Chard, Thomas to my friends.'

'Mr Chard it is then. What can I get you?'

'A pint of your very best bitter please.'

The barman's face remained expressionless. 'All my beer is the very best.'

Chard pointed to Dic Jenkins and his two companions. 'I am sure it is but I will have the same as those gentlemen are drinking.'

The barman muttered something then went to the beer pump and drew a pint with a very full head. He placed it in front of Chard who looked at it and stared with an expression of extreme dissatisfaction.

'I suppose you want me to top it up?' he grumbled.

Chard nodded very slowly, this time being certain to hold the barman's gaze. The latter looked away and topped up the glass ensuring that the full pint replaced the original two inches of froth.

After handing over payment and getting only another grunt in return, Chard looked at Dic Jenkins' companions. One of them was stoutly built, in his thirties but with black receding hair. The other had the appearance of an academic with round framed spectacles and dark hair with grey streaks that made him look quite distinguished. They noticed Chard staring and turned their backs on him.

Chard risked speaking to the barman once more.

'Is Gwen in tonight?' he asked.

The barman turned and shrugged.

'*Wn i ddim,*' was his response, then he turned away.

Realising that he was far from welcome, and that coming to the Ivor Arms had been a bad idea, Chard quickly finished his drink and left the pub, slamming the door behind him.

*   *   *

The next morning a still disgruntled Chard was interrupted at his desk by Constable Preece who passed on the information he had gleaned the previous evening.

'Well that's certainly interesting, Preece. If Blake is the man in the river then who is the person they buried?'

'There would have been an inquest on the train crash itself, sir, but not on the specific causes of death. However, somebody would have been asked to identify the body and witness the death certificate.'

'True,' agreed the inspector. 'Go to the registrar first thing on Monday and find out who identified the body. Then we will track them down and pay them a visit, hopefully on the following day.'

The rest of the morning passed relatively quietly apart from the disturbance of a prisoner who was being taken from the cells for transfer to Cardiff prison. The two-horse police van had arrived ready to take him and the prisoner had seemed calm enough until he saw his transport. He then started to panic and had to be restrained by the two officers who held him whilst Constable Jackson beat his legs savagely with his truncheon.

At midday Chard decided to have a stroll around the market. The noise coming from the town had been building all morning and he had been looking forward to finally seeing if the market was really as good as Sergeant Morris had claimed. Leaving the station he crossed the road into Church Street and entered a maelstrom of people. He was used to markets. Shrewsbury was the county town for Shropshire and had its own market, after all, but this was in another league altogether. It was as if the entire population of the South Wales valleys had descended on the town. Chard had to physically squeeze through groups of shoppers to make any forward progress between the lines of market stalls. The stalls here sold ornaments, clothing, toys, medications of unknown provenance and a variety of bric-a-brac. He took in the variety of people crushed around him. Butcher's boys carrying trays of meat to their stalls, well-dressed ladies grabbing their children by the hand for fear of them wandering off to grab the nearest toy, women in shawls with pinched anxious faces trying to find a bargain so that they could feed and clothe their families, hard faced out-of-town traders looking to make a quick profit: all life was here. A man in a long white coat was calling out extracts from *Old Moore's Almanac* to encourage shoppers to buy the copies on his stall. Chard felt a bump on his right hand side. He turned but then was quick to realise that it had been a distraction whilst someone tried to pick his left hand pocket. Swinging around he managed to stop the theft but failed to grab the culprit who slipped away into the crowd.

Rather than continue into the main Market Street which was bound to be even busier, Chard turned left into the indoor market. Here it was the smell of various foodstuffs that assaulted the senses. There was the rich aroma of different cheeses coming from a dairy produce stall, which was at odds with the strong smell of raw meat from the many butchers' counters which in turn mixed with the sickly sweet smell of hot fruit cordials being sold from a stall nearby.

As he went further inside the waft of the local delicacy of faggots and peas hit his nostrils and he suddenly felt hungry. He opted to buy some Welsh cakes from a stall, though he had to queue to be served. Chard had often bought them from a Welsh-owned bakery in Shrewsbury and they were a particular favourite of his. He bit into one, letting the crumbs fall onto the flagstones below, and put the rest of the bag in his pocket for later in the day. Chard noticed that he was starting to pick up the odd word of Welsh. He had mimicked '*diolch*' which he had deduced meant 'thank you' and seemed to have got away with it, which put a smile on his face. On he went, passing stalls selling bone china, haberdashery and books. It was still very busy with crowds of people but at least the wider spacing between stalls in this part of the market gave slightly more room to manoeuvre. Also it was less noisy. The traders here were obviously well-established with permanent stalls, so there was less need to bark out for customers. He was now in the fresh produce market and this time it was the smell of vegetables and fruit, some of the latter quite exotic having been imported via Cardiff docks, that invaded his senses. In just a few more presses through the masses he was back at the familiar sight of Penuel Square.

Chard took a breath of fresh air. The streets were still very busy but it felt much less hectic than what he had just experienced. He was just about to turn and take a short cut back to the police station when he heard a loud bang followed by a shout of alarm.

There were other shouts and a scream as people in the street jumped back onto the pavement as a horse-drawn butcher's cart came careering down the road. The eyes of the horse were open wide with fear and it was looking for a means to escape from the noise that had frightened it. Chard suddenly noticed a figure that seemed to be wandering in the road directly in the path of the oncoming cart. He recognised the young lad, Dilwyn Evans, who he had met outside the station on his arrival in Pontypridd. The boy seemed in a stupor, unaware of any danger.

'Look out!' yelled the inspector.

Dilwyn heard him but just stopped and stared blankly. Chard's reactions then took over. He sprinted the few yards to the boy and hurled himself full length, hitting the waif with all his force just before the horse reached the spot where the lad had been standing. The hooves miraculously missed the inspector and he only just twisted his legs to one side in time as the cartwheels flew by. Two men were running past now aiming to catch the out of control animal, but it was Constable Davies who had been patrolling up Taff Street that headed it off and grabbed the trailing reins. The chasing men caught up and between the three of them they managed to get it back under control.

Meanwhile a group of people had gathered around Inspector Chard and the boy.

'Well done, mister, you saved that boy's life,' commented a concerned man in a shopkeeper's apron.

'It was slates falling off a roof that startled the horse,' informed another man, pointing down the street.

'You brave man,' smiled a very pretty young woman in a lemon yellow dress, touching his arm. 'Are you alright?'

'What about the boy?' said another older lady.

'Yes, how is he?' asked Chard who was aching abominably in the right shoulder where it had impacted on the road.

'He's alright,' advised a well-dressed man in a dark blue jacket, 'but he seems very drowsy.'

The man reached into the boy's pocket and gingerly fished out a small broken bottle from which a sticky residue trickled. 'Cough medicine. It looks like he's had nearly the whole bottle.'

Chard sat up and looked at the lad. 'I suppose it had morphine in it?'

The man with the bottle looked at what was left of the label.

'Yes, as is usual with these remedies. I will take him up to the infirmary.'

As the boy was lifted to his feet Chard suddenly felt someone grasp his hand and start pumping it vigorously.

'Well done sir, well done. What is your name if I might ask,' requested a florid-faced man in a bowler hat.

'Thomas Chard. Inspector Thomas Chard. I am out of uniform at the moment.'

Several people then helped him to his feet whilst a recently-arrived Morgan the reporter scribbled frantically in his notebook.

'There's no need to make a fuss, honestly. Just doing my duty.'

Chard then noticed the reporter and with wisdom born from experience he beat a hasty retreat back to the police station.

CHAPTER TEN

Tuesday morning found Inspector Chard and Constable Preece outside the door of Taff Vale House in Treforest. The registrar had revealed that the body buried as Michael Blake had been identified by Mr Graham Dunwoody of the Taff Vale Ironworks. An appointment had been made to speak to the manager of the company, Mr James Roberts, who also happened to be the chairman of the new local authority.

The weather had worsened over the weekend with torrential bursts of rain and even though it had eased slightly the water still dripped steadily off the inspector's umbrella and the constable's raincape. Smoke from the Taff Vale Ironworks' chimneys and those of the Forest Iron & Steel Works high above Treforest swirled beneath the heavy cloud cover forming a dark noxious canopy.

A servant answered the door. He took the dripping cape and umbrella from them before leading them through to a large office where an imposing-looking gentleman sat behind a polished mahogany desk. He rose to greet the policemen, nodding to the constable whilst shaking Inspector Chard's hand.

'Inspector Chard, I presume. Very pleased to meet you.'

'You presume correctly, sir, and this is Constable Preece. I have the pleasure of meeting Mr Roberts I take it?'

'Yes indeed, please take a seat,' said the manager, pointing to a chair. 'How can I be of help?'

The two senior men sat whilst the constable remained standing at the door.

'You used to have a gentleman working for you by the name of Michael Blake I understand. He was believed to have died in a train crash.'

'Well, yes, he did die in a train crash. I recall the matter quite well. He had failed to turn up for work the previous week then suddenly we had word that he had died in the infirmary. They wanted someone to identify the body so I sent my under manager, Mr Dunwoody.'

'I wonder if I might have a word with him.' enquired the inspector.

'Certainly, however I do wonder what all this is about,' responded Mr Roberts.

He hit a brass bell on his desk and the sharp sound resulted in a knock on the door pre-empting the entry of a short young woman with blond hair wearing a matching patterned grey blouse and skirt.

'Yes Mr Roberts?'

'Go and find me Mr Dunwoody, Miss Hawkins, and be quick about it,' he commanded.

The woman rushed off and within a few minutes there was another knock on the door and in came a timid-looking man with the merest of wisps of hair on his balding head, a florid complexion and anxious eyes.

'Yes Mr Roberts?'

'Take a seat please, Dunwoody. These gentlemen would like to ask you about Michael Blake. Do you remember him?' asked the manager.

'Yes I do. Most unpleasant. I mean his death was unpleasant, though in truth he was a rather coarse man.'

'He was not popular then?' enquired Chard.

'No. He was a chargehand here in one of the foundries. Some of the men were rather afraid of him. He could be a little difficult to get on with,' answered Dunwoody nervously. 'May I ask what all this is about?'

'I will come to that presently. How long had he worked for you?'

'Not that long really, about six months I think. He came from London and had good references.'

'I understand that you identified the body,' continued Chard.

'Yes, I did,' answered the under-manager, nervously rubbing the back of one hand with the other.'

I was called in to see Mr Roberts here and I was sent up to the infirmary.'

'When you got there you had no doubt that the body was that of Michael Blake?'

'W-w-well,' stammered Dunwoody, 'he was about his build and wore the similar sort of clothes that I had seen him wearing outside of work. I tried looking at his face, but it was just too awful.' He suppressed a shudder.

'So how did you know it was him, man?' interrupted Mr Roberts.

'It was his pocket watch. It was with the body and it was definitely his because it had his name engraved on the back,' replied the under-manager.

'Did you count his fingers?' asked Chard intently

'I don't know what you mean.'

'Neither do I, Inspector,' interjected Mr Roberts.

'He was known to have been missing a finger so it would have been useful if you could have confirmed that the body in the hospital did as well.'

'I am afraid I didn't look. It just didn't occur to me,' garbled Dunwoody apologetically.

'You see, we believe that we've just dragged Mr Blake's body out of the River Taff,' continued the inspector. Mr Dunwoody turned very pale.

'Don't worry sir, you won't have to look at the remains, there's not much left to identify. We can't be absolutely sure it's him, but there is enough suspicion to order an exhumation of the body you identified in the hospital,' explained Chard.

Chard shook hands with the two men and Constable Preece opened the office door for them to leave. Mr Roberts followed them out to the front door where Chard was given his umbrella and Preece his raincape. The thick walls of the house-cum-office building had shielded them from the noise of the ironworks which became more apparent as they came outside and the sky was still full of the dark smoke from the chimneys.

'Does the ironworks continue to run all day and night?' enquired Chard out of curiosity.

'Not at the moment,' answered Mr Roberts. 'To tell the truth the industry is in decline. There's too much competition. We no longer have night shifts and some of the men are only on five-day weeks. Hopefully things will pick up in future.'

Chard shook his hand once more and the policemen returned to the station to arrange the paperwork to request an exhumation.

*   *   *

The following week Constable Preece was sitting at a desk in the police station writing up an arrest report relating to a drunk and disorderly charge when Inspector Chard strode into the room looking grim.

'How did the exhumation go, Inspector?' asked Preece.

'Thoroughly unpleasant, Constable, as one might expect. However, it has moved us forward. One leg had been severely fractured, the jaw and part of the skull had been smashed and …' he paused for effect '… all his finger bones were still there.'

'So we know he wasn't Blake then, sir.'

'Correct. Which means that presumably, if the train crash

victim had Blake's watch on him then it is likely that he must have killed Blake sometime in the previous week. So now we need to try and find out his identity.'

'Yes sir, but where do we start?' asked the constable.

'There is only one place. We need to go to the infirmary. Finish whatever you are doing and we will leave in the next ten minutes.'

*   *   *

The workhouse in Pontypridd struck terror into the hearts of the old and infirm of the poorer classes. It wasn't necessarily because the life there was harsher than any other workhouse, in fact compared to many it was more compassionate. It was the shame, the social disgrace of having to resort to the lowest form of charity that made people fearful. It meant that you were so poor, or so lacking in family or friends that you could not afford to eat, care for yourself or have shelter. The only way of surviving was to submit yourself to the indignity of having to dress in workhouse clothes, perform menial and often laborious tasks and obey harsh rules restricting the personal freedom that everyone else took for granted. All in exchange for a bed in a dormitory, some heat in winter, basic subsistence meals and if the workhouse was compassionately run, some basic medical care.

After a courtesy visit to the governor of the workhouse, Inspector Chard and Constable Preece were shown to the infirmary where they were greeted by Miss Roper and then shown into the office of Dr Henderson.

'Dr Henderson, this is Inspector Chard and Constable Preece. They would like to have a word with you about the dreadful train crash two years ago,' explained Miss Roper.

'Thank you, Miss Roper. That will be all.'

The pretty auburn-haired clerk left the room and Constable Preece could not help but give an admiring glance as she passed.

Dr Henderson lifted his bulky frame to stand and greet his visitors. He shook hands with the inspector and offered both officers a seat before settling back down, looking at them over his grey drooping moustache with great curiosity.

'Well gentlemen, how can I be of assistance?'

'We are interested in the identity of one of the victims,' explained Chard, whilst indicating to Preece that he should start taking notes.

'In what way? They were all identified,' answered the doctor.

'Yes, but we have reason to believe that one of them was not who he appeared to be.'

'That is rather intriguing. Do continue, you have my full attention,' smiled Dr Henderson.

'Do you recall a casualty who had a badly broken leg but more particularly had severe damage to the jaw and skull? I would imagine that his face would have been quite disfigured.'

The doctor nodded slowly. 'Yes, I recall that poor chap very well indeed despite it being two years ago. Frankly if he had lived, he would never have walked properly again and would have been hideously disfigured.'

'Did he say anything whilst he was here?' continued the inspector.

'Not a word. When I first examined him he was barely alive. There was the merest twitch in his fingers. I remember that he was one of the last patients that I looked at that night. One arm was moving, possibly just muscle spasms, but I had hoped he might pull through. Unfortunately, he didn't make it through the night. One of the staff found him dead next morning before I came on duty.'

'We have spoken to the gentleman who identified the body, a Mr Dunwoody.'

'Yes, well we needed to get the deceased victims identified as soon as possible in order to notify families and so on. We had a name from a pocket watch that was with his clothing.'

'So we understand.'

'We kept the body in the makeshift mortuary for two days before someone came forward. Word had got around that we were looking for the relatives of a Michael Blake. It so happened that the name was well known in certain quarters as belonging to somebody that worked at the ironworks. We got in touch with them and they sent Mr Dunwoody.'

'I understand that he didn't spend too long identifying the body,' prompted Chard.

'Exactly so, Inspector. He seemed a very timid man and was very eager to leave as soon as possible. Apparently Blake often wore a pocket watch very similar to the one we found and indeed it did have his name inscribed on it. In fairness he was so disfigured I doubt even his own mother could have recognised him.'

'Apart from his missing finger,' pointed out the inspector.

The doctor raised an eyebrow quizzically.

'The real Michael Blake was missing a finger,' explained Chard. 'I am afraid the body was not correctly identified.'

The doctor looked shocked. 'This is terrible. Yet no one else has come forward looking for an unnamed casualty or for another Michael Blake. So how did he come to have that watch?'

'That is exactly what we want to find out. You see we pulled the body of the real Michael Blake out of the river last week. By the way, what happened to the watch?' asked the inspector.

'When Mr Dunwoody told us that Blake had no next of kin, the watch was sold to a pawnbroker in order to provide basic undertaker costs for the burial. It could be anywhere by now.'

'That is a pity. Did he have anything else to identify him on his person?'

'There was an empty wallet with nothing in there to give a clue. Not even his railway ticket,' answered the doctor.

'That is strange,' said Chard, pausing to consider what line of enquiry he could pursue. 'I am grasping at straws here, Doctor, but perhaps someone else here noted something about his identity. Who was the first person to deal with the victim?'

'You might want to talk to Miss Roper. I remember that on the day she organised the arrival of the casualties and dealt with the various visitors,' suggested the doctor.

'Visitors?'

'Yes. There were the ministers, priest and vicars. Then we had some volunteer helpers, including local doctors in private practice. We also had extra staff sent from Porth hospital. It was quite a task to deal with it all.'

'Well, Doctor, we've taken up enough of your time. I think we might have a word with Miss Roper on our way out.'

'My pleasure, gentlemen,' replied Dr Henderson, hefting himself from his seat to shake their hands.

The two policemen left the office and walked across to the end of the infirmary ward where Miss Roper was talking to one of the bed-ridden invalids. He was a craggy faced old man with laughing eyes and the pair appeared to be sharing a joke.

The young woman suddenly noticed the policemen approach and said in a clearly false stern voice, 'Mr Jarvis, you are too familiar. You really must be better behaved.'

As the inspector and constable came nearer she nodded in the direction of the patient.

'This is Jarvis, one of our oldest inmates. He is an old

rogue and only pretends to be ill so he can be coddled,' she explained, loud enough for the patient to hear.

Chard could tell from the smile that she was finding it difficult to conceal, that she actually liked the old fellow.

'Can I help you?' she asked.

'Yes, you may be able to,' answered the inspector as Constable Preece got his notebook out once again.

Miss Roper brushed an auburn strand of hair from across her eye and stepped a few paces away from the beds so that they could talk more freely.

'I take it that you recall the big train crash of two years ago?' asked the inspector.

'I am not likely to forget it,' she answered.

'In particular can you remember one of the casualties? It was a man with a badly damaged leg and a disfigured face. I understand that it took some time for someone to come forward and identify him,'

'Yes, I can remember exactly who you mean. I found his name on a pocket watch when I went through his clothes in the morning, after he had passed away.'

'We know about the pocket watch and an empty wallet. Is there anything else that you can recall about him?'

'Not really. It was as you described, but there's nothing else I can add. Why are you so interested in that particular victim?'

'I am afraid that we are certain that it wasn't his watch, Miss Roper, so we are trying to find out how he came to have it. Tell me, do you remember when he was brought in? Perhaps the watch had been found on the ground at the scene of the crash and it was wrongly assumed that it belonged to him,' suggested Chard, unsure if that possibility would make the puzzle better or worse.

'Well I certainly remember him being fetched in,' smiled

Miss Roper. 'He had been transported in a carriage by a slim, very elegant young man in a grey frock coat.'

'Do you know how that had come about?'

'I seem to recall that the gentleman said he had been alerted to the crash whilst travelling nearby and had gone to help.'

'I assume you will not have remembered his name.'

'You assume correctly, Inspector, but I do remember that he said he was an acquaintance of Mr Crawshay and staying at Forest House. He wanted to remain a while in the infirmary which I normally would have refused but at the mention of Mr Crawshay's name …'

'Yes, there's no need to explain. I understand the influence that the Crawshay name has in these parts,' said Chard with a sympathetic expression. Francis Crawshay, the great industrialist, was deceased but his son Tudor Crawshay carried on his works and was a powerful man in the social hierarchy of South Wales.

'Why did he want to stay?' continued the inspector.

'Just to see how the patient responded, whether he lived or died, I suppose. Anyway he stayed for a while until Dr Henderson cleared him out with the others as we were getting so busy. They were just getting in the way.'

'You mentioned "the others". Who were they?'

'Our local vicars and ministers, a Catholic priest, a reporter who had sneaked in behind my back and some volunteers who just came to help. In fact as I remember there were two of them talking with Mr Crawshay's acquaintance as they left.'

'Do you know who they were?'

'I cannot remember, but I do seem to recall something about them having been with the Catholic priest when he was notified so I would guess that they were his parishioners.'

Chard scratched his sideburns in thought. 'Who else had contact with the patient?' he asked.

'Apart from Dr Henderson and myself there were two porters, both inmates, one of whom is no longer with us and the other died of illness last year. Also our Nurse Harris who is not on duty today, but I can speak to her on your behalf tomorrow if you would like. She has worked here for years and has a good memory so I am sure that if I have missed anything then she will remember.'

'That would be most kind,' thanked the inspector. 'You have been very helpful so we won't keep you any further.'

'My pleasure, Inspector.'

Constable Preece pocketed his notebook as the pretty young woman turned and walked towards Dr Henderson's office.

'Do you think it will do us any good trying to trace this man that fetched the victim in sir?'

'Sadly not, Constable. It is probably a dead end. We will have to forget the watch as a bit of a red herring. We know that the real Blake was not a popular man so perhaps we need to find out a bit more about him.'

'Oi! Copper!' came a whispered yet urgent call.

The two policemen both frowned and glanced at each other before turning and walking towards the nearby bed occupied by the old man called Jarvis.

Jarvis gave a wink. 'She's a lovely girl but thinks that because I'm old I'm deaf as well. Well she's wrong. I can see and hear as good as a man a quarter of my age.'

'It's Jarvis, isn't it? Why address us in that manner and why are you talking so quietly?' asked Chard.

'It's like this. We aren't allowed any alcohol in here and I miss a tot of rum. I thought that if I do you a favour then perhaps you would show some favour to an old veteran of the Crimea by sneaking me in a snifter or two.'

'You cheeky blighter!' interjected Preece.

'Like I said, sonny, a favour for a favour,' snapped the old man.

Before an indignant Preece could respond, Chard raised a finger to stop him.

'Very well Jarvis, my curiosity is piqued,' said the inspector, 'so what is this favour?'

'I heard your conversation and I can tell you a lot more about that bloke with the mashed-up face. Do we have a deal?'

'In the very unlikely event that what you have got to say is of interest then I will see what I can do,' promised the inspector, who chose to ignore the look of shock on his constable's face.

'I was in the infirmary when they fetched the casualties in. I had been in a nice warm bed, but then had to move into a makeshift bed on the floor across the way.'

'Go on …' encouraged the inspector.

'That pocket watch they found. It wasn't with him when he came in,' asserted the old man, pointing his finger to emphasise his statement.

'How could you know that?' Chard's face showed his cynicism.

'Because the porter, Evans, was a thief. He was the one that stripped the patient and put him into bed. The next day he disappeared.'

'So he would have taken the pocket watch if he was a thief,' interrupted Preece.

'Exactly, that's my point. The next morning they found an empty wallet, didn't they?'

'Ah!' exclaimed Chard 'I see what you mean.'

Constable Preece gave the inspector a puzzled look.

'What our old friend here is telling us, Constable Preece, is that if the pocket watch had been there when the casualty was brought in, then the porter would have stolen it at the same time as he stole the contents of the wallet,' explained the inspector. 'So the pocket watch must have been placed there sometime between the time the patient was first put into the bed and the following morning.'

Chard looked at Jarvis intently. 'Do you recall anyone going near the body other than the porter and the nursing staff?'

'Yes, I do. Exactly as Miss Roper said. There was that fancy fellow in a frock coat that came in at the same time. Then there was the other two. The young couple, a foreign-sounding lad and a gorgeous dark-haired lass. Lovely frame on her,' he added with a lecherous smile.

'I didn't realise that they went close to the patient.'

'Yes, all three went behind the screen to the bedside.'

Chard glanced across at his constable. 'It looks like we've got three suspects,' he proclaimed with a beaming smile.

'Do we still have a deal?' asked the old man.

'Yes, I promise,' replied the inspector, 'though goodness knows what trouble it will cause if I get found out.'

'As you have promised, and I take you to be an honourable man,' added Jarvis, 'I will tell you a little more. Another strange thing happened that night.'

'Such as?'

'I've been here for many years and I know how things are. We have a nurse at night who puts her feet up in Dr Henderson's office most of the time and just walks around the infirmary once an hour, on the hour. It has always been the same. That night, though, there was someone else wandering about. I heard footsteps and it was so unusual that I kept it in here,' the old man explained, tapping the side of his head.

'Who was it?' asked the inspector with interest.

'No idea. I didn't look. I mind my own business, see.'

Chard scratched his sideburns and looked exasperated. 'So let me get this correct. You have made me promise to fetch you a "little snifter" on the basis that you've given me three real suspects and now you've told me that there may, or indeed may not, have been an unknown intruder who, if they exist, could have placed the watch there as well.'

'That's right and a promise is a promise,' smiled the old man smugly.

Chard gave a grunt. 'Come on Constable, I've had enough of this old rogue.' He gestured to Preece in the direction of the door. 'No wonder he survived the bloody Crimean War,' he added as they walked away.

*   *   *

Jenny Norton left the church less troubled than when she had gone in. Finally she had felt able to tell Father McManus about her troubles. Not that she burdened him with all her worries, but she had to tell him about the most important thing in her life. It was something she should have done a long time ago. Perhaps in future times society would accept such a relationship but not here, not now. The priest would not, indeed could not, reveal her secret as she spoke to him in the confessional. That said she didn't think it was a sin and her suspicion was that Father McManus was of the same mind. Her mind was still troubled though and after returning to her home and closing the door she wept.

CHAPTER ELEVEN

Inspector Chard sat at his desk in a state of high dudgeon. He had just returned from the inquest into the death of the real Michael Blake. Heavily influenced by the opinion provided by Dr Ezekiel Matthews, the coroner passed an open verdict. In other words, the death was suspicious but there was not enough evidence to give any other clear verdict. This outcome meant that Chard had to treat this as an open case, which meant that he was pleased that he could be doing some active police investigating, but it also meant that there would be a lot of pressure to solve it quickly. The problem was that this case might be extremely difficult to solve. Granted there were some leads. If the old man in the infirmary had been telling the truth then three people had been near the train crash victim and could have planted the watch. Then again there could have been an additional night visitor. To be completely thorough one could add the two porters, one of whom had died, Miss Roper, the nurses and even Dr Henderson. The key was to find a link between the suspects and Michael Blake. The first steps would be to try and identify the three visitors who had come to the infirmary and stood near the body. According to Miss Roper two of them had some sort of connection to the local Catholic church, so that would be an obvious line of enquiry. The other was an elegantly dressed gentleman who was allegedly staying at the Crawshay's residence. Surely if anyone had an opportunity to place the pocket watch amongst the clothes of the injured man then it would be him. Though if the old man was right then he must have slipped it into the clothes after the porter had stolen the money from the wallet. Yet it was a possibility, so he would need to follow it up. Conflicting thoughts rushed through the inspector's mind as he sat tapping his fingers on the desk. Finally he got to his feet and opened his office door just as Constable Jenkins was fetching him a fresh batch of reports to sign.

'Sorry Constable, I have more important things to do. Get me the directions to the Crawshay residence and arrange some transport. I have cages to rattle.'

* * *

May Roper stared through the window of the infirmary at the raindrops running down the pane and gathered her thoughts. Dr Henderson had spoken to her about his conversation with Inspector Chard. Clearly the infirmary records would need to be corrected and May would be responsible for the necessary administration such as notifying the registrar. May was intrigued and quite excited. As a child she often got into trouble at home with her strict parents through the reading of 'penny dreadfuls' leant to her by friends. As she got older she progressed to the less lurid and slightly more respectable writings of Wilkie Collins and the adventures of his protagonist Walter Hartright in *The Woman in White*. Other 'sensation novels' like *Lady Audley's Secret* followed. The one novel that really lit up her imagination however was *The Female Detective* by Andrew Forrester. May took her work very seriously but when she had free time May could often be caught daydreaming that she was the book's heroine, Mrs Gladden. Obviously that was all fiction but here she was connected to a real life mystery. 'Perhaps no one would mind if I helped just a bit,' she muttered to herself. 'It wouldn't be interfering, just helping that poor policeman.'

Unaware of the discussion that had taken place between Jarvis and Inspector Chard, May pondered how the pocket watch belonging to the real Blake could have turned up in the clothes of the crash victim. She assumed that the injured man must have taken it from Blake. Ideally she would like to speak to the gentleman who brought him in to confirm if he had actually seen the watch at the site of the crash. However she couldn't very well just turn up at the Crawshay residence unannounced. Then again, there were the other two visitors that left at the same time as him. They were behaving very strangely so perhaps they knew the injured man. She smiled to herself, 'I know where I'll start.'

*　　*　　*

Jabez Grimes took a long draw of his cigarette, leaned back in his chair and considered the news he had just received. As he blew out a plume of blue smoke a slow smile spread across his face as he realised the possibilities. There was not much in the way of news that escaped his network of eyes and ears. He smelled a scandal and for him that meant profit. Taking his gold plated pen from its holder on the desk he scribbled a long note, and called for his servant.

*　　*　　*

Chard dismounted from his horse, patted its nose and tied the reins to a convenient fencepost outside Forest House. He was annoyed with Constable Jenkins when he came out of the front of the station to be presented with the horse rather than the covered gig he had been expecting. Fortunately, the constable had thought to provide a riding cape to keep off the rain, but Chard made a mental note to specify next time exactly what type of transport he required. The inspector could ride but admitted to himself that he was not a natural horseman and he was thankful that the mare was only fourteen hands high and relatively docile. It was kept in the White Hart stables on a retainer fee for use by the superintendent or inspector of the police station. Chard had kept the animal on a slow trot on what would have been a pleasant ride had it not been for the inclement weather and the dark oppressive industrial smoke that held beneath the cloud cover. He looked around at the pleasant well-kept grounds which had a private tram road running through it which led to the Forest Iron & Steel Works situated high above Treforest. The house itself looked very functional rather than ornate as befitted an industrialist thought Chard. He approached the front door and pulled on the brass bell pull. Seconds later the door was opened by a haughty-looking manservant who looked at him from top to toe and then gave a derisory snort.

'Can I help you, sir?' he offered in a tone that did not infer that he meant it.

'I am Inspector Chard of the Glamorgan Constabulary. Is Mr Crawshay at home?'

'Might I ask, sir, for some identification? Sir does not appear to be in uniform.'

Chard reached into his pocket, brought out his warrant card and showed it to the servant.

'Very well, sir,' he said with a false smile. 'I am afraid Mr Crawshay is not in residence. He has gone to the Continent on business and will not be back for some considerable time.'

'Perhaps you can help me?'

'Perhaps, sir.'

'I am trying to identify someone who has stayed as a house guest of Mr Crawshay. Very elegantly dressed, I understand.'

'I am sure all of Mr Crawshay's guests are elegantly dressed, sir.'

'Young, slim, stayed here about two years ago around the

time of the train crash,' snapped Chard who was getting very irritated.

'Ah, why didn't sir say so earlier? Yes of course that would be one of Mr Crawshay's business associates, young Mr Dorsett. I am sorry sir, I am forgetting myself, I mean the Honourable James Dorsett. He often stays here as he is a significant investor in the Forest works.'

'Is he staying here at the moment?'

'Not at the moment sir, you have not long missed him, but he is returning next week. Might I suggest sir tries the company offices at Castle House on Monday?'

Chard gave a grunt. 'Thank you,' he snapped before turning on his heel towards his horse.

'My pleasure, sir,' replied the servant, this time without the false smile.

The inspector took the reins from the fencepost and mounted just as a raindrop slipped uncomfortably down the back of his neck. Damn it, he thought. Never mind, there might be better luck tracing the other two. He mounted the mare and set off in the direction of the Catholic church.

It was only a relatively short trot to his destination and soon he was tying up the reins outside the presbytery. The weather hadn't improved and in the distance the foundry chimneys of the Taff Vale Ironworks were still belching out columns of black smoke making the atmosphere more oppressive. He knocked on the door which was opened by the housekeeper and after showing her his identification he was led into the priest's study. The housekeeper took Chard's hat and raincape and left him alone in the room. Some moments later there was a sound behind him and Father McManus entered.

'Good day to you, Inspector, how can I be of help?'

Chard looked into a face that was kind and compassionate. He took an instant liking to the cleric.

'I am trying to locate two of your parishioners, Father,' he answered as he shook the priest's hand. 'Do you recall receiving the news of the big train crash that happened about two years ago?'

'Yes, I received a telegram about it,' he replied in a sad voice. 'It was a terrible business.'

'Was there anyone with you at the time you received the telegram?'

'Yes, a young lady, Jenny Norton.'

'I am looking for a young woman and a young man who went to the infirmary to help after the crash. I understood they were with you when you got the news.'

'Well only Jenny was with me, but of course, there was Jack.'

Chard looked questioningly. 'Jack?'

'Jack Ross, he is a neighbour of Jenny's. They both work at the Taff Vale Ironworks.'

The inspector's ears pricked up as the priest continued.

'Yes I remember, Jenny got a hansom cab for me. I briefly noticed both of them in the infirmary, though we didn't talk as I was busy with the casualties, giving last rites and so on.' The priest's expression showed the pain of the memory.

'Thank you, Father. That is all I really need to know.'

'May I enquire what your interest is in them? I can't say I really know Jack, but Jenny is a lovely soul and a pillar of our congregation. She has had a hard life and bears a lot of sorrow.'

'In what way, Father?'

'I am sorry but that is something that I cannot discuss.'

Chard nodded, gave a smile of thanks and shook the priest's hand once more before leaving the study. Father McManus noted disappointedly that the inspector had avoided answering the question regarding the police interest in his two parishioners.

At the front door Chard took his hat and cape from the housekeeper and looked forward to his forthcoming return visit to the ironworks. It could wait until the next day when he would have Preece with him to take notes. Tonight he would find somewhere to enjoy a nice beer, obviously not the Ivor Arms, and gather his thoughts for the next stage of the investigation.

* * *

May Roper had walked home from work as fast as she possibly could. Luckily the rain had eased to a slight drizzle so the plan that had excited her all day could definitely go ahead. A small set of stone steps led from the pavement up to the front of her house. Underneath the front window her bicycle (to which her father had strongly objected) was sheltered from the damp by a sheet of tarpaulin.

She opened the door, dropped her wet umbrella and rushed to the living room door where she called out loudly.

'Mam, just leave me some food to heat up. I have an errand to run. I might be some time. It is infirmary business,' she lied.

'Your father will be annoyed when he gets home,' came the admonishing reply.

'I am twenty years of age but they treat me like a child,' May said quietly to herself as she ran up the stairs. When May reached her room she quickly changed into her riding skirt. It had tiny lead weights sewn into the hem for the sake of modesty. If she was to come home on the bicycle later wearing anything else her father would erupt. After tying a bonnet to her head and putting on a light coat she went out, uncovered her bicycle, carried it down the steps and set off for the Catholic church.

* * *

Father McManus was surprised to receive a second unexpected visitor that day from outside of his flock of parishioners. His housekeeper had introduced her as a young lady from the infirmary who was seeking his assistance.

'Good evening, Father McManus. My name is Miss Roper, I wonder if you could help me trace two of your parishioners?'

'Would this be anything to do with the train crash two years ago by any chance?' asked the priest.

'Why yes, actually it would,' answered May, suddenly very unsure of herself.

'Then it is quite reasonable to ask that you give me the reason why,' insisted Father McManus frustrated that the police inspector had been unwilling to discuss the matter with him.

May thought quickly. In her experience and in every one of the novels she had read the police were always very slow to do anything. Perhaps this time the police had been efficient and had already spoken to Father McManus. She couldn't lie to a man of God but perhaps there was a middle path she could tread.

'Administration, Father. I keep all the medical records and it is important that we keep everything as accurate as possible.' Which was of course true.

'There was an error at the time of the crash and the wrong name was allocated to a victim. It has been brought to our attention and I now need to correct it.'

May shuffled uncomfortably as she fought to control her nerves. 'There was a young man accompanying a young lady who indicated that she knew you. The lady gave me her name but I am sorry to say that I failed to make a note of it. They were stood near the victim in question and just might have some knowledge of his real name so that I can correct our records.'

Father McManus looked doubtful. 'I think I should tell you that I have had a visit from the police earlier today asking me about the same two parishioners and the same incident.'

'They take these sorts of mistakes ever so seriously, Father,' she replied, 'due to the costs incurred in exhuming and reburying the body. Then there is the question of tracing the next of kin. The man we originally thought it was might have gone missing, so the police will have to try and trace him.' May took out a dainty handkerchief from her sleeve and pretended to dab her eyes. 'I am in so much trouble, Father. The police will blame me for wasting their time and I will probably lose my job ...' She gave a little wail and pretended to cry into her handkerchief.

'There, there ...' comforted the priest. 'I am sure it is not that bad. The police inspector I spoke to seemed such a nice gentleman.'

'If only I could find out the crash victim's name first, before the police, I am sure I could redeem myself.' May opened her eyes wide and looked hopefully into Father McManus's eyes in the same manner that she often used to try and get around her own father when he was in a bad mood.

Father McManus reflected that he had not been informed by the police inspector that their interest was of any serious nature and this young lady seemed in such distress.

'Very well, Miss Roper. I don't think I would be doing any harm by giving you the name of the lady in question and her address. However, I do not think it would be proper to give you the name and address of the young man. It would not be right for you, a young lady, to go unaccompanied to a single working man's house unaccompanied and unintroduced.'

The priest called for the housekeeper to fetch him writing materials and he sat down to write out Jenny Norton's name and address. He handed the note to May with an avuncular smile.

'Thank you ever so much, Father. I promise that I will not trouble the lady too long. I just need five minutes of her time.' Grasping her note tightly, May made her grateful farewell and set off for the little house in Park Street before dusk fell.

CHAPTER TWELVE

May rapped firmly on the door of the terraced house and adopted a confident posture. Back ramrod straight, eyes fixed ahead and a stern expression. This wasn't the worried, nervous young thing that she had portrayed for the benefit of Father McManus. Instead this was the Miss Roper that ran the administration of the infirmary competently and efficiently.

The door was opened by the statuesque, imposing figure of Jenny Norton. Although strikingly beautiful in a dark blue patterned dress, with her dark hair let down for the evening, cascading over her shoulders, May noticed that her eyes were red-rimmed as if she had been crying. She stood there holding the door waiting for May to speak.

'I am terribly sorry to call on you this evening without prior notice, Miss Norton. My name is Miss Roper and we met briefly some time ago.'

'I am afraid I don't recall …'

'It is a matter of some delicacy. Father McManus gave me your address. Perhaps I could come in just for a few minutes? I will not trouble you any longer than is necessary,' said May putting a foot forward over the threshold.

Jenny was slightly taken aback but the mention of Father McManus and the confident nature of this young visitor led her to allow the girl through. There was no internal hall or passageway in this small house, the door opening straight into the living room.

'What is this delicate matter and how can I help you, Miss Roper?' asked Jenny wearily.

May glanced around the room, principally looking for a chair as she was expecting to be offered to sit. The room was lit by a gas lamp on the wall by the front window, next to a rocking chair with a small table alongside. On the table was a note with a torn, open envelope. A small fire glowed in a simple fireplace on the right hand wall below a mantelpiece supporting a row of decorative china plates.

Suddenly Jenny reached out, grabbed the note and threw it on the fire.

'I repeat, Miss Roper, how can I help you?'

'We met two years ago at the time of the train crash that happened near Devil's Bridge.' Clearly the offer to sit was not going to materialise.

'Did we?'

'Yes, we did. I am the administration clerk for the infirmary, and you came as a visitor to offer your help.'

'I remember coming to the infirmary but we were not needed,' answered Jenny rather curtly.

'By "we" I take it you mean yourself, the young workman and the gentleman.'

'I came with Jack Ross my neighbour, but I don't remember any gentleman. What is all this about?' Jenny turned towards the ornate dresser with brass drawer handles that stood against the opposite wall to the fireplace. She started to fiddle with the Napoleon mantel clock that rested in front of the dresser's mirror, not looking at May as she replied.

'Surely, Miss Norton, you must remember the gentleman. He was very striking.'

'I do recall him actually. I am not at my best today and sometimes my memory fails me. He gave me a lift afterwards but I don't remember his name.'

'I had the impression at the time that you all knew each other already.'

Jenny turned and looked directly in May's eyes.

'Jack might have known him but I don't understand how that could possibly be the case. How would a gentleman know a workman unless he was in his employ? I certainly hadn't met him, not previously and not since. Now please, either tell me what this is about or leave.'

May hadn't thought out exactly what she was going to say at this point so spoke on the spur of the moment. She was to regret it.

'We found a pocket watch and we now think it might have been stolen …' May paused to see if the words would have a reaction with the intention of continuing the sentence to say that perhaps Jenny had seen someone suspicious at the time. The pause however was too long, and the reaction was too quick. The blood rushed to Jenny's cheeks, she drew herself up to her full height and stepped forward until she was inches from May's face. May was not short by any means and Jenny was only an inch or two taller but she looked strong and fierce.

'Are you accusing me of being a thief?' she yelled full into May's face and the smaller girl stepped back. 'Get out of my house this instant!'

May hastily ran to the door and grabbed her bicycle which she had leant against the outside wall. Not even bothering to mount the bike, she ran pushing it alongside as the slammed door reverberated down the street.

The rain had started to fall heavier so to compound the misery of having made such a mess of her enquiries May was getting soaking wet. To make matters worse dusk had fallen and the street gaslights would not be lit until 9pm so visibility was very poor.

Because of this, as she cycled home down a neighbouring street May failed to notice the worried man removing the note that had been pinned to his front door.

He looked nervously right to left down the street. Suddenly there in the murky distance, blurred by the rain was the outline of a large man. The figure seemed to be tapping the side of his leg gently with a hammer. The house owner shuddered, went inside and locked his door.

*　　*　　*

It was a happy Thomas Chard that sauntered through the streets that evening. Not even the persistent rain could dampen his spirits. His investigation now had a clear focus. It could not be a coincidence that at least two of the people who could have planted the watch worked at the same premises as Michael Blake. It was not yet lighting up time so visibility was poor due to the rain which fell without respite. Nevertheless, Chard's stout umbrella and his thick overcoat were doing a fine job of protecting him from the elements. He passed through Penuel Square and onwards to the end of the street, turned right over the road bridge that stood alongside the Old Bridge and glanced down at the river that had risen significantly due to the heavy rain.

'Where to go next?' Chard muttered.

Light shone through the windows of the Maltsters Arms that overlooked the river, but the inspector decided to walk on by and take his first look at the Glamorgan Canal. Ignoring the Ivor Arms to his right he continued a little further until he could see more lights shining through the gloom ahead.

'This looks promising,' he said to himself.

Near to a hump-backed bridge stood the Llanover Arms and the Queens Hotel. Walking up to the latter he stood by a canal wharf where several barges were tied up. Tarpaulin was stretched across some of their decks covering their loads, others remained open to the elements.

Chard stood for a while just watching the raindrops splash on the black waters of the canal with just the sound of the rain hitting his umbrella for company.

He heard a snort and a rattle of iron-shod hooves from somewhere behind him and looked to see that there was a stable close by where the barge horses sheltered. Chard walked across and smelled the damp hay. He felt very content in the moment but realised that he couldn't really just stand there in the rain indefinitely so resolved to warm himself with a small whiskey.

After some deliberation the inspector chose to walk into the Llanover Arms. The front door opened into a corridor with a door to the left and another to the right. Opening the left hand door he found a drinking room occupied by a group of young and boisterous bargemen. Quite incongruously in the corner, in a large wooden chair, sat a well-dressed old lady knitting whilst chatting to an elderly friend. Closing the door, Chard crossed the passageway and took the other option, entering into a small, friendly-looking bar.

There was one tall portly man in the process of having his glass refilled from a bottle of Scotch. Chard waited his turn then asked the bewhiskered barman for a drink.

'Do you have any Irish whiskey please?'

'Certainly sir, we have Jamesons if that is alright with you?' replied the bewhiskered barman.

'Excellent, I'll take it neat.' replied Chard. He felt a tap on his shoulder.

'What is wrong with Scottish whisky?' asked the man who had just been served. His voice was slightly slurred but the accent was clearly from north of Hadrian's Wall.

Chard turned to face the man. 'Nothing at all. It is just that I don't have a taste for it,' he replied as pleasantly as possible.

'Then you don't drink it properly. You need to add a little drop of water to get the smell of the peat into your nose,' the Scotsman explained, wagging his finger and pointing to his nose.

'Now Jock, leave the man alone. I am sure he just wants a quiet drink.'

'Och, I am just trying to educate the man,' he replied flailing an arm haphazardly and nearly catching Chard with it in the process.

'Constable Donachie, will you please settle yourself down on the bench over by the window. *Eisteddwch* now.'

'Dinnae use that language to me,' replied the Scot who nevertheless staggered away and sat quietly on the bench seat across the room.

Chard looked at the barman with curiosity. 'Why did you call him Constable?'

'Canal police, isn't it,' he answered as if all should be clear.

Chard looked nonplussed.

'New here, are you?'

The inspector nodded. 'Only been here a couple of weeks. What do you mean by canal police?'

'The Glamorgan Canal runs its own police force, just to deal with canal matters, see? Theft of stock, drunkenness and fighting, that sort of thing. It helps out the ordinary police. They just fine or fire the culprits. That's why I don't mind having Jock in here. You've heard the canal lads in the room next door?'

Chard nodded again, 'Yes. They are a bit rowdy but otherwise seem to be behaving themselves.'

'That's part of our own unofficial rugby team. Play on a Saturday afternoon they do. Sometimes they get a bit out of hand but a word from Jock keeps them in order.'

'He doesn't look capable,' commented Chard.

'If you meet him at another time you might think differently. He has gone quiet for the moment but I admit he might start up again when he wants another drink.'

The inspector paid for his whiskey, knocked it back in one

and left, rather than stay and risk an altercation. He was sure that the superintendent still hadn't forgiven him for getting involved in a brawl on his first night.

There was a nice warm glow in his throat from the whiskey as he made his way out through the front door and into the rainy night. The lamplighter had been around whilst he had been inside and every few dozen yards there was a glow of gaslight through the downpour. Chard considered giving the Ivor Arms another try but decided against it. It was perhaps better to call it a night and head back to the New Inn.

The walk back towards Taff Street was uneventful except for the faulty street lamp by the Old Bridge which left the road in complete darkness causing Chard to miss the curb edge and tread in a puddle. He felt the unpleasant sensation of the water flowing over the edge of his shoe and into his sock.

'Bollocks!' he swore out loud. As he did so, the inspector made out the shape of someone ahead moving furtively. Approaching the left turn into the town's main street the gaslight made the outline clearer and Chard smiled to himself. There was only one person who moved so suspiciously as a matter of course. He couldn't be sure due to the poor visibility, but it had to be Dic Jenkins. The inspector had cut his evening short and had time to indulge his curiosity, so he followed, keeping at a distance.

Past Penuel Square, Dic turned down into Gas Lane. At this point Chard was getting bored and resolved to carry on ahead to the New Inn and a nice warm, dry room. It was likely that his quarry was not up to anything, he probably sneaked around like that all the time.

Then, barely visible, two shadowy forms drifted out of the darkness and stalked wraith-like in the direction taken by Jenkins. Some feral sense was alerted within Chard and he immediately collapsed his umbrella and broke into a run.

By the time that Chard caught up, Dic Jenkins was already on the floor. The two assailants stood over him with their backs to the inspector. Both were young, probably less than twenty years old, but dangerous nevertheless. Poorly clothed for the inclement weather and looking in need of a good meal, they were probably opportunistic thieves. The slightly taller of the two had his fist raised to hit the fallen man.

'No you don't!' shouted Chard, making a grab for the raised hand. The hand broke free and the punch went down, but the inspector had done enough to cause the blow to miss. Meanwhile the other thief had kicked Jenkins hard in the chest causing him to shuffle backwards on the floor until his back came up against the bottom of a brick wall.

The youth, whose hand Chard had tried to grab, now turned to face him. Reaching inside his jacket he pulled out a short-bladed knife.

'You should keep your nose out, butt. Now we'll have your money as well,' he snarled.

Chard held up his umbrella to defend himself as the thief slashed with the knife at his fingers. Chard stepped back causing the blow to miss. The other assailant now turned to join in. He threw a wild punch at the inspector's head which Chard easily avoided.

'Too slow sonny,' he taunted, stepping to one side placing the second youth between himself and the one with the knife.

Dic, in the meantime, struggled to his feet.

Another punch came at Chard's head, again it missed. The inspector tried to grab the arm as it went past with his right hand whilst holding the umbrella in the left. The attempt was unsuccessful, but his opponent was still shielding him from the youth with the knife.

Chard was expecting the next punch and rather than dodging it he stepped into the blow, leading with his fist which connected with the thief first with an almighty crack as it broke his jaw, knocking him out cold.

Dic Jenkins looked at the fallen youth lying on the ground and gave a big grin, followed by an urgent shout.

'Look out!' he yelled as the thief with the knife crept up behind Chard.

The knife came down but in one swift movement the inspector had turned to the side and used his foot to trip up the thief who fell full length in a muddy puddle. Dropping the umbrella Chard quickly knelt on the thief, twisting his arm behind his back and causing the knife to fall to the floor. Hauling him to his feet Chard called out to Dic,

'Come on Jenkins, help me get this scum up to the station. The other one can stay there. It'll be a while before he wakes up.'

There was no reply. Chard looked over his shoulder but Dic Jenkins had vanished in the rain.

CHAPTER THIRTEEN

The next morning it was a surprised Mr Dunwoody that welcomed Inspector Chard and Constable Preece into his office.

'Please take a seat. I am sorry that Mr Roberts is not here to welcome you, gentlemen. He is at a meeting with our bankers in Cardiff. How can I be of assistance?' he enquired, rubbing his hands in his usual timid, obsequious manner.

Chard looked around at Dunwoody's office, it was well furnished but not to the grand standard of that belonging to Mr Roberts. He took a seat whilst Constable Preece remained standing.

'It is connected to our previous visit, Mr Dunwoody. I can confirm our earlier suspicion that the man you identified in the infirmary as being Mr Blake was actually someone else.'

'Really, who?'

'Sadly we do not yet know. We recovered the body of the real Mr Blake from the river.'

'How terrible. Are you sure?' asked the little man clearly dismayed.

'Yes, we are sure,' confirmed Chard. 'However, we are currently concentrating on trying to find out the identity of the man you incorrectly identified.'

The under-manager went red in the face. 'How could I have made a mistake, though? There was his watch.' He put his head in his hands briefly, then suddenly announced confidently. 'I have it. They must have known each other.'

'Perhaps sir,' responded the inspector, not wanting to get into a discussion of possible theories with the little man. 'However, returning to the identity of the man in the bed, we do have a possible lead. You see there are two of your employees that were at the infirmary on the day that the train crash victims were admitted. A Jenny Norton and a Jack Ross. They may have noticed something on the day that could help us.'

'Why were they at the infirmary?' asked Dunwoody.

'They thought the infirmary would want volunteers,' answered the inspector.

'That sounds like our Miss Norton. There couldn't be a more helpful young lady. Jenny came here some time ago and joined as a junior clerk working on the wages but she is so gifted with figures that she now works alongside Miss Hawkins on the main company accounts.'

'What about this Jack Ross?'

'I can't speak for his character,' Dunwoody sniffed. 'Damn foreigner, you know, for all that he speaks good English. He works in the small foundry we use for producing cast iron goods.'

'Perhaps we could start with him first, if you don't mind?'

'Of course, of course,' answered Dunwoody, getting to his feet.' Follow me, gentlemen. I will lead the way.'

They exited the room and went down a corridor into a small office where Chard recognised Miss Hawkins who was busily working at her desk. Opposite her sat a strikingly beautiful woman with dark hair who looked up briefly and caught his eye. He paused for a second but then moved on in the wake of Mr Dunwoody with Preece following behind.

As they left through a door at the back of the room Lizzie Hawkins leant across her desk and whispered to her friend.

'That's those policemen I was telling you about. I couldn't catch what they were saying last time they were here, but it did send Mr Dunwoody into a bit of a flap. It must be important for them to come back here.'

'We'll see,' was the only reply as Jenny returned to her work.

*   *   *

Out in the open air Chard stared up at the chimneys that spewed black smoke into the sky. There had been a short lull in the continual rain so the policemen had been happy to leave their respective raincape and overcoat at the front door of Taff Vale House. Chard was regretting that decision now, though, as particles of soot started to fall on his finely tailored jacket.

'You mentioned pulling Michael Blake from the river, Inspector. Did he drown?' enquired Dunwoody as they passed one of the furnaces. 'Open verdict, Mr Dunwoody, so there may or may not have been foul play. We are looking into the matter.'

There was a sudden thump through the ground as a steam drop hammer impacted on white hot metal in one of the workshops. Both policemen flinched at the unexpected sound.

Mr Dunwoody smiled benignly. 'You will get used to that. It is quite noisy but not as much as it once was, I'm afraid. We have ten puddling furnaces but only four are now in operation. That is why we have reduced the hours of our remaining workers.'

'Is business that bad, sir?' asked Constable Preece.

'I am afraid so. We only produce wrought iron and a small amount of cast iron,' answered Dunwoody sadly. 'Our main contracts used to be for railway tracks but they have gradually switched to steel. Up at Crawshay's Forest Works they produce wrought iron and Bessemer steel and I understand even they are having a hard time due to competition from elsewhere.'

'What do you produce with the wrought iron now, Mr

Dunwoody?' continued Preece as they walked on towards a smaller foundry in the distance.

'It is still used for railway couplings, nuts, bolts, steam pipes, etc. You see wrought iron is more resistant to corrosion than steel but with the Bessemer process steel is less labour intensive to produce and therefore cheaper,' explained the small man who suddenly stopped, his expression distracted and pensive.

Chard raised an eyebrow in his direction. 'Mr Dunwoody, would you like to say something?'

Dunwoody sighed. 'I don't know if I should mention this, I really don't.'

'Is it to do with Mr Blake?' asked the inspector.

'Yes, but it really isn't my business,' pondered Dunwoody rubbing his hands nervously.

'I think we need to hear it,' insisted Chard.

'Very well,' agreed Dunwoody. 'I told you previously that Michael Blake was not well liked. To be honest he was a brute of a man and there were many scared of him.

I understand that there was someone that he had close dealings with outside of the works.' Dunwoody paused, uncertain of himself.

'Please do continue,' prompted the inspector.

'I would rather that this is confidential. I do not want it known that I have discussed this with you.'

'I do not reveal my sources unless absolutely necessary,' assured Chard.

'Well, there is a man in the town called Jabez Grimes. I understand that he is a most disreputable individual. If anyone caused harm to Blake then he is likely to be behind it. There, I will say no more, but it is to him that you should direct your attention.' With that he walked ahead once more and led them to the cast iron foundry. The relatively small cylindrical furnace was about fifteen feet high and stood outside the building. One man prodded with a long metal tool into an opening at the rear of the furnace to encourage the flow of the impurities, the slag, which being lighter than the metal, rested on top of the metal liquid. This done, it formed a small waterfall of sludge down an almost vertical chute on to the floor of the yard, resulting in a small dirty yellow pool which was left to cool. The furnace roared in accompaniment, with yellow smoke billowing above. At the front of the furnace the molten iron started to flow down a longer chute with a gentle gradient.

'Come this way, gentlemen,' encouraged Mr Dunwoody as he led them to some stone steps alongside the foundry where they were able to look through a window at the workers making the cast iron. In fact there were several large windows around the building and a large open door at one end to help disperse the acrid fumes within. From their viewing platform the policemen could see where the chute from the furnace led into the foundry. Molten iron flowed bright yellow, so intense it was like liquid sun, down an open chute into a metal bucket. Some slag still floated on top and one of the workers used a metal scoop to skim it off the top to land on the floor creating a fountain of sparks.

'That's Ross there, about to attach the yoke,' pointed out Dunwoody.

Two metal rods joined at one end now formed a yoke around the metal bucket. Two men then grabbed the yoke with large thick leather gauntlets, their eyes shielded from the glare by darkened goggles. They then carried the yoke, backs bent with the weight, towards the moulds and carefully tilted the bucket so that the molten metal flowed into the draining holes set into the moulds. More acrid smoke came and as they walked away flames could be seen flickering from the moulds as the liquid settled into the cast.

'It's much easier to make cast iron than wrought iron, you see,' explained Dunwoody. 'It is a very practical method for making parts of machinery that are not subjected to shock loads as well as cisterns, manhole covers, ornamental works and so on.' The under-manager led the way down from the stone steps and around to the large open door just as the furnace was being shut to allow the chute to be scraped clear of debris from impurities.

'Ross! These gentlemen would like to have a word with you,' said Dunwoody as soon as they got into earshot.

'Yes, Mr Ross, if you wouldn't mind stepping outside,' added the inspector. To Chard, the small drops of soot in the air were less unpleasant than the sulphurous fumes that assailed his lungs in the foundry.

Ross looked questioningly at Dunwoody, but took off his gauntlets and goggles without argument and walked out into the yard.

'We'll be alright on our own now, Mr Dunwoody. After a quick chat with your man here we will make our way back to your office before speaking to Miss Norton.'

'Miss Norton?' queried Ross, speaking up for the first time.

'None of your business, Ross,' interjected Dunwoody before turning to the inspector. 'Very well, I will make the necessary arrangements.'

Chard watched Dunwoody go before turning his attention to Jack Ross. The worker wore a long leather apron over his trousers and shirt. A dampened scarf was wound around his neck and he wore a flat cap. He appeared alert and confident, holding the inspector's gaze. It was also evident that he cared about his appearance because the young man sported a very neatly trimmed black moustache and even with his cap on one could see that he used hair oil.

Preece stood behind with his notebook at the ready.

'My name is Inspector Chard and I need you to help me with my enquiries.'

'I will help you if I can. What is it about?' asked Ross, the trace of a foreign accent quite noticeable.

'What is your real name, Mr Ross?' asked the inspector, changing the conversation.

'I am sorry, I don't understand.'

'Let me make it easier for you. *Come si chiama*?'

Ross smiled again. 'Giacomo Rossi *sono*. So you speak Italian, Inspector?'

'Just a little,' replied Chard, his face expressionless. 'Let's keep this in English though. Why change your name?'

'It just makes my name easier to pronounce. It can be difficult being a foreigner here.'

'How long have you been in the country?'

'About three years. Ships regularly transport coal between Cardiff and Genoa. I had done the trip several times but decided to try living in South Wales. I thought I might make my fortune.' He gave a sardonic laugh. 'It didn't work out.'

'What was the name of the ship you came in on and, remember, we can check if we need to.'

'The *Cielo Azzurro*,' replied the Italian.

'Did you come to Pontypridd straight away?'

'No, I spent some weeks working in Cardiff, on the docks. I heard there was plenty of work in Ponty so I came to take a look, but everyone else seems to have had the same idea which is why I work in this shithole. What is all this about?'

'You would have known a Michael Blake, who was a chargehand here?'

'Yes, I knew him. Why?'

'What was your working relationship with him?'

'I didn't like him. He was not a pleasant man,' replied Ross, maintaining direct eye contact throughout.

'When the train crash happened two years ago you volunteered to help at the infirmary.'

'I accompanied Miss Norton, but we weren't needed.'

'You were aware that Mr Blake was reported to have died in the crash?'

Ross shrugged his shoulders. 'So I was told.'

'The man they said was Blake has turned out to be someone else.'

'What has that got to do with me?'

'I have reason to believe that you saw the victim before he died. He was a man with a disfigured face.'

'Was that him? I saw such a man and it turned my stomach so I left.'

'I understand there was another man there with yourself and Miss Norton,' prompted Chard.

Ross turned his head and spat on the ground. 'Yes, a fancy-dressed gentleman, soft skin, probably never worked in his life.'

'Did you know him?'

'Do I look as if I keep company with that sort?' answered Ross angrily.

'Mind your manners, Ross, or I'll take you down to the station,' threatened the inspector.

'By the way, Blake has been pulled out of the river.' Chard introduced the statement suddenly whilst watching for a reaction.

Ross held the inspector's gaze and a smile slowly spread across his face. 'So?'

'We think that there may have been foul play involved. So

I find myself wondering who might have wished him harm?' asked Chard.

'Just about everyone that knew him, Inspector. As I said, he wasn't a pleasant man, but I know nothing about how he came to be in the river.'

'Why don't I believe you?'

'Because I am a foreigner. We are the first people to be blamed for everything. At least I am not a Jew or you would have me in prison already,' reacted Ross angrily.

Chard wondered if it was a genuine reaction or just a way of deflecting questions.

'Did you have any dealings with Blake outside of work?'

'Never,' snapped Ross.

'Do you know anybody who did?'

The Italian hesitated before replying. 'No. Is that all, Inspector?'

'One last question. When you were at the infirmary that day, did you see a pocket watch on or near the man with the disfigured face?'

'Once again the answer is no. Now if I may …'

Chard nodded his assent and watched as Ross picked up his gauntlets and goggles and returned to the foundry.

'Did you get all that, Constable? Including the name of the ship?'

'Certainly did sir,' replied Preece. 'I also noted the name that Mr Dunwoody gave us, a Jabez Grimes.'

'Well done, Preece, I will want to find him in due course. Now let's get back over to Mr Dunwoody's office.'

The two men walked back through the yard, flinching again as a steam drop hammer sent vibrations through the ground.

Dunwoody was waiting for them in the office occupied by Jenny Norton and Lizzie Hawkins.

'I have explained to Miss Norton that you would like a word, Inspector. Miss Hawkins has asked if she might remain with her friend. These young ladies are not used to talking to policemen.'

'I would prefer if we spoke to Miss Norton on her own, Mr Dunwoody. As you say, there is nothing to worry about,' replied Chard firmly but with a pleasant smile.

Lizzie Hawkins looked disgruntled for a second before getting up from her desk and giving Jenny's shoulder a sympathetic stroke. The short blonde then followed Dunwoody out of the room leaving Jenny alone with the two policemen.

Both men took a seat, with Preece taking his notebook out once again.

Chard looked across at Jenny. Her face was cold, imperious and stunningly beautiful.

'My name is Inspector Chard and I need to ask you a few questions.'

'Mr Dunwoody tells me that it is something to do with me being at the infirmary on the day of the train crash,' replied Jenny. Her voice was clear and melodic.

'That is correct. You see there was an injured man there who was assumed to be Michael Blake. In fact Mr Dunwoody subsequently identified him as such. However, he was wrong.'

Jenny gave a wry smile, the first time that her face had shown any expression since Chard entered the room. 'So that is why he seemed so flustered today. What has that got to do with me being at the infirmary?'

'If that man wasn't Michael Blake, I need to find out his real identity. You were seen close to the injured man in question on the day the casualties were brought in.'

'I am not sure I would remember,' answered Jenny.

'This man had a very badly disfigured face.'

'Yes, I do recall. It was horrible. So that was the man that was thought to be Michael Blake?'

'Yes. Tell me, could you have seen that it wasn't Michael Blake?'

'No Inspector, but I would have had no reason to suspect it was. I would have barely spoken to Blake in all the time I had worked here and the face of the man in the bed would have been unrecognisable to the poor man's own mother. None of us knew that Blake had been in the train crash until Mr Dunwoody told us days later and I had no reason to connect Blake with the person I had seen in lying in the bed.'

'Did you notice a pocket watch on or near the disfigured man?' enquired Chard.

Jenny thought back to the visit from Miss Roper the previous evening. She stared directly into the inspector's eyes. 'No. Definitely not,' she replied firmly.

'I understand that you were with two other people. Jack Ross was one and the other was a Mr Dorsett I believe?'

Again the same questions thought Jenny. 'If you say so. Jack was certainly with me until he rushed off. I recall the other gentleman but I wouldn't have remembered his name.'

'Why did Jack rush off?'

'I don't know. He seemed to have been upset by the sight of the injured man. I can't say I blame him. Jack is my neighbour and although he seems very carefree and confident I think that he can be very sensitive.'

'I did wonder why you speak of him so informally, Miss Norton.'

'As I said we are neighbours. It would not be acceptable for me in my position to be so familiar with a foreign man of the working class in any other capacity. I am sure you understand that, Inspector.'

'I certainly do, miss. No disrespect intended.'

Chard subconsciously scratched his sideburns. He was finding Jenny's stare discomforting.

'Were you aware that a man's body was fetched out of the river the other day, Miss Norton?'

'There was some local gossip about that, Inspector, not that I engage in tittle-tattle.'

'Would you be surprised to hear that the body was that of Michael Blake?' asked Chard, looking for any kind of reaction.

Jenny stiffened. 'Oh dear! How shocking! I understand the man wasn't liked but why should he drown himself?'

'It is likely that someone put him in the river. We don't think it was an accident.'

'Are you sure, Inspector? It sounds so terrible.'

'In truth we are not one hundred per cent sure. That is why we are trying to find out all we can about him,' conceded Chard.

'As I have explained, Inspector, I barely knew the man. He only arrived some months before he disappeared and I had already been here for two years or more at the time.'

'So I understand.' Chard hesitated before continuing. 'Miss Norton, may I ask something personal that has engaged my curiosity?'

'You may, Inspector, but I might decline to answer,' her face returned to the cold imperious look that she had at the start of the conversation.

'It's just that I spoke to Father McManus about you …' There was a momentary flinch in Jenny's austere expression, '… and he seemed very protective towards you as does Mr Dunwoody and indeed Miss Hawkins. Why is that?'

Jenny's lip started to tremble as she began to answer. 'I was orphaned at a very young age. A convent took me in, looked after me and taught me to read and write. They found I had an aptitude for numbers and that gave me a start in life. Now if you don't mind …'

Chard noticed that a tear had started to form in the corner of her eye. He rose from his chair, prompting Preece to do the same.

'I am sorry to have bothered you, Miss Norton. That will be all. We can see ourselves out.'

The policemen gave a knock on Mr Dunwoody's office door to say they were leaving, gathered their coat and raincape and made their exit.

'What do you think, Constable?'

'Well sir, we are looking at someone who could have a motive for killing Blake and who could have planted the pocket watch. If we are only looking at the three most likely to have planted the pocket watch, then the most likely to have a motive would be Ross. He would have had most contact with Blake, being a working man.'

'Yes Preece, but what concerns me is what if the person planting the watch, who may or may not be one of the three we are looking at, was planting it on behalf of someone else? This whole puzzle is a real rat's nest.'

'What is our next step then, sir?'

'I think it has to be tracing this Jabez Grimes character.' Chard gave a sigh as fresh drops of rain started to fall. 'Oh well, back to the station. Paperwork first. It is piling up everywhere. Grimes will have to wait until tomorrow.'

CHAPTER FOURTEEN

When Chard entered the station next morning he was greeted by Sergeant Humphreys.

'The superintendent is in early this morning, sir. He wants to see you as soon as you go in.'

'Thank you, Sergeant,' acknowledged Chard. The inspector went to his office, hung up his hat and coat then marched across to his superior's office. He knocked on the door and was commanded to enter.

'Ah, Chard, I think we need to have a little chat.'

'Do we sir?' Chard saw that the superintendent, resplendent in his uniform as always, was particularly grim-faced.

'I believe that after the debacle of your first night in this town I had some words with you about brawling in public. Do you recall, or has it somehow slipped your memory?'

'Oh, I remember it well sir,' Chard replied, standing to attention and staring just over Superintendent Jones's shoulder. He had been told years ago by an old soldier never to look a senior officer directly in the eye when being reprimanded.

'Then why do I find that the other night you were brawling in the street once again? I was informed that you fetched a prisoner into the station the other night. If there are miscreants that need arresting then the brawling is done by the constables. That is their purpose. Your purpose is to bring dignity to your office and uphold the reputation of the station.'

Chard felt incensed at the unfairness of the accusation and broke with his strategy of not looking the superintendent in the eye. 'I had no option, sir. There were two assailants attacking a man on the ground. I incapacitated one of them and the other pulled a knife. I brought that one in as the other man was unconscious,' replied Chard, red in the face.

'May I ask then, Inspector, where is the man that you knocked unconscious?'

'By the time the constables went to pick him up he had recovered and disappeared,' answered Chard, quite certain of where the conversation was leading.

'In that case, where is the knife that the man you arrested allegedly pulled on you?'

'There is no allegedly about it, sir,' answered the inspector, hardly controlling his anger.

'Calm down, Inspector. I am merely playing the part of the magistrate here,' cautioned the superintendent. 'I repeat, where is the knife?'

'The thief I left on the ground must have taken it with him when he recovered,' answered Chard miserably.

'Well at least we have the evidence of the witness, that is to say the person who you found being attacked. Is that the case?'

Chard realised that the superintendent already knew the answer but was just making him suffer. 'No sir, he ran off,' admitted the inspector.

'Which is why I had to let the miscreant go this morning. Pointless keeping him here if we aren't going to get a conviction. You weren't in uniform so he could argue that he thought he was being attacked. He will deny any knife, any accomplice and any other victim. Shoddy police work, Chard, and I won't have it.'

'Yes sir,' answered Chard fully admonished. 'If that's all sir?' The inspector turned towards the door and was on the point of opening it when the superintendent called him back.

'No Inspector, that is not all.' As Chard turned he saw that Superintendent Jones's severe expression had softened into a gentle smile. 'I just read in my journal how you saved that small boy's life last week by diving in front of that horse and cart. Well done.'

'Thank you sir,' answered Chard, surprised at the change in tone.

'That is all. Just chase up that uniform.'

'Yes sir.' The inspector left the office still feeling puzzled and went to find Constable Preece.

'Constable, I want you to spend the morning trying to find out what you can about this Jabez Grimes. Have a word with the newspaper office, ask the local authority, the post office or any businessmen you know. I need an address and any information on what he does for a living. In the meantime I have to get on top of my paperwork.'

'Certainly sir,' replied Preece who rushed out of the office, eager to please his superior.

* * *

It was after midday when Preece returned to the station. Taking out his notebook for reference he knocked on the inspector's door and entered.

'Any luck, Constable?' enquired Chard, relieved to have something to take his mind off the routine paperwork on his desk.

'It's all a bit strange, sir. Jabez Grimes has an office on Morgan Street amongst the firms of solicitors, accountants and so on. He also is believed to own several other properties across town. Yet nobody seems very clear on exactly what he does or what his business interests are.'

'That is strange. I thought everybody knew everybody's business around here,' responded Chard whilst scratching his sideburns.

'That isn't all that is strange, sir. It was some of the reactions I got when I asked. Particularly from some of the more prominent gentlemen around town, I might add.

Don't get me wrong, sir, most told me everything they could, which was little enough, but others just clammed up as soon as I mentioned his name.'

'Then I am intrigued. From the sounds of it, this Grimes fellow is a man of substance so why, according to Dunwoody, would he have dealings with Blake? You have tried your best but I think I need to find out a little more about him. If you give me the address on Morgan Street I will go there this very afternoon. I don't think I will need you with me though. If he has anything to hide he will probably just deny knowing Blake and at this point I just want to get the measure of the man.'

'Very well sir,' agreed Preece, slightly disappointed.

'Don't look so glum, Constable, I have something at the back of my mind that may become necessary, and my reasons for not taking you will become clear.'

*   *   *

The office premises in Morgan Street were not particularly large or impressive, but it was situated on what was considered to be a very desirable location not far from the town centre, and indeed not far from the police station. The door was opened by a young maid who asked Chard to wait in a comfortable downstairs room whilst she informed her master of his visitor. After a five minute wait the inspector was led upstairs and into a small but comfortable office.

'Good morning, Inspector. Please take a seat,' Grimes spoke politely but without getting up or offering a handshake.

Chard took an instant dislike to the man sat behind the desk. There was something about his manner, something indefinable about the way he looked that the inspector found profoundly unsettling. Grimes was slouching in his chair, smoking a cigarette with one hand whilst the other rested lazily on the armrest. He was jacketless with a bright red waistcoat from which a gold watch chain dangled.

'How can I help you?' he offered, his insincere broad smile breaking through the elegantly trimmed black beard.

'I understand that you used to know a man called Michael Blake.'

'Michael Blake?' Grimes paused, 'No I don't think so.'

Chard frowned, knowing full well that the man opposite him was not telling the truth.

Without prompting, Grimes continued. 'Then again you could mean Mickey Blake. Yes, I knew old Mickey.'

The inspector realised that Grimes was toying with him. Still the insincere smile remained.

'Who told you that I knew Mickey Blake, Inspector? Was it a mutual friend of his perhaps? I would like to know, really I would.'

'I am afraid that is confidential,' answered the inspector.

'A pity. I would like to thank them for putting you in touch.' Grimes' eyes were dark and predatory.

'Would it surprise you to know that Blake's body was fished out of the river recently?' asked Chard, anticipating a facial reaction of some kind. It was a reaction that never came.

Grimes blew a ring of cigarette smoke in the air, and waved his hand lazily in a nonchalant manner. 'No it wouldn't.'

Chard was slightly taken aback by the reply.

'The inquest was earlier this week,' continued Grimes.

'How do you know that? The papers haven't reported it yet.'

'I don't need the papers to keep me informed. I make it my business to know everything, Inspector.'

'What exactly is your business, Mr Grimes?'

'Oh, I like to invest here and there. I own a few properties as I am sure you already know. My more detailed interests are a private matter.'

'Very well, but if you don't mind I would be obliged if you could enlighten me as to your relationship with Mr Blake.'

'Mickey came here from London and was looking for work. We met by chance in the town and he seemed a decent fellow with similar social interests to my own so I gave him a reference so that he could gain employment at the ironworks.'

Chard felt he was being toyed with once more. He knew Grimes was lying and the businessman realised that he knew. There was no option for now other than to keep playing the game.

'Yet Mr Blake was of a different social class to yourself, so how did you have similar social interests?'

'Oh, you really haven't been here very long. The social norms in Ponty often don't apply. It is very egalitarian here, you know. We were both keen on charity and looking after our fellow man.'

'I am pleased to hear that you were both so altruistic. Are you aware of anyone that might have meant Mr Blake harm?'

Grimes paused as if genuinely perusing an idea, but then leant forward with both elbows on his desk and replied, 'I cannot imagine anyone wanting to harm such a kind, generous man.' His eyes were deliberately wide with mocking fake innocence and Chard decided that he was wasting his time.

'Thank you for your time, Mr Grimes. I will see myself out,' snapped the inspector, rising to his feet and making an exit. He pulled the door behind him as he went through but, disappointingly, it didn't slam.

Grimes got up from his desk and smiled, this time genuinely, as Chard stormed off.

It was perhaps a little imprudent of him to get under a new police inspector's skin, but he couldn't resist it. He was too powerful to be touched by a mere policeman and the sooner

Chard realised it the better. If he proved too troublesome then he could always be removed, one way or another.

*   *   *

It was an angry Thomas Chard that strode into the station and commanded Constable Preece to follow him into his office. 'You will remember me saying that I might have something in mind for you?'

'I do, sir,' responded Preece.

'I have decided to put my idea into practice so I will change the working rota. Take the rest of the afternoon off. I have a special job for you to do tonight instead,' said Chard.

Preece was intrigued. 'What is it, sir?'

'I have just been to see Jabez Grimes and I didn't like what I found. I know scum when I see it and by heaven it was sat behind his desk smoking a cigarette. There is something rotten about that man and I want to know what it is.'

'I did try to find out all I could this morning, sir.'

'Yes I know you did, Preece. I had a feeling that my meeting with him wouldn't go well. That is why I want you on duty tonight. This morning you were in uniform talking mainly to the professional class of person in a formal capacity. You found out very little and some were clearly avoiding your questions.'

'That's right, sir, and I can't understand why that should be.'

'My proposal is that tonight you go out of uniform and talk to the underbelly of society. If Grimes is the sort of person I perceive him to be then someone somewhere must know something.'

'Out of uniform? Isn't that rather irregular, sir?'

'I doubt the superintendent would approve. We don't have a detective department in this station but it will come one day, of that I am sure. Well, are you up for it? I would happily do it myself but Superintendent Jones has had a fairly robust discussion with me this morning and I do not want to be misinterpreted as trying to be difficult.'

Preece looked doubtful. Chard recognised the concern in his face and sought to reassure him.

'Do not worry, Preece. If by some unlikely chance something goes wrong with this exercise I will take full responsibility.'

'It isn't that, sir. I am concerned that surely someone will recognise me. I have done enough patrols in the town for people to know I am a policeman. As for the underbelly of society, I am sure that a fair proportion of them will have been through our cells at one time or another.'

'I think you are overestimating the risk of being recognised. The only real risk would have been if you had come with me to interview Grimes and then accidentally bumped into him tonight. When you are on patrol people, unless of course they really are "regulars", look at the uniform not the face. Then there is your build. No offence intended here, Preece, but out of uniform I would imagine you don't really look like a policeman.'

Preece looked offended.

'I mean compared with Sergeant Morris, for example,' added Chard quickly, realising that such an extreme comparison was actually less offensive. 'Then there is your deportment,' continued Chard.

'What is wrong with it, sir?' asked Preece, starting to feel self-conscious.

'Nothing. That's the problem. You do stand and indeed walk like a policeman.'

That at least started to make Preece feel a little better.

'You need to slouch a lot more and shuffle your feet a bit when you walk,' continued the inspector.

'You mean like this, sir?' Preece bent forward slightly and tried to walk in a slovenly manner across the office floor.

'A good try but that's a little bit too much. Go home and practise in front of a mirror for a couple of hours. That is if you are up for it.'

'I will give it a go, sir.'

'Good chap, Preece. I look forward to receiving your report in the morning.'

CHAPTER FIFTEEN

That evening, Danny Preece stood on the Tumble deciding where to try his luck first.

He wore a flat cap, muffler, the oldest jacket he owned and a pair of trousers that he usually reserved for gardening. A smudge of dirt was smeared across his face to add to his slovenly appearance. It seemed busier than usual for a Friday night and the public houses were in full swing. There was also one of Oscar Wilde's plays being put on at the Clarence Theatre and a variety of carriages, hansom cabs and broughams were dropping off their passengers outside. Danny had spent a good half hour in front of a mirror at home trying to get his walk right, so now was the time to put it into practice. He pulled his cap further over his face, slouched forward and walked in a slovenly manner across the road from the Clarence to the Bunch of Grapes. The pub was one of the busiest in town. The entrance was on the left hand side of a large bay window through which Danny could look into the saloon bar. It was clearly very raucous and getting into a quiet conversation with someone would undoubtedly be difficult in that room. The policeman entered into the long, narrow corridor and decided to go to the lounge bar at the back of the premises. It was not quite so busy here and although all the tables were occupied there were few people standing at the bar. Maintaining his slouched posture, and still concerned that he might be recognised, Danny made his way to the bar and attracted the attention of the barman. The burly custodian of the bar in black waistcoat and white apron looked at him in a far from friendly manner.

'Oi! What's your game?' he snarled before Danny could open his mouth to order a drink.

'What do you mean?' asked Danny, doing his best to put on the accent of a friendly simpleton.

'We don't serve scruffy beggars like you in here. Get in the saloon bar, or preferably go home and have a bath. Your face is filthy.'

Danny was shocked for a second. As a policeman no one would ever dare to talk to him like that. He felt indignant, yet somehow pleased that he hadn't been recognised.

'Sorry,' he replied, raising a hand in acknowledgement of the perceived error.

Danny shuffled out and moved back down the corridor into the saloon bar. Getting in was a tight squeeze as the patrons were packed tight. Customers jostled for position as they attempted to get served and it was a while before Danny could force himself to the front.

'Pint of bitter please,' he called out above the hubbub, this time using a gruffer tone to disguise his voice. He felt far more confident of being served without question in this bar as it was clearly patronised by a rougher clientele. Danny paid for his pint and then held it aloft to avoid spillage as he squeezed his way back through the crowd waiting to be served. Finding a rare bit of space in which to stand he looked around to see if there was someone unsavoury enough that he could latch onto and draw into conversation. He really wasn't sure how to go about it. As Danny scanned the room he did see someone familiar that stood out like a sore thumb.

He nudged the nearest man to him and asked casually ''Ere butty, who's that over there by the far end of the bar, then?'

The man to whom he spoke, turned and replied with fetid breath, 'Who'd you mean?'

'Him, over by there. Dressed a bit nobby for in here, isn't he?' answered Danny. He pointed at a tall thin man in a black frock coat who leant between the far end of the bar and the wall and was occasionally buffeted by people trying to get served. The man had a glass of whisky in his hand and it clearly wasn't his first of the night.

'Never, seen 'im in here before,' replied the man with bad breath, who then turned away.

'I know where I have seen him, though,' muttered Danny to himself. He had recognised the individual as Mr Bolton the solicitor, and had only asked the man with fetid breath in order to try and discover what he was doing here. A man of his station would not normally be found in such premises, probably not even in the lounge bar. Danny also had the impression that he was normally a sober, upright pillar of society yet there he was clearly looking worse for wear, red in the face and looking as if he had the weight of the world on his shoulders. As Danny watched, the object of his scrutiny knocked back his whisky and started to move away from the bar like a salmon swimming against the tide. As he made the door, Danny thought about following him but as he turned slightly to one side he inadvertently bumped against a man's elbow, spilling some of his drink,

'Oi, watch it!' came an angry retort.

Danny looked into the face of a middle-aged man with bushy eyebrows and an angry expression. His exclamation had been very loud and to the young policeman's consternation several people had turned to stare.

'Sorry, I'm really clumsy. Let me get you a fresh pint,' offered Danny.

'That's very decent of you. I'll have a pint of porter.'

Danny got back to the bar with difficulty as he was still holding half a pint of his own unfinished drink, but he did manage to get served and return to his starting point without spilling any of the precious liquid.

'Thank you butt,' said the bushy-eyebrowed man, who had

finished the rest of his original drink whilst Danny was at the bar. 'My name is Dai Lewis by the way.'

Danny shook his outstretched hand and quickly made up a name. 'Bryn Edwards,' he announced.

'Nice to meet you. Hold on, though, don't I know you from somewhere?'

Danny hunched forward slightly so that the peak of his cap hid more of his face.

'No, can't do. I'm new here. I start work at the Maritime colliery next week,' he replied. 'Actually I was looking out for someone who I was told would be a useful contact about town,' he added, eager to change the conversation.

'Who's that then?'

'Jabez Grimes was the name I was given. Quite a man about town or so I've heard.'

Dai Lewis scratched his head. 'Never heard of him. If he's a man about town he doesn't come in here or I'd know him. Are you sure I don't know you from somewhere?'

'I'm sure,' replied Danny, quickly gulping down the remainder of his pint. 'I need to be moving on now, though. Good to meet you, Dai.' With that he gave Lewis a hearty slap on the shoulder and pushed his way to the door.

Once he got outside Danny took in a deep breath of fresh air, free of tobacco smoke. It had started to rain again so he decided to cross the road and try the Clarence Hotel next as it was the nearest obvious choice. As he stepped off the pavement he heard a noise coming from a doorway a little further down the street. It sounded like an altercation. It was too dark to see exactly what was going on as the street lamp was on the other side of the road and could not fully illuminate the opposite pavement. Stealthily he moved nearer.

'Just leave me alone,' came an anguished cry as someone ran out from the cover of the doorway and into the rain, heading down towards the town centre. As soon as the gaslight from the street lamp fell on him Danny immediately recognised the man. It was Bolton the solicitor from the Bunch of Grapes. As he considered following the fleeing man another figure stepped out from the doorway. For a brief second Danny made eye contact with a large man, scarred on the left hand side of his face. The policeman halted momentarily and in that time the scarred man had turned, moving swiftly down the street and into the shadows. Danny gave chase, unsure what to do if he caught up. He was much smaller and not carrying his truncheon which he would normally use to subdue a bigger opponent. After a few yards, however, there was no need to contemplate the issue. The large man had disappeared into the rain, as had Mr Bolton.

Danny retraced his footsteps back to the Clarence Hotel as he had originally intended. He was pleased to get into somewhere dry but would have preferred somewhere that wasn't immersed in a fog of blue, swirling cigarette smoke. The Bunch of Grapes was smoky but it was like a fresh pine forest compared with this bar. Danny had only ever been in the Clarence twice before and each time he had vowed never to come back. He looked around at his fellow patrons. One thing was for sure, the clientele in the bar of the Clarence and that of the adjoining elegant Clarence Theatre were never likely to mix. Not that it was as bad as a couple of the establishments in town. The Vic, for example, was a hell hole which is why he intended to leave it as a last resort. Danny made his way to the bar which was not overly busy and bought himself a pint of pale ale. He stood near to the doorway as the far end of the room held an attraction that was not to his taste. A large cage was set up on the far wall, occupied by four capuchin monkeys who screeched constantly until quietened by food or indeed drink, given to them by customers. Danny watched as a very short fellow, who couldn't be more than five-foot tall, ordered a packet of pork scratchings from the bar and started to feed them to the unfortunate creatures. When the little man had finished and returned closer to the bar Danny decided to strike up a conversation. He checked his slovenly posture and deliberately spoke with a slightly slurred voice, pretending he had drunk more than he actually had.

'Not many pubs have got creatures like that, do they?' he asked.

The man grinned good-naturedly. 'Have you seen them before?' he asked.

'No,' lied Danny. 'I am new in town. Name's Bryn.'

'On your own are you?' enquired the little man with a raised eyebrow.

'Yes, but I am looking to find an old friend, Jabez Grimes. Do you know him?'

'Can't say I do, *bach*, but perhaps it might be worthwhile if I were to introduce you to someone else.' The man pointed to two women across the room, one in her twenties and the other probably double her age. They were both attired in low cut dresses of cheap material, and their cheeks were heavily rouged.

'Mother and daughter. I've 'ad both of them,' leered the little man. 'At the same time,' he added.

'I don't think I need to meet them,' answered Danny hurriedly, repulsed at the thought. 'I really need to find Jabez.'

'You get me wrong, *butty bach*,' assured the man who was undoubtedly their pimp.

'Megan and Sian know everybody. I am sure they will know this Jabez of yours. Come over and just meet them,' he encouraged.

Against his better judgement Danny followed the man over towards the two slatterns.

'*Shwmae* girls. This young man is on his own in town and is looking for his friend, Jabez Grimes. I am sure you must know him?' Danny failed to see the sly wink that the pimp gave to the women.

'Of course we do, don't we Sian?' laughed the older woman.

'Oh yes, we know him. Where were you meant to meet up?' asked the younger woman.

'He doesn't know I'm here. It's a surprise, but I don't exactly know where to find him. I would be obliged if you could tell me what he is doing nowadays. He is always up to something, a bit of a lad if you get my drift. Nothing too hot for him to handle.'

'That's us. We're hot to handle,' giggled Sian.

'Do you know where he hangs out at night?' persisted Danny.

'We can do better than that, we can show you,' suggested Megan.

The two women took the beer glass from his hand and put it on a nearby table. Then they each took an arm and started to lead Danny towards the door.

'Really, there's no need to take me, I just need directions,' he argued.

The women continued to pull and soon he was outside in the fresh air and the rain.

'It's not far. Let's hurry. We're getting wet but we'll soon be under cover,' said Megan.

Prompted by the rain and the women's urgency to get under cover, Danny allowed himself to be led down the road past the front of the adjoining theatre towards the town centre. A few yards further on the women pulled him into an alley.

'Up here, it's a short cut and because the alley's so narrow it will give us cover from the rain. Quickly now!' insisted Megan.

It was pitch black inside the alley which sloped steeply

upwards and Danny froze when he felt what he thought was a rat run over his foot. They were a few yards into the alley when the women suddenly pushed him against the wall. He felt a hand grab his testicles and a moment later he also felt a pricking sensation at his throat.

'Now then, love. How about you paying for some fun?' Megan whispered in his ear.

'I don't want any fun,' replied Danny through gritted teeth as the pressure of Sian's grip increased.

'I was talking about you paying and us having the fun,' taunted the older whore.

'Now you be a good boy and keep still. Then Sian won't have to squeeze harder and I won't have to slit your throat.'

Danny nodded as best he could with the knife at his Adam's apple and he felt a hand reach into his inner pocket and remove his wallet.

'Good, now turn around with your face against the wall.'

Danny slowly turned, feeling the point of the blade gently tracing its way around his neck without breaking the skin. As his nose touched the wall the pressure vanished. He waited for a moment then turned as he heard the sound of the women's footsteps vanishing in the darkness. There had not been much money in the wallet and Danny had been wise enough to leave his warrant card at home. If he had said that he was a policeman then there was no doubt that Megan would have used the knife. It took a little while for Danny's nerves to settle down before he slowly walked back down the alley towards the main street. The young policeman felt utterly despondent. He had been entrusted with a challenging task, one that he felt was within his capabilities but he had failed. There was no way he could recount this humiliating incident to his colleagues for they would make him a laughing stock. How could he have been so naive to have allowed the women to lead him into the alley?

Once back on the main street Danny pondered under a street lamp. He still had a couple of coins left loose in his pocket so could try one more premises but that would be it before a long walk home in the rain. Thinking that perhaps the Butchers Arms would be worth a go he walked towards the town centre. As he approached, Danny glanced down the alley at the side of the building which led to the footbridge across to Ynysangharad Fields. He suddenly stopped. There was something wrong but he couldn't be sure what it was. There was a street lamp on the corner of the alley which gave some light but the rain still made visibility difficult. Then Danny realised what it was. The end of the footbridge was visible from the alley and there was a shape that shouldn't be there. Someone was standing on the bridge railings. Quickly but stealthily Danny went down the alley towards the shadowy, motionless figure. As he got within a few feet Danny recognised the man. It was Bolton the solicitor. He was bareheaded, stood stock still on the railings staring into the water, rain and tears rolling down his face.

Danny spoke gently. 'Mr Bolton sir, are you alright?'

There was no reply. Bolton just stood there staring into the river whose waters had risen with the heavy rains. The rail on which he stood was only two or three inches wide but he supported himself by holding onto a post that formed part of the bridge's framework with his right hand.

The policeman went to reach for the man's arm.

'No, leave me alone. I am going to jump,' commanded the solicitor firmly.

'If you do, Mr Bolton, then you might just survive, you know. Normally the river is shallow enough for you to break your neck but with the water level being high you are more likely just to get wet,' said Danny, underplaying the ferocity of the river's current.

'I will drown.'

'Not if I jump in and save you, which I will,' lied Danny gently, only too aware of his own inability to swim. 'Now tell me, what has brought you to this state of affairs?'

'Who are you?'

'I am just someone who wants to help you.'

'I am beyond help,' replied Bolton mournfully.

'No one is beyond help.'

'I am a ruined man. I cannot face another day of this perpetual torture.'

'I saw you earlier this evening. It looked like a man was threatening you.'

'He works for the devil that has ruined me, a man called Grimes.'

Danny's ears pricked up. 'Do you mean Jabez Grimes?'

Bolton turned his head to look at Danny. 'You have heard of him? I am surprised. He doesn't normally make himself known to people outside of his immediate circle.'

Danny tried again to grab the solicitor's arm.

'No! Keep away!' he yelled.

'Alright sir, I won't try to grab you again, but please tell me more so that I don't fall into your state of despair.'

Bolton grimaced. 'That isn't likely. He picks his prey well, and they all have money. You see I have a weakness for gambling and it was that bastard Blake that I met in the music hall that introduced me to him.'

'That wouldn't be a Michael Blake? Big fellow?'

'Mickey Blake, he called himself. He used to collect debts for Grimes then suddenly he was replaced by the animal you saw earlier.'

'I see,' answered Danny, thinking about diving for Bolton's legs.

'Blake lured me into joining the Fortuna Club, a discrete

gaming room for gentlemen. Of course the games are rigged and gradually all the members fell into debt. Too much to repay.'

'So why not go for a loan from a bank?'

'It's too much and Grimes is so much cleverer than that.'

'How do you mean?' asked Danny, trying to keep the conversation going long enough to allow him a chance to pull the man back off the railings.

'Those in debt have to attend every gaming night. The clever bit is that on occasions he runs a fair game and some of us win and reduce our losses, but of course never enough to free ourselves entirely. Nevertheless there is always the chance that we will reduce our indebtedness at the cost of one of the other members. In that way he turns us against each other but maintains a hold over us.'

'Why bother with the gaming, though? Why not just bankrupt you or just take regular payments off you under threat of violence.'

'Because it is all about power. We have to turn up at the club. He will swan around pretending to be our benefactor. He feeds off our fear. I was threatened earlier because I refused to go to the last gaming session. Those who don't turn up can end up crippled. It's just that I've had enough. He recently made me include false evidence in a court case in lieu of some of my debt. I can take the shame no longer.'

Danny had edged just that little bit closer and went to grab Bolton's legs at the very moment that the solicitor let go of the post and jumped. The policeman's fingers could only brush the cloth of Bolton's trousers as the man fell, plunging into the water below. Danny caught sight of a flailing arm briefly before the torrent took the body downstream into the darkness.

CHAPTER SIXTEEN

Chard woke bleary-eyed after very little sleep. He had been disturbed in his room the previous evening by a worried member of the hotel's staff who advised him that a dishevelled maniac claiming to be a police officer was causing havoc downstairs.

He was refusing to leave and insisted that he wanted to speak to Inspector Chard.

The inspector had rushed to the hotel foyer as soon as he could to find Constable Preece dressed in dirty civilian clothes and in some distress. Having been told very briefly what had happened Chard instructed the disconcerted hotel staff to give Preece a very strong drink. He then told the constable to get home afterwards and give a full report in the morning. The inspector then went with all speed to the police station and formed a search party. They found the body about a mile downriver around three o'clock in the morning. From what they could make out by their oil lamps it appeared that Bolton would have hit some rocks during the fall before being carried under and drowned. It had taken some time to get the body to the mortuary and find the caretaker to open up, so Chard did not get back to his room and some much needed sleep until five o'clock.

This morning did have one saving grace. The superintendent was away from the station on other business. So Chard could at least arrive a little later. As he looked in the mirror he pondered on whether he could miss out on shaving. In fact, he thought why not grow his moustache permanently to give his sideburns some company?

Pleased with that personal decision he quickly washed and dressed before making his way downstairs. At the bottom of the hotel staircase he glanced around for sight of the lady proprietor. Mrs Miles would certainly want a word about him telling the staff to serve what looked like a rain-sodden itinerant in her bar the previous evening. Seeing that the coast was clear Chard made his way out through the door and into the street where, for a change, it wasn't raining.

*   *   *

May Roper sat in her room at Tower Street and put her book down. She was feeling decidedly miserable. It had been three days now since her embarrassing attempt to emulate her heroines by getting involved in a real life mystery. Today she would enjoy a midday walk around the town and treat herself to luncheon at the Silver Teapot in Market Street. From now on she would concentrate on sensible matters and put all thoughts of crime detecting behind her.

*   *   *

Chard sat at his desk whilst Constable Preece, properly attired in uniform, stood opposite him. The inspector shuffled the papers he had been reading then put them back down on his desk.

'That seems to be a good and thorough report, Constable.'

'Thank you sir,' replied Preece, feeling rather guilty because it wasn't completely thorough, or entirely accurate. He had decided to leave out the incident with the prostitutes as too embarrassing and not entirely relevant to the main event of the evening. Neither had he mentioned that he was, in effect, in disguise. The report just mentioned that he was off duty and was looking for a friend in the town.

'However,' continued Chard, 'we have to consider carefully how we next proceed.'

'In what way, sir?'

'Bolton jumped into the river because he owed money to Grimes. He had belonged to a private gambling club which he attended regularly and occasionally won money back off the other members. Bolton was under Grimes' control and was being threatened by his "bruiser". The final straw was having compromised his integrity as a solicitor as a favour to Grimes. Correct?'

'Yes, that's correct sir, so we need to go after him,' affirmed Preece.

'It is not as straightforward as that though is it, Constable? We don't have Bolton as a witness. It is just hearsay from yourself. We know neither the court case nor the false evidence to which Bolton made reference. Also, you saw what you thought was an altercation between Bolton and the man working for Grimes but we don't know who he is and could you honestly stand in a witness box and swear that he was threatening him?'

'No sir, but there's the gambling …'

'Not illegal in a private members club,' interrupted Chard. 'For that matter we don't know where the gambling takes place. Are you sure he didn't mention it?'

'Quite sure, sir. He just said it was called the Fortuna Club and it was a gaming room.'

'Ah, very apt,' commented the inspector.

Preece looked puzzled.

'Fortuna was the Roman goddess of chance and of fate. They would pray to her for good luck but the goddess was capricious and just when things would be going well in life she could suddenly bring disaster. In this case death.'

Chard scratched his sideburns and paused before

continuing. 'Of course if it really is a private members club then it has to have a full list of its members. If it hasn't then the gambling would be illegal. We need to find out where this gaming room is.'

'There's also the Blake issue, sir, the reason why we were looking into Grimes to begin with,' reminded Preece.

'Yes, Constable, that's correct. We now have a very definite link between Grimes and Blake. Also it might be more than a coincidence that Blake disappeared and suddenly there is this scarred fellow turning up and taking his place.'

'Do you want me to go looking for the gaming room location tonight, sir?'

'No, that won't be necessary. You did enough last night. I will make my own investigations in the days to come. It has been a busy week so we can restart in earnest on Monday. We can have a trip out to the offices of the Forest Iron & Steel Works where we should eventually get hold of the elusive Mr Dorsett.'

* * *

May Roper had enjoyed her walk through the bustling Saturday crowds. The market had been full of lively distractions that had lifted her mood. The weather had improved with the sun making an appearance every now and again from behind grey clouds that for a change did not seem to be carrying the promise of heavy rain. All thoughts of following in the steps of her fictional heroines had disappeared and May had no intention of reawakening them. Fate, however, had other ideas.

Entering Penuel Square, May had no doubt about her next port of call. The window of the bicycle showroom. The rumour that she had heard was correct and on display in the window was the brand new 1895 Ladies Popular Rover Bicycle.

It cost £16, which made buying it out of the question. As she stood admiring it a voice close by spoke.

'It is a beauty, isn't it?'

May looked up and in the reflection of the window she could see that there was a young man behind her wearing a straw boater and a blazer. The young woman turned and instantly there was a flicker of recognition in her eyes. Even after two years she recognised the face and the mildly accented voice. Or at least she thought she did. Yet there was no recognition in the eyes of the handsome young man before her as her auburn hair was largely obscured by her hat which was tied in place by a pretty scarf, and after all they had only met briefly two years earlier.

'I am so sorry to have interrupted your thoughts, and without having first introduced myself. Please do forgive me. My name is Mr Ross. Jack if you prefer.'

The name also triggered May's memory, yet the man she was thinking of had been dressed in workman's clothes, not wearing smart and presumably expensive attire.

'You are rather forward, Mr Ross,' she replied. 'Do you have an interest in bicycles?'

He gave a quite captivating smile. 'I tried a Raleigh Racer once at a showroom when I briefly lived in Cardiff. They let me ride it in their yard but I kept falling off.' He laughed and May could not but help smile. At the same time she thought what her fictional heroines would do in this situation. They would use their feminine wiles.

'I am on my way to the Silver Teapot for luncheon, Mr Ross. If you wish to continue our conversation you may accompany me,' invited May, feeling rather brazen as she spoke.

'Well certainly Miss ...?'

'Roper.'

'... and your Christian name?'

'Miss Roper will do fine, Mr Ross.'

They walked side by side in more or less complete silence until they reached the Silver Teapot tearooms in Market Street. Once there they were offered a table by the front window and Jack ordered tea and sandwiches for them both.

Once the waitress had moved on, Jack gave a smile and spoke softly to May. 'Now may I call you something less formal than Miss Roper?'

'You don't remember me do you?' asked May.

'I am sorry?' responded the confused Italian.

'We met briefly two years ago, at the infirmary, though you were dressed somewhat differently.'

'I don't recall …'

'It was after the terrible train crash. I am the administration clerk at the infirmary.' As she spoke May untied the scarf that held her hat in place and removed a hair clip so that her auburn hair fell loose.

'Ah yes, now I do remember,' admitted Jack.

'Oh, I am glad that you do, because there is something that troubled me that day and it won't go away.'

'What might that be?'

'The reaction of your companion, the young lady, when she saw the gentleman that came in the carriage. It appeared as if she knew him but she denied it. I also think I saw some reaction from yourself.'

'Then you were mistaken. Why does this interest you so much?'

'Because there was a mistake made in identifying one of the crash victims and I am responsible for the administration of the infirmary.'

'I am aware of the mistake. The police have interviewed us about it at our place of work. It wasn't a very pleasant experience but they were satisfied with our account,' snapped Jack.

'I think your friend had something to do with it.'

'With what? The mistake you made? That is ridiculous. I am sure Jenny, I mean Miss Norton, had nothing to do with it. She is without doubt the most gentle, honest and irreproachable person I know. Is this suspicion on your part just because of her reaction to seeing the gentleman with the carriage? If she recognised the dandy fellow then it would have been from the same place that I recognised him.'

'Really? Where would that be?' asked May firmly.

'In the wooded area behind our works, by the river, talking to one of the other employees. I saw him a couple of times,' affirmed Jack.

'Who was he talking to?'

'A man called Michael Blake.'

May's mind started to race and her heart beat faster. This was important information and she would have to tell it to the police. She paused the conversation to sip her tea, gaining a moment to keep composed.

'Oh, I see,' May replied with a smile. 'I can see now that my suspicions have been unfounded. I am afraid I have been rather silly,' May explained with a false, disarming giggle.

Jack visibly relaxed and he gave a confirming nod followed by a reassuring smile. 'Well, I am sure you meant nothing by it. However, I feel I must be on my way, so if you will excuse me?'

Without waiting for an answer Jack got up from the table and left the tearoom leaving May feeling quite pleased with herself. A feeling that was slightly dampened when she realised that he had left her to pay the bill.

*   *   *

Chard had decided to retire to his room early. Having only had a couple of hours sleep the previous night the last thing he wanted to do was to have a night on the town. He had just settled down to read a newly published novel, *The Time Machine* by HG Wells, when he was interrupted by a knock on his door. Giving a huge sigh he got up and answered the door to a servant who passed him a sealed note. Puzzled, he opened it and read the contents. 'Please come to the Ivor Arms tonight. Come alone and not in uniform. Urgent. Gwen.'

Annoyed at having his evening interrupted, yet intrigued, Chard changed his clothes and set off through the town. Although it was a Saturday night it was still relatively early and although the streets were getting busy there was none of the rowdiness that might be expected later in the evening. The walk to the Ivor Arms was uneventful but Chard felt slightly apprehensive. Why the mystery, and why come alone? He had hardly been welcome on his last visit and had vowed never to go again. In all possibility this could be some sort of trap and he was walking right into it. The inspector reached inside his pocket to check he had his police whistle to summon assistance if needed. He had spotted Constable Scudamore on patrol by the Old Bridge and he would be in earshot if required.

Chard turned the handle of the pub's door cautiously. It needed a shove to open it. As he walked in the busy room fell silent and everyone turned to look at him. The inspector took a few steps towards the bar feeling slightly unnerved. Suddenly someone started to clap slowly, which was picked up by others, then by the whole room. The grim barman poured a pint of beer, put it on the bar and gestured towards Chard before grunting and disappearing down to the cellar. Gwen appeared from nowhere with a broad smile on her face and took the inspector's arm.

'We heard how you saved Dic and read in the paper about how you threw yourself in front of that horse to save young

Dilwyn. Everybody has been feeling guilty about how they treated you the other night and they wanted to make up for it.'

The landlady led Chard across to the bar where he was greeted by Dic Jenkins who came forward and shook his hand firmly. 'Thank you, butty. Sorry about the other night.'

'Do you mean when I came in here or when you ran off in Gas Lane?'

The man's face with its spectacular bulbous nose and drooping moustache looked guilty. 'Both really,' he confessed, looking at the floor in embarrassment. 'It's just that we didn't know what sort of person you were. Gwyn, the barman that is, told us that a policeman was coming to spy on us. As regards to me retreating, shall we say, in Gas Lane I don't know what to say. It was just instinct see, butt. Yes that's it, my natural self-preservation.' He looked back into Chard's face as if that explained and excused the whole situation.

'Very well,' accepted the inspector a little stiffly.

'Good, good,' he repeated, handing Chard the drink that had been left for him on the bar. 'Now come around to the other side and meet my butties.'

The inspector followed Jenkins to where his two companions from the other evening stood with welcoming expressions.

'This here is Dai Books the librarian,' introduced Dic as his distinguished-looking bespectacled friend came forward to shake the inspector's hand. 'Also, we have Will Horses who has the best hansom cab in the town.'

The younger, stoutly built man came forward. 'Pleased to meet you properly, Mr Chard. Any time you need some transport that's faster than anything else the police can provide then just let me know.'

'Thank you, I'll bear that in mind. There's no need to call

me Mr Chard by the way. If I am out of uniform and off duty in here than I am happy to be called Thomas.'

'That might take some getting used to. Not used to calling policemen by their first name see. We'll probably stick with Mr Chard, at least for a while. No offence,' explained Dic. Dai Books and Will Horses did seem reasonable fellows, though unless there was a miracle of fate in determining their life choices he assumed those were their nicknames.

The inspector raised his glass to the room and took a hearty swig of beer before explaining that he would be unable to stay very long as he had little sleep the previous night and was quite exhausted. Three hours later he entered his room at the New Inn and contentedly fell asleep fully clothed.

CHAPTER SEVENTEEN

Chard had slept for most of Sunday so was fully refreshed by the time he walked into the station on Monday morning. A sudden thought occurred to him as he walked towards his office.

'Constable Jenkins, you don't have a relative called Dic Jenkins by any chance?'

'No sir, can't say as I do,' answered the constable as Chard walked past his desk.

'Hmm. Good, I suppose,' replied Chard. 'Constable Preece, in my office please,' he commanded as he continued through.

Preece followed his inspector and closed the door behind them.

'We will be setting off for Castle House in the next half hour so don't get tied up with anything else. I also need to think about how I am going to approach the search for the gambling room so make sure I am not interrupted between now and then. I want no distractions.'

'Certainly sir, I will make sure that none of the lads interrupt ...'

Just then there was a knock on the office door and Sergeant Morris entered, his huge frame filling the doorway.

'Sorry to interrupt, sir, but the superintendent wishes to see you. He has a visitor with him.'

'Who would that be, Sergeant?'

'Colonel Grover, the clerk of the council, sir.'

'Very well, Sergeant. I will come straight across.'

Chard dismissed Preece and then made his way across to his superior's office.

'Ah, Inspector Chard. I take it you will not have met Colonel Grover?'

The inspector gave a polite smile to the elegantly dressed man of military bearing that stood across the room. The colonel sported a magnificent beard that spread halfway down his chest.

'I have not yet had the pleasure,' Chard replied offering his hand.

Colonel Grover shook the proffered hand warmly. 'Pleased to meet you. Are you any relation to the hero of Rorke's Drift by any chance?'

'I am afraid not,' replied Chard, noting the disappointment in the colonel's eyes.

'May I ask why you are not in uniform, Inspector?'

'Problem with the stores in Cardiff, sir. It should be arriving any day now,' answered Chard, not mentioning the fact that he had made no effort whatsoever to chase the matter up.

'Damn shame. Appearance is everything. Do you not agree, gentlemen?'

'I certainly do,' answered the superintendent swiftly, 'and so does my inspector. Isn't that correct, Chard?'

'Certainly, Superintendent. I can't wait for my uniform to arrive,' agreed Chard, as he felt his senior officer's stare burning into him. 'May I ask the purpose of your visit, Colonel?' he asked, changing the topic of conversation.

'Yes, of course. The superintendent and I were just discussing it before you came in. As you will be aware, we are a new local authority and we want to show that the Pontypridd Urban District is a model of society. Fortunately the crimes in our community are usually of the meaner sort. Very rarely do we have the most serious offences. Yet we find that in our inaugural year an open verdict has been delivered on what may in fact be an unsolved murder. We want the matter sorted either way, Inspector, but quickly.'

'I am working on the matter myself, Colonel.'

'Very well, but what progress have you made?'

'I am sure you will understand that I cannot go into too much detail, Colonel, but I have a number of leads. My enquiries are ongoing and will be completed as soon as is humanly possible.'

'Can I have your word that you will pursue this matter above all else?'

'You have my word as superintendent and that of my inspector,' interposed Superintendent Jones. 'No other case will take precedence.'

'Thank you, gentlemen. The council will be very pleased to receive your assurances when I make my report at tonight's meeting.'

Satisfied with the outcome of his visit, Colonel Grover bade both police officers farewell and left the room.

'Inspector, the eyes of the council are upon us. Do not let me down. What are these leads of yours?'

'Well sir, we know that the deceased was involved in collecting gambling debts.'

'Gambling is a terrible sin that leads to destruction,' interrupted the superintendent sanctimoniously.

'Quite so,' agreed Chard. 'So we will be looking at the person on behalf of whom he was collecting the money as well as the associated debtors. There are also three other people of interest. Two of them can definitely be linked to the victim via his place of employment. The third is an unlikely suspect at the moment but we have yet to conduct an interview. I intend to do that later today.'

The superintendent nodded approvingly. 'I can see that you have been busy, Chard. Go to it then and do not get sidetracked. We have given our word.'

'Yes sir,' replied the inspector, mindful that it was the

superintendent that had given Colonel Grover both their word without asking for his agreement.

Chard left Superintendent Jones's office and returned to his own. As he passed Constable Preece he snapped out a command.

'I am back to where I started upon arrival here this morning, Constable. We leave in another half hour. I am not to be interrupted. Understood?' Without waiting for a reply the inspector marched into his office and closed the door.

Fifteen minutes later Chard was scratching his sideburns, deep in concentration, when there was a hesitant tap on his office door.

'Damn and blast!' he cursed, thumping his desk in annoyance. 'Come in!' he shouted.

Tentatively, Constable Preece poked his head around the door. 'I'm really sorry to bother you, sir. I know you didn't want to be disturbed but the young lady is very insistent.'

'What young lady, Constable? What are you talking about?'

'The young lady from the infirmary, sir. According to my notes it is Miss Roper. We interviewed her recently.'

'Yes, I remember. What about her?'

'She is outside at the front desk with Sergeant Humphreys. Apparently she has some information that is pertinent to our enquiries and wants to talk to you in person.'

Chard felt his temper recede as he pondered on the reason for the woman's visit.

'Very well. Send her in.'

A minute later May Roper was escorted into Chard's office by Constable Preece who then returned to his desk. The young lady wore an olive green skirt with a matching jacket covering a white high-necked blouse. Her auburn tresses cascaded from beneath a fashionable small green hat onto her slim shoulders.

'Please take a seat, Miss Roper. I understand that you have something to tell me.'

Chard watched as May took a seat and stared at him earnestly.

'Yes, Inspector. It is to do with your enquiries regarding the man that we believed to be Michael Blake.'

'Please go ahead.'

'You recall that I told you about the three people that visited the infirmary on the day of the crash.'

'Yes, a young man, a young woman and a gentleman of quality. We now know who they are.'

'I was convinced that somehow they knew each other.'

'Well, Miss Roper, you did say at the time that the young man and woman arrived together.'

'Yes, but the connection of which I was uncertain was with regard to the other man. You see I now know that he was connected to the real Michael Blake.'

Chard was thrown by this revelation.

'And how do you know that?' he asked, leaning forward in his seat.

May smiled at the realisation that she now had the inspector's full attention.

'It was all down to sheer chance. I happened to be in town and accidentally bumped into the young man. I nearly didn't recognise him for he was dressed very smartly, not at all like when he came to the infirmary.'

'That was a very long time ago. How did you notice him in the first place?'

'As I said, it was sheer chance. In fact he didn't recognise me at all. I suppose that your recent visit to see us just jogged my memory,' explained May. She had decided not to mention her unannounced visit to Jenny Norton which had been the real incident that had kept the issue fresh in her mind.

'Very well, Miss Roper. What happened next?'

'He invited me to take tea with him,' answered May, blushing at this barefaced lie.

'You agreed to that?'

'Yes, but only because I realised that he may be able to tell me something pertinent to our, I mean your, case. I wouldn't normally agree to take tea with someone to whom I have not been introduced.'

Chard started to look rather concerned. 'I hope you have no illusions about wanting to involve yourself in our investigations, Miss Roper.'

'No, nothing like that,' she lied. 'Anyway, it transpired that I was right in my suspicion that they had seen each other before. According to Mr Ross, the other gentleman in question had been seen meeting with the real Michael Blake in the wooded area next to the river that lies behind the Taff Vale Ironworks.'

'Did Mr Ross say why the other man was meeting Blake?'

'No, Inspector. Mr Ross said he didn't know.'

'May I assume that you gave your name to Mr Ross, perhaps even where you live?'

'I did remind him who I was and my position in the infirmary as a precursor to asking him about Blake, though I certainly did not give him my address.'

The inspector scratched his sideburns and gave May a steady stare. 'You do realise that if Mr Ross was somehow involved, then you could have put yourself in danger?'

'Not likely, Inspector. We were in a busy tea room.'

'I didn't mean then, Miss Roper. Until we resolve this case you need to take particular care. Please do not go around unaccompanied in quiet areas and definitely do not approach any of the people involved. Do I make myself clear?'

'Perfectly clear,' replied May feeling admonished and a little nervous, but above all indignant that the information she had provided seemed unappreciated. 'I will say good day then, Inspector.'

The young woman got up and left the office, leaving Chard sitting pensively at his desk. He hadn't meant to be so hard on Miss Roper but he knew it was important to dissuade her from interfering and possibly putting herself at risk. At least he now had further questions to put to Mr Dorsett. The inspector grabbed his coat and hat then strode out of his office.

'Come on, Constable, let us crack on!'

Preece immediately got up, followed the inspector into the station yard and waited for the young stable boy to fetch them the gig.

The weather was warm, dry and in the area close to the station the air was relatively fresh apart from the horse manure piled in the corner of the yard. Soon the two police officers were on their way, past the Tumble and onto the Tram Road. The broad thoroughfare was quite busy that morning with wagonettes, broughams, carts, four-horse omnibuses and even a phaeton amongst the vehicles travelling in both directions. The fresh breeze and improved weather had lightened Chard's mood and he felt inclined to pass the journey in conversation.

'I have noticed, Constable, that there appears to be an awful lot of people with the same surnames in South Wales. I exclude foreigners like myself of course,' he added with a chuckle. 'I mean everywhere you go there is a Williams, Jones, Evans or Davies.'

'Quite so, sir, and we have Rees, Morgan, Matthews and Bevan as popular names but it doesn't mean that they are related. I mean sometimes they are, obviously, but not going way back. I just think it's something you'll need to get used to, sir,' replied Preece.

Their conversation was halted by the sight of a cart that had stopped, partly blocking one side of the road. The old horse pulling its heavy load had collapsed and lay juddering on its side as the owner with the help of a passer-by was freeing it of its harness. It was a sombre sight but not uncommon and the policemen continued on their way in silence.

Castle House stood close by the old stone three-arched Castle Inn Bridge, near to the weir at Treforest. A large, sturdily built property on the corner of a terrace, it housed the offices of the Forest Iron & Steel company well away from the noise and smoke of the industrial site itself. Constable Preece held the reins of the gig whilst the inspector went to the door. He used the door pull which was answered by a tall, officious-looking man in a sombre dark suit.

'Good morning, my name is Inspector Chard and I am here to see Mr Dorsett.' As he spoke, Chard fetched out his warrant card before the man could make a comment about his lack of uniform.

The office employee glanced at the card and gave a sniff before smiling insincerely. 'Did you have an appointment, sir?'

'I did not consider it necessary. I called at Forest House and was told that he would be here this morning. I had assumed that he would have been informed that I wished to talk to him. Could you advise him that I am here?'

'If only I could, sir.'

'You mean I was misinformed?'

'Oh no, sir. You would have been seen by my cousin who works at Forest House and he would never misinform.'

Chard remembered the man and he didn't like him either.

'Then why can't you tell Mr Dorsett that I am here?'

'Because I don't know where he is, sir. He was here, of course, so you were not misinformed, but you missed him by about five minutes.'

Chard cursed inwardly at the time he had spent talking to Miss Roper.

'So where has he gone?'

'I am afraid I don't know, sir. Mr Dorsett is a significant investor in our company but I am not part of his household. You are welcome to come in and wait but I have no indication that Mr Dorsett will be returning today.'

'Do you know where he will be tomorrow, by any chance?' enquired Chard, not confident of a helpful answer.

'Actually I do. He will be at the main works tomorrow morning. I assume that you would like an appointment this time, sir?' There was an air of sarcasm in the man's voice but Chard had no option other than to nod in agreement.

'Yes, that would be most obliging.'

'Very well sir. I will send a message to the site and Mr Dorsett will be notified when he arrives there tomorrow. Shall we say he will expect you at perhaps eleven o'clock?'

'Yes, that will be fine. Thank you. I bid you good day.'

With that Chard returned to the gig and sat alongside Constable Preece, with a face like thunder. 'Back to the station, Constable, and don't say a word.'

The journey passed in complete silence and Preece was delighted to get back to the station. As they entered Sergeant Humphreys gave what passed as a smile (given his missing front teeth) .

'Parcel arrived for you, Inspector. I've put it on your desk.'

Chard gave an ill-mannered grunt and headed straight for his office. On entering he saw that a large package was indeed resting on his desk. For a moment he was intrigued but then realisation crept in and he gave a sigh.

'My bloody uniform,' he groaned.

Taking out his pocket knife he quickly cut through the wrapping to reveal that it was indeed two pairs of uniform trousers, two jackets, a raincape and an inspector's cap.

Chard stepped into the common room and sighted Sergeant Morris who he called to his side.

'Sergeant, my uniform has arrived. I do not wish to be disturbed for the next fifteen minutes. Make sure that I am not bothered by anyone. If the superintendent wants me then tell him I am occupied on urgent business but will attend him very shortly.'

'Will do sir. I perfectly understand,' confirmed the sergeant.

Confident in the ability of Sergeant Morris to keep him undisturbed, Chard started to change out of his civilian clothes and into his uniform. The navy blue trousers were a comfortable fit, perhaps a little long in the leg, but a local tailor could easily make an adjustment. The military cut tunic in navy blue with black braid was not as long as the superintendent's frock coat style and carried less elaborate decoration. Nonetheless there was significant 'frogging' – black tassles and cords which were purely for show as the garment fastened with discrete hooks and eyes. Chard stretched his arms and walked across his office. The tunic was a perfect fit. He next took up the cap. It lacked the band of silver wire that decorated the cap of Superintendent Jones but had the same badge of a crown. The inspector absent-mindedly brushed his upper lip where his moustache had grown into a recognisable feature and started to relax. He checked his posture and had a final walk across his office before stepping out into the common room.

As he did so Sergeant Morris was already waiting for him to appear.

'Superintendent wants to see you, sir. I did as instructed and said that you would be along shortly, and ...'

'Yes, Sergeant?'

'... very smart if I might say so, sir.'

'Thank you, Sergeant,' replied Chard as he headed for the

superintendent's office for the second time that day. As he knocked and entered his superior's office he was surprised to see that the superintendent had yet another visitor. Though he was not as surprised as Superintendent Jones who, at the sight of Chard in uniform, had dropped the pen he had been holding.

'Inspector Chard, I believe you have met Mr Roberts,' stated the superintendent, regaining his composure.

Chard shook the visitor's hand. 'Good to see you again, sir. Tell me, are you here with regards to the ironworks or as chairman of Pontypridd Urban District Council? Colonel Grover came to see us this morning.'

'I am here with regards to the ironworks and what I have to say is most confidential. I would not want any of this to be mentioned outside of this room,' answered Roberts, the worry clearly reflected in his facial expression.

'You can be assured of our discretion,' interjected the superintendent.

'You must understand that our industry is not doing particularly well at the moment and money is tight. It has caused me to start looking at our accounts more closely and whereas I cannot be certain, I have my suspicions that some money is being drained from our accounts. The problem is that I cannot be absolutely sure as to how it is being done and I do not want to alert the culprit by charging in and giving them time to cover their tracks.'

Superintendent Jones shrugged. 'It is difficult to know how we can help, Mr Roberts. If we do not have direct evidence of a crime then we cannot arrest anyone. After all we are a police force and not a detective agency.'

Roberts looked crestfallen. 'Then again, sir,' interrupted Chard, 'I do have rather a talent with figures, even if I say so myself. I would be quite interested in taking a look.'

Roberts's face brightened. 'I would be most grateful. I do not wish to drag our auditors in on mere suspicion because inevitably word would get out to our investors.'

'Perhaps we can make some arrangement …'

Chard was suddenly cut short by an agitated Superintendent Jones. 'Inspector, are you forgetting the meeting that took place this morning? We have both given our word that nothing is to interfere with the Blake case. Until it is solved you must not take on any other work.' The superintendent addressed Mr Roberts apologetically. 'I am sorry Mr Roberts. I can agree to my inspector taking a look at your problem, but only after we solve the mystery surrounding Mr Blake's demise. At the moment it would distract our enquiries and we might never get to the bottom of it. I would ask you to remain patient. I will be exceedingly disappointed if Inspector Chard cannot solve this case in the next two weeks.' Chard groaned inwardly as the superintendent continued. 'Then he will be free to look at your issue.'

'Very well,' agreed Roberts, 'I suppose that will have to do. Two weeks then.'

Their meeting concluded, Roberts made his farewell leaving the two police officers to themselves. 'Sorry to have put myself forward on that occasion, sir. I do intend to prioritise the Blake case,' apologised Chard.

Superintendent Jones smiled benignly. 'You were just being conscientious. Just think a little more, eh? By the way, very glad to see you in uniform. That will be all.'

The superintendent gave a dismissive wave and Chard returned to his own office, eager to track down the elusive Mr Dorsett the following day.

CHAPTER EIGHTEEN

The following morning Chard stood outside the entrance of the Forest Iron & Steel Works on the hillside high above Treforest. From his position he could see the smoke rising from the furnaces of the Taff Vale Ironworks in the valley far below. Chard felt tense as he approached the main entrance, which consisted of a pair of large black doors with the name of the company on the brickwork above. The fact that he had missed his quarry the previous day had annoyed him and the anticipation that the same thing might happen yet again was playing on his mind. The inspector, resplendent in his new uniform, nodded to Constable Preece who gave the doors a thump with the side of his fist. Seconds later an elderly man with grey hair, wearing a long dust coat, opened a small entrance built into the double doors and let the policemen through. Once inside they were greeted by a short man with an upright posture who exuded an air of importance. Dressed in a tweed suit with matching waistcoat he checked the time on his pocket watch as he walked briskly towards them then snapped the watch casing shut as he began to speak.

'Good morning officers. Inspector Chard, I assume. We have been expecting you. My name is Walters. I am the chief clerk.'

'Yes, well, actually it is Mr Dorsett that I have come to see,' explained Chard, his frustration rising as he could see another delay coming his way.

'Yes, so I understand, Inspector. The Honourable Mr Dorsett is currently out in the yard inspecting the works. If you wait here I am sure he won't be too long.'

Chard scratched his sideburns and then made a decision. 'No, I think not. Constable Preece will wait here with you. I will go and find the Honourable Mr Dorsett myself. Point me in the direction where I might find him.'

'Very well, Inspector.' Walters pointed into the distance. Although the weather was dry and mild the view ahead was still obscured by the fog of dust from the yard. 'Can you see over there, that slight rise in the ground in front of the third blast furnace?'

Chard nodded in confirmation.

'Well, he will probably be just the other side close to our wrought iron workshop. He is smartly dressed and will be easy to identify,' explained Walters.

Chard thanked the chief clerk and then made his way out into the yard. The ground trembled as a steam driven drop hammer made contact with a molten ball of iron in another of the workshops. Although he'd had a similar experience at the Vale Ironworks Chard nevertheless felt his heart jump as he walked past. He felt himself involuntarily increase his pace across the yard and soon came to the rise of piled up earth which Walters had pointed out. The dirt beneath him started to slip as the inspector clambered up and he was forced to put his left hand down to steady himself. Once over the top and having gingerly made it down the other side, the heat from the nearby blast furnace hit him. It caused the dust to catch in his throat and he was momentarily distracted from noticing that someone was walking towards him. Almost framed by the red hot heat and smoke coming from the blast furnace, the man looked as though he was walking out from the mouth of hell itself. Wearing a long black riding cloak, high riding boots, a top hat and carrying a cane, the figure moved with an easy grace that seemed so incongruous to the surroundings.

'Inspector Chard, I assume?' asked the man, holding out a gloved hand.

Chard took the hand and looked into the face before him.

For such an environment it seemed remarkably out of place. Around the yard men toiled industriously, their grizzled faces worn by hard physical work and the heat and dust of the environment. Yet here was this young man with a face so delicate that it would not be out of place on a china doll. The inspector recovered his thoughts, then responded to the introduction.

'Yes indeed and you, sir, must be Mr Dorsett.'

'Indeed I am,' smiled the young man. 'Hot here, is it not?'

Chard smiled back. 'Rather too hot for me.'

'Our men pour limestone, coke and iron ore into the top of the furnaces from the loading platforms at the back. We then have engines that blast air into the furnaces to heat the temperature to around two thousand degrees Fahrenheit. Molten iron and slag are then removed from the base of the furnace.'

'I was told that you were well informed about the industry, Mr Dorsett.'

'Yes, Inspector, I find it fascinating. It is why I keep coming here. Mr Crawshay is often away and he does not mind me staying on occasion at either Forest House or at his hunting lodge. Now, Inspector, would you satisfy my curiosity and tell me why on earth you wish to talk with me? I am quite intrigued.'

'Perhaps we can discuss that in the relative quiet of an office somewhere?' suggested Chard.

'Certainly, we can go back to the entrance and use the chief clerk's office. However, I was in the process of finishing my inspection. Would you care to join me as I take a look at the wrought iron workshop?'

This seemed like an instruction rather than a request but Chard nodded his agreement and followed Dorsett past the nearest blast furnace and behind a strange cylindrical steel pot about twenty feet high.

'I see that curious look, Inspector. That is a Bessemer converter. It transformed our industry. Molten iron from the blast furnace is put in the top. Then compressed air is blasted through openings near the bottom to burn out excess carbon and impurities. The problem for Bessemer was that his process couldn't get rid of phosphorus so that meant that only phosphorus-free iron ore could be used, which meant sourcing it from Scandinavia or Wales.'

'So presumably that is why the industry has flourished here,' suggested Chard.

'Quite. However, nigh on twenty years ago a Welshman by the name of Sidney Gilchrist Thomas came along and solved the problem. He discovered that adding limestone to the Bessemer converter caused the phosphorus to float to the top of the Bessemer converter where it could be skimmed off. This method resulted in phosphorus-free steel.'

'That must have been of great benefit.'

'It depends, Inspector, on where you have invested your money. Suddenly you could use iron ore from anywhere to make steel so naturally the price dropped due to market forces. Steel manufacturers could source the cheapest price for their raw material from anywhere they wanted and so initially made greater profits, whilst iron ore producers in Wales found that their profits fell due to increased overseas competition.'

'So as steel manufacturers this company will have been a great investment,' said Chard thoughtfully scratching his sideburns.

Dorsett gave a patronising smile. 'Commerce is not a simple matter, Inspector. You see, now that any iron ore can be used you don't need to have your manufacturing sites located in Wales or Sweden. They can be based in Germany,

America or anywhere else. So we now have considerable overseas competition. In addition, there is a move towards the "open hearth process" which a German called Siemens first developed thirty years ago but which is only now becoming very popular. It produces steel from pig iron in large shallow furnaces in very large quantities.'

'So the business is struggling?'

'The whole industry is struggling, I am afraid. In fact the one side of the business that is holding its own is the manufacture of wrought iron. Steel is far easier to produce but we maintained one wrought iron workshop here because there is still a demand. There are some products which need the greater resistance against corrosion.'

The men had stopped by a very large open-sided building with a corrugated roof and a stone-flagged floor.

'This is the wrought iron workshop. The hammer is about to drop by the way.'

Chard heeded the warning and put his hands over his ears just as the hammer landed on a mass of white hot metal sending sparks flying and a sound wave that reverberated through the floor. The hot metal, now in a rectangular shape, was then dragged with what looked like long-handled tongs by two muscular men in leather aprons across to the rolling mill.

'That will now be rolled into bars before going to the finishing mill,' explained Dorsett.

'It certainly is very labour intensive,' commented Chard.

'As I explained earlier, making steel is easier and cheaper but there are enough key uses to keep wrought iron profitable for at least the short term.'

Dorsett turned and started to walk back across the dusty yard towards the main entrance with Chard following behind.

'I still find it unusual for someone in your social position to be so interested in the detail of the industry,' probed the inspector.

'You are referring to my honorific title, I suppose. Yes, it is unusual and my family does not approve. Perhaps that is why I do it. I like to live in as inappropriate a way as possible without forfeiting my inheritance. That is why I try to stay away from my father's estate in Herefordshire. He is Lord Abcote and in poor health. I am afraid of overstepping the mark if I am too often in plain view.'

'I am sorry to hear that your father is not well. It must concern you.'

Dorsett stopped and turned to face the inspector.

'I will share a confidence with you, though it is not exactly a secret in my home county. My father and I do not see eye to eye on most things. We have not spoken with any affection for many years. I am his sole male heir but I am sure that he would like to see me fall foul of some scandal so that he would have an excuse to disinherit me.'

'Tell me, are you at risk of falling foul of a scandal?' asked Chard in a tone that seemed jocular. There was a pause as the inspector waited for a reply.

Dorsett looked at the ground and tapped his riding boot with his cane as he reflected, before looking back at Chard and giving his response. 'Regretfully always.' He then gave a hearty laugh and slapped Chard on the shoulder. 'Come, Inspector. I am joking.'

The two men walked on to the entrance archway before entering through a door in the right-hand adjoining building. They found themselves in a small office. Constable Preece sat on a stool in the middle of the room and stood to attention as the inspector entered. On one side of the office a young woman with a pockmarked face worked at a desk on which rested a typewriter and several metal filing boxes. Natural light came from an adjacent window which had a small oil lamp on its sill for evening use.

Chard was amused to see that on the other side of the office Mr Walter's desk was fixed two feet higher than that of his secretary so that his short frame could look down on his subordinate. A candle holder, paperweight, pen and ornate inkwell rested on his desk whilst Walters himself sat scrutinising an open ledger.

'Walters, could you leave us for a few minutes please?' asked Dorsett.

Walters indicated to his secretary and both departed, leaving Dorsett and the two policemen to discuss matters in privacy.

'Inspector, would you mind?' asked Dorsett as he handed his cane to Chard in order to allow himself to remove his long riding coat which was covered in dust.

The inspector took the elegant cane, the top of which he had observed was embellished with a silver leopard's head, whilst Dorsett hung up his coat and brushed the small amount of residual dust off his jacket with the back of his hand. He placed his top hat on the chief clerk's desk and turned to the policemen looking as elegant as ever. Chard handed back the cane and then became aware of his own appearance. His new uniform was absolutely covered in dust so that it looked grey than navy blue.

'Well then, Inspector, down to business. How can I help you?'

Chard composed himself. 'Firstly I just want to reassure you that this is just a routine enquiry and part of our normal procedures.'

'I am reassured. Please go ahead.'

In the background Constable Preece had taken out his notebook and stood pencil at the ready.

'I am sure that you must remember a train crash that occurred in this area about two years ago.'

'Indeed I do. In fact with the help of my coachman we took one of the casualties to the infirmary.'

'I am very glad you remember, Mr Dorsett. Do you recall the identity of the man in question?'

Dorsett frowned and spoke apologetically. 'I am very sorry, Inspector, but I have no idea who he was. I had him taken to the infirmary, saw him put into a bed but left soon afterwards.'

'I see. Do you remember seeing a young man and woman, also visitors like yourself at the same time?'

'I certainly remember the young woman. I gave her a ride in my carriage to Treforest but I do not know who she was.'

'You had not seen her previously?'

'No. I cannot say that I had.'

'What about the young man?'

Dorsett waved an elegant manicured hand dismissively. 'Impossible for me to say. I might have seen him somewhere I suppose. Had he worked here at some time?'

'Possibly, Mr Dorsett, quite possibly,' said Chard, giving a brief glance at Preece who noted the idea.

'So then, Inspector, do not leave me in suspense. What is this all about?' asked Dorsett giving another disarming smile.

'We thought that the injured man that you fetched to the hospital was a man called Michael Blake. Unfortunately he did not survive the night.'

'Then I am sorry.'

'Does the name Michael Blake mean anything to you?' asked Chard giving Dorsett a penetrating stare.

'It isn't one that I recall,' he replied but was unable to meet the inspector's gaze.

'He was a charge hand at the Taff Vale Ironworks.'

'If he was a common workman then I am hardly likely to remember,' came the quick reply.

Chard instinctively felt that Dorsett was beginning to lose his composure.

'Also, how would I know someone working for the Taff Vale Ironworks?'

'Precisely, Mr Dorsett. That is what I want to know.' The inspector sensed that he had his quarry now and he wasn't going to let go. It was time to play his trump card.

'I have a witness who can confirm that you met clandestinely with a Mr Michael Blake by the river close to the Taff Vale Ironworks.' Chard felt slightly guilty because the information that he had was only second hand so technically he did not have a testifiable witness at this stage.

Dorsett went silent for a moment then with a speed and suddenness that shook Chard, slammed the heavy head of his cane down on the desk.

'Damn it!' He stayed still for a moment before taking a deep breath and calming himself. 'Yes, I met with Blake. What of it? There is no law against it.'

'No,' answered Chard. 'There isn't. However, we fished the real Blake out of the river recently. You knew him. It was also you who fetched someone to the infirmary with an item belonging to Blake which led to the misidentification.'

'I don't know what you are talking about. What item? I didn't even know that Blake was dead until you told me just now. I assumed he had just left the area. Neither did I know that the man I had fetched in had been identified as Blake. You are just quoting me a mere coincidence.'

'I don't like coincidences,' replied Chard. 'What was your business with Blake when you were spotted talking together?'

Dorsett hesitated before replying. 'I hope that what I am about to say can be treated in confidence.'

'It depends what it is. However, I can assure you that I am no purveyor of idle gossip.'

'I needed to find out the financial state of the Taff Vale Ironworks. My investments are financed by my allowance from my father and I need to be astute financially to keep myself in the manner to which I have become accustomed. When my sickly father eventually passes and I get my inheritance then money will not be a problem but for the meantime I have expenses that must be covered. At the time I met Blake I was considering selling my shares in Forest Iron & Steel Works if I could buy the Taff Vale Ironworks shares cheaply and perhaps gain a majority holding. Then I would have stripped the assets to make a profit, closed it down and then bought back the shares in the Forest works.'

'How would Blake know about the Taff Vale's financial state?' asked the inspector.

'He saw the orders coming through and whether their regular products were increasing or decreasing in the stockyard. He also knew when men were being laid off or when they were having their hours cut. I think he also had another contact inside the works but he wouldn't say who it was.'

Chard scratched his sideburns in thought. 'Your explanation will remain between us. It does appear reasonable, but we may need to speak to you again. Are you planning to leave the town in the next week or so?'

'I have no such plans at the present time, Inspector.'

'Very well. We will take our leave.' Chard nodded to Preece who put his notebook away. As they moved towards the door Dorsett called Chard back.

'Wait, Inspector. One more thing before you go.'

Chard turned, his senses alert to the possibility that something of significance might be revealed. There was a pause, heavy with anticipation, before Dorsett continued to speak.

'When I met with Blake I was very careful indeed. There is only one way that I could have been spotted.'

'Enlighten me, Mr Dorsett.'

'Either someone was following me personally, or they were following Blake. Now why would that be?'

CHAPTER NINETEEN

May Roper had finally finished her day's work after a carrying out a complete inventory of the infirmary's stores. The weather was pleasant so she refused the offer of a lift home from one of the workhouse administrators and instead set off on foot towards her home in Tower Street. The way that Inspector Chard had spoken to her still rankled. He hadn't been the least bit grateful at the information she had provided and that was so unfair. Frowning as she ran the conversation over and over in her head, May neglected to look where she was going and stumbled on an uneven pavement. Fortunately she was able to regain her balance without falling completely to the floor, but May was annoyed and embarrassed for herself as she looked around to see if anyone had noticed. Luckily there was no one facing her direction but May suddenly recognised someone with their back to her who was standing on a street corner. She thought for a moment before deciding to go up to the man and talk to him. As she made her way in his direction the man looked up and noticed her. Appearing startled he turned away and went to the entrance of the next street as quickly as he could before disappearing around the corner. Hitching her skirt slightly, May moved as fast as she could without actually breaking into a run and followed the man into the same street. 'Evans, wait I want to talk to you!' she cried, but to no effect. Giving a last glance behind, the man went down a small alley that was littered with refuse and disappeared.

*　　*　　*

Later that evening Chard strolled out in his comfortable civilian clothes down Taff Street, turned right over the

New Bridge, and headed for the Ivor Arms. It was a clear evening, a little chilly perhaps, but the cool breeze fed fresh air into his lungs and it felt good. Earlier in the day, when Chard had returned to the police station from the Forest Iron & Steel Works, he had looked in a shoddy state. Having asked Constable Preece to go in ahead of him to check that Superintendent Jones was ensconced in his office, Chard had swiftly entered his own room, changed into his other uniform and wiped his cap clean. Once more resplendent, he then took the dust-covered original to be laundered in the town. Having returned, the inspector considered Dorsett's final words. Perhaps Ross had been following him, or indeed following Blake. Had Miss Norton been following either of them? Did Miss Norton spot Dorsett with Blake, or was that a lie given to Miss Roper by Ross? Was the spotting of Dorsett by Ross pure accident after all? Was Dorsett flat out lying? Then there was the involvement of Grimes. The man had got under his skin. Where was this mysterious gambling club? The questions went round and round in his head all afternoon. Certainly Ross needed looking at again and he could not help but feel that Dorsett was not telling the whole truth. Chard felt stressed which was why he had decided to try and unwind by going to the Ivor Arms where he could sit quietly in a corner and relax with a beer whilst clearing his thoughts.

Entering the comfortable warmth of the bar the inspector spotted a free table by the window and placed his hat there to claim the spot whilst he went to order a drink.

'Good evening Mr Chard,' came the greeting from Dai Books who was stood at the far side of the bar talking to Gwyn the barman. The latter turned, gave a sniff and then plodded across to serve the inspector.

'Good evening Dai,' responded Chard before turning his

attention to the barman who stood ready to serve him. 'A pint of stout tonight please.'

Gwyn gave a grunt in acknowledgement and pulled a pint of dark beer through the pump into a glass tankard. Chard paid for his drink and took it back to his table, not offended by the barman's brusque manner on this occasion. Sitting comfortably, the inspector started to reflect once more on the myriad questions that had been tormenting him. However, before he could really formulate a strategy on how next to proceed he was interrupted by a welcome from across the room.

'Well, Thomas, how lovely to see you again so soon.'

Chard looked up to see the stately frame of Gwen moving towards him like a force of nature. There would be no deflecting her from coming to speak to him, that much was certain.

'Hello Gwen. You gave me such a fine welcome last time that I felt comfortable coming here again. I thought I could have a quiet sit down and reflect on my problems.'

'Problems? I bet I can sort them out for you,' the landlady offered brightly.

Chard smiled. 'Sorry, but I can't discuss cases and don't forget that I want a clear distinction between myself as a policeman outside this pub and myself as an ordinary customer in here.'

'Is there any problem that isn't work-related then?'

'Not at the moment but thank you for asking.'

'Alright, but can I ask you something else?'

'If you must, Gwen, but then, and I mean no offence, I would like to get back to my thoughts.'

'I have been quite curious as to what has brought you here. Most people in positions such as yours would have come from the local area like Superintendent Jones. I would have thought someone moving for advancement would have gone to a big city like London or Birmingham.'

'Large cities don't appeal to me and I didn't move for advancement.'

'So what was the reason?'

'I don't really want to talk about it,' answered Chard defensively.

'I am only asking because others will wonder and will start to make things up. I just want to be able to silence them if they come up with anything untoward.' The landlady had a kind smile and was obviously very skilled at getting people to confide in her.

Chard suddenly realised that perhaps it would be worth parting with some personal information in exchange for something else.

'Very well. If I tell you, will you promise to keep the details confidential and never, ever ask me about it again?'

'I so promise,' replied Gwen making a quick sign of the cross.

'There will also be a quid pro quo. I will ask you a question which you must answer.'

'Is it something personal?' asked Gwen, somewhat worried.

'No, but you mustn't enquire why I am asking.'

'Very well, I agree.'

'Then I will try to keep it as brief as possible, and remember, after I have spoken there are to be no further questions.'

The landlady nodded her head in agreement and so Chard commenced his tale.

'After being orphaned I was brought up by my mother's sister and her husband. My aunt then died years after I left home. After my aunt's funeral my uncle asked if, in the event of his death, I would take care of his money and papers. He showed me where they were kept and told me that I was named as his executor in his will. I was very surprised at this because we had never really got on. In my opinion he had not treated my aunt well so I rarely visited. However, I felt that I had some obligation to him so I agreed. A year later he became ill and it was clear that he would not survive. He was in hospital, so I went to the house and took the locked case containing his money, plus a folder containing his will and papers; and in addition all his unpaid bills so that I could deal with them.'

Chard paused and took a long gulp of his beer. He looked disconcerted and Gwen felt guilty at having raised what seemed to be a traumatic issue.

'That was very kind of you,' she said sympathetically.

'But subsequently I was accused of theft by his sisters,' explained the inspector. 'I was appalled and then I read the will. To my horror I found that my uncle had lied and I was not named as the executor. I returned the locked case with everything else to the sisters who banned me from the subsequent funeral. I was in no position to argue.'

'Oh my Lord. That must have been terrible for you.'

'My close friends realised that I had acted in good faith and my motives were honest but rumour sticks and my reputation in the wider community was shattered. I had been very friendly with a young lady of my acquaintance but I was disappointed with her reaction when the accusation first came out and it made me realise that she was not the one for me.'

'Oh dear. I am so sorry. I should never have asked. I can see now why you felt you wanted to get away to pastures new for a time,' said Gwen softly.

Chard took another swig of his drink, paused a moment in thought, then pulled himself together before addressing the landlady.

'Time for your part of the deal. Remember, you mustn't enquire why I am asking this question.'

'Yes, I remember. A deal is a deal. What do you want to know?'

'If I want to gamble heavily in this town where would I go? There must be some people who are known to gamble heavily, so where do they meet?' Chard had felt awkward about using his new acquaintances to help his enquiries. In a way it was a breach of trust. The only way he could justify it to himself was by exchanging something personal in return.

'Oh dear, Thomas. How did you start gambling?'

Chard held up a finger to remind the landlady of her promise.

'Sorry I won't ask again,' came her response. 'I understand that money does exchange hands in the billiards room of the Butchers Arms from time to time. There is a man called Bill Bevan who used to be a regular here. I had to ban him for trying to push the other customers into stupid bets. I understand he is now at the centre of things in the Butchers.'

'Thank you, Gwen. Let us talk no more about things. I will just sit here and reflect.'

'Very well but if you need to talk about your problem you know I will always give you a sympathetic ear.' The landlady gave Chard an affectionate squeeze on his arm before returning to her duties.

The inspector took a slow sip of his beer and considered how best to approach the lead he had been given. If he could infiltrate the town's gambling community he might just find the location of the Fortuna club.

CHAPTER TWENTY

The following evening Chard stood before the mirror in his hotel room. He mixed two teaspoons of black powder in a bowl of hot water until he achieved a consistency similar to toothpaste. Then very carefully he applied the mixture to his sideburns and moustache. Whilst the substance dried the inspector took a handful of hair oil and slicked back his dark brown hair which now gleamed black and gave off a sickly sweet aroma. After ten minutes or so he washed his facial hair which had now also changed to a deep black colour. A common enough product, the beard dye had been bought at midday from a barber's shop in the town. As a final touch the inspector applied wax to his moustache, twisting it into fine points. He didn't think that anyone in the Butchers Arms would necessarily recognise him as a policeman as he still hadn't been in the town for any great length of time, but he didn't want to take any chances. Satisfied with his changed appearance Chard picked up one of his two purchases from earlier in the day. Firstly he put on a very long black coat that he had picked up from a pawnbroker's and then he added a dark grey cap which he pulled low on his forehead.

Although the Butchers Arms was only across the road from the New Inn Chard had not become a patron. It just felt a little too close to his accommodation. Despite being a popular venue in the town, the bar of the Butchers Arms was quiet as Chard walked in through the heavy oak door. He was impressed by the quality of the furnishings. Thick marble pillars, ornately carved chairs with red cushioned seats and brass fittings abounded. Half a dozen male patrons stood by a long bar counter that ran the length of one side of the room but there were no other customers other than Chard himself.

Adopting a confident demeanour he walked briskly to the bar and ordered a whiskey from the sturdily built custodian.

'I understand you have a billiards room here,' he enquired as he paid for his drink.

'Up those stairs, second door on the right,' replied the barman. 'There's a boy there who will run orders for your drinks,' he added helpfully.

Chard took his whiskey, exited the bar via the indicated staircase and easily found his way to the billiards room.

Cigarette and cigar smoke swirled in the light emanating from the gas lamps that illuminated the three tables in the room, though only one was the focus of the occupants' attention. Seven men stood watching as two others played. A ginger-headed, freckle-faced youth was at the table and Chard watched as he racked up points. One of the spectators moved the brass marker on the scoreboard that was fixed to the wall and looked smug. He was a big man, tall with a pot belly, and a bald head framed by a circle of unkempt hair. The suit he wore reflected a distinct lack of taste with its large blue and brown checks suited to that of a fairground barker. As a contrast to the scorekeeper's expression the rest of the spectators wore deep frowns as the score continued to grow. Swiftly the youth at the table moved from shot to shot, barely taking time to take aim.

'He's getting too cocky,' murmured Chard to himself. This proved to be the case as a rushed shot saw the red rattle in the jaws of the pocket.

The smugness temporarily vanished from the scorer's face as the other player came forward to take his turn. He looked nervous and a little unsteady on his feet. Potting the red had been left as an easy task which he easily accomplished, but after it had been re-spotted the following stroke failed to score. The red ball had been left tight against the cushion with his own cue ball left teetering on the edge of the middle pocket. A groan came from the spectators and the smugness returned once more to the man in the check suit.

'Harris to play next, leading Stevens by 265 to 230. Now, gents, do you want to raise your bets? I am willing to offer 2 to 1 against Stevens reaching the target of 301 first.'

Grunts of dissatisfaction came from the onlookers. There were no takers of the offer. Clearly most, if not all, had their money riding on Stevens and had reconciled themselves to losing it. Chard meanwhile scratched his sideburns thoughtfully. Billiards is largely a game of patience. High breaks are easy to make if you bide your time and go for them when the position of the balls are right and not before. Although Harris was next at the table it was unlikely that he would make much of a score on his turn. Stevens had left his own cue ball, which had a black spot on it, hanging right over the pocket so would be bound to go down for two points but under the rules of billiards it would then stay off the table. That would leave just the red and Harris's own cue ball on the table. With the red tight against the cushion there wasn't much that he would be able to do, yet Chard had guessed from what he had seen that Harris didn't have the temperament to play safe. He would be bound to try, and then leave an opportunity open for his opponent. The inspector decided to make a bold move.

'I will lay a crown on Stevens,' he announced, stepping forward.

Everyone turned to face him and the room went silent until the pot-bellied scorer spoke.

'You came in quietly. We hadn't noticed you. Come forward, stranger.'

The small gathering parted to let Chard through to the

table. When he got there he threw a silver crown coin onto the baize.

'There's my stake,' he said confidently.

'Then you are welcome,' said the scorer as he bent forward to take the money.

Chard grabbed the man's wrist as soon as he touched the silver coin. 'I hadn't finished talking. I will lay a crown on Stevens but only if I take the shots for him.'

The man froze for a second, looked as if he was going to argue vigorously but then glanced back at the money on the table. 'I am willing to accept but these other men have bet on Stevens so he and they would have to agree. What say you, Stevens?'

'I can take this ginger-headed arse yet. I just need to get into my rhythm.'

At this one of the onlookers stuck his head in front of Stevens's face. 'Don't lie, you idiot. If we had known you were going to drink before coming to the table we would never have put our money on you.' The man turned to the scorer. 'Go on, Bill. If this stranger is confident enough to risk his money then I am happy for him to take over. Anyway, you told us that Harris had hardly ever played before. What do you reckon boys?'

There were yells of support backing the man up so the man who Chard now assumed to be Bill Bevan straightened up and held up his hands apologetically. 'I am sorry you feel that way. I hadn't met Harris before and his dear grandmother, who I met by chance, told me that the young lad wanted to have a try at playing a serious game of billiards. I wasn't to know he was any good was I?'

'In that case, why is it that you are the only one of us that bet on him to win?' called out another punter.

'Just my charitable nature to give him some encouragement,'

came his excuse to a disbelieving audience. Seeing that things could turn nasty he decided to acquiesce to the mood of the room. 'Alright, the stranger can take over, for what good it will do him.'

Bevan turned towards Chard, spat on his own hand and held it out for the inspector to seal the bet. He took it, his palm feeling uncomfortably damp before removing his cap and throwing it casually onto a chair. The long coat remained on as Chard walked to the cue rack and checked each in turn before selecting one that had a good tip and no warping.

'What's your name, man?' asked Bevan.

'Smith. Nathaniel Smith,' lied Chard.

'Very well, back to the table then. Harris to play next.'

The ginger lad was very fidgety and settled down to take his shot and as Chard had anticipated he went straight for the easy pot of the other white for two points. Ignoring the sensible shot of playing safely against the red he then attempted a very difficult pot in the corner pocket which missed. The red ricocheted towards the bottom cushion in a more or less central position with the cue ball only about three inches away.

Chard smiled as his own white 'spot' ball was now replaced at the top end of the table. Taking careful aim he played a very gentle stroke sending his ball rolling slowly down the table to glance against Harris's white ball and then onto the red, scoring two points for a cannon. The inspector was now in a classic position for a decent break. With all three balls close together near to the bottom cushion it was relatively easy to keep nudging his ball against the other two, raising his score by two points on every stroke. It was intensely boring to watch, unless of course money was resting on it, but it was the means to gain a stranglehold on a game. Bevan's face became grimmer each time he moved the brass score marker.

Eventually the continual cannons had to end, as the balls fell in line with each other making the shot impossible. Chard's eye was in, though, and he potted the red for three points, then went deliberately in off the red for another three point hazard. His cue ball was placed back at the top of the table and he played another slow ball down to once again touch both of the other balls for another cannon. The score had now risen to 298 with only three needed. The room was silent with an atmosphere that could be cut with a knife. Potting the red looked relatively easy but Chard paused, balancing his natural competitiveness against his main objective. Twitching slightly as he ran the cue along the back of his hand, he deliberately fluffed the shot. The men in the room groaned, apart from Bevan who gave a sigh of relief. Harris now returned to the table but this time he had learned his lesson. Instead of rushing every shot he calmed down and, though preferring the hazard to the cannon, his aim became unerring. He potted a succession of reds and then finished his break hitting a cannon with his ball also going into the pocket off the red for a five-point score.

'Harris wins 301 to 298,' called a triumphant Bevan.

Money exchanged hands as the losing punters paid their debts and Chard shook hands with Harris before retrieving his cap. The inspector deliberately hung around looking regretfully at the table and as he had hoped Bevan eventually came up to exchange words with him.

'Hard lines there. Nathaniel, did you say? I thought my man was going to lose.'

'Yes, so did I. Call me Nate by the way. Did I hear them call you Bill?'

The pot-bellied man held out his hand, this time not covered in saliva. 'Bill Bevan's the name. I'm the man to see if you want a fair wager.'

Chard found it hard not to raise an eyebrow in disbelief. Bevan had clearly fetched the billiards player Harris to the pub for the sole intention of fleecing the other punters. He would be the last person Chard would trust to arrange a fair wager.

'Are you new in town, Nathaniel?'

'I am just passing through. Thought I would stay a couple of nights before moving on up to Merthyr.'

'As Lady Luck has blessed me this evening why don't you join me for a drink downstairs in the bar?' offered Bevan with a conviviality that Chard knew wouldn't have been there if the man had lost his money.

Chard accepted the invitation and the two men retired down to the bar where Bevan bought the inspector a whiskey and himself a large brandy.

'So then, Nate, I take it you're a betting man.'

'I do like to make the occasional wager if the odds are fair,' replied the inspector.

'Well then, it is fortunate that we have fallen in with each other for I am the ideal man to be acquainted with in this town.'

'Why is that?'

'Why? Why? My dear Nate! It's because I am at the hub of gaming. I give the fairest odds whether it be horses, greyhounds or boxing. You name it and Bill Bevan is the man to come to.'

'Cards.'

'Pardon?'

'I said cards. You said name it and I just did. Cards.'

'Certainly. Cards it is. I can get a game arranged in a couple of days with some of the local lads. As soon as the miners and ironworkers get paid they will be up for a game.'

'I am talking about a serious game, you understand,'

explained Chard. 'Five guineas buy-in, with credit of at least double that amount.'

Bevan spluttered into his drink. 'You can't be serious.'

'I am perfectly serious. I don't want to waste my time playing cards for trifling amounts. That game of billiards was just a bit of fun. I make my living playing poker or blackjack.'

Bevan scratched his bald pate. 'I am sorry but that scale of game is not something that I can arrange.'

'A pity …' Chard paused whilst he swirled the whiskey in his glass before taking a long sip, '… however, if you could find me an introduction to somewhere that can accommodate me?'

'Well, Nate, there is somewhere in the town but there are two problems. Firstly, I doubt my name could get you in, and secondly it's somewhere you should stay clear of. I hear people get badly into debt there and some have come to a bad end.'

'You let old Nate worry about that.' Chard reached into his wallet and pulled out a gold half sovereign. 'Now where do I go?'

CHAPTER TWENTY-ONE

Half an hour later Inspector Chard lurked in the shadows of a shop doorway, biding his time. An evening mist had settled on the town and the occasional gas lamps shed an eerie glow on the small sections of street that they illuminated. One of the advantages of the usually unwelcome administrative tasks of the inspector's job was that he knew exactly who would be on the various shifts and where they would be patrolling. Eventually Chard was pleased to hear heavy unhurried footsteps approach along the pavement. As a tall figure appeared out of the mist Chard called out softly. 'Constable Jenkins! Over here!'

Jenkins responded to the call by looking in the direction of the doorway, but unable to identify who was trying to attract his attention, he cautiously drew out his truncheon.

'Who's there? Come out where I can see you.'

Chard stepped forward. 'Put that truncheon away, Jenkins. It's me. Inspector Chard.'

Jenkins stared at the man in front of him. It sounded like the inspector but …

'I am in disguise, Jenkins. I've only waxed my moustache and changed my clothes for goodness sake.'

'Oh yes, sorry sir,' apologised the constable.

'Sergeant Morris is at the station tonight, yes?'

Jenkins nodded his affirmation.

'Tell him he is to gather together as many of you as he can in the next fifteen minutes and then get down here. If you hear my whistle then you are all to come running.'

Jenkins looked puzzled. 'Certainly sir, but where will you be?'

Chard pointed up the street into the mist. 'In the Victoria.'

Jenkins looked concerned. 'Wouldn't you rather wait for us first, sir?'

'No, I want time to look around in there first. I will only call for you if needed.'

'Very well, sir. I'll get going.'

Chard watched his constable disappear into the mist, straightened his cap and then walked towards the Victoria.

Despite its deservedly bad reputation, it was often very busy outside the Vic as people made their way down the alley that ran alongside the pub in order to access the Empire Music Hall that stood behind it. On this night, however, there was no show taking place and it was quiet on the street as Chard went to the threshold and made his entrance. An oppressive atmosphere pervaded the compact bar as soon as he walked in. There was a smell of stale beer, unwashed bodies and cheap tobacco. A man stood behind the bar opening a new bottle of whisky. Chard noticed that he had a small club tucked into the waistband of his barman's apron. Two customers sat on stools at the bar. Big men, hard men. They somehow managed to exude menace even though they were merely sitting. A group of four others, older but with a lifetime of sin etched in the lines on their faces sat drinking whisky and smoking cigarettes. One of them, small in stature, looked up at Chard as he walked past and noticed the grim determined look on the inspector's face.

'Cheer up, you miserable bastard. Life's too short, mun,' he called out in a manner that wasn't meant to be friendly.

'Aye, and so are you,' retorted Chard.

The reaction on the man's face was something to behold and his three companions roared with laughter.

'He's got you pegged there, Will,' chortled one and they all laughed again. The indignant Will made to get up and confront Chard but the others grabbed his shoulders and pushed him back down.

Chard felt his nerves on edge but knew that it was important to keep an outward show of confidence so he gave the issue little regard and walked to the bar. He glanced at the bottles of spirit on the shelf behind the bar and looked for one that actually had a label on it.

'Irish whiskey, please, from that Bushmills bottle at the back.'

'I've got this one here at half the price,' offered the barman, pointing at an unlabelled bottle full of a murky amber liquid.

'No thanks. I'd rather keep my eyesight,' responded the inspector.

The barman grunted and took Chard's money in exchange for a glass of the Bushmills, which the inspector tasted cautiously to ensure it was the real thing and hadn't been adulterated.

Just then there was a slight draught in the room as the door opened and a man rushed in. Dressed in a smart coat with the collar turned up, a scarf around the lower half of his face and a hat pulled down low on the forehead so that he was unrecognisable. Not bothering to acknowledge anyone in the bar he went towards a beaded curtain in the corner of the room and disappeared through it. Chard was curious but no one else paid any attention. He leant at the bar sipping his whiskey, in one way pleased that nobody was trying to draw him into a conversation. Conversely he needed to find out how a gambling club could be running from these rundown premises. As he was contemplating whether to attempt to break into a conversation with the two men sat on the nearby bar stools his attention was drawn to another man, face hidden, who came straight in only to disappear behind the curtain without a word.

'That must be it,' the inspector told himself under his breath. Indeed over the next half hour, and two whiskeys later, another half dozen or so people, a couple of whom seemed strangely familiar by their gait, had followed in the same curious manner. 'How many others had already gone through earlier?' thought Chard.

'I think I might have a wander through the curtain,' he said to the barman with a questioning intonation. The response was a wink and a nod. Still clutching his glass of whiskey he made his way past the table occupied by the four seated customers to the doorway with the beaded curtain and strode through. Unfortunately it wasn't obvious that there was a step immediately on the other side leading downwards and a big step at that. Chard fell spectacularly onto the floor of another room, his glass of whiskey falling from his hand. Fortunately the glass didn't smash but the precious liquid splashed across a patterned carpet.

'We've got an eager one here, haven't we? He can't wait to get down on all fours,' giggled a feminine voice.

Chard raised his head to find he was level with a dainty ankle. Looking further up he was faced with a pair of very shapely legs in a pair of bloomers.

Suddenly another pair of legs, this time adorned in gartered stockings, came alongside and a different voice spoke. 'You've spilt your liquid all over the floor. I hope you aren't going to do that later. Never mind, you can buy another drink for yourself and for me and Maisy too.'

As two pairs of hands helped him to his feet the second voice spoke again. This time it called out loudly so that it could be heard through the beaded curtain into the bar. 'Frank, send through another whiskey and two large gins, the customer is treating us. We'll put it on his bill.'

Chard started to focus on his surroundings. He was in the

company of two rather pretty whores, both quite young. One wore the bloomers and the other the stockings with garters accompanied by lace drawers. Both wore corsets over which their ample bosoms spilled.

'You don't mind buying us drinks, do you?' teased the one presumably called Maisy as she tickled him under the chin.

'No, not at all,' he replied, straightening his cap which had become askew from his fall.

'Good,' said the other girl, who had a wicked smile, 'because we've got to wait. All openings are currently being filled.' She pointed to the other side of the room. There were three curtained booths from behind which the inspector could now hear the grunts and groans of ardent copulation.

Something suddenly struck Chard. Clearly this was an illegal brothel, but if these were the only booths, and unless the girls were working 'two up' there must be yet another room. His thoughts were interrupted as the barman came in with a tray and placed the ordered drinks on a small table next to the girls. Chard smiled like a simpleton as Maisy pushed him into a chair and sat on his lap. The room was dimly lit and it was only as he was being nearly smothered by Maisy's breasts that he noticed a small door in the far corner guarded by a big man with a scarred face.

A feeling of excitement came over him, not due to the wandering hands of his new lascivious friends but from the realisation that he had found the location of the gaming club.

Thoughts of at least being able to raid the premises for running a brothel were broken by the sudden appearance of a figure rushing into the room. He didn't bother to look where he was going and his foot caught Chard's outstretched leg. The stranger stumbled, only just keeping his balance. As he did so the scarred man guarding the far door called out, 'You're late. He has been waiting for you.'

'*Fa'n cuolo!*' came the foreign retort. 'I've just tripped over this arsehole,' he added, turning to face Chard. For a few seconds their eyes met, a pause, then dawning recognition.

'You idiot!' yelled the stranger at the scarred man whilst pointing at Chard. 'That's a peeler.'

'Ross!' shouted Chard as absolute pandemonium erupted. The whores screamed and leapt off the inspector's lap. Yells of dismay at coitus interruptus came from the booths. Ross ran towards the door guarded by the scarred man, and more alarmingly, the latter took a hammer from his pocket and charged towards Chard. The inspector felt that discretion was the better part of valour and leapt to his feet. Taking a running jump up the entrance step and through the beaded curtains he collided with the table around which sat the man called Will and his companions, sending their drinks flying. Without stopping he made it to the door of the pub, at the same time managing to pull out his police whistle. He gave three blasts and turned to face the four men facing him, noticing that the scarred man was still by the beaded curtain. The two men at the bar stools looked with interest but stayed where they were for the moment, though one had casually picked up a beer bottle just in case. Suddenly Chard felt a push in the back as Constable Jenkins barrelled into him followed by Sergeant Morris and three other constables with truncheons drawn. That was the signal for all hell to break loose. The man with the beer bottle smashed it against the bar so that its jagged edges became his weapon. The barman handed the other customer at the barstool his club before ducking under cover. Will, meanwhile, drew a wicked-looking knife.

Seeing he was no longer outnumbered, Chard went on the attack and grabbed the nearest man intending to put him in an arm-lock. However, one of the other drinkers came to the man's aid and Chard became embroiled in a three-man tussle.

Whilst this was taking place the barstool customer without the broken beer bottle flexed a pair of huge biceps and made to grab the throat of Sergeant Morris, but the policeman contemptuously swatted the man's arms away and punched him in the ribs before putting him in a bear hug. Close by, Constable Jenkins, the trained boxer, punched the man with the broken bottle so hard in the chest that he fell back against the bar counter and collapsed in a heap. Another opponent threw a punch at Jenkins but he ducked and weaved as the blow went harmlessly over his shoulder. The man called Will jabbed ineffectually with his knife. Jenkins hit Will with a left jab to the ribs but it was still two against one and he narrowly avoided a kick to the groin. Constable Jackson had entered the room looking for an easy target for his truncheon. He laughed seeing Chard struggling with his two opponents and ignored him but when he saw Will was vulnerable to an attack from behind he swung his truncheon low and upwards crushing the man's testicles, sending him screaming to the floor.

Fortunately for Chard it was Constable Morgan that came to his rescue, hitting the thigh of one of the assailants a mighty blow with his sturdy truncheon and causing him to stumble away. The other opponent bit down on Chard's left wrist with rotting teeth, causing a spasm of pain to shoot through the inspector. The man's success was short-lived though as Constable Morgan struck him on the collar bone, a terrible crunching sound evidencing the fractured bone.

'Thanks, Morgan. Now we need to get through there quickly,' shouted Chard indicating the beaded curtain as best he could whilst nursing his injured wrist.

The scarred man meanwhile had seen enough. Apart from the huge sergeant and his opponent, who were mutually trying to crush the life out of each other, there was no one else fighting the police. They were either on the ground, had run out through the front door or, as in the case of the barman, were cowering behind the counter. Constable Matthews was the only policeman not to have engaged in the fight. His only contribution so far had been to wave his truncheon menacingly and snarl without actually hitting anybody. However, he was the first to notice the retreating man with the scarred face who held a nasty-looking hammer and so he had started to give chase even before Chard had called out. Leaping through the curtains he caught up with his quarry and hit him on the back with his truncheon. To his surprise the fugitive hardly seemed to notice and before he could strike another blow a heavily perfumed figure became wrapped around him as Maisy attempted to slow the constable down.

The scarred man took advantage of the delay and slipped through the door. Constable Matthews shrugged the girl off as he heard a bar being slid across the door on the other side.

'Break that door down,' yelled Chard as he ran into the brothel. He noticed that the curtains around the booths had been pulled back and the occupants had fled. Apart from Maisy, so had all the other working girls.

Meanwhile back in the bar, the giant Sergeant Morris and his worthy opponent were both still face to face, trying to squeeze each other to death. The veins on their temples were showing blue and swollen against their red faces, eyes were bulging and every so often one of them would arch backwards in pain before forcing every sinew into regaining an advantage.

'Enough?' asked the sergeant. The two men looked into each other's eyes. There was a mutual nod and they released each other. They stood apart for a moment, then the bar customer made a run for the door. Sergeant Morris let him go with just a boot swung at the man's rear end as he passed. The sergeant watched his erstwhile opponent stagger out into the street and then followed his police colleagues through the beaded curtain.

'Ah, Sergeant, good. We are having some trouble with this door. Can you oblige?'

Sergeant Morris just nodded and then ran at the door, hitting it with his shoulder. There was a splintering sound and then the door sprang open. They were in yet another room, this time though it was lavishly furnished. In the centre was an oval table covered by a baize cloth with beautifully carved chairs set around it, some of which had been knocked over. A mahogany table containing bottles of brandy, whisky and a decanter of port stood in one corner whilst two smaller tables carried partly-filled glasses. Another small table had been knocked over and now lay on its side on the deep pile carpet amidst broken glass and a damp patch of spilled alcohol. At the far end of the room was an open door.

'See where that leads, Matthews!' ordered Chard. The constable returned a minute later.

'It goes into a props room for the music hall next door and that has a door leading to the alley outside.'

'So they all got away then, sir,' said Sergeant Morris regretfully.

'No, not quite,' responded Chard pointing to an object that had been left behind on the floor.

It was an expensive cane with an elaborately designed silver leopard's head and he knew who owned it.

CHAPTER TWENTY-TWO

Chard was annoyed with himself at being late getting to his office. Although the hair oil had been easy to wash out the previous evening, the dye in his moustache and sideburns had proved a nightmare to remove. There were still patches of jet black when he awoke, made more obvious by the daylight and it had taken a fair degree of scrubbing and trimming before he was satisfied with his appearance. At least he was back in his uniform and could get rid of the long black coat which smelled of tobacco and stale beer.

The inspector had barely sat down at his desk when there was a knock on the door and Constable Preece popped his head into the office.

'Thought I had better let you know that somehow the superintendent has already heard about your exploits last night, sir.'

'Thank you, Constable, it seems that news travels fast.'

'I don't know who told the superintendent, but I heard from Fisty, I mean Constable Jenkins. He popped in first thing to tell me about it, even though he isn't on duty this morning. He said it was a fair old scrap and the boys were full of *hwyl*.'

'Full of what?'

'*Hwyl*, sir. It's a Welsh word and hard to describe but let's say in this case it means fighting spirit'

'In that case I can't argue with the statement. Yes it was good but I don't know what the superintendent is going to say.'

It didn't take Chard long to find out because an hour later he was called to his superior's office.

'I understand you were brawling again last night, Inspector,' stated Superintendent Jones, his face giving no indication of emotion.

'If you mean I was in a physical altercation then, yes sir, that is true.'

'This time I understand that you involved a fair few of your colleagues as well. Is that true?'

'I cannot deny that some of our men assisted me as was their duty,' replied Chard starting to feel a little uncomfortable.

'Answer me honestly, Inspector. Were you in uniform?'

'No sir, it was necessary for me to be out of uniform in order to assist my enquiries.'

'Then let me ask you one more thing, Inspector. Had you been drinking during the course of the evening?'

Chard looked at the stern stare coming from the superintendent and felt both indignant and apprehensive as he gave his answer.

'I admit that I had imbibed a small amount of alcohol though I was in no way intoxicated.'

'So why is it that reports reached my ears this morning, from certain sources, that a drunk off duty police officer instigated an unplanned raid on an honest business premises and assaulted several of its customers?'

'Hardly an honest business premises, sir. We uncovered an illegal brothel.'

For a second a smile appeared on the superintendent's lips but then vanished.

'Ah, I see,' he replied. 'So how many arrests were made?'

Chard looked sheepish. 'None, sir.'

'None?' queried the superintendent with a raised eyebrow. 'Come now, there must have been whores and of course their customers. How can you claim it was a brothel if you cannot produce the customers?'

Chard looked a picture of abject misery. 'I confess that all the customers and all but one of the whores got away, sir. The one we caught denied everything and I had no real evidence against her so I let her go.'

'Did you not recognise any of the customers before they got away.'

'No sir.'

Superintendent Jones barely suppressed an ironic laugh. 'Probably a good job too. Judging by the source of the complaint I received I am guessing that one of their patrons was someone of significant social standing. Ha!' he guffawed before straightening his expression.

Suddenly Inspector Jones slammed his fist down on his desk with significant force. It was done so unexpectedly that Chard's heart missed a beat.

'Listen, Inspector, I don't give a damn that you raided that hell hole or that you might have caught some dignitary or other with their trousers around their ankles. I can maybe even forgive the fact that you were not in uniform, but what I find absolutely intolerable is that you gave your word that your absolute priority, in fact your only priority, would be the Blake case. Instead you have only achieved closing down a brothel with no actual arrests.'

'That is both unfair and incorrect,' interjected Chard. 'You clearly do not have all the facts, sir.'

'Then enlighten me, Inspector.'

'I was indeed working on the Blake case. You will remember me telling you of the link with a gambling club?'

'I do,' confirmed the superintendent.

'Well I was in plain clothes in order to locate its whereabouts and whoever complained about the raid obviously failed to tell you that it was actually taking place in a room beyond the brothel.'

Superintendent Jones grunted. 'So you have made some progress in the case.'

'Not as much as I would have liked, sir. The purpose of finding the gambling club was all about establishing links to Blake. As you are aware it is not illegal to run such an enterprise if there is a full list of gentleman members and it is properly constituted. Locating it was the first problem. It was finding the brothel that allowed me to access the place. Grimes is not the licensee of the Victoria, at least not officially. In the unlikely event of a legal club having been set up then we could have accessed the members list which would have been most useful. However, if there wasn't a members list, which seems likely, then we could have arrested Grimes for illegal gambling. Either way, we could have used what we found to exert pressure and find out more about Blake's activities leading to his death. It was just necessary to catch the gambling taking place, particularly with Grimes present.'

'So how many gamblers did you detain?'

'I regret to say that they all got away, sir.'

'Say that again Inspector, for I fear my ears may be deceiving me,' responded the superintendent with barely concealed anger.

'They got away, sir, but our efforts were not entirely in vain,' answered Chard quickly in an effort to placate his superior.

'Really?' asked the Superintendent in disbelief.

'We didn't physically catch anyone there but I know two people who were present and they are now my prime suspects. I only recently spoke with the Honourable James Dorsett who had been seen talking to Blake. He reluctantly admitted that he knew the man but failed to mention that it was connected with Blake's employment as a debt collector for Grimes. However, I admit that my evidence of it is circumstantial.'

'You said that you knew he was there last night.'

'Oh yes, he was definitely there. I found his cane but he may have been one of the customers in the booths with the ladies and dropped the cane when he made his escape via the gambling room.'

'Why didn't the gamblers come into the room via the exit rather than enter through the Victoria?'

'Simple enough, sir. They would have to have come through a door into the props room of the theatre. If they had been noticed then it would have looked very suspicious for several people to be clandestinely slipping in there. However, it is not unusual for strange people to flit in and out of the Victoria especially with a brothel in the back. I also think that Grimes would have wanted it that way. Remember that the whole thing for him is about power over the individuals. Making them walk through a room of thugs and then a room of debauchery would make some of them feel humiliated.'

'Very well, but you mentioned there were two suspects.'

'The Italian foundry worker, Jack Ross, is my other suspect. I do not understand how he would have the money to become involved with Grimes but I saw him and he gave no indication when interviewed previously that he knew Blake through his gambling connections.'

'How do you intend to proceed then, Inspector?'

'I think I have enough on Ross to drag him in to the cells. He will have some difficult questions to answer. As for Dorsett, I will track him down and return his cane in exchange for some truthful answers. He may or may not be the murderer but he is definitely hiding something.'

Chard scratched his sideburns with his left hand.

'Inspector, what have you done to yourself?'

Chard glanced at the wrist that had been bitten the previous night. It was red and swollen.

'It was bitten in the fracas last night, sir. It is rather painful.'

'Then get yourself to the infirmary and get the wound dressed. It looks as if it may have become infected. That will be all for now. Just ensure that you keep me informed of your progress.'

∗   ∗   ∗

It was actually after midday before Chard finally found himself walking through the gates of the workhouse on the way to the infirmary. On the way he had made a detour into the White Hart to make a small purchase which he slipped into the inner pocket of his uniform jacket. The workhouse buildings still appeared grim and foreboding but the sky was a beautiful shade of blue interrupted by wispy white clouds and the air was unusually fresh. Chard was in good spirits apart from his throbbing wrist. The temperate weather and the fact that he felt he was finally making some progress in the Blake case had lightened his mood.

'*Prynhawn da*, Inspector,' said a voice from a few yards to his right.

Chard turned to see who had hailed him and recognised a familiar figure in workhouse clothes leaning on the handle of a sweeping broom.

'Ah Jarvis, I take it that was some kind of greeting and nothing unpleasant.'

'It means good afternoon, Inspector. Have you come to see me over our unfinished business?' He gave a wink and then cackled. 'You've taken your time mind. I was beginning to think that you weren't a man of your word.'

'Actually I have come to get an injury dressed in the infirmary,' explained Chard. Jarvis's face dropped and he started to look angry but before he could say anything the inspector stopped him by patting his pocket. 'However, coincidentally I do have a little something here for medical purposes.' Chard casually glanced around before pulling a half bottle of brandy from his inside pocket and passing it discreetly to Jarvis who stuffed it down his trousers.

'God bless you, sir. I never doubted you for a minute. A true gentlemen if I may say so.'

'Never mind the blather, I need to get on.'

'Very well Inspector, but I do have something else to add which might or indeed might not be important. I probably should have mentioned it last time but I thought it might be worth holding something back just in case you didn't return with the ... well, you know,' added Jarvis. 'Not that I really doubted you of course.'

'It doesn't sound like it,' replied Chard sarcastically. 'So what didn't you mention before?'

'The tattoo.'

'What tattoo?'

'The tattoo that the man with the smashed face had. I noticed it when they took him away for burial.'

'What did it look like?' asked the inspector curiously.

'It was a tattoo of a pistol on the right hand side of his chest,' replied the old man, tapping the side of his nose.

'I wish you had mentioned it earlier. We still don't know exactly who the man was. If the tattoo helps identify him then that might tie in somehow with the murderer of Blake,' snapped an annoyed Chard.

'I will suggest one more thing to you, Inspector. Ask down the docks in Cardiff what the tattoo means. That's where you'll get the answer.' With that the old man wandered off leaving Chard pondering this new information. Feeling slightly irritated the inspector made his way to the infirmary.

'Good morning sir, how can I help you,' came a friendly

greeting from a nurse of mature years who immediately recognised Chard's importance from his uniform.

'Good morning nurse. It's something fairly minor. I have had a bite on the wrist and I have been advised to get it checked, just to be on the safe side.'

Chard did as he was told and then waited for the nurse to return with Dr Henderson.

'Ah Inspector Chard, what have you been up to, eh?' he asked through his drooping grey moustache.

'A less than co-operative miscreant, Doctor. I assume it isn't too serious?' enquired Chard as he showed the doctor the injury.

'No, nothing to worry about there. Just needs a good cleaning, a salve and proper dressing. It'll heal in a few days. Our nurse will sort that out for you.'

'Thank you Doctor, but whilst you are here, could you answer me a quick question about that man who died? You know, the one everyone thought was Michael Blake.'

'Certainly Inspector, ask away.'

'Did he have a tattoo on the right hand side of his chest?'

The doctor frowned and scratched his head. 'I can't say I remember, Inspector, it was over two years ago now and my memory isn't quite as good as it was.'

'Let me jog your memory. I understand it might have been a tattoo of a pistol.'

The doctor pondered then suddenly his eyes lit up. 'Oh yes, I remember now. It didn't seem important at the time.'

'Very well, it means that it might be worth me checking with other police forces to see if anyone with that tattoo has been recorded as missing. Thank you, Doctor.'

Dr Henderson left Chard in the competent hands of Nurse Bayliss who cleaned and dressed the wound with a neat bandage. He was about to leave the infirmary when he accidentally came face to face with May Roper who was returning from an errand for Dr Henderson. She was wearing a matching claret skirt and short jacket over a white high neck blouse decorated with a large green brooch. May's eyes narrowed as she recognised the man before her.

'Good morning, Miss Roper,' greeted the inspector touching his cap politely.

'Good morning to you also, Inspector Chard,' she replied coldly and made to walk past.

Chard felt a little guilty about the offhand way he had treated her when they had last met so tried to make amends.

'Thank you for the information about the gentleman, Mr Dorsett. He did admit to knowing Mr Blake, so that was most useful.'

May's expression softened and was replaced with a look of eagerness. 'Why was he meeting with him? How were they connected? Is he the murderer?' she garbled.

Chard suddenly wished that he hadn't said a word. 'I am sorry but I can't tell you. He gave a reason why he met Blake but that is all I can say.'

The cold look of annoyance returned to May's face. 'Very well Inspector, I will wish you good day.' The auburn-haired young woman turned on her heel whilst the inspector shook his head and also made to leave. However, before he could take a step, May called over her shoulder.

'By the way Inspector, I saw Evans the other day. I hadn't seen him in ages.'

Chard stopped momentarily. 'Yes, young Dilwyn Evans was sent up here after nearly getting run over in the street.'

'No, I mean Evans the porter here at the workhouse. The one that vanished the night of the train crash,' replied May without turning around.

Chard chased after her, which had been her intention.

'Miss Roper, wait a moment. I had forgotten all about him. It might be useful to ask him a few questions. Where did you see him and what does he look like?'

'What was the purpose of the meeting between Blake and the man, Dorsett?'

'I am not here to play games Miss Roper.'

'Neither am I,' replied the young woman fiercely.

Chard puffed out his cheeks in annoyance before giving in. 'Dorsett wanted to find out about the Taff Vale Ironworks as a business. It was due to his interests as an investor. That is all.'

'You don't believe him though, do you?'

'I have given you the answer that he gave me. Now you give me some answers about this Evans.'

'Very well, I saw him on the corner of a street off the Graig hill not far from here. I called to him and he recognised me but he made off. I followed him but he disappeared down an alley.'

'Thank you. If you can give me a description we will keep a sharp look out for him. Is there anything remarkable about his appearance?'

'Oh yes,' replied May. 'He is a large man, with a powerful body but he is very easy to recognise because of his face. He has horrible scars down the left hand side of it. Two parallel deep grooves from his chin to just below the corner of his left eye.'

Chard stood for a moment taking the information in before touching his cap once again.

'Thank you, Miss Roper. Most helpful,' he said rather brusquely before turning around and walking hurriedly out through the door.

*   *   *

Chard had arrived back at the station looking very flustered. Entering his office, he hung his cap on the door hook before turning around and kicking a wastepaper basket across the room. Unknowingly to the inspector Constable Preece had risen from his desk, followed him to the door and had witnessed the undignified display of petulance.

'Everything OK, sir?'

Chard turned, feeling a little embarrassed at his lack of decorum. 'No Constable, it is not. I felt that I was making some progress on the case with my suspects narrowing, but now I find that I missed another line of enquiry.'

'In what way sir, if you don't mind my asking?'

'It turns out that the fellow with the scarred face that works for Grimes is almost certainly Evans, the porter that disappeared the night of the train crash.'

'Coincidentally, he now appears to be doing Blake's old job,' commented Preece, catching on to the obvious implication.

'Exactly, and so far we have made an assumption that because Blake went missing a week before the crash he must have been killed a week before the crash. What if he hadn't? What if Evans had stolen the wallet from the train crash victim when he was admitted to the infirmary, left the workhouse that night, killed Blake for reasons unknown, then broke back into the infirmary to plant the watch?'

'That seems a bit far-fetched to me, sir.'

'Nevertheless it is possible. I don't like coincidences and something tells me that Evans must be involved. Get the men out looking for him, especially in the Graig area. I want him arrested on sight.'

'Very good sir,' replied Preece who made to leave the inspector's office.

'Another thing, Preece. Send a message down to our colleagues in Cardiff. Ask them if they know of any significance regarding tattoos of a pistol on the right hand side of the chest. Apparently it is worth asking down the docks. Hopefully it means nothing that will complicate this case any further because I need something to reduce the suspects in this case not add to them.'

CHAPTER TWENTY-THREE

The Llanbradach Arms stood above the east bank of the River Taff upstream of the Machine Bridge at Treforest. The small yard at the back looked down on the Taff Vale Ironworks on the opposite bank, the shadowy outline of which was occasionally visible by moonlight. No sound could be heard from the small row of cottages that adjoined the pub. They were all in darkness, the occupants had either retired to bed in preparation for a hard day's graft on the following morning or alternatively were in the drinking establishment themselves. At the front of the building the Glamorganshire canal lay dark and silent. In the morning, barges would be travelling from the canal lock by the Newbridge Chainworks, half a mile to the north, before passing the pub then disappearing under a nearby hump-backed bridge on their way to Cardiff.

Inside the Llanbradach the atmosphere was warm and convivial. In a fog of pipe and cigarette smoke, and in an aroma of strong ale and tobacco, a dozen or so men laughed, joked and exchanged stories. One man however chose to sit alone and leaned back in his chair with his legs, clad in expensive riding boots, resting on a stool. He wore a long black riding coat, black riding britches, with a contrasting bright red waistcoat over his shirt. In one hand he held a cigarette on which he puffed thoughtfully whilst in the other he cradled a glass of expensive brandy. Putting down his glass on a small side table, Jabez Grimes took his pocket watch from his waistcoat and checked the time. There was still enough time to finish his drink before having to leave, he decided. The raid on the Victoria was an unfortunate interruption of his activities but hardly disastrous. Everyone had escaped the clutches of the law and no charges could be brought but there needed to be a new location for future gambling. All of the men over whom he held power had been told that meetings and any payments due were to be suspended until he contacted them again. However, there was one more payment to be extracted that could not wait. Evans had been instructed to lay low for the time being but in this case it was something that Grimes wanted to deal with himself. Not that his financial wellbeing depended on it, there were many more investments in dubious activities that provided a steady flow of income, but there was joy to be had in exercising power over individuals with secret weaknesses that only he knew.

Ten minutes later Grimes finished his drink, stubbed out the remains of his cigarette and made his way to the door. The landlord bid him farewell as he made to leave which Grimes acknowledged with a dismissive wave of his hand. Once outside he walked to his horse which had been left tied to a post outside the pub and gave it a pat on the nose before walking a few yards to the edge of the canal. Following the towpath just a little further to the nearby hump-backed bridge he walked beneath it and undid his britches. Grimes released a sigh of relief as he emptied his bladder into the canal, the warm urine steaming as it hit the water.

'Mr Grimes?'

The sudden sound made him jump and grab the edge of his britches in an effort to regain his dignity. Grimes turned to see who had crept up on him so quietly.

'What the devil are you doing here, you stupid bastard,' he snarled. 'I nearly pissed myself. You will pay for that, by God you will.'

'This can't go on. I've had enough.'

'You've had enough when I say you've had enough. You are my creature and it will remain that way until you are no longer of use to me.'

'No, I won't let this go on. If no one else will stop you, then I will.'

Grimes laughed and turned away. 'Leave what you owe me on the towpath then piss off. Talking of which, I hadn't quite finished what I was doing when you turned up,' he added undoing his britches fully once more.

Unexpectedly Grimes felt a crushing pain on his skull and suddenly, against a background of agony everything went black and he felt himself falling. More pain came, he felt sick and wanted to cry out but was unable to do so. His vision was gone but his attacker's voice was perfectly clear as it cursed him time and time again. Then Grimes passed out, not feeling the remaining blows that crushed his skull like an eggshell, leaking blood and brain tissue over the towpath.

His assailant stood there for a moment gasping with the physical and mental effort of the grisly task before vomiting, which added to the slippery mess beneath them. It took two heaves to get the body in the canal where it lay floating lifelessly and out of sight.

* * *

Jack Ross stood, with a holdall containing his essential belongings, on the Machine Bridge, watching the moonlight glint on the River Taff as it flowed on its southern course to Cardiff. He didn't want the police paying him any attention, it was too risky, but what had happened in the Victoria made it inevitable. That Inspector Chard was going to ruin everything, so for now he needed to keep a low profile. The question being how to do that? Obviously he couldn't be seen at the ironworks or return to his house, but how then could he talk to Jenny? There was no way he could move on without telling her of his feelings. He would risk one more night in the town before moving on, hiding out in the wooded hillside on the eastern side of the valley beyond the church of St Mary's. In the morning he would discreetly get a message to Jenny and ask her to meet him that night for perhaps the last time. Unfortunately she would have left for work by then so he would have to send it to her at the ironworks. It was a risk but his heart could give him no other option.

Suddenly Jack was alerted by the sound of footsteps and he automatically dropped to his knees. Someone was running but he was unable to identify who it might be as here on the bridge there were no gaslights. As the footsteps got nearer it was obvious that the other person was running on the other side of the road though they remained invisible. Then a shaft of moonlight breached the passing clouds and illuminated the fugitive's face momentarily before it disappeared once more into the darkness.

* * *

It was very early the following morning when Dai 'Kipper' Jones knelt at the front of his barge smoking his favourite clay pipe. There were three barges in total, all low-sided, packed with anthracite coal and tied together whilst being pulled by a heavily muscled working horse that trod patiently along the towpath.

'That's a good lad, Samson, we're off to a grand start this morning, aren't we?'

Kipper often talked to his horse, usually asking it questions to which he did not expect answers. The barges glided gently past the Duke of Bridgewater pub and on to where the foundry smoke from the early morning shift at the ironworks could be seen across the river. Then came the Llanbradach pub, its doors closed and windows shuttered, the landlord yet to rise and start his working day.

'We'll stop there for a drink on the way back, eh Samson?'

As Samson approached the hump-backed bridge he suddenly stopped and started to whinny.

'Now, now, old fella. What's the matter with you, you daft bugger? It's only a little bridge to go under, isn't it?'

Samson would go no further but as he stopped, the momentum of the barges meant that they still continued to glide slowly along. Kipper's eyes were on the horse and the sudden bump as the barge hit an obstacle caught him unawares so that his pipe nearly fell out of his mouth. Then the smell from the towpath hit him.

'Oh, my Lord! Samson, we need to get the constable.'

*　　*　　*

Chard noticed that there was some excitement at the station when he arrived. A number of the men had gathered in the yard and were surrounding a newly painted two-horse police van which seemed an unusual object of fascination. Deciding to ignore the gathering he went inside where the gap-toothed Sergeant Humphreys stood at his desk writing some notes in a ledger.

'Good morning, Sergeant. What's all the fuss in the yard? The prison van from Cardiff wasn't due today was it?'

'No sir. Apparently it's ours,' he replied with what would have been a beaming smile if he had front teeth. 'They've sent it up from Cardiff for our use.'

'And just where are we going to keep it?'

'I understand that the superintendent has had permission to extend the station. In the meantime the gig will go to the White Hart stables and we'll keep the van here.'

'Oh, I see.' Chard left the sergeant smiling at his desk whilst he went to his own office feeling a little put out that the superintendent had not mentioned anything about it when they had last spoken.

On the way to his office Chard had a quick word with Constable Preece who was standing by the station noticeboard.

'Be ready to leave in an hour, Constable. We're going to the ironworks to pick up Jack Ross today and nothing else is going to take priority over that.'

* * *

It was only a short time after his pronouncement that Chard received news of the dead body found in the canal.

'Damn and blast! Come on, Constable Preece, the fates are against us once more it seems.'

Putting the new police van to use for the first time, the two men arrived at the scene within half an hour of receiving the message. On arrival they saw a small crowd of curious onlookers gathered outside the Llanbradach Arms looking towards the towpath as it disappeared under the small hump-backed bridge. Standing right next to the bridge was a large, bumptious-looking man defying the onlookers to come any nearer.

'What's the matter, sir?' asked Preece in response to a groan emanating from his inspector.

'Constable Donachie of the Glamorganshire Canal Police. I came across him once in different circumstances. I hope he's sober this time.'

Fortunately this proved to be the case and, as a bonus, he failed to remember their previous encounter.

'Good morning, officers. Everything's under control for you,' greeted Donachie, his Scottish accent less pronounced than it had been under the influence of drink. 'I would of course have been able to deal with this myself but I am just paid to deal with pilfering and the odd fight, not something this messy.'

'Yes, we were told that there is a dead body and that there probably has been foul play,' said Chard.

'Och, unless the man repeatedly smashed the back of his own head in, then there certainly has been foul play.'

'I take it you haven't moved the body.'

'I had to, there wasn't an option. The canal had to be cleared so as not to disrupt the barges going through. It took myself and a couple of volunteers with boathooks to drag the body to the side of the path and heave him up. It wasnae pleasant either, I can tell you.'

'Very well, Constable Donachie, we'll take it from here, but thank you for your assistance.'

'Aye well, the landlord was kind enough to offer me a free whisky when this was over, so I'll go and take him up on it now. I dare say that you'll need one too after you've finished. The corpse is there under the bridge, help yourselves.'

The policemen made their way to the towpath and walked under the bridge, the smell nearly making them gag.

It was light enough under the small bridge to spot the body, lying face down and sodden from the time spent in the canal.

'The back of the head has been pulped,' commented Chard to Preece who was looking distinctly queasy. 'Mind where you step, by the way, Constable, that's one hell of a mess on the towpath.'

Chard bent down towards the body but realised that it would have to be turned. 'Right then, you take his legs and I'll take his shoulders and we'll flip him over.'

The task wasn't an easy one as Chard had to stretch awkwardly to avoid getting gore on his uniform, but eventually with one strong heave they turned the corpse and Chard could at last see the victim's face.

'Grimes! I wasn't expecting that,' he uttered, scratching his sideburns as he tried to work out the wider implications. 'We'll need to get him in the van, so get a couple of volunteers to help. So much for running the Fortuna club. It looks like the goddess took a dislike to him,' added the inspector with a grimace.

Preece was only too happy to get away for a moment and went to the crowd outside the pub to persuade two of the more curious onlookers to come and help.

Soon he returned with two elderly but strong and wiry individuals who, after the promise of a pint of beer or two, agreed to lift the body and put it in the van.

'Right, Constable Preece, we'll take the body up to the mortuary chapel at Glyntaff as it is close by.'

'They'll be getting fed up with seeing us there, sir.'

'Yes, we need our own mortuary setting up at this rate. I'll speak to the superintendent about it when we get back. In the meantime we also need to get a telegram to Dr Matthews. It is pointless our returning all the way to the police station if we've got to come back out again. There'll be someone at the cemetery offices who can sort that out for us, I'm sure.'

*　　*　　*

Fifty yards away, across the canal and the road, a figure with coat closed and cap pulled down over the face walked towards a small corner shop. The owner, a lady of mature years in a shopkeeper's apron, stood outside the premises, observing the drama being played out across the other side of the canal. As the customer opened the shop door, causing a bell to ring, the shopkeeper turned and followed the man in.

'I understand they've found a body over there,' she said in what was meant to sound like a confidential whisper, but which was actually quite loud.

The man nodded but seemed unconcerned with the news.

'A pencil, some writing paper and an envelope please,' he asked in a slightly foreign accent.

'One of my regulars called in ten minutes ago and said that they reckon it was murder,' continued the shopkeeper, trying to start a conversation as she handed the items over.

The customer nodded, paid for his purchases and left without responding to the news, leaving her disappointed.

*　　*　　*

It transpired that it was to be a two-hour wait for the policemen before Dr Matthews was able to make an appearance. Chard had to endure a long discourse from the cemetery authorities on the disruption being caused to the normal day-to-day running of their facilities. They felt that the police should make their own arrangements for the examination of murdered corpses elsewhere. Thankfully, when the atmosphere had somewhat calmed down the administrative staff had offered some refreshment to the policemen and they were able to pass the time in reasonable comfort whilst they waited for the doctor.

'So, Constable Preece, as we have some time to wait, perhaps you can enlighten me about something.'

'Certainly sir, what do you want to know?'

'I have on occasion spotted some of the men sniggering when I pronounce Welsh place names.'

Preece looked embarrassed. 'Nothing meant by it, sir. You are very popular with the lads.'

'I'm glad to hear it, but it doesn't really answer my question.'

'Well, it's just that you try hard but you don't seem to get it right.'

'For example?'

'You can't pronounce the double 'l' sound for instance. So when you say Gelliwastad as if it is an English word it sounds funny.'

'So how do I make the 'll' sound?'

'Try placing your tongue on the roof of your mouth near the teeth as if to pronounce an 'l', then blow voicelessly.'

'I'll remember that, Constable, but if you think I'm going to try it here in front of you, you've got another think coming. I'll give it a go back in my rooms,' answered the inspector with a smile.

'To be fair you've got the 'ch' sound right though.'

'Yes, I soon picked that up. It's just like in the name of the composer Bach. I do get confused by the letter 'y' though. Sometimes it sounds like a 'u' and sometimes an 'i'. Why is that?'

'To be honest I am not sure myself, sir. Having been brought up with the language I just take it for granted.'

'Seems odd to me.'

'No more odd than some of the quirks in the English language, sir,' responded Preece defensively.

There was a period of silence before the inspector turned their thoughts back to their work. 'What is your opinion, Constable, on the implications arising from the demise of Mr Grimes?'

'Well sir, the immediate thought is that it must be something to do with the raid you did on the Victoria.'

'I agree, but what difference did my raid actually make?'

'Well it stopped the gambling and the brothel.'

'Yes, but only temporarily until they find somewhere else. What else?'

'You now know that Ross and Dorsett had not been entirely truthful when you interviewed them.'

'Exactly. That has to be relevant.'

The discussion was interrupted by a cheerful voice that they immediately recognised.

'Good day gentlemen. I must say your appointment to this town has been excellent news for my fees. Bodies are turning up everywhere aren't they?' exclaimed Dr Matthews.

'I'm glad it's good news for somebody,' responded Chard in a friendly tone.

'Best get things started, then. Let the dog see the rabbit, as they say.'

'Agreed. This way, then. They've put the body in here.' Chard led the doctor through to the white-tiled room where the corpse now lay on a table covered by a cotton sheet. Preece followed behind and took out his pencil and notebook.

Dr Matthews' nose started to twitch as he put down his medical bag and then pulled back the sheet to reveal the head of the victim.

'I had the staff place him face down for your inspection so that you wouldn't have to turn him to see the wound.'

'Thank you, Inspector. Most considerate,' replied Matthews, his little moustache moving with every twitch of the nose. The doctor reached into his medical bag and took out a small metal probe with which he prodded the corpse's skull.

'Nasty. Very nasty,' he proclaimed. 'A number of very hard blows with something solid.'

'Anything more definite as to what was used?' asked the inspector.

'Something a couple of inches across perhaps, possibly with a square edge, though it's difficult to say because some of the blows have clearly overlapped.'

'I assume he was definitely dead before going in the water?'

'Oh yes, no doubt about it. Normally I would have to wait until I checked the lungs, but the damage to the skull is so great that I am confident it was the blows that killed him. I will of course perform a full post mortem, but you needn't wait while I do it. You will get my full report early next week.'

'Thank you, Doctor. In that case we will be off. I think it's about time we started arresting suspects and I know just where to begin.'

CHAPTER TWENTY-FOUR

Lizzie Hawkins could not help but be curious. Mr Dunwoody had come into the office that lunchtime bearing an envelope addressed to her best friend Jenny.

'Miss Norton, the staff in this office, including myself, are not here to act as postal messengers for your convenience. Please ensure that personal messages go to your home address and not to this business.'

'I am afraid I do not know what you are referring to Mr Dunwoody,' replied Jenny frowning. 'I am not accustomed to receiving messages at work as you well know.'

Dunwoody, trembling slightly as he usually did when agitated, passed the note over and Jenny looked at it with disinterest.

'Well?' asked Dunwoody as Lizzie looked on expectantly.

'Well what, Mr Dunwoody?'

'I think that Mr Dunwoody wants to know what is in the message,' suggested Jenny's blond-haired friend.

'Just so, Miss Hawkins. If I have been interrupted from my work then I would like to know why.'

Jenny paused a moment, grimaced, then taking a letter knife from her desk, slit open the seam of the envelope. Her face expressed no emotion whatsoever as she unfolded the contents, read the message, then folded the paper back up again before re-inserting it into the envelope.

'It's personal and it won't happen again,' she stated, looking firmly at Mr Dunwoody, then putting the envelope in her desk drawer and slamming it shut.

Dunwoody blustered. 'Very well then. Just make sure it doesn't,' he replied before turning on his heel.

'Well?' asked Lizzie.

'Well what, Lizzie?'

'We have no secrets from each other do we?'

Jenny's face remained emotionless. 'As I said, it's personal.'

*　　*　　*

Inspector Chard and Constable Preece found themselves once again at the door of Taff Vale House having secured the horses of the police van to a tree outside the premises. They knocked at the door which was answered by a servant who, after they had stated their business, led them inside.

The two officers were shown through to Mr Roberts' office where he looked quite pleased to see them.

'Delighted to see you. I assume you are here with regard to my delicate little "problem"?'

Chard looked blank in response whereas Preece suppressed a little smile.

'With regards to the accounts,' prompted Roberts, whispering in case he was overheard.

'Ah I see,' replied Chard as he caught on, 'No, not yet. I am afraid we are still after our murderer. We feel we have enough circumstantial evidence to warrant bringing one of your employees in for questioning.'

'Who would that be?' asked Roberts, obviously disappointed that his own issue was not going to be dealt with at the moment.

'Jack Ross, who works in the cast iron foundry.'

Roberts gave a bellow, 'Dunwoody!'

A few seconds later the red faced little man nearly stumbled through the door as he rushed to answer the command.

'The inspector here wants a word with that man Ross who works for us.'

'C-certainly,' stammered Dunwoody. 'This way, gentlemen.'

The two police officers followed Dunwoody out through the rear of Taff Vale House and into the works yard where the thump of steam hammers and the heat and smoke of the ironworks beckoned.

*　　*　　*

Jenny Norton caught sight of the policemen as they passed through the building and held her breath. Hopefully she would be away from this place soon and living in comfort, never having to work for the likes of Dunwoody again. The tension was unbearable yet she was determined that no one should know her secret.

It was fortunate for Jenny that Dunwoody had left the building to accompany the policemen, for a few seconds later a servant came by looking for him.

'There has been an envelope delivered just this second, Miss Norton. I should really pass it through Mr Dunwoody but as it is addressed to you and he isn't here I suppose he wouldn't mind me giving it to you directly.'

'You are right. I am sure he wouldn't object,' lied Jenny. Lizzie Hawkins found it hard to restrain from making a comment.

The servant passed over the envelope and Jenny looked at the front, recognising what this second message of the day might contain. She went to the corner of the room this time, tearing the envelope open with her fingers, and read the contents. Her heartbeat sounded loud in her ears as she took in the implications.

'What is it?' asked Lizzie.

Jenny put the note back into the torn envelope and pushed it inside her blouse before returning to sit at her desk.

Once more her face was like marble sculpture, beautiful but impassive.

'Nothing,' she replied.

*　*　*

'Jones!' shouted Dunwoody into the cast iron foundry workshop where the clanking of metal and hiss of the furnace made it difficult to be heard from across the room.

'Yes, Mr Dunwoody,' answered two men at once.

'Either of you, I don't care which. Just tell me where Ross is.'

'He hasn't turned up,' answered one of the men called Jones. 'Not sight nor sound.' 'No idea why he isn't here,' added the other Jones.

Dunwoody turned to Chard. 'Sorry, Inspector, you had best try his home address. Follow me back to the main building and I'll get it for you.'

'Damn!' cursed the inspector as Dunwoody led the way back into Taff Vale House.

*　*　*

The policemen and Mr Dunwoody had been talking loudly as they returned from the yard. They went into Dunwoody's office and could easily be overheard.

Lizzie noticed the look of relief on Jenny's face when it became clear that they were going to leave and it was a matter of concern for her, as her friend had not seemed quite herself. It was soon after the policemen departed that Jenny excused herself and left the room, leaving Lizzie on her own. Curiosity aroused to a level that she could no longer control, Lizzie moved across to Jenny's desk and whilst listening carefully for her friend's return, she carefully opened Jenny's desk drawer and took out the mysterious first envelope. Heart beating like a drum, she slipped out the enclosed note and read it as quickly as she could before putting it back in the envelope and carefully returning it to the drawer which she closed quietly. Her mind was in turmoil for she wanted to ask Jenny about the contents but couldn't say anything without revealing that she had looked at her friend's personal correspondence. A moment later Jenny returned but seemed too wrapped up in her own thoughts to notice Lizzie's flushed appearance. It was Dunwoody that noticed the change in the blonde clerk's mood later that afternoon.

'Miss Hawkins, please note on the payroll records that our employee Ross failed to turn up today and frankly is unlikely to remain working here at all. The policemen that came here want to question him and he is likely to be the murderer they are after. Miss Hawkins, are you listening? You don't seem quite yourself? Is there anything wrong?'

Lizzie made to say something but paused and then replied. 'No, Mr Dunwoody. There is nothing wrong at all.'

*   *   *

Park Street was relatively quiet when Inspector Chard and Constable Preece arrived outside Jack Ross's small terraced house. All of the houses in Park Street were in shade as the retaining wall of the railway on the opposite side of the narrow road loomed above them. There was a hansom cab parked outside the entrance to the small Treforest railway station waiting for fares and a cart was parked outside the ironmonger's shop further up the street, but no other vehicles. A couple of women, shawls around their shoulders despite the pleasant weather, stood gossiping outside the nearby grocery shop and a young errand boy rushed along the far pavement, message in hand, no doubt being paid an extra penny for the speed of his delivery.

'Do you see anything inside?' asked Chard as Preece peered through the front window.

'Not a sign of movement inside,' answered the constable who then brought his fist down to hammer three times on the front door. There was no response.

'We know he lied to us before and he is connected to two murder victims. Kick it in,' commanded Chard.

Preece was not of the physical stature of his colleagues at the station and it took four attempts to splinter the door and shatter the lock. Cautiously, the constable entered first, drawing his truncheon as he did so. The front room was sparsely furnished, a table, two chairs and a box with a cloth over it being the sum total of items present. The small kitchen at the back seemed to have been the main room of habitation with pots and pans stacked on shelves, a comfortable chair, a low table on which rested a two-day-old newspaper and a pile of dirty crockery in the sink. The inspector tapped Preece on the shoulder and pointed upwards.

'Mr Ross, if you are in here I advise you to come down now,' shouted Chard up the small staircase. No reply came. 'On you go, Constable. I'll be right behind you.'

The staircase creaked as Preece slowly made his way upwards, his truncheon held firmly in his right hand. Chard waited a moment then followed his constable, fairly confident that they would find nothing in the bedroom. The inspector was correct in his assumption for both the bedroom and the small ante-room were unoccupied. The bedclothes lay ruffled on the bed, the single wardrobe had a few clothes in it, and there was a wooden chest with additional clothing but noticeably there were no personal items at all.

'Our bird has flown, Constable,' grunted Chard.

'The superintendent won't be happy, sir.'

'You needn't state the obvious, Constable,' admonished the inspector, scratching his sideburns. 'I am not going to go back empty-handed, so there's only one thing for it. We'll go after that dandy bugger, Mr Dorsett.'

So, after leaving the small house and pulling the front door back into place as much as possible, the policemen returned to their vehicle and climbed back on board. Constable Preece picked up the reins and with a slight tap of the whip they set off on the short journey to Forest House where, at this late time in the afternoon, they hoped to find their quarry.

Their journey only took ten minutes and as soon as they arrived the inspector took no time in jumping down off the van, leaving Constable Preece to tend to the horses.

'I'm standing no nonsense off that haughty bastard of a servant this time,' he muttered to himself as he marched to the door absent-mindedly brushing down his uniform as he went.

Chard rang the bell and as anticipated it was answered by the same manservant as the previous time he had called.

'Yes sir?'

'Take me to Mr Dorsett right now.'

'I am afraid not, sir,' answered the servant calmly.

'Do you not understand that I am here on police business?' demanded Chard.

'Of course sir,' came the obsequious smile. 'I can tell from the uniform.'

'Then take me to Mr Dorsett.'

'Before we continue, sir, would you mind moving your vehicle to the rear of the building? Having a van marked 'Police' outside my master's house is rather unseemly.'

'I don't give a damn. I want to see Mr Dorsett immediately.'

'He isn't here, sir,' answered the manservant politely, clearly enjoying the inspector's growing rage.

'Then where is he? Castle House? The Forest Iron & Steel Works? Where? You had better give me a straight answer or I'll have you down the station for wasting police time.'

'Oh perish the thought, sir,' he answered quite unperturbed. 'He is at Abcote House.'

'Where?'

'Abcote House, near Glasbury-on-Wye. He left this morning in quite a rush. It was most unexpected.'

'When is he expected back?'

'That I must admit is rather strange, sir. He said that he would not be returning.'

*   *   *

It had been a very stony silence as Inspector Chard and Constable Preece made their way back to the station, for other than advising the constable that Dorsett had also disappeared, Chard said not a word.

'I assume that the superintendent has gone by now, Sergeant.' asked Chard as he marched purposefully into the station.

'Yes sir,' replied Sergeant Humphreys. 'Until Monday. I was just about to go off shift myself, if that's alright sir?'

Chard paused whilst he remembered the rota he had worked out to cover for their temporary lack of a third sergeant. 'Yes, I've got Constable Jackson down to cover desk duties for tonight and Sergeant Morris is on duty tomorrow. Just hang on a little while until Jackson turns up and then tell him that he is only to contact me at my rooms if there is an emergency. I will be busy packing tonight and will be out of contact tomorrow, returning to duty on Monday.'

The inspector turned to Preece and spoke to him for the first time since leaving Forest House. 'I am sure that nothing much is likely to happen over the next couple of nights. Evans and Ross have probably left the area by now so it will be a while before we can get hold of them. Just to be on the safe side, though, I would rather have you here to keep an eye on things. I'll change the rota so that you get tomorrow night's shift with Sergeant Morris because if Evans is still around then maybe a Saturday night might be the time to get a lead on him.'

'Where are you going then, sir?'

'Off on the trail of Mr Dorsett. I want to know why, the morning after the murder of Grimes, he has decided to dash off so suddenly.' Chard turned his attention to the desk sergeant.

'Humphreys, another thing, find me a spare set of handcuffs.'

'Right you are, sir,' he replied with his toothless grin.

Chard walked through to his office and opened the top right drawer of his desk. Extracting a tin box he emptied the contents until he found the spare key to the armoury cupboard. Constable Preece had followed him into the room looking concerned.

'Are you sure it's wise to go after Dorsett on your own, sir? I mean if he is the killer you could be placing yourself in considerable danger.'

The inspector ignored the comment and walked past his constable who then followed behind as Chard went to the armoury cupboard, unlocked it and selected a .455 Webley and a dozen cartridges.

'I shall be completely fine, Constable.' There was a cough from the sergeant's desk. 'Ah, the cuffs. Thank you, Sergeant.'

Preece made another attempt to try and persuade the inspector not to go alone but was rebuffed.

'Get yourself home, Preece, and be ready for tomorrow night, just in case.'

With that final command Chard left the station heading for his rooms at the New Inn, some busy packing and an early night.

CHAPTER TWENTY-FIVE

That evening Lizzie Hawkins paced up and down in the parlour of the comfortably furnished home where she lived alone. She really could not decide what to do. Her feelings for Jenny Norton were overwhelmingly strong. Tall, dark and statuesque as well as being beautiful and clever, she was everything that Lizzie would like to be. Yet there was the note, that shocking note that read, 'Meet me at midnight outside the vestry at St Mary's. The truth can't be hidden. I love you, Jack.' Surely Jack and Jenny weren't lovers? Jenny had never mentioned any interest in men. Was that what the phrase, 'The truth can't be hidden' meant? Then there was that second note. If only Jenny hadn't kept that with her. Lizzie had managed to stop herself saying anything to Mr Dunwoody even though he clearly recognised that there was something wrong. Lizzie stopped pacing for a moment and fidgeted with her necklace as she considered her options. She could tell someone about the note. After all, Jack Ross was wanted by the police and Jenny could be putting herself in trouble by aiding a fugitive. Her silence about the note might mean that Jenny was already in trouble with the police. She could of course do nothing at all, but then could end up in trouble with the police herself if it became known that she had seen the note and done nothing. Also what if Jenny and Jack ran away together? The garbled thoughts ran quickly through Lizzie's brain as she tried to make sense of it.

Lizzie resumed her pacing across the carpet. What if Jack didn't really love Jenny and it was just a ruse to entice her somewhere lonely so he could kill her? The police suspected him of murder and surely that would make sense? Yes, the best thing would be to report it to the police that Jenny was being drawn into this against her will and was in danger. That way Lizzie would be saving her life and Jenny would be ever so grateful to her when she realised how close to peril she had been.

Lizzie gave a sigh of relief as she settled on her course of action and walking into the hallway she grabbed her coat and set off for the police station.

✻　　✻　　✻

Inspector Chard entered the Ivor Arms and looked anxiously for the one person he hoped to see there. Although the original intention had been to pack for a train journey as soon as he had got back to his rooms, several problems had occurred to him. Having consulted his Bradshaw's Railway Guide, Chard realised that the quickest way to get to his destination by train would involve travelling from Pontypridd to Cardiff, then changing for a train to Hereford, followed by a Midland Railway train in the direction of Hay-on-Wye, and getting a connection at Three Cocks junction for Glasbury. On arrival there the inspector would have to get a cab to Abcote Hall and persuade the driver to wait for however long it took to confront Dorsett. The whole journey there and back, including the time at Abcote Hall, would certainly take longer than a day and would necessitate an overnight stay. Further problems would arise if Dorsett had to be taken into custody and the cab driver refused to transport a felon. Additionally Chard did not want to involve the local constabulary, particularly if Dorsett had influence with the local magistrates and travelling on a train in uniform would be bound to draw attention. Fortunately an alternative option sprang to mind.

'I suppose you'll be wanting a drink,' grunted Gwyn the barman.

'Not tonight, thank you,' replied the inspector, walking straight past to where Will Horses was sipping a beer.

'Will, I need to talk to you.'

'*Shwmae*, Mr Chard,' responded Will.

'Are you and your cab fully employed this weekend, Will?'

'Saturday has me busy all day picking up fares here and there but Sundays are quiet.'

'How would you feel about me hiring you and your cab to go up to Glasbury-on-Wye tomorrow?'

Will looked intrigued but shook his head. 'The horse can't do there and back in a day. He needs looking after and it's my livelihood.'

'I'll hire you for the Sunday as well and cover accommodation. Hopefully I'll get reimbursed by the station, but if not I'll cover the cost myself.'

'It must be important and I won't refuse the money,' agreed Will, holding out his hand. 'I won't overcharge you though, it'll be a fair price,' he added.

Chard took the hand and shook it to seal the agreement. 'I would stay for a drink with you but I have to pack. Pick me up at eight in the morning outside the New Inn.'

'Then I'll be off after this one myself. Tomorrow will be a long day.'

'Hopefully it will be an eventful one as well,' added Chard as he turned and left.

*　　*　　*

Constable Jackson stood behind Sergeant Humphreys' high desk at the entrance to the police station and cursed Inspector Chard. Another turn on the night shift, albeit indoors. At least he was then off until the Monday morning, even though that had a drawback as he was allocated a very early start.

Most of the other officers were out walking their beats apart from Constables Scudamore and Morgan, both of whom Jackson considered to be too self-righteous, never inclined to take short cuts or stretch the law to their benefit. He knew he wasn't popular with them or any of his other colleagues but that was their lookout. Against regulations he had fetched a hip flask of whisky into the station and he patted the bulge it made inside his uniform jacket as he anticipated drinking the warming liquid once he was confident that Scudamore and Morgan were fully occupied.

His anticipation was interrupted by a loud bang as Constable Matthews came in from his beat holding a struggling, scrawny individual by the scruff of the neck.

'One for the drunk cell, Jackson. Name is Meredith. Threatening behaviour with an offensive weapon.'

Matthews tossed a six-inch knife on the desk and Jackson gave him a key for the cell in return before opening the station ledger and making the entry.

'Tell him that if he starts making a racket I'll pay him a visit with my fists,' said Jackson loudly as Matthews disappeared towards the cells with his inebriated burden.

'Excuse me,' came a timid voice from someone who had entered whilst the policemen had been distracted.

Jackson looked around to see a short blond-haired woman standing in the doorway. She wore a long coat but no hat or bonnet and had a worried expression on her face.

'Well, well. Who do we have here?' asked Jackson, leering.

'My name is Miss Hawkins and I have a friend who is in trouble.'

'If she looks like you, darling, then I am not surprised.'

Lizzie felt the anger rise within. 'Don't you dare talk to me like that, Constable, or I will take your number and report you to your inspector. Men like you disgust me.'

'There's no need to get like that, woman. What is it that you want anyway? If you are just here to waste my time then you can clear off.'

Lizzie was on the point of turning around and going home but concern for her friend overrode her instinct to leave.

'I understand that you are looking for a man called Jack Ross.'

Jackson stared at her as his expression changed from one of hostility to one of interest. 'Yes we are,' he confirmed.

'I happen to know that he has sent a note luring my innocent friend to meet him tonight.'

'Where is this note? Show it to me.'

'I don't have it. I was only able to take a quick look at it. I think my friend is in danger.'

'What did the note say, exactly?'

'As I remember, it said, 'Meet me at midnight by the vestry of St Mary's, Jack,' answered Lizzie, being careful not to mention any part of the note that might make it sound that her friend was complicit with the arrangement.

'How do you know that was from Jack Ross, and why would he be writing to your friend?' asked Jackson suspiciously.

'Because they are neighbours and both work at the ironworks. Also my friend doesn't know anyone else called Jack who would write to her.'

'How do you know that?'

'Because we are very close and she has no secrets from me.'

'If she has no secrets from you then how come you had to sneak a look at this note then?' commented Jackson snidely.

Lizzie blushed with embarrassment, unable to reply.

'Alright, what is your friend's name?' continued the policeman. 'You haven't mentioned it so far.'

'Jenny Norton, but she has done nothing wrong.'

'If she is innocent she wouldn't be agreeing to meet a man

on her own at midnight,' responded the constable with as much sarcasm as he could muster. 'Nevertheless we will do something about this, so go home now, please, and leave the rest to us.

'Very well, but remember that no harm is to befall my friend,' warned Lizzie as she turned and left.

Jackson watched the woman leave and then started to muse about what advantage could be gained from the information he had been given. There was no sergeant on duty due to there being a staff shortage and, for something as important as this, he should send one of the other constables down to the New Inn to wake up the inspector. Then Chard would organise the arrest and get all the credit. However, the inspector had been very insistent that he wasn't to be interrupted unless it was something very urgent and it could be argued that a bit of hearsay from a woman walking in off the street didn't fall into that category.

'I'll catch the bastard myself,' muttered Jackson under his breath.

Just then, having locked the drunk away, Matthews was on his way back to duty patrolling the town centre.

'Busy up the Tumble tonight, Matthews?'

'Very. And not pleasant,' grunted the normally cheerful constable.

'As I am acting desk sergeant as it were, what if I was to say that you could stay here in the warm for a bit and have a nice cup of tea?'

Matthews was taken aback by this friendly manner coming from Jackson and eyed him suspiciously. 'What's the catch?'

'No catch at all. I just need you to watch the desk for a couple of hours whilst I go out. I've had a message that one of my informants has got something important to tell me,' he lied. 'Just to prove it's official business, I'm going to get Morgan to come with me.'

Matthews paused and thought about the comparative merits of a couple of hours patrolling the Tumble or staying in the station drinking tea. 'Fair enough,' he decided.

Jackson gave a cunning smile and went to get Morgan who after an argument, agreed to go along.

* * *

It was ten minutes to midnight and Jenny Norton walked along a deserted Park Street that was lit every fifty paces by a gas lamp. Her footsteps echoed as she made her way down towards Taff Vale House, then across the Machine Bridge where no gaslight fell and below which the River Taff flowed on its way to the weir. Onwards she hurried, to the Cardiff to Merthyr Road, which ran over the small hump-backed bridge above the canal close to the Llanbradach Arms, causing her to shiver at the thought of the murder committed beneath. By now the whole of Treforest knew of the terrible event, as the news spread as soon as people came home from work that day. There was a well-positioned gaslight on the corner of Cemetery Road, lighting up the shuttered windows of a small shop, but beyond it there was darkness. Rather than turning right towards the cemetery, Jenny walked uphill towards the tower of St Mary's, the oldest church in the Pontypridd area, which could be made out in the fleeting moonlight. She came to the large iron gates which were closed but unlocked and gave them a push. There was a terrible creak as they opened, which sounded unnaturally loud to Jenny's ears, and she glanced behind to check no one was following her. It felt strange walking up the steep path through the graveyard towards the church. As a Catholic, Jenny had never been in the grounds of this Anglican church before and was unfamiliar with the position and shapes of some of the grander gravestones and memorials that edged the path. They became strange, threatening shapes in her imagination and the light night breeze that ruffled the leaves of the trees that edged the graveyard added to the eerie atmosphere. Something scuttled through nearby undergrowth and Jenny froze, her hand resting over her heart. After taking a moment to regain her composure she continued slowly up the path, cautious not to stumble in the dark. The path turned to the right and Jenny could see the steps and great wooden door of the church looming above. Unfortunately she had no idea where the vestry was located so she stood for a moment not knowing whether to walk to the right or the left of the main body of the church. Jenny reasoned that the logical place for a clandestine meeting would be as far away from the road as possible, so walked around to the left of the building.

'Jenny, over here,' came a whisper.

The sound startled the young woman, who stumbled and was only saved from falling by reaching out a hand that luckily fell against a gravestone, which allowed her to steady herself.

'Jack? What is this all about? I fear I know what it is from what you wrote in your note but please tell me.'

'Jenny, there is so much I want to say and to ask you,' answered Jack, coming forward and resting his arms on Jenny's shoulders. 'The only reason I have stayed here for so long is you. Every day I can think of nothing else but you and I have never had the courage to talk to you like this. I have things to ask of you and things that I must confess ...'

There was a pause that seemed to last an eternity, but no sooner did Jack start to form his next words in his mouth than there was the sound of heavy boots crunching on gravel. Both Jack and Jenny jumped in alarm as a shape could just be made out in the darkness from the direction that Jenny had just come.

'Right then, you little bastard. I am Constable Jackson and you are under arrest. I do hope you are not going to come quietly,' came a threatening voice.

Jack and Jenny were trapped between the wall of the church building on their left and the churchyard wall just a few feet to their right. The vestry covered any escape behind them and Jack already knew that the door was locked.

'I haven't done anything,' argued Jack.

'Then why have you lured this young lady here at midnight? You murdered that man down by the canal and you were going to do for her next,' accused Jackson.

Jack looked pleadingly at Jenny though she could barely see his face, 'No that's not true, you don't understand …'

'I didn't know he was following me, honestly Jack,' protested Jenny.

Jack glanced at the holdall containing his possessions which lay nearby and then made his decision. Leaving the bag where it lay, he suddenly ran head down at the constable. Jackson gave a callous laugh as he saw what was being attempted and casually stepping to the side out of the way of the Italian's charge, he brought his truncheon down hard on his shoulder. Jack gave a yelp of pain and crashed to the ground. In a moment Constable Jackson had him handcuffed and had shouted for Constable Morgan who had been sent to cover the main gate in case Jack had evaded capture by the vestry.

'We came in by the lychgate at the back of the churchyard,' explained Jackson to Jenny. 'You've been a stupid little girl, so sod off home. We've got what we want,' he added, hauling Jack roughly to his feet.

'Look what I've found,' proclaimed Constable Morgan as he picked up Jack's holdall.

'Good. Fetch it with us,' ordered Jackson.

The two policemen and their prize disappeared into the darkness, leaving an emotionally shattered Jenny alone in the graveyard wondering what to do next.

CHAPTER TWENTY-SIX

When Inspector Chard walked out of the New Inn the following morning, oblivious to the arrest of Jack Ross, he was pleased to find that Will was true to his word and an immaculately maintained hansom cab was waiting for him at the appointed time.

'Good morning, Mr Chard,' greeted Will, who stood stroking the lean, powerfully-muscled black stallion that was harnessed to the cab. He wore a long coachman's coat with a slightly battered top hat and leather boots.

'Good morning, Will,' answered Chard. 'What's your real surname by the way?'

'Owens, Mr Chard, but I'm happy enough with my nickname.'

Chard had considered travelling in civilian clothes but reasoned that it might be more beneficial to wear his uniform, particularly if there were problems getting accommodation. In his right hand the inspector also carried the cane that Dorsett had left behind in the Victoria on the night of the raid. 'Right, let's be on our way,' he called as he threw his case inside before climbing into the cab.

Will gave his horse a final pat before going to the rear of the vehicle and climbing up to the driver's seat. With a slight shake of the reins the hansom set off at a gentle pace heading north.

The first stage of the journey was uneventful as they made their way up the Merthyr Vale until they reached the heavily industrialised town itself. There were several grand buildings but on the outskirts Chard could see evidence of dire poverty. Poor overcrowded housing, overflowing sewers, shoeless waifs and crippled beggars were all signs of a society where the drive for profit had ridden roughshod over the lower classes.

Will's horse needed rest and feed but they carried on through the town until they reached a coaching inn on the other side, below the Cantref reservoir.

'Merlin will need a good rest now, Mr Chard, before we take on the hardest part of the journey. It will be hard going for him until we are over the Beacons but I reckon we can make Brecon town itself for our next stop if we take it easy.'

The customers of the inn thought it peculiar that a uniformed police inspector was happy to share a table with a mere coachman but the two men ignored their stares and enjoyed a hearty lamb stew with chunks of fresh bread whilst the horse, Merlin, was fed and watered by the inn's stable boy.

Feeling fully refreshed they set off on the second and most demanding part of the journey as the road led upwards into the Brecon Beacons. Chard was in immeasurable good spirits as they travelled along in bright sunshine under a clear blue sky. The waters of the Cantref reservoir, which had only been completed nine years previously in order to supply Cardiff with fresh water, rippled with the gentle breeze that came down the valley. Then, not much further ahead, a complete change of environment as there was a vista of dust and heavy industry completely incongruous with the natural surroundings. It had been decided that the Cantref reservoir was not sufficient so the construction of the Beacons reservoir was now underway, although it was not due to be completed for another two years. The inspector was pleased when they left the construction site behind them and were able to return to the wild scenery of the higher hills. Merlin was struggling now, not being used to such a gradient for a continuous period and soon after getting a glimpse of Pen-y-Fan, the highest point of the Beacons, Will pulled up on the reins for an unscheduled stop.

'Sorry, Mr Chard, but I suggest you get out and stretch your legs for a bit. Poor old Merlin is knackered.'

Chard got out, taking Dorsett's cane with him. He rather liked the feel of it in his hands and he did admire the way it was capped with the heavy silver leopard's head. Using it to support himself across the rough ground away from the road, Chard walked a little while until he came across a stream. Bending down he scooped a handful of cold water and enjoyed the refreshing shock of rubbing it into his face.

'How is the horse doing?' asked Chard on returning to the hansom.

'Merlin's alright now he has had a breather. Not far to the head of the pass and then its downhill to Brecon,' answered Will climbing back to his driving seat.

Keeping up a steady pace, they soon reached the highest point of their journey, which revealed exceptional views of the countryside on the other side of the pass. Merlin, appreciating the change in gradient, sped up and had the travellers pulling into the yard of a coaching inn at Brecon town just in time for luncheon. Once again Chard shared a table with Will and they dined heartily on a heavy meal of steak pie, peas and new potatoes, washed down with a pint of ale.

Almost reluctantly, for their bodies felt more inclined to lie down and rest, the two men resumed their journey, which now at least would no longer involve steep hills for their steed. Moving onward they came, after some time, to the little village of Three Cocks, which had a small railway junction and an inn where Chard considered that they might spend the night after their visit to Abcote Hall. Here they asked for directions to Glasbury-on-Wye as it was not a great distance away. Chard also assumed that the locals would be familiar with Abcote Hall's location, which proved to be the case. Soon they were crossing the wide but shallow River Wye on a small bridge before turning onto a narrow road leading deeper into the countryside where they finally reached their destination.

Abcote Hall was surrounded by a large boundary wall with the entrance to the grounds guarded by large ornamental wrought iron gates, alongside which stood a stone gatehouse. Will pulled on the reins and it was only a few moments later that a stocky man in a tweed jacket came out and asked them their business. Satisfied with Chard's uniformed appearance, backed by his warrant card, the gatekeeper opened the gates and let the carriage through, advising them to drive to the left of the main building where their horse could be fed and watered in the mews. After thanking the man for his advice they drove on along a well-maintained roadway through extensive grounds, the grass of which had evidently been kept low by a large flock of sheep which could be seen happily chewing and bleating off to their left. In the distance to the right Chard could also make out, beyond a fence, a herd of deer with a sharp-eared buck standing stock still, his head turned in their direction.

The inspector was unimpressed when the Hall itself came into view. Large and imposing it might be, but it looked squat, ugly and without any architectural merit.

Will dropped Chard off close to the front of the building before carrying on around to the mews.

Chard approached the main entrance to the Hall, feeling glad of his decision to wear his uniform. The last thing he wanted now was to be treated dismissively by another bloody awkward servant who was too big for their boots, especially after such a long journey. Indeed those fears seemed to be justified when he was met at the door by a tall, gaunt manservant, very sombrely dressed, who exuded a patronising air even before he spoke.

'Good afternoon, sir. The master had not informed us

that we were to expect a visitor. May I ask if sir has an appointment?'

There was something about the tone of the servant's voice that just seemed to light a fuse within the inspector's head. He had become fed up with being lied to by suspects, talked down to by servants and generally feeling continually on the back foot. Chard had decided he was not having any of it.

'No, I don't have a bloody appointment and I don't need one. Here is my warrant card,' snarled the inspector extracting it from his jacket pocket, 'and I want to know where Mr James Dorsett is right now.' Chard pointed threateningly at the manservant. 'Before you say one word, let me warn you that any obfuscation on your part will lead me to lay a charge of obstruction. So where is he?

Strangely the man smiled in a manner almost predatory. 'That path, two hundred yards, by the river', came the succinct reply with a sarcastic 'sir,' added on for good measure.

Chard gave an accepting grunt and, taking the leopard headed cane with him, set off down the indicated path which led around the other side of the building and on into the grounds beyond a stand of trees. Once past the trees Chard came across a small wooden bridge carved and painted in Chinese fashion which crossed a tributary of the Wye that ran through Lord Abcote's land. Looking from the bridge to his right Chard spotted what appeared to be his quarry. Wearing waders and in the water up to his knees was indeed James Dorsett. In his hand he carried a split cane fishing rod and as the inspector watched, he drew back his arm causing the silken line to unfurl above and behind him. Smoothly his arm moved forward only to stop suddenly, causing the line to shoot forward across the water and then halt in mid-air. Back came the arm once more to repeat the action and when Dorsett finally released his grip on the forward motion his cast was propelled even further to land the artificial fly at its tip delicately on the water. Chard could not help but admire the skill and elegance of Dorsett's casting action and he continued to observe quietly as the fly floated for a few seconds on the surface of the water, flowing gently downstream. In a sudden violent explosion of action there was a disturbance on the water, the fishing line went tight and the rod bent savagely. Dorsett raised his right arm high and worked with the spare line in his left hand to control the tension being exerted by the trout which now broke the water and leapt a foot into the air before racing away from the river bank, taking more line with it. Now it had to be given more time to tire itself but without losing the tension on the line. As the inspector started to walk off the bridge down towards the fisherman, Dorsett kept the line tight whilst moving slowly back towards the bank where he had left his net. Gradually the fish began to tire and soon it could be seen coming back to the surface, gradually losing its fight against the pull of the line. Still unaware of his audience, Dorsett netted the fish, extracted the hook and having extracted a small wooden club from within his clothing, he brought it down forcefully on the head of the trout which jerked spasmodically before stiffening.

'Is that what it was like when you killed Blake and Grimes?' asked Chard, who had stepped silently to within a few feet.

'Inspector Chard, Good Lord! What are you doing here?' came the response as Dorsett turned in surprise, still with the short club in his hand.

Chard was surprised that the man spoke not in shock and fear, but almost in delight as if the inspector had walked in as a surprise guest at a birthday party.

'What was it you said about people being killed? Blake I understand, but Grimes? Has Jabez Grimes been killed?'

'I assumed you would be in a position to know. After all he

was killed Thursday night and you decided to vanish from the scene yesterday.'

Dorsett, paused and then his attractive androgynous face started to laugh.

'So you thought it was me and have come all this way,' he gave another laugh, holding his side. 'Oh, it really is too much, Inspector.'

Chard started to get angry at being the source of the amusement. 'I think you forgot this,' he snapped, throwing the cane at Dorsett's feet.

'Oh good, so pleased that you have come all this way just to give it to me. I had missed it.' The laugh had least subsided to an almost childish giggle.

'Do you deny leaving it in the back room of the Victoria?'

'Not in the least, Inspector,' came the reply, the amusement now contained. 'I am certainly guilty of forgetfulness and undue haste.'

'What were you doing there?'

'Well, just to put your mind at ease, I hadn't been in that rather disgusting brothel in the adjoining room.'

'I assumed you had not.'

'I will admit that I was playing cards with a few friends, but I obviously will not say that I was playing for coin. Unless of course you can prove otherwise?'

Chard declined to respond as indeed he had no actual evidence.

'I also wish to apologise to you, Inspector.'

'Would that be in respect of your relationship with Blake?'

As they spoke Dorsett casually sat on the river bank and started to remove his waders.

'Yes, I had fallen behind with some, shall we say 'investment losses' and at that time Mr Blake was a go-between, until he disappeared. Not a pleasant fellow. Did you see his replacement by the way?'

'You mean Evans.'

'Yes. Scarred face. It was Blake that did that to him, or so I hear. Hit him with a belt buckle.'

'You can't have enjoyed being chased by people like Blake.'

Dorsett, having removed the waders, now put on a pair of shoes and regained his feet.

'Actually, in a way I did. It felt exciting at times and a break from the normal responsible life that my family want me to lead. I was never really in danger of not being able to pay but, sometimes, if my father had been late paying my allowance, then I would have to temporarily get loans against my commercial investments which can take a while to turn into actual cash.'

'So why involve yourself with a parasite like Grimes and his sordid little gambling club in a place like Pontypridd? You could gamble openly and freely in one of the established clubs in any of the big cities?'

Again an amused laugh came from the young man. 'For the very reason that it is a sordid little club. Let us be frank, Inspector, though if you arrest me for illegal gambling I will deny what I am about to say. I do like to play cards, but to do so openly as a member of a club would have met with the disapproval of my father and the rest of the family, risking him changing his will and disinheriting me. Also, I liked the thrill of being in that environment. I was secretly cocking a snook at my family whilst fooling that arse Grimes that he had power over me, which of course he never did. I used to pretend that I was struggling with debt when I never really was and on occasion he did run a fair game which was often to the detriment of the other gamblers, apart from that young Italian fellow.'

'You mean Ross?'

'Yes, he was good. Really good. He obviously had been caught up in Grimes' web at some stage for he owed him money, so had to keep turning up, but he got a lot back too off the other gamblers. I don't know why he didn't just up and leave town and start somewhere else,' explained the young man who had now picked up his trout, put it in a canvas bag and handed it to the inspector. 'Take this, will you, whilst I carry the rest of my equipment and we'll take it to the Hall. We can give it to cook for supper, though she'll probably put poison in it.'

Chard had a good mind to tell Dorsett where to put his trout but as the suspect was being so open and indeed affable, he agreed to comply taking both the bag and picking up the cane that he had thrown down.

'Is your cook that bad?'

'No, she's excellent, but the staff all hate me. I think you'll find out why soon enough.'

As they walked back to the Hall thoughts whirled in the inspector's mind. If Dorsett was never really in debt then what would the motive be for killing Blake and Grimes?

'How did you travel here, Inspector? It can be quite a journey.'

'I hired a hansom cab. My driver took it around to the mews.'

'The police force must pay better than I imagined.'

'Out of my own funds, actually. I am fortunate to be acquainted with the driver. I thought it would be more discreet to take you into custody as handcuffs tend to draw attention on a train.'

Again the laugh which just served to irritate the inspector. 'You really are a card. I am inclined to let you take me in just for the fun of the scandal but I have other plans which will become clear in due course.' Dorsett stopped for a moment, turned to Chard and gave him a conspiratorial wink.

'Oh, by the way, I am afraid that you have failed so far to deduce my real dark secret, the one sin that my father would never forgive if he had known.'

'Do enlighten me,' said Chard, thinking that perhaps he might have an idea.

Dorsett laughed again, leaving Chard wondering why the man seemed so unnaturally happy.

'It can wait,' teased the young man as they walked up the steps to the Hall door which was opened by the same humourless individual that had greeted the inspector.

'Ah, Bennett, put my equipment away and give the contents of the bag that the inspector is holding to Cook with my compliments. Then make sure that the inspector's driver is made welcome in the servants' quarters.'

The servant grimaced, 'Yes, my lord,' before carrying out the instructions with clear ill humour.

The entrance hall had a grim, depressing feel to it and things were not improved when they entered a large drawing room which was darkened by black drapes across the windows.

'I notice that he called you "my lord".'

'Yes, Inspector, my father has passed on to the other side. I am the new Lord Abcote,' Dorsett announced triumphantly. 'He died rather suddenly.' There was a pregnant pause and the new lord saw the expression on Chard's face. 'Don't worry, Inspector, I have many faults but patricide is not one of them. It happened on Thursday when I was still in Pontypridd and it is the reason why I left so quickly yesterday. All of this is ...' Dorsett spun around, his arms indicating the extent of his wealth, '... mine. Not that I give a damn about this ruin, mind. I intend to sell it all off and the decrepit staff with it.'

'My condolences on your loss, my lord,' offered Chard with a hint of sarcasm.

'Well, I hated the old bugger and he hated me. His funeral is to be a quick one at my insistence. Monday, in fact, so if you do arrest me then at least I'll have an excuse not to be present. However, let us talk about this after we've dined. If you go through those doors and up the staircase to the second door on the right you'll find a guest room where you can refresh yourself after your journey. Bennett will call you in due course and fetch you to the dining hall.'

Chard had to admit to himself that he was tired after the journey and needed a rest. He also needed to get away from Dorsett for a little while in order to reflect on what had been said. 'Very well, my lord,' he agreed.

'You can drop the honorific, Inspector, I am not used to it myself yet, though I soon will be,' added Dorsett as Chard walked away.

* * *

At the police station in Pontypridd Sergeant Morris was giving final instructions to his men before they went out in the town for their Saturday night beat.

'Very well, men, you are aware that this is not an ordinary Saturday night for us. We have a main objective and that is catching the man Evans. He will be easy to recognise for he is an ugly bastard.'

'How does that make it easy, Sergeant? There are hundreds of them,' joked Constable Matthews.

'Yes, and you are one of them, Matthews,' retorted the sergeant. 'Now in all seriousness, there is a danger that he might be armed but the inspector has taken the only pistol from the armoury and I don't want to issue rifles because we don't want to alarm the general populace. If any of you spot him then blow your whistle and the nearest man will do likewise and come running. The chances are that Evans will try and run rather than fight, but if he does pull out a firearm then just keep your distance and watch where he goes. Is that understood?'

'Yes, Sergeant,' came the uniform response.

'Good, now we will spread out through Ponty, with every man within whistle range of another. Jones takes the Queens area by the canal basin; Evans the Maltsters, the bridge and if you keep your ears open you should still be in range to cover Fairfield. Matthews, you can take Penuel Square and Gas Lane; Jenkins Taff Street from Penuel to the Butchers Arms. Davies, you'll have from the Butchers to the Clarence. I will cover the Tumble with Constable Preece and finally Scudamore can do the Graig up as far as the workhouse. Is that clear?'

There was a unanimous 'Yes, Sergeant' before the men all broke off to get ready to patrol their assigned beats.

Preece waited until the other constables had dispersed before approaching his senior. 'I have an idea, Sergeant.'

'Well go ahead, Preece, what is it?'

'Either Evans has killed Grimes and stolen enough money from him to have fled or he is innocent of that crime and now without funds having lost his employer.'

'He might still have killed Blake, though, even if he didn't kill Grimes.'

'Either way, if he is still in the area then he would be trying to lie low during daylight hours but even then he would have to eat. So I've been trying to think where would a big hard lump of a man find employment at night where he would also have access to food?'

'Pubs are the first thing that come to mind,' suggested the

sergeant, 'but then there would be the risk of being spotted by members of the public.'

'Exactly, and that is the reason why he can't just start robbing people. Firstly, we would be alerted to his approximate whereabouts because his victims would easily recognise him and reports would be flooding in. Secondly, if he just filched money somehow without being seen, he would still need to go somewhere to obtain food and risk being spotted.'

'Go on, Preece, you've clearly thought this through.'

'It would have to be some kind of employment where workers are hard to find, so get taken on with no questions asked and where the public generally have no inclination to go. That would suggest something like the coal mines, though underground work would not suit such a big man and, again, there was the need to easily obtain food,' reasoned Preece.

'So what have you come up with?'

'There is only one place that fits the bill, Sergeant, and I understand it even has a night shift.'

'Well then, Constable. Lead the way.'

CHAPTER TWENTY-SEVEN

It was some time before Bennett came to inform Chard that Lord Abcote requested his presence in the dining hall, but at least it had given the inspector time to rest and to reflect. The more he considered Dorsett's explanation and general demeanour, the more he felt inclined to believe that the man, however irritating he might be, was telling the truth. If as seemed likely, he would be returning to Pontypridd without Dorsett in tow, at least there would be one less suspect to muddy the waters. Still keeping the pistol inside his uniform, just to be on the safe side, Chard made his way to the dining hall where his host awaited him at a large table of polished oak resplendent with silver cutlery and crockery of the finest bone china. Dorsett had dressed formally and as always, elegantly, for the meal and he rose to greet his guest. 'I do hope you have rested, Inspector. I have taken the liberty of assuming that you will accept my hospitality and stay the night. Your driver seems more than comfortable in the servants' quarters and I have instructed Bennett to take your case to the guest room.'

'Thank you, my lord. That is most kind. By the way I have your cane. I was getting so used to carrying it that I took it with me up to the room.'

'Then you must keep it, Inspector. I have another one of exactly the same design and that one has a slight mark on the leopard's head. I owe you something for the inconvenience to which I have put you.'

'Very generous, my lord, but it would be a rather expensive gift and I don't think it would be something that I could accept.'

Dorsett laughed. 'A mere trifle. I am now rich beyond your imagination, Inspector. Apart from what you see before you there are also extensive investments in America, but more of that later. Let us eat and we will talk of other matters afterwards, over our port and cigars.'

Chard sat and made himself comfortable as the first course was served, wild mushroom soup.

'Mind the "destroying angels",' warned Dorsett seriously, followed by a laugh on seeing Chard frown. 'It's alright, Inspector. I wouldn't poison you, though Cook might poison me.'

The soup was delicious as was the main course, fillet of trout cooked with parsley and shallots accompanied by duchess potatoes.

'Perhaps we can discuss matters further now, my lord,' suggested Chard.

'Soon, Inspector, but not before dessert,' admonished Dorsett with a wag of his finger as a steaming hot apple pudding with cream arrived before them.

Eventually, the meal finished, Dorsett rose and patted his slim waist with a sigh, 'I think we will retire to the library, Inspector, where all will be revealed.'

* * *

Sergeant Morris and Constable Preece walked in front of the White Hart and the Greyhound on the Tumble and ignored some of the less serious offences that were currently taking place. A drunk urinating against the side of a building, who would normally have received at least a clip across the head, was surprised to see the police officers go past without even a word being said. Two men swinging their fists at each other, neither able to land a blow due to their inebriation, were similarly ignored.

Even one of the well-known town prostitutes who was

caught unawares when Sergeant Morris's huge figure suddenly loomed over her was shocked as there was no command to move off the street. Thus the two officers proceeded until they stood outside the new abattoir.

'Ever been in there, Sergeant?'

'No, Constable, I can't say as I have. I suggest that you stick with me. We'll go in through that door at the front and if your guess is right and he is actually in there we'll just have to hope we catch him before he runs out the back.'

Constable Preece stepped forward and with both arms pulled open the large wooden door before stepping into the slaughterhouse. The inside was dimly lit for the first few feet and they entered without being noticed, the noise of the door opening having been drowned by the clanking of chains as a small team of workers worked busily at the far end of the building. The animals herded into the pens and slaughtered during the day had been gutted and hung to drain. Now the carcasses were being moved via chains and pulleys to be skinned and butchered before being put into the cold store which was to the right of where the policemen currently stood. The workers' voices echoed as they laughed and joked despite their grisly tasks, unaware of being watched.

'No sign of our man. It appears that your supposition was wrong, Constable,' whispered the sergeant.

'He might be out the back. Let's just wait a mo …' Preece stopped mid-sentence as there was a sudden creaking noise to their right as the door of the cold store opened and out stepped Evans. For a moment nothing happened and time seemed to stand still as the wanted man stared into the faces of the two policemen, then suddenly there was a roar, as Evans took something from inside his work jacket, pulled his arm back and threw. Sergeant Morris sensed rather than saw the heavy object flying towards him and dodged as it flew past his left shoulder. Evans moved quickly and in that split second, when the sergeant's attention was occupied with the need to evade the thrown object, he bolted for the door. Sergeant Morris made a grab for the felon's arm but failed to get a firm hold and the man made his exit.

'Come on, after him,' yelled the sergeant to Constable Preece as he made after the fugitive and began to blow his whistle in order to alert his men on the Graig and in the town. It was clear that his alert had been heard for the faint echo of other whistles confirmed that the constables were converging in the sergeant's direction.

Evans could be seen running through the Tumble, scattering bystanders as he went and heading into the town. Sergeant Morris realised that he wasn't going to catch his man but suddenly became aware that Preece hadn't overtaken him.

'Preece, where the hell are you?' he shouted with authority, but there was no reply and no sign of the young constable. Just then Constable Scudamore came into view, running down from the Graig hill and the sergeant gesticulated that the fugitive had run down into the town. Rather than follow Scudamore and continue the chase, Sergeant Morris retraced his steps and re-entered the abattoir where he found the group of workers huddled close to the entrance. The sergeant pushed through and looked at the object of their attention and gave a gasp.

'Sweet Jesus!'

*   *   *

The new Lord Abcote poured a glass of port from a Waterford Crystal decanter and handed it to Inspector Chard who was seated comfortably in a fine red leather armchair in the well-furnished library.

'Cigar, Inspector?' offered Dorsett.

'No, but thank you. I do occasionally indulge but it detracts from the port in my opinion.'

'A man after my own heart. I do agree with you. Perhaps later then.' Dorsett sat down facing the inspector. 'So, are you now satisfied that I am not the man you are after?'

'Possibly, but was there not a risk that Grimes would reveal your gambling habit to your father?'

'A small risk, I concede, but I took great care not to reveal my relationship with him to my family and I doubted that whatever influence in South Wales Grimes had, it would not extend this far north. Even so, given that you are also presumably looking at the same culprit having killed Blake, then I suggest I must be discounted for I had no concerns about that individual, other than that he was rather vile.'

Chard nodded thoughtfully. 'That is quite a presumption. It could have been two different killers, though I admit that just one is more likely. Returning to the murder of Grimes, you have mentioned that you had a darker secret than the gambling about which your father would have disapproved. Would not Grimes have known about that?'

Dorsett's handsome face creased with a broad smile. 'Not a chance. It has remained a secret that no one has discovered.'

'So perhaps you will enlighten me.'

'Soon, very soon, but first, assuming that you exclude me from your enquiries, where does your investigation lie?'

Chard scratched his sideburns. 'That is another assumption of yours but I'll run with it, for the moment.' The inspector paused whilst he took a sip of the excellent port before continuing. 'My thoughts return to the watch planted on the train crash victim. Whoever put it there has to be the prime suspect in the murder of Blake and therefore probably Grimes. The Italian, Ross, has a link to both, as does the porter who you know as Evans, then there is the young woman Miss Norton who had a slight connection with Blake, though none as I know of with Grimes.'

'Then why suspect her?' laughed Dorsett.

'There is something about her that I can't put my finger on. Call it a policeman's hunch.'

Dorsett started to laugh again, so much so that he held his ribs and continued until there were tears in his eyes. Chard looked astonished and felt conflicting emotions of confusion, anger and concern. Eventually anger took precedence and he downed his port and stood up to confront his social superior.

'Explain, damn you!'

Dorsett used his arms to indicate that the inspector should calm down whilst he regained his breath. 'I do apologise, Inspector. Please sit back down and I will indeed explain. You have been very patient and I have been rather toying with you.'

Still looking flustered, Chard complied and regained his seat whilst Dorsett poured him another port.

'The reason for my laughing will become very obvious. You see my dark secret, the unforgiveable sin in my family's eyes, is that nearly three years ago during what was intended to be a singular visit to South Wales, I met and fell in love with a Catholic. I am speaking of course of Miss Norton. My family are ardent Protestants and any suggestion of me wanting to marry a Catholic would have resulted in my having been disinherited immediately. As a result we have had to be extremely secretive and the only person aware of our relationship has been Father McManus. Our clandestine meetings have been amongst some trees by the riverbank close to the ironworks, where I would creep up on her in the dead of night in case anyone else was around before finally holding her in my arms. The meeting at the infirmary that time after the crash was pure coincidence and we had to pretend that we didn't know each other.'

'So that was the main reason why you kept finding an excuse to come to Pontypridd, not the gambling.'

'Correct, Inspector, though I wasn't lying when I said that I did enjoy the thrill of cocking a snook at the family by getting involved with Grimes's unsavoury club.'

'So now you are free to marry?'

'Yes, Inspector, though I would appreciate it if you would keep it to yourself. I have agreed to renounce my faith and adopt Catholicism but I am keeping that decision under my hat until after the funeral. I have arranged for a quick burial in the local church which will take place on Monday morning, straight after which I will disgust my family by leaving for Cardiff immediately, arriving in the evening. I sent a message to Miss Norton as soon as I heard of my father's death telling her to pack her essential belongings and to catch the evening train to join me.'

'Why Cardiff?'

'Next morning we will travel for Bristol and then to America where we will marry and start a new life. I can appoint my agents to deal with the selling of the property and travelling back across perhaps twice a year to deal with anything that needs my personal attention.'

'You have done remarkably well to have kept your secret for so long.'

'Exactly, and that is why I was laughing. We are in love but Miss Norton hasn't been able to tell anyone other than Father McManus.' Dorsett's face became solemn. 'In fact it must have been a terrible strain on her all this time. I am so pleased that we can now be open about it, well after the funeral at least.'

Chard finished his port. 'Thank you for being so candid, though to be honest, my lord, it would have saved a considerable amount of time and effort if you had told me this earlier. However, considering how much you would have lost financially if it had leaked out before your father's death, I do have a degree of sympathy for your situation.'

'Enough not to arrest me for obstructing your enquiries?' asked Dorsett jokingly, though with a serious look in his eyes.

'Perhaps,' replied the inspector.

*　　*　　*

Evans ran in a mad panic for he could hear police whistles shrieking both behind and ahead. As the fugitive came level with the entrance to the Clarence Theatre he could see the bulky frame of Constable Davies coming his way. The policeman was large and solid but slow. Evans easily ran around him but then found himself trapped. A row of hansom cabs were lined up in the road leaving no opportunity to get off the pavement. Davies was now behind, blocking a retreat, and coming out of the gaslight ahead at a fast pace was Constable Jenkins who had become an easily recognisable figure amongst the men of the town due to his boxing prowess. Like a stag trapped by the hounds Evans stared wide-eyed looking for an escape. Realising the only real option, Evans took a quick sprint forward towards Jenkins but then dived down the alley alongside the Victoria and headed for the Empire Music Hall. Jenkins gave chase followed by Davies and Scudamore who had just arrived. As the policemen barged into the hall they found the doorman lying on the floor having been bundled over by the fleeing Evans. The Hall itself was packed, the bench seating was full and, as it had not been modernised for thirty years, there were still tables in the centre and additional standing was allowed, giving a cluttered crowded feeling more akin to a football match than a theatre. The audience was in good humour and a talented young lady performer was mimicking the famous Marie Lloyd and her infamous risqué songs, the assemblage joining in with '… and she'd never had her ticket punched before …' and similar well-known lyrics.

'There he is, trying to hide by that table in the corner!' shouted Scudamore and the constables, who by now had also been joined by Constable Matthews, charged into the crowd eliciting shrieks and curses from the customers impacted by the sudden rush of bodies.

Evans jumped onto the stage, causing pandemonium as the performer leapt back terrified, and the band came to a discordant screeched halt. Jeers and boos with the odd thrown bottle and beer glass began to be directed at the police officers as they chased their man onto the stage and behind the curtain into the wings.

'Down there!' yelled Jenkins as they saw a door closing down a small flight of wooden steps. Crashing down the steps and shoulder first into the door they found themselves in the props room which they recognised from the recent raid.

'Damn,' exclaimed Davies. 'He's either gone out through that side door and double backed into the alley behind us, or he has escaped up into the back rooms, into the Victoria and out through the front door.'

'OK. Me and Fisty will take the Vic and you two get back into the alley,' decided Matthews. He indicated to Jenkins who followed him into the rear of the pub whilst Davies and Scudamore went the other way.

Meanwhile Evans was blessing his luck, for having run through the gambling and brothel rooms he was now in the bar of the Victoria and heading for the street.

Once there he felt sure he could get back to the Graig hill where he could hide amongst the back alleys that he knew so well. The fresh air hit his face and a moment later so did a fist with the force of a steam hammer that broke two teeth on impact. By the time that Jenkins and Matthews arrived thirty seconds later Evans face resembled something like pulped fruit and an enraged Sergeant Morris had both his hands around the man's throat whilst two customers from the pub were trying to pull him away.

Alarmed at the sight of their huge but usually calm and gentle sergeant in such a fury, Jenkins and Matthews ran and helped pull him off from the unconscious Evans.

'Sergeant, please stop. He's had enough!'

The big man turned to them with tears running down his cheeks. 'You don't understand. He's killed our Danny.'

CHAPTER TWENTY-EIGHT

On the Monday morning Jackson was in the station for his early shift and being briefed by Sergeant Humphreys.

'… of course the hammer he threw smashed Danny's skull. Sergeant Morris was distraught and nearly killed Evans when he caught him. They took Danny up to the infirmary, got Dr Henderson out of bed and he did find a faint pulse …'

'So, he'll live then?' asked Jackson with a degree of disinterest that was oblivious to the sergeant.

'They doubt it. He couldn't be moved yesterday but they hope to get him to the hospital today, though the move will be a dangerous one. If he dies then I doubt Evans will make it to the hangman. Of course his arrest is going to overshadow your catching of Ross,' needled the sergeant.

'How come? Has he confessed to the killings of Grimes and Blake?'

'It's difficult for him to confess to anything with missing teeth and a broken jaw.'

'Then I just need Ross to confess first,' snarled Jackson.

'Talking of Ross, there's a message about him that came in somewhere. It's a reply to a query sent off by Danny but he obviously won't be reading it now. I'll go and get it.'

Whilst Humphreys wandered off to find the message Jackson reached up and grabbed one of the keys from behind the sergeant's desk.

'It's a reply to the query about the ship that Ross used to get here about three years ago,' announced Humphreys as he returned. 'Apparently he lied about where it came from. It did come from Italy but the port of departure was Naples not Genoa.'

'Then he must have been lying for a reason. I might have a word with him about that.'

'No you don't,' snapped the sergeant. 'Inspector Chard will want to speak to him first.'

Jackson gave a grunt and walked away without comment and only a few minutes later Jack Ross was woken from slumber on his hard wooden bed by the cell door crashing open.

'Right, you lying little eyetie bastard. You are going to confess to the murder of Jabez Grimes,' he snarled.

Ross opened up his arms in supplication. 'I have done nothing. I don't know what you are talking about,' he cried.

'Liar,' yelled Jackson, spittle dripping from his mouth. The policeman hit Ross full in the face causing blood to flow from the prisoner's nose and lips.

'No, stop!'

'Then confess. What was all that money in your holdall? You stole it from Grimes, didn't you?'

'No, the money is mine!' shouted Ross.

Jackson grabbed the young Italian's arm and twisted it behind his back. 'I'll make you talk.'

*　　*　　*

Inspector Chard had set off for the station in a settled state of mind. The decision not to arrest Lord Abcote had been one that he was bound to have taken. The scandal, without strong evidence would have been incalculable and if the man was proven to be innocent then it would have meant the end of Chard's career. At least the inspector had received an excellent breakfast and the journey back to Pontypridd on the Sunday had been very leisurely. There had been no complaint from Will Horses who the previous evening had enjoyed a dalliance with one of the Hall's maids. Almost reluctantly Chard had accepted the gift of the cane which remained in his rooms on the self-justification that somehow it might still be pertinent to the investigation.

Having arrived back late on the Sunday evening the inspector had no inkling of the events of the weekend and neither did Superintendent Jones, who was entering the station just as Chard arrived. Their salutations were interrupted by Sergeant Humphreys who came to meet them straight away and snapped to attention.

'Superintendent Jones, Inspector Chard, I need to inform you of some serious matters that have occurred this weekend; terribly serious in fact.'

Jones turned to his inspector. 'Chard, you have been here have you not?'

'I have not sir. I have been pursuing a suspect out of the county and only got back last night.'

'Did you get your man?'

'No sir, but I have eliminated one if not two suspects, leaving just Evans and Ross,' explained the inspector feeling that this was sufficient justification.

'Begging your pardon sir, but we've got them both in the cells,' interjected Humphreys with no expression of joy on his face.

'Excellent,' guffawed the superintendent, 'well done.'

Chard however sensed from Humphreys's demeanour that there was something amiss. His expression became serious as he spoke to the sergeant. 'Humphreys, there's something wrong isn't there?'

'Yes sir,' answered the sergeant sadly, unable to look Chard in the eye. 'It's young Constable Preece.'

There are moments in a person's life when the world seems to stand still and the air is heavy with a feeling of dread. It happens when there is a tragic family loss such as when parents have lost a child. Times when the awful truth is known before the words are spoken. The heart is crushed and the sense of loss is overwhelming. Chard felt those sensations before Sergeant Humphreys said any more.

'He was injured during the arrest of Evans and was sent to the infirmary. I am afraid that just before you arrived news came that he has passed away,' continued Humphreys, his voice unsteady. There was a stunned silence as the shock set in and then they quietly walked inside, Chard cursing himself for not being there and Superintendent Jones lost in thought as to how to respond. 'I will go to visit his mother in Treforest and break the news of …' Before the superintendent could conclude his sentence the three men were startled by a terrible scream coming from the cells. The two senior officers rushed towards the sound coming from behind a cell door and pushed it inwards. Ross was curled up on the floor clasping his left arm to his body and whimpering whilst Jackson was stood astride him, truncheon raised and ready to strike.

'What is going on?' barked Superintendent Jones loudly.

'He's broken my bloody arm,' spat Ross through his teeth that were clenched in pain.

'He attacked me, sir,' lied Jackson, taken aback by the sudden appearance of his superiors.

'Get out, Jackson!' ordered the superintendent. 'You will be dealt with later.'

As Jackson left, Chard, turned to Sergeant Humphreys who had followed behind. 'As duty sergeant you shouldn't have let this happen. Get the prisoner cleaned up and then report back to me.'

'In fact report to both of us, in my office, in the next fifteen minutes,' added the superintendent. 'I want a full description of everything that has happened this weekend. Leave nothing out.'

Both the superintendent and the inspector had snapped particularly harshly at Humphreys, their anger an outlet for the inner turmoil they felt over Preece's death.

Shamefacedly the sergeant waited for his superiors to leave the cell, locked it with the key left behind by Jackson, then rushed off to find a constable to attend to Ross.

'Come, Inspector, you can start by telling me exactly where you have been this weekend. It had better be good.'

Once in the superintendent's office, Chard went over his reasoning that led him to travel in pursuit of Dorsett, grunting in agreement when the inspector mentioned that he had paid for the journey out of his own funds. When it came to the revelations provided by the new Lord Abcote the superintendent was shocked and disgusted. 'What a terrible way to deceive his family,' he exclaimed. 'His poor deceased father in particular,' he added. 'Well, he certainly is a rogue in my eyes, Inspector, but you were correct in not arresting him without sufficient evidence. Is he now no longer a suspect in your eyes?'

'That is correct, sir. His explanation covers the behaviour of both himself and Miss Norton. The culprit must be Evans or Ross but we will see what Sergeant Humphreys has to say about their arrest.'

The two senior officers did not have too long to wait until the sergeant arrived to give them a full explanation of the weekend's events, from the arrest of Ross in the churchyard to the tragedy of Constable Preece's injury, which left the three of them in silence.

'Sergeant Morris was at the lad's bedside when he drew his last breath. He has taken it pretty badly. We all have,' he added pointedly.

Straightening his posture Jones gave a slight cough and

brought them back to the other issues. 'At least we have caught the prime suspects, the men need to be commended for that.'

'The good work by Jackson in arresting Ross does not excuse him breaking the prisoner's arm though, sir. We'll have to send Ross up to the infirmary under guard to get it looked at,' commented Chard.

'Agreed, Inspector, but he needs to be questioned properly as soon as possible, as does our other suspect.'

'I can make a start with Evans and I had best do so before somebody follows Jackson's example,' suggested Chard.

✳   ✳   ✳

Chard had yet to return his pistol to the armoury and as he opened the cell door he subconsciously patted his uniform pocket to ensure it was still there. However there was no cause for concern, for there was no fight left in Evans. He lay on the hard wooden bed of the cell staring at the ceiling and did not get up as the inspector entered. Chard stared at the man's heavily beaten face, one eye swollen and closed, nose broken, lips split, flesh a mixture of purple and black bruising, yet the inspector felt no pity.

'You know that the constable hit by your hammer has died.'

Evans grunted but eventually responded, mumbling through his damaged mouth. 'I didn't even know it had hit 'im.'

'Nevertheless you will hang,' emphasised Chard.

'So, is that all you came to tell me?'

The inspector shook his head. 'No. I thought that as we can't hang you more than once you might as well tell me the truth and admit to the killing of Grimes and Blake. If you do then I'll get you some medical attention and make sure that you get to the scaffold in one piece.'

'So you want me to lie to clear up your case? Very well, I killed them.'

'I don't want you to lie. I want you to tell me the truth.'

'You can't have it both ways,' Evans laughed sarcastically causing the dried cut on his lower lip to start bleeding afresh. 'I never killed that bastard Blake or Mr Grimes.'

'Though you are aware of Grimes having been murdered.'

'Word gets around in this town and why would I bite the hand that feeds me?'

Chard scratched his sideburns as he paused for thought. 'So how did you come to work for Grimes and, whilst we're at it, why did you speak of Blake with such venom?'

'I was in debt from having to pay for medicine for my sick wife. When she died I earned money doing some debt collecting myself but then one day I was collecting from someone who also owed money to Mr Grimes. Blake turned up at the same time and we quarrelled over who should get the money. We fought along the length of the street with everything that came to hand and all the people in the houses came to stand on their doorsteps to watch. Eventually he got me with that belt buckle of his across the face. Then he hit me with a loose brick from a collapsed wall and down I went.'

'What happened next?'

'I gave it all up. I lost my bottle and couldn't carry on. I was still in debt and too injured from the fight to do any manual work for a while so I threw myself on the mercy of the parish and entered the workhouse. They gave me light work in exchange for my food and a roof over my head. Then when I was stronger I was put to work as a porter at the infirmary.'

'Until you stole from a train crash victim,' added Chard seriously.

'Well he wasn't ever going to need it was he? His face was smashed up more than mine,' chuckled Evans grimly. 'There was enough there to pay off all my debts and start afresh. I was surprised to hear a few days later that Blake was dead and even more surprised when I got an offer of a job from Mr Grimes.'

'You had never met Grimes before?'

'No, he must have heard that until Blake came along I was well known for my work, so he put me to chasing debts or putting pressure on people. I sometimes broke a limb here or there but never had to kill anyone and Mr Grimes always paid me fairly. He was a good man.'

'Then your idea of a good man is far different than mine,' snapped Chard. 'That's all for now but I will be back after I've spoken to Ross.'

'That foreign lad, well I can tell you that he isn't what he pretends to be. Don't turn your back on him,' shouted Evans as best he could as the inspector closed the cell door.

On his way back to his office Chard was intercepted by Sergeant Humphreys who mentioned the information he had given to Jackson about the ship used by Ross. 'We've also had this just come in from Cardiff, Inspector,' added the sergeant, giving him an envelope.

Chard took the correspondence to his desk, opened it and after reading and digesting the contents he left the room and found Humphreys once again.

'Has Ross been taken up to the infirmary yet?'

'Yes, Inspector. Accompanied by Constable Morgan.'

'Then if anyone wants me, that is where I'll be.'

* * *

The weather had taken another unpredictable change for the worse and instead of the early morning sunshine the town was now shrouded in cloud with a light splattering of rain. Nevertheless, Chard had opted to walk the few hundred yards to the infirmary confident in the sufficiency of the raincape to keep his uniform dry. When the inspector reached the workhouse gates he spotted May Roper standing outside the infirmary door. As he approached he could see that tears were silently rolling down her cheeks and she was trembling. Despite noticing the inspector and acknowledging his presence with a slight nod of the head May continued to look into the distance at nothing in particular.

'We often have deaths here, Inspector, but I am afraid that seeing that young man pass away was just too tragic. I was on an errand but just had to stop for a while to gather my thoughts,' explained May, wiping her tears with a small cotton handkerchief. Chard sensed the young woman's vulnerability and instinctively wanted to put an arm around her to give comfort, but held back.

'Yes, Miss Roper, it has been a terrible tragedy and we all feel the loss,' acknowledged Chard sadly. 'I just wish I had been around when it happened.'

'I take it you were not on duty at the time then, Inspector.'

Chard felt guilty and unjustifiably ashamed as he explained. 'Actually I was, but I was chasing after Mr Dorsett once more. On this occasion many miles away and at the time that poor Danny Preece was injured I was probably dining lavishly at a country house.'

May could see the hurt in the inspector's eyes and felt sorry for him. 'I am sure there would have been nothing that you could have done and I know that you wouldn't have been off after Mr Dorsett without good reason.'

'Thank you. It's very kind of you to say that,' replied Chard, genuinely grateful.

'As you did try to be so helpful in the past and I was, I am sorry to say, rather offhand, I think that you deserve to know that Mr Dorsett is now Lord Abcote and very wealthy. His strange behaviour and that of Miss Norton was due to their love affair which had to be kept quiet whilst his father was alive in case he lost his inheritance.'

Not used to gossip, but well versed in romantic fiction where young ladies were swept off their feet by dashing aristocrats, May was intrigued to hear the details and the inspector gladly obliged. After describing the Hall and the planned marriage of the two lovers across the ocean in America, May suddenly noticed the time. 'Oh, I am sorry, Inspector, but I must rush off. I was due to run an errand for Dr Henderson just before you arrived. I might see you again when I come back. Constable Morgan is at the far end of the ward,' May added as she turned and set off.'

As Chard entered the infirmary's ward he could see the conspicuous figure of his constable standing close by a bed at the far end.

'How is the prisoner, Constable Morgan?' Chard demanded as he approached.

'Fairly drowsy, Inspector,' answered Morgan, his expression sombre. 'They've given him some morphine.'

'Yes, had to do it. It was a bad break,' interjected Dr Henderson who had lumbered towards them whilst they were speaking. 'I've set it in a splint now so that's all that I can do, but I wouldn't move him for a couple of hours until the drug wears off.'

'I take it I can talk to him?' asked the inspector.

'Yes of course, but he is still drowsy so you might not get full answers.'

'Get your notebook out then, Constable, and I'll have a word.'

Chard took a chair and sat next to the bedside of Ross who looked back with slightly dilated pupils.

'You've been telling me lies, Ross.'

The prisoner looked back almost uncaring and answered slowly. 'I told your officer the truth before he broke my arm.'

'You said that the *Cielo Azzurro* sailed from Genoa, but it didn't, did it? It sailed from Naples.'

'Maybe, I can't remember. That's not a crime.'

'True, but put together with a few other things it starts to build a picture around you that causes me concern.'

'What other things?'

'For a start there is all the money that was found in your possession. You have enough to gamble with and are, so I am told, quite proficient in that respect. There is enough to give you a reasonable lifestyle here or indeed to move on out of the clutches of Grimes and yet you have placed yourself in a dirty manual occupation as a foundry worker. I find that very strange.'

Ross gave no response other than an expressionless stare.

'Then we have the tattoo.'

'What tattoo?' murmured Ross.

'The one on the train crash victim. It's the reason why you left the infirmary in such a hurry, realising that they had found you,' answered Chard with a self-satisfied smile.

'I don't know what you're talking about'

'You know very well who. The Camorra.' Chard glanced up Constable Morgan who was looking puzzled. 'It's a criminal organisation based in Naples,' he explained. 'A pistol tattooed on the right side of the chest is a recognised symbol of one of the senior families, isn't that right Ross? One of our colleagues down in Tiger Bay in Cardiff found out by asking some sailors from an Italian vessel.'

The prisoner nodded slowly.

'So,' continued the inspector, 'here we have an Italian who has lied where he has come from, changes his name, takes up a menial job unnecessarily, has more money than he lets on and is afraid when a member of an Italian crime family turns up on his doorstep.' Chard glanced again at his constable who again looked puzzled. 'Therefore,' he continued, 'the obvious implication is that you were either clever or stupid enough to steal from the Camorra and they don't like allowing people to go unpunished so they sent someone after you. Am I or am I not correct?'

Ross answered quietly. 'Yes, but I have not committed any crime here.'

'We'll see about that. It looks to me that there is a large amount of indirect evidence building up against you. You gambled with Grimes, probably initially just to pass the time, and Blake knew about it because he collected the debts. Possibly Blake found out your secret and threatened to tell the Camorra so you killed him and took his watch. By chance you then had the opportunity to hide the watch on the train victim who by an act of fate was someone probably sent to kill you. Why you killed Grimes I don't know. Perhaps it was something to do with our raid and having spotted you at the gambling den but whatever the reason you disappeared the night that Grimes was killed.'

'I did not murder anyone,' insisted Ross drowsily.

'The one other thing that puzzles me is why, when you knew that the Camorra had traced you two years ago, you didn't move on. They clearly haven't sent anyone else, but they might have done. So why stay?'

'Jenny. I love Jenny,' answered the Italian sadly. 'Tell me, did she betray me to you? Is that why your men were waiting in the graveyard?'

'No, she didn't,' answered the inspector, 'but I have some bad news for you.' Chard hesitated, wondering whether to say anything, but then continued, 'Miss Norton is to be married to James Dorsett, now Lord Abcote. She leaves on the train for Cardiff tonight and will be emigrating to America.'

As soon as Chard's words registered with him Ross gave a startled sob and through grief and the morphine still present in his system, passed out.

* * *

When Ross awoke he found May Roper standing next to the bed. He noticed that the policemen were no longer there but when he tried to move he found that his uninjured arm had been handcuffed to the bedpost.

'There was no point in them waiting around with nothing to do, so they've gone out for a while but they should be back in half an hour,' explained May to the puzzled Italian.

'How long have I been asleep?'

'About three hours. I should have gone home by now but I want to see Inspector Chard when he gets back.'

Suddenly things started to flood back into the patient's memory and he started to become distraught.

'Calm down, Mr Ross. I will get a nurse.'

Ross steadied himself and started to control his breathing. 'No, there's no need. It's just that Inspector Chard said something upsetting to me which can't be true. He must have been lying. I think he was just trying to play with my mind in order to unsettle me.'

'What was that?'

'He said that Jenny, my Jenny, who I have loved ever since I came here, is to be married to someone else.'

'I am afraid I do believe that is true and it is a relationship that has been going on secretly for some time,' explained May as gently as she could.

She walked away only to be alerted five minutes later by

the sound of Ross shouting as he tried to free himself from the handcuffs. As the realisation of the wasted years and pointless emotional anguish struck home his mood had changed from despondency to anger, with a ferocity that only a rejected lover could contemplate.

'The bitch! After all I've done for her! The murderous bitch!' he yelled followed by a string of oaths in Italian that May was grateful that she couldn't understand.

'What do you mean murderous?' she asked, interrupting his venomous tirade as he thrashed about on the bed in anger.

'I saw her the night Grimes was killed. I had packed up to leave town and was crossing the Machine Bridge late at night when I saw her running away in the pitch darkness from the direction of the area where Grimes was murdered. She had no other reason to be there, none at all! Then there was that business with the watch all that time ago. I know that I didn't plant it on the body so it had to be Jenny or her lover. If she didn't plant the watch then she is still the one that killed Grimes. I would never have given her away, never, ever, but she has betrayed me.' The young man's anger then collapsed and he started to sob quietly, turning away so that May couldn't look at him.

'She's leaving for Cardiff this evening. She must be stopped,' exclaimed May, but Ross was no longer listening. The young woman ran quickly to Dr Henderson's empty office, wrote a brief message and put it in an envelope. Then she ran towards the door, passing the note to Nurse Harris who was just about to start her shift.

'Give this message to Inspector Chard as soon as he comes in. He said he'll be back inside the next half hour and that is less time than it would take for me to find him myself. This is extremely urgent, Nurse Harris,' emphasised May as she ran out of the door.

CHAPTER TWENTY-NINE

Chard patted Merlin on the nose as he introduced Constable Morgan to the horse's owner.

'This, Constable Morgan, is Will Owens and this beautiful creature of his is called Merlin.'

'*Shwmae* Constable,' greeted Will who received the same salutation in response.

'I thought you might have given him a rest after our journey,' commented the inspector.

'He has been in the stables all day, Mr Chard, doing bugger all. I thought we might park ourselves here outside the station for a couple of hours in case of the odd fare or two this evening, but that will be the limit of his exertions. Do you need taking anywhere?'

'No, Will, we're on our way up to the infirmary but as it has stopped raining, for a little while at least, we're happy to walk. It isn't far and there's no particular hurry so we can take our time.'

Standing inside the railway station yard and with their backs to the road, the policemen didn't see the cab that trotted quickly down the Graig hill and turned right just behind them onto the Tram Road. Neither did they glimpse the auburn-haired passenger, her face set with grim resolve.

* * *

Jenny checked around the rooms of her little terraced house. She had paid handsomely for the large wooden chest with her clothes and essential belongings to be taken the hundred yards from her house to Treforest Station. What remained, the furniture, ornaments, kitchen utensils and general bric-a-brac could just be left behind. The new owners would be welcome to them. She picked up her coat from the bed and put it on and then added her matching wide-brimmed red hat. Finally, after all this waiting, it was over. She had broken the news to her employers that very morning. Mr Roberts was surprised, Mr Dunwoody was shocked and upset and Lizzie just collapsed into tears. Still, this was her dream, and soon she would be Lady Abcote.

Her thoughts were suddenly broken by a series of loud knocks on her front door. Puzzled by the interruption, Jenny went downstairs and opened the front door.

'Oh, it's you,' she exclaimed as her face drained of colour. 'You were the one person that I thought might turn up at some time or other.'

May, standing on the doorstep, unsure of how she was going to approach this difficult situation, looked surprised at Jenny's reaction. 'You don't know why I'm here.'

'Of course I do,' answered Jenny.

* * *

Inspector Chard and Constable Morgan had walked back to the workhouse with barely a word spoken, each lost in thought over the death of their colleague. They entered the infirmary and headed directly for the bed where their prisoner was secured.

'Do you believe Ross then, sir?' asked Constable Morgan.

'I believe that he was clearly besotted with Miss Norton but as for everything else, I think he is still hiding something.'

'Inspector!'

Chard turned to see a nurse, looking quite anxious, walking quickly towards him.

'I have an urgent message for you, Inspector, from Miss

Roper,' she declared, handing him an envelope. As Chard ripped it open she added 'I am quite concerned because Miss Roper spoke to me in a manner that was rather brusque and a little impolite which is so unlike her.'

As Chard started to read the note his face started to drop and having finished he rushed up to the bed where Ross lay and, grabbing him by the shoulders started to shake him.

'Ross, answer me! Is it true? Did you tell Miss Roper that Jenny Norton killed Grimes?'

The prisoner, his face held only inches away from that of the inspector, nodded slowly. Chard let the man go before turning to his constable. 'The stupid girl!' he exclaimed. 'She's gone to try and delay Jenny Norton from catching the train. Come on, Constable, there's no time to lose. We'll run down to the railway station and hope that Will is still there. I pray we're not too late.

*   *   *

Jenny led the way through her living room into the small kitchen followed by a hesitant May. She stopped and turned by the kitchen window, her hand resting on the small kitchen table laden with stacked plates and cutlery. 'I knew that you were working for Grimes the first time you came. He has, or rather had, people everywhere. Did you really believe that I would think it was sheer coincidence that you should turn up unannounced on the same day as I got Grimes's blackmail note? You were there to judge my reaction, to get me rattled.'

May stood confused but aware of the need to delay Jenny for as long as possible, did not deny the accusation.

'I was tempted to tell the police about your visit when they interviewed me at Taff Vale House, but then that might have brought things out in the open,' continued Jenny. 'I assume that Grimes must have taken you into his confidence so you now want your price.'

May tried to look confident as she stared at the imperious, beautiful woman before her and nodded.

Jenny turned away, facing a kitchen dresser which stood against the right hand wall, its ledge bearing storage jars and bowls, staying there for a few moments without saying a word. When she turned back around her eyes looked sorrowful, a decision had been made.

'Very well, the money no longer concerns me, but although you know what I did, you won't know the reason. Once I've paid you then I want that to be an end to it so perhaps, if you hear my story, you will understand as only a woman can and trouble me no further.'

'I am prepared to listen. Take your time,' encouraged May.

Jenny's shoulders sagged as she leant against the dresser and began her tale. 'I was only ten years old when my gin-soaked mother threw me out on the street. I never knew who my father was and never will. For two years I scavenged rotten food that had been thrown away at the markets and slept in doorways, then one day I thought my luck had changed. A woman saw me begging in an alley and offered to take me somewhere where I would be given food and shelter.'

May could see that this tale was becoming difficult for the other woman to recount for her eyes were becoming red-rimmed.

'I was taken to a large house where I was given hot food, the first I had tasted in months. Then a maid took me to be bathed and I was given a beautiful dress to wear. I felt so lucky.'

'What went wrong?' asked May, noticing from Jenny's expression that it wasn't a happy memory.

'It was a month before they put me to work. It was a child

brothel. I was twelve years old!' The explanation came out with a loud grief-laden sob.

May was shocked and she waited as Jenny dabbed her eyes with a silk handkerchief before composing herself and continuing.

'For three years I was used as their prize child whore. Thankfully I wasn't made to work as often as some of the others but it was unpleasant enough. Some of the men were kind but most were not, particularly one of my regulars who would delight in frightening me. I used to call him Satan for he was the devil himself.'

'How did you escape from that life?' asked May, becoming so involved in the tale that she was starting to forget the reason why she had come.

'I pretended I was happy with being a whore until they eventually came to trust me, to such an extent that they finally let me go out without a man guarding me. At the time I don't think they were too concerned about me running. By then I was fifteen years old but looked older, so I was outgrowing a child brothel. Anyway, one day I was passing a convent and I just ran in. It was as simple as that. They ran a home for reformed street girls which was very strict but I was overjoyed after the life I had lived. Over the next four years they brought me up as a good Catholic and gave me an education. I found that I had an aptitude for figures and soon was helping to run things. Eventually though, I just wanted to get as far away from London as possible. With good references from the Catholic Church I was able to get a post here and I started a new life.'

Jenny stood up and walked across the room, poured herself a glass of water from an enamel jug and took a sip before continuing.

'All was happy, then suddenly someone came to Pontypridd

who knew me. It had been maybe six years since he had last seen me and at first he wasn't sure, but I was. It was the man I called Satan. He threatened to tell everyone my past and ruin my life. I thought he wanted money so I agreed to meet him late at night. The thing is he didn't want money. He demanded just one act of coupling "for old time's sake" and then the matter would be settled for ever. So to my shame I agreed and I lay there in the dirt whilst he grunted over me. I can still smell his stale breath and the stink of his body.'

May put a hand on the iron cooking range that was on the right of the doorway where she stood, to steady herself, shocked at the other woman's revelation.

'Then, when he got up and was pulling up his trousers, I told him that I never wanted to talk to him again. He just laughed and said that he would have me once a week or everyone would know what a whore I really was.'

May gasped.

'I suddenly snapped and became like a mad woman. His back was to me so I picked up a heavy, sharp stone off the ground and grasping it with both hands I hit him as hard as I could. I aimed for his skull but hit his neck. I must have broken it for I think I heard a crack and he fell to the ground silently. It was a terrific struggle to move him but I am very strong and once in the current the river took him easily.'

'But they found Grimes in the canal,' interjected May, thoroughly confused.

Jenny looked surprised, 'I'm talking about Blake. That's why you're here isn't it? It was clear in the note Grimes sent that Blake had told him he was meeting me just before he went missing. When the train crash body was identified as Blake it allayed his suspicions but then when the real body was discovered he put two and two together. Then you came and started asking about my visit to the infirmary which made me realise that he must know that I was the obvious one to have planted the watch. It had fallen out of Blake's clothes when I dragged him to the river and something made me keep it. I was taking it to Father McManus to confess what I'd done when the news of the crash came in and I saw a God-given opportunity. Why are you looking surprised?'

May took a step back into the kitchen doorway.

'My God! You didn't have a clue about this did you? You've only been guessing! Why did you think I had anything to do with killing Grimes?' Jenny's expression had changed once more, this time from sorrow to a fierce anger.

'Jack Ross saw you running away late at night from the direction where Grimes was killed. He said you had no other reason to be there,' answered May.

'My God! I thought no one had seen me! So that's why Jack sent me the note to meet him at the church. Yes, I was running away from Grimes's murder but ...' Jenny paused, clearly flustered, her mind in turmoil. 'Very well, how much do you want?

Quickly now, I am in a hurry.'

May continued to back away. 'I don't want money,' she replied automatically and not thinking of the implications declared 'The police are on their way.'

Jenny gave an unladylike curse as she realised her folly. In a panic she reasoned that she needed to get away. James would understand and forgive her, she knew he would, though had there been an option she would have done anything to have stopped him from finding out. Perhaps if she could get away and hide somewhere until she could get a message to him they would still be able to start a new life in America. Still, there was one particular problem. The only person that she had confessed to was right in front of her.

May, realising that her words could have put herself in

danger, started to retreat slowly through the living room towards the front door.

Jenny grabbed a knife from the cutlery that lay on the kitchen table and as May saw the look in her eyes she turned and grabbed for the handle of the door. Then she felt pressure in her back together with a sharp agonising pain that made her open her mouth in a silent scream. Her legs just seemed to collapse from beneath her and she felt very faint.

Jenny, her face impassive now, grabbed May by the ankles and dragged her away from the door. After fetching her small valise Jenny stepped over the prone body and walked as quickly as possible towards the station.

CHAPTER THIRTY

The distinguished-looking businessman in frock coat and top hat was just about to enter the cab when a figure in uniform suddenly barged him out of the way and a voice yelled up to the driver.

'Will, it's a matter of life and death. Get us to Park Street and drive as if the devil is at your back!'

'No problem, Mr Chard.'

The two policemen hurled themselves into the cab, leaving the furious businessman to shake his fist as Will cracked the whip and Merlin set off out of the station yard. Soon they were flying down the tramway, hurtling at the gallop past the astonished passengers of horse-drawn omnibuses and other vehicles as they went. At the turn to Fothergill Street the cab nearly overbalanced, throwing the two passengers together, before the left hand wheel came crashing back down safely. Onwards they thundered down Park Street until Chard knocked the roof of the cab and the driver above pulled the reins to fetch the cab to a screeching halt. Leaping out into the road, Chard led the way to Jenny Norton's house followed closely behind by Constable Morgan. A sharp knock on the door gave no answer.

'Morgan, look through the window. Can you see anything?'

The constable peered through the front window which had net curtains making it difficult to see inside.

'Not sure, sir, but I think there may be someone on the floor,' he reported hesitantly with his face pressed close to the glass.

It would be usual for an inspector to command a constable to break a door down but Chard was not about to adhere to protocol for his heart was beating in panic. Taking a step back he gave an almighty kick at the edge of the door close to the lock, resulting in a load crack as the door frame splintered. A second kick resulted in it swinging open.

'Miss Roper!' Chard cried seeing her prostrate body lying on the living room carpet, a blood-soaked knife protruding from her back. Both policemen knelt alongside the young woman's body and Constable Morgan grabbed her wrist.

'I can feel a pulse, sir. She's still alive.'

'Good, but she'll need help. You stay here and keep her as comfortable as possible but do not try removing the blade. Keep talking to her even if she doesn't respond. I'll send Will for medical help and then get after the bitch that did this.'

Chard rushed out into the street and yelled to Will who was waiting anxiously to find out the reason for their dash from Pontypridd.

'Will, there's a young woman in there who will die without urgent medical help. Do you know of a doctor nearby?'

'There's a Dr Argyle. I've taken him to his house several times. I'll set off straight away.' Without waiting for a response the whip cracked once more and the cab thundered off to get help.

Chard watched it go for only a moment before crossing the street and heading for the station entrance, his face a mask of grim resolve.

* * *

From her position on the southbound platform of the small station, Jenny had been able to lean on the station retaining wall, look down on Park Street and observe the arrival of the policemen. Her heart was pounding as thoughts began once more to flow through her mind as to her best course of action. The train was due any minute now. Once on it she would have time to think things through properly, but for now it was best to stick to pretending that she wasn't there when May Roper called and that the girl had been murdered by an opportunistic burglar who had known the house would be unoccupied. It didn't seem very convincing but there was nothing else for it. Then Inspector Chard had appeared and could be heard shouting to the cab driver to find a doctor. Jenny's heart leapt into her mouth. If May Roper lived, or was even able to talk before dying then there was no hope. She would have to pray that the train arrived on time and then try and hide somewhere in Cardiff until she could discreetly contact James. In the distance there was the faint sound of a train approaching so she stared hopefully northwards towards Pontypridd and for a moment her heart lifted because the inspector was still in the street below. Then came disappointment as she realised that the sound was coming from behind. It was the northbound train heading in the opposite direction, up the valley. She turned around to see the smoke billowing from its funnel as it came into view a few hundred yards away. Quickly she looked back praying for a similar apparition heading for Cardiff but what she saw was a grim-faced Inspector Chard running onto the platform, and he saw her. Now there seemed no escape and sheer panic set in. There was one single chance to get away but it had to be snatched in the moment. If she could somehow cross the station and get on the northbound train before the inspector could get on the other platform then maybe, just maybe, she could escape and hide for the time being in one of the mining towns in the Rhondda Valley. Dropping her valise, Jenny turned and ran off the sloping end of the platform down to the ground level of the rails then started to run across to the other side. It should be easy to make it across in front of the northbound train but with the inspector thirty yards behind he would be stranded the other side of the train and unable to stop her boarding. There had been no other passengers on the other platform so with luck the train would set off immediately. The probability that the uniformed inspector would be able to draw the attention of the train driver or guard by just waving his arms or that a signal could be sent further up the line did not enter her panic-stricken head. The train was starting to slow as it approached the station and Jenny's judgement was correct. She was easily able to run in front of the train whilst Chard was still at the platform edge, but then her foot caught the rail, made slippery by the rain earlier in the day and she fell.

* * *

Chard saw Jenny stumble as she made her bid for freedom but felt sure that the murderess had got away so he ran back along the platform waving and shouting across the line before running up over the small footbridge and down the other side. By the time he got there the driver had already left the engine, together with his fireman, and they were looking anxiously back down the track. Chard ran past them and found the train guard kneeling by Jenny who lay deathly pale on the ground, her mouth moving but no sound coming out. The lower part of her dress was torn and blood was pumping from where her lower right leg used to be.

The train guard heard Chard approach and turned around, his face full of anguish.

'I don't know what to do,' he croaked.

'She is in shock, just hold her and talk to her for a moment whilst I try and stop the bleeding,' answered the inspector removing his belt. Hitching the injured woman's skirt higher he put the belt just above the knee of the severed limb and pulled it tight. 'This will slow the blood flow. Now go and find something thinner like some string or ripped material and a piece of metal rod, or a gentleman's cane that I can use to twist the tourniquet tighter. Then send someone down to Park Street, there will be a doctor arriving there shortly to deal with another medical emergency. Do you understand all that?'

The guard, somewhat calmed by a uniformed official who seemed to know his business, nodded in confirmation, then dashed off, leaving the inspector alone with Jenny.

'I don't care for what you've done, Miss Norton, and I dare say you'll hang but I won't let you die. Not here, not now.'

* * *

It was two days before the medical staff at Porth hospital gave permission for Inspector Chard to interview their patient. When he finally was permitted access he found Jenny Norton asleep on her bed with her head on the pillow. Her complexion was very pale yet she still looked serenely beautiful. Constable Morgan stood discreetly a few paces behind with a notebook and pencil to hand.

The nurse that had accompanied Chard gave her a gentle shake of the shoulder and Jenny awoke, looked up at the inspector and gave a little sigh before using her arms to push herself into a sitting position.

'You know, I feel as if it's still there,' she said, indicating the part of the bed where her lower right leg should have been making a ridge beneath the blanket.

Chard said nothing. The stabbing of Miss Roper on top of Danny Preece's death had filled him with anger and he had entered the hospital determined that no pity would cloud his judgement. Yet, despite himself, as Jenny Norton spoke he felt a degree of sympathy for someone so beautiful who had been maimed for what remained of her life.

'You are not the first visitor I have had today, Inspector.'

'So I understand. Lord Abcote was here this morning, I believe.'

Jenny raised her left arm and presented her hand to the inspector, displaying a diamond engagement ring. 'I didn't know whether he would stand by me, but I shouldn't have doubted his love. I know everything will come out at my trial so I decided to tell him all, expecting him to disown me, but instead he insisted that we marry regardless,' she explained smiling sadly.

'After what you have done, he must love you very deeply,' commented Chard who was genuinely surprised that a member of the aristocracy would want to marry a murderess and former prostitute, however beautiful.

'How is Miss Roper?' asked Jenny.

'Alive. Thankfully you missed the vital organs and medical help arrived in time. I haven't interviewed her yet but I intend doing so tomorrow if the doctors will allow me.'

'Good, I am glad she survived. It was a moment of madness, I just panicked.'

'It would have been a pointless death when you would have hanged anyway for the murder that you did commit. Did you realise that there was a witness to you fleeing the scene?'

'Oh, Inspector,' exclaimed Jenny, giving a tired ironic laugh. 'Let me stop you there. I assume that you are under the same allusion as Miss Roper was when she came to my house,' she added as her face took on a look of tragic resignation. 'As Miss Roper is alive, there is no harm in my telling you exactly what I told her for she will reveal all and I will go to the gallows anyway …'

There was a pause whilst Jenny waited for some words of comfort from the inspector. None came.

Jenny gave a heavy sigh. 'Just ask the nurse for a chair, sit down and listen ...'

* * *

It was early evening when Inspector Chard, accompanied by Sergeant Morris, knocked on the front door of the small but neat terraced house. He had waited for Sergeant Morris to come back on duty for he felt the sergeant needed something to take his mind off Danny Preece's death.

After what seemed an eternity the door was opened cautiously and on seeing the identity of the callers there was a panicked attempt by the occupant to slam the door shut. However Chard had anticipated the reaction and jammed his foot in the door to prevent it closing.

'I can see by the look on your faces why you are here. You had best come inside.'

All three went through to a cosy, well-presented parlour and sat in comfortable chairs as Chard recounted his interview with Jenny Norton. 'Miss Norton has confessed to the killing of Michael Blake and the wounding of Miss Roper. She will hang for the former crime so has no possible motive to lie about the murder of Grimes,' stated Chard assertively. 'Grimes had put two and two together and although he did not know the reason why Miss Norton had murdered Blake he felt sure that he held enough information to provide the police with circumstantial evidence that would be bound to lead us in the right direction. So, being the man he was, he decided to blackmail her. Miss Norton was prepared to pay for the time being because she knew that her fortune was soon to change and that her forthcoming marriage would provide her with a new life overseas. However, on the very night that she was due to make payment she turned up at the appointed place and the appointed time, only to see you smashing Grimes's brains out, Mr Dunwoody.'

'I see you have the truth of it,' confessed Dunwoody, tears forming in his eyes. 'I never saw her, though.'

'Miss Norton was only glad to see the back of her blackmailer so wasn't going to report it. There would have been a need to explain what she herself was doing there at dead of night.'

'Will I hang? Oh dear, I will, won't I?' cried Dunwoody despondently. 'I had taken so much, you know. Threats from that man Evans, then I had to re-mortgage my little house. I was in so much debt, yet that devil Grimes would squeeze and squeeze. I had to turn up to his silly card games on pain of violence but even when the gambling was fair I couldn't compete with the likes of that Italian and that dandy. The last straw was when I found myself stealing from the company. I had been doing it for months but I suspect the auditors were closing in.'

'They were indeed,' confirmed Chard. 'Mr Roberts had been to see us, though we had not yet identified the culprit.'

'I knew where Grimes used to drink occasionally and so had taken a small hammer from the foundry. I went out for several nights just waiting for him to turn up at the Llanbradach Arms and then finally I was in luck. I didn't know if I had the courage to go through with it but he spoke to me so dismissively, as if I was nothing but a worm. He turned his back on me and I hit him. Then I kept on hitting, I couldn't stop myself.' Dunwoody put his head in his hands and collapsed into tears.

'Did you get that, Sergeant?' asked the Inspector.

'Yes sir,' confirmed Morris, putting his notebook away. He looked compassionately at Dunwoody and took his arm with a light touch. 'Come along with us now, sir. We won't use the handcuffs, gently does it.'

EPILOGUE

(i) Three weeks later

'O bydded i'r hen iaith barhau.'

The Welsh national anthem, written and composed by two sons of Pontypridd, Evan James and James James, concluded and the crowd erupted into a cheer as the ribbon was cut, officially opening the new fountain in Penuel Square.

'At last. It's been finished for weeks; can't see why it's taken this long,' muttered Constable Matthews.

'Silence in the ranks!' snarled Sergeant Morris as loud as he dared without attracting the attention of Superintendent Jones. However, there was nothing to fear, for the superintendent, having shaken hands with the dignitaries present was in good humour and had just pulled Inspector Chard to one side.

'The men are looking particularly smart today and of course I include you in that praise, Inspector.'

'Thank you, sir, though the armbands are a sad reminder of our loss.'

'Yes indeed, Inspector. We won't forget him.'

Danny's funeral had taken place two weeks earlier at Glyntaff. It had been a grey, rainy day, the miserable weather in concert with the deep sadness of the mourners. After the coffin was lowered into the damp earth by Sergeant Morris and three constables, the committal service was performed by the vicar of St Mary's whilst the superintendent himself comforted Danny's mother. Afterwards the mourners sang the powerful Welsh hymn 'Cwm Rhondda' before dispersing quietly.

After a difficult silence when neither man knew what best to say, Superintendent Jones gave a little cough and changed the topic of conversation.

'I have been having some discussion with the chief

constable in Cardiff this week. He is quite impressed that we have sent three prisoners for trial on capital charges with strong evidence for conviction in every case. In addition he has received glowing correspondence from Mr Roberts of the Taff Vale Ironworks thanking us for having discovered who was embezzling money from the company. I have been commended and that praise must also fall on you, Inspector.'

Chard shook his head. 'Much of it was luck. I took a number of wrong turns. Evans's deed was right in front of Sergeant Morris; Jenny Norton told us about Dunwoody and it was Miss Roper who was the most convinced that Jenny Norton was a murderess.'

'Not of the right murder, though, and if you hadn't arrived in time to get her medical assistance then we would have no evidence against Miss Norton regarding Blake's murder. Until we had her full confession we were relying solely on what she told Miss Roper. How is she by the way?'

'Recovering physically, but mentally there will be scars for some time. However Constable Morgan has got into the habit of taking her flowers on a regular basis so perhaps that might help her state of mind.'

Superintendent Jones smiled. 'You see, sometimes some good can come out of the most terrible of things. Talking of which, as a result of the discussions I mentioned I have been given a number of assurances. Firstly, an increased complement of officers, which is long overdue. Secondly, the station is to be extended to give us more facilities and finally the temporary mortuary in the workhouse is to be improved up to a full hospital standard with a separate room for police examinations. I am hopeful that Dr Matthews will agree to be our permanent medical officer for such matters as Dr Henderson will no doubt wish to limit himself to workhouse business.'

'Will the increased complement of officers allow for a separate detective unit, sir?' asked Chard.

'We'll see, Inspector. We'll see.'

*   *   *

The small prison chapel had a congregation of six. Unusually the prison governor was present together with a male prison guard, both standing just inside the entrance. Two stern-faced, heavily built women in the dour uniforms of prison warders stood to attention closer to the altar.

'... I now pronounce you man and wife,' concluded the Catholic priest brought into the prison especially for the service.

Lord Abcote, dressed fastidiously in frock coat with a red cravat and red carnation in his buttonhole, stared entranced by the beauty of his new wife. Jenny stood alongside him, dressed in a plain but clean prison shift, balanced clumsily by means of a simple wooden crutch to which she was not yet fully accustomed. The groom went to give his wife their first married kiss and one of the women warders glanced at the governor. He shook his head, so Jenny was pulled away and James, Lord Abcote, could do nothing but watch his love being led away, stumbling, the crutch banging against the stone floor as she went from the chapel back to her cell.

(ii) AUTUMN 1895

Thomas Chard leaned comfortably against the bar in the Ivor Arms. He held a pint of beer in his right hand whilst humming a tune.

'You seem happy,' called a voice from behind him and Chard turned to see Gwen approaching, a broad smile on her face.

'I've been looking at houses for rent and I might have found one for a reasonable price. I can't keep staying at the New Inn indefinitely.'

'You do seem to be settling in now, don't you? I even heard you pronounce Llantrisant properly the other day. We'll make a Welshman of you yet,' teased the landlady.

'Yes, well I had some advice from Danny Preece,' replied Chard sadly.

'Come now, Thomas, tell me all about the trial of the Norton woman,' insisted Gwen, quickly changing the conversation. 'There was only the briefest of accounts in the paper.'

Chard gave a wry smile and putting his beer down, began to recount what had happened at the crown court.

'It was like something out of a melodrama. Let me set the scene for you,' said Chard as Gwen listened intently. 'There is a hubbub of anticipation as the judge enters the courtroom. Everyone rises and waits for him to take his seat before they too can settle. The accused is called for, but instead of coming directly into the dock from the cells below, as is customary, there is a noise behind everyone from the entrance to the courtroom. Silence descends on the room as slowly a beautiful young woman, dressed in purest white appears in a wheelchair pushed by a burly woman prison warder. The wheelchair has an audible squeak with every rotation of its wheels, the sound deafening in the eerie silence as all eyes are fixed on the spectacle.' Chard paused and sipped his beer.

'Go on, Thomas. Don't stop there,' encouraged Gwen,

'At the foot of the dock the accused is helped from the wheelchair, handed a simple crutch and made to hobble up the steps to take her appointed place. There are cries of "shame" coming from the gallery as the onlookers sympathise with her difficulty. She now stands erect and proud like Boadicea brought before the might of Rome. It is a wonderful piece of theatre and all twelve men of the jury are already swayed in her favour.'

'Surely the evidence against her was compelling,' exclaimed the landlady.

Chard ceased his dramatic story telling account and gave a shrug. 'You would have thought so, but Dorsett had obviously been very busy behind the scenes. We had the carefully arranged entrance, stage managed to perfection. Then there was the small matter of Lady Abcote being on trial, not some common factory girl, and with social unrest bubbling below the surface did the aristocracy want to have one of its own branded as a murderer? The prosecutor deigned not to mention that Jenny Norton had been a child prostitute so the motive for Blake's murder was kept from the court, though at least the fact that she had committed the act of killing Blake and had stabbed Miss Roper was laid before the jury. Also, because Jenny Norton had made a confession they informed Miss Roper that her testimony would not be necessary. I would have liked her to have insisted on appearing but she is still very shaken from the ordeal and was only too eager to take the opportunity to avoid the trial. To my surprise I was notified via the chief constable that the prosecution also considered my testimony to be unnecessary as the barrister had all the evidence he required.'

'Then what happened? Surely the facts could not have been denied.'

Chard gave a sarcastic laugh. 'The defence barrister, the finest in the country, performed like the most gifted actor of his age and presented the killing of Blake as a gentle young woman protecting her honour against a savage beast of a man, her only crime being the hiding of the body by pushing it into the river. There was no mention that we believe he was still alive when he went into the water. The prosecuting barrister had said nothing about the incident involving the placing of the watch on the other body so it wasn't mentioned by the defence either.'

'What about the stabbing of Miss Roper?'

'Ah, yes, they couldn't get around that one. Her barrister described it as "a regrettable moment of madness and unrepresentative of her normal character" and proclaimed that "had not God Himself dealt His holy retribution on her and delivered sufficient punishment by taking her limb, leaving her disability as a reminder of her unfortunate action?" Nevertheless, she would have had to have been found guilty but then the barrister threw something else in that he wished to be considered by the judge and jury.'

'Such as?'

'He went on to describe the murder of "an upright, influential local businessman", in other words Jabez Grimes. He gave every gory detail, describing it like something out of the worse type of penny dreadful horror. The courtroom was aghast and it contrasted with the description given of the allegedly self-defence killing of Blake. Then he revealed that the killer had been caught, not by the forces of law and order, but through the brave testimony of the defendant, Miss Norton.' Chard took another sip of his beer. 'Sad to say there was a tiny element of truth in that,' he added ruefully. 'So to sum up, she was found not guilty of the deliberate murder of Blake but guilty of wounding Miss Roper. Taking her help in the conviction of Dunwoody into consideration she was given only five years and not even hard labour.'

'It's a wonder that the press didn't make more of a story of it,' commented Gwen.

Chard shook his head. 'Not when the newspapers are owned by men of the same social standing. Anyway their attention seems to be fully on the scandal around the trial and conviction of Oscar Wilde.'

'Well, I think she should have gone to the gallows like that swine Evans and that man Dunwoody,' stated the landlady emphatically.

'Well sometimes Lady Luck, or Fortuna as the Romans called her, smiles on you and other times her shadow will fall and do you down.'

'Stuff and nonsense. Everyone suffers for their sins in the long run, however much they think they've got away with things, so no more talk of Lady Luck and such rubbish,' insisted Gwen.

'Very well, let's change the subject to something else,' agreed Chard, reaching for his beer once more.

The landlady smiled mischievously. 'Well, Thomas, I think it is about time that you found yourself a wife. You can't be settling into a house here and not have someone to cook and clean for you, let alone your other needs,' added Gwen with a cheeky wink. She saw his worried expression and patted his arm. 'Don't worry, I'm not talking about myself, but I'll be keeping my eye out for a suitable companion for you, and I'll find one, you see if I don't.' The landlady gave him another pat of reassurance on the arm as she got up and walked back into the kitchen. Chard gave a mournful sigh, finished his beer in a single gulp, walked to the bar and ordered another.

*   *   *

Jack rubbed his arm as he waited on the railway platform for his train. The break had healed well and there was now only the occasional twinge when he lifted something particularly heavy. He glanced down at the bag at his feet. This time he had plenty of time to pack, there had been no rush, but there was little that he needed to take with him in order to make a fresh start, just what remained of his money, a change of clothes and a deck of cards. It would have been possible to resume his life in Pontypridd but the place just held bad memories for him now and he needed to try and forget what a fool he had been over Jenny. The Camorra had not sent anyone else after him so they had either lost his trail since losing their man or they had just given up. Just to be on the safe side it wasn't worth travelling south to Cardiff and the coast, at least not for another couple of years, so he considered it might be worthwhile going north to the industrial town of Merthyr Tydfil. If he could find a fair card game there then maybe he could recoup his losses of the past two years. His time in Pontypridd had been wasted, squandered on unrequited love, but it could have been so much worse. He had only narrowly escaped detection by informants of the Camorra in Cardiff before coming to Treforest and, if their assassin had eventually recovered from the terrible injuries caused by the train crash, then potentially the hunt would have been on once again. That was why he'd had to break into the infirmary that night. The man was too weak to fight against the pillow over his face and it was over with quickly. Fortunately no one saw him, though for a moment he had been concerned that one of the patients moving amongst their bedclothes might have meant that he had been heard. Yes, it had been a lucky escape, thought Jack as his train came into view.

AUTHOR'S NOTE

It might seem an odd choice to base the location of a Victorian crime novel in what might be considered a small town in South Wales. Yet crime existed outside of Whitechapel and the fog-filled streets of London.

Even in the 1890s the role of the detective had not established itself in most police forces and although the technique of fingerprinting had been discovered it was still in its infancy and not commonly used. Urgent communication in the first half of the 1890s was primarily by telegram. Telephones had become available in the 1880s but they were only just beginning to spread from the major cities and were prone to technical problems. Their use would spread later in the decade but even then they would be few and far between in the valleys of South Wales.

During the nineteenth century there was tremendous social upheaval as the industrial revolution led to considerable growth in communities that needed a ready supply of labour to exploit local natural resources. Of these, coal was undoubtedly king and towns in the south of Wales expanded rapidly as workers, both skilled and unskilled migrated from other parts of Wales, England and overseas, all seeking a better life. Other heavy industries grew up alongside and the infrastructures of towns had to be improved to cope with the expectations of the new communities. Pontypridd was one such town and situated at the confluence of the rivers Taff and Rhondda it developed exponentially as a market town as well as a hub of industry.

The police force was largely undermanned, having to cope with the inevitable social disorder as hard-working miners, navvies and ironworkers let off steam on a Saturday night. Drunkenness and drug dependency were commonplace in the

1890s throughout Britain with many opiate-based products freely available to all levels of society. In the darkest depths of society it would be reasonable to suspect that for the desperate there would have been prostitution, illegal gambling and loan sharking. Yet, at the other end of the scale there were also strict codes of respectability. High society attended glittering balls, the theatre and charity functions. The poorer classes by and large held to their own moral codes of Christian virtue and established a reputation for being friendly and tolerant to strangers. It was also generally a polite society and although some of the conversations in this book may sound a little stilted to our modern ears it should be remembered that the English language has become much more informal over the last fifty years compared to say French, Spanish or Italian, where it is still customary to say 'Good day sir,' to a shopkeeper before making a purchase.

It is worth saying a few words on the Welsh language. During the Victorian age there had been a steady decline in its usage as official documents and most parts of structured social life were dominated by the English language to an extent that the use of Welsh became discouraged. Thankfully over the last fifty years there has been much done to try and revive the language and I hope that this continues to be successful. On the topic of language, I resisted the temptation of including too many colloquial words and phrases particular to South Wales (of which there are many) and apologise if this omission disappoints some readers.

I have attempted to keep as historically accurate as possible with regards to the town of Pontypridd itself (allowing for some deliberate 'artistic licence' here and there) but I have certainly understated two things in particular which both had a bearing on social structure. Firstly, public houses, for although a substantial number are mentioned in the novel, there were actually many more. Secondly, Nonconformist chapels, of which I have only mentioned Penuel as a significant local feature. In fact there were many, and indeed there still are, with members of Protestant congregations often defining themselves as 'church' or 'chapel'.

It might surprise the reader to know that there really was a Father McManus, a Superintendent Jones and a Mr Roberts, as well as other quoted names in this novel though my characterisations are pure fiction. Similarly, the train crash at the start of the book was an actual historical event and the casualties were indeed taken to the workhouse infirmary. It might seem strange that a 'Poor Law Infirmary' should be used to supplement a hospital but in an age when the National Health Service was not even an idea it was quite commonplace.

Ironically the workhouse was eventually demolished and a hospital now stands in its place. As to the other locations mentioned in the book, many of the streets remain as they were in 1895.

The Taff Vale Ironworks, Forest Iron & Steel Works, Newbridge Chainworks and Treforest Tinplate Works could also be found in 1895, though little trace of them now remain. Some, but by no means all of the public houses still exist in some form or another, occasionally with a change of name or internal alterations. Sadly the Ivor Arms does not. There was an Ivor Arms in the distant past but my description of it and its occupants are pure invention.

Older residents of Pontypridd remember Penuel Chapel, the old Police Station, the New Inn and the scene of Grimes's murder with the canal flowing past the Llanbradach but sadly these locations are no longer with us. Neither is the Catholic church of St. Dubricius, though a much grander church was subsequently built early in the last century close to the old Taff Vale House and named St. Dyfrig's.

Yet several other locations do remain. The river still flows under the Old Bridge, New Bridge (later widened and renamed as the Victoria Bridge), Machine Bridge (which has another alongside it) and the Castle Inn Bridge (referred to on Ordnance Survey maps as Castle Bridge), before flowing over the weir close to Castle House. St Mary's Church and its graveyard are as they were and the fountain still stands in the middle of what was Penuel Square.

Finally, for anyone who might be interested in researching the period of history when this novel has been set, and of the town of Pontypridd in particular, I would begin by highly recommending a magnificent book, *Victorian Pontypridd* by Don Powell (Merton Priory Press ISBN 1-898937-23-0) which covers a wider historical timescale and in far greater depth than provided by this work of fiction. Also worth mentioning is *Old Pontypridd & District in Photographs*, published by Stewart Williams (ISBN 0-900807-34-5). There is, of course, the town itself and in particular the Pontypridd Historical and Cultural Centre. For an insight into day-to-day life in a Victorian industrial environment I can thoroughly recommend the Ironbridge Museums in Shropshire, and the Blists Hill site in particular. There are very many internet sites of course that deal with the history of South Wales and Victorian life in general, far too many to mention here, but one of particular interest is the Facebook page of the Virtual Museum of Police in Wales.

I hope this book gives as much pleasure to the reader as it gave to me in writing it.

L.S.